FALLON'S
WAKE

FALLON'S
WAKE

RANDY LEE EICKHOFF

A TOM DOHERTY ASSOCIATES BOOK
NEW YORK

FALLON'S WAKE

This book is printed on acid-free paper.

Design by Jane Adele Regina

A Forge Book
Published by Tom Doherty Associates, LLC
175 Fifth Avenue
New York, NY 10010

www.tor.com

Forge® is a registered trademark of Tom Doherty Associates, LLC.

ISBN 0-312-86762-X

First Edition: February 2000

Printed in the United States of America

0 9 8 7 6 5 4 3 2 1

For R.T.

Ich halte für die höste Aufgabe einer Verbindung zweier Menschen diese:
dass einer dem andern seine Einsamkeit bewache.

—RILKE

and for
Rennie Shattuck
who led the Boston expedition

MY THANKS

Quelle âme est sans défauts?

—ARTHUR RIMBAUD, *Une saison en enfer*

PART ONE ◆ Ireland

1

THE SKY HAD BEEN RED IN THE MORNING BUT BY NIGHT IT TURNED black and a storm churned up the mountain called Long Woman's Grave from Carlingford Lough, lashing the small, whitewashed cottage and littering the yard with leaves and small cones from the trees standing around the cottage on three sides. The air had cooled now, although a soft rain still fell bringing with it a tangy smell of pine needles. Inside the cottage, Fallon had placed a new block of peat on the smoored fire and used the billows to pump the fire into life. Now he sat contented, reading by the fire, enjoying sips from the cup of tea at his elbow and the warmth of the fire and the sound of the rain dripping from the eaves. The room was cozy, a bachelor's room lined with bookcases overflowing with books. When he raised his eyes to their titles, his mind read them in the dim light: Rousseau's *Confessions*, Larkin's Red Branch Cycle, Lawrence's *Sons and Lovers*, *The Fox*, the sets of Dickens and Balzac, Yeats, some in collectors' first editions, a rare copy of Joyce's *Ulysses* rescued from a farmhouse attic near Armagh. Music rolled softly from a tape player on a small corner table while Miss Sheba lay in his lap, purring contentedly, eyes half-closed. The Victorian lamp gave off a soft glow through the roses delicately entwined on its globe. A faint scent of toasted cheese reminded him of his light supper.

Haunting notes from a tin whistle nearly hid their approach

across gravel in front of the house, but Miss Sheba heard them, a low growl emanating from her throat as she leaped lithely from Fallon's lap to the mantel, her black fur gleaming in the light from the peat fire. Fallon placed a leather bookmark between the pages of Arthur Rimbaud's *Une saison en enfer*, carefully placed it beside the mug of tea on the small table near his elbow, then rose and slipped the Baby Browning from the hidden shelf beneath the mantle, stepping to the left of the door. He checked the pistol, slipping the safety off.

They moved quickly, throwing the door open while simultaneously sliding into the room, ducking to miss the low beam and fanning out to each side, crouched, pistols trained on the empty chair. Miss Sheba snarled, drawing their attention as Fallon slipped behind them.

"Good evening. Don't," he murmured warningly as they started to turn toward the sound of his voice. They froze. The tall one straightened, shaking his head in disgust. The tin whistle died and Phil Coulter slid into "The Rose of Mooncoin," the notes from his piano falling like silver leaves into the room.

"Do it, Johnny," the taller one said after glancing over his shoulder. "The bugger's got us." He tossed his pistol onto the chair.

"Ned," Johnny said.

"You won't make it," Fallon said softly. Johnny hesitated, then tossed his pistol after his partner's.

"How'd yuh know? Yuh owe us that," he said, the Ulster vowels long and harsh in his words. He started to turn, dropping his hands, then stopped as Fallon raised the Browning.

"Do you take me for a fool, now?" Fallon said.

"Sure, sure, now. Be careful with that," Ned said nervously, stepping back and raising his hands.

"On the floor. Hands straight in front of you."

"We was only having a bit of fun," Johnny protested. "'Twas himself sent us. MacCauley."

"He said how good yuh were," Ned explained.

"And now you know," Fallon said calmly. "The floor."

Johnny swore, dropping to his knees, gingerly lowering himself to the floor. Ned hesitated, glanced into Fallon's eyes, then followed his partner. Fallon stepped between their legs and quickly searched them. Johnny had a flick-knife in his pocket. Fallon tossed it into a corner. Ned had a small Beretta in an ankle holster. Fallon took it and slid it into the back pocket of his trousers and moved away from them.

"You may sit up, now," he said. "But keep your hands in your laps where I can see them."

"Bleedin' bastard," Johnny muttered. He rolled to a sitting position and glared at Fallon standing over him.

"You're alive," Fallon said. "You don't have to be." Ned slid backward across the floor until his back could rest against the bookshelves.

"What does he want?"

"MacCauley? I dunno. He just said to bring you."

"Where?" Fallon asked.

"Yuh have to be blindfolded," Johnny said sullenly. Fallon stared at him; a tiny flush crept up Johnny's cheeks. Ned shook his head disgustedly.

"Don't mind him. Leaves his good senses in the jakes when he shats. Will yuh come?" Ned asked.

"I'm finished. MacCauley knows that," Fallon said.

Ned regretfully shook his head. "Now, then, yuh know how it is. Yuh were part of us for a long time. Once in, always in. If yuh don't come with us now, he'll only send others. More next time. Yuh've had a good time of it, now, ain't yuh? What? Two, three years?"

"Forty-two months," Fallon automatically answered.

"There, now. Yuh see? Yuh see what I mean? Don't yuh? It's a good rest yuh been havin'. And sure, haven't yuh been deservin', now? I was sayin' that to me mate here while we were comin' out. 'Johnny,' I says, 'yuh know that Tomas Fallon has been restin' a good while now, while others have been dyin' in the North. Yuh canna be tellin' me that a man like that isna tired of all that peace and quiet.'"

"That's what you were saying, is it?" Fallon said. Ned vigorously nodded.

"Aye. An' may God strike me where I'm sittin' if it ain't so."

"So you came in with guns. Not very friendly."

"Ah, well." He smiled sheepishly, rubbing his nose with the flat of his hand. "That were a mistake, yuh see." Johnny cleared his throat. Ned gave him a warning look, and he slumped back against the wall, staring at the floor between the toes of his engineer boots.

"Will yuh come wit' us, now?" he asked.

"I won't have to wear a blindfold?"

Ned laughed, nodding at the pistol in his hand. "I think we can forget the blindfold, don't yuh, Johnny?"

"MacCauley will have our balls," he answered dourly.

"Better than being dead," Fallon said. "Dead's a long time." He backed to a hook beside the door and removed a jacket, shrugging into it while keeping the Browning trained on them. "Shall we go?"

Johnny glanced at their pistols in the chair. "Our guns?" Fallon smiled and shook his head. "No, I didn't think so," he said resignedly. He walked to the door, opened it, and stepped out into the night. Ned followed, pausing at the door. He turned.

"Yuh're a hard man, Tomas Fallon," he said.

"You're alive," Fallon said, lifting the pistol. "For now."

Ned nodded thoughtfully and turned to follow his partner. Fallon closed the door behind them.

2

THEY HAD LEFT THEIR CAR, A BLACK FORD CORTINA, PARKED BEHIND a stone wall across the graveled yards from the cottage. They walked toward it through the cold night air, their breaths appearing in tiny clouds above their heads. To the north, the lights of Warrenpoint glowed softly against the low-lying clouds along the coast. Johnny drove while Ned sat quietly in the front seat beside him. They turned south toward Dublin and rode in silence through the night. When they reached the city, Johnny turned off the main road, taking the backstreets, weaving his way back and forth across the River Liffey. When he was satisfied no one had followed them, he pulled up in front of a warehouse and killed the engine. They sat for a long minute, listening to the metal ping as it cooled. Finally, Ned opened his door and stepped out. Fallon slipped out behind him and motioned Johnny to his side. He took a deep breath, smelling the water and rotting fish. A ship eased down past the wharf, sounding its foghorn, strange, lonely like the cry of a loon. He glanced back the way they had come, but the street was empty, long serpentine lines of tire prints running through glazed pools of blue-white light from the lamps. He looked at the pair waiting in front of him.

"You know the way," he said, gesturing with the pistol. They exchanged glances, then Ned stepped forward and opened the Judas gate. Fallon followed them into a small yard. Broken crates had been piled at one end. The old cobblestones were wet from the fog and glistened from the single light over the warehouse door. Ned slid it open. Bales and packing cases of all shapes and sizes were piled high, filling the interior. A light shone at the far end. They moved toward it. Rats squealed and scurried away, then turned to see if the men followed them, their eyes glowing redly in the dark.

A man sat at a trestle table, quietly waiting as they approached.

"Hello, Tomas," Seamus MacCauley said.

"Seamus." Fallon motioned his two companions off to the side. MacCauley's eyes flickered toward them then slid impassively back to Fallon.

"It's been awhile. How've you been?"

"Not bad," Fallon answered. "You're getting gray. Your hair was darker then."

"My heart was lighter then." MacCauley laughed. A fit of coughing struck him, doubling him over. "Damn," he said, straightening. He ran his hand over his thinning hair. Deep wrinkles gouged his forehead and trailed down over his cheeks. Heavy pouches sagged beneath his eyes. His face looked bloated and gray. He wore an old leather coat like the old ones connected with the IRA had worn. A battered fedora lay on the table in front of him. Two men stood silently in the shadows just beyond the pool of light cast by the single bare bulb suspended from the ceiling over the table. Straw spilled from an open wooden packing case on the floor beside the table. A red cross had been painted on the sides of the boxes, marking them as medical supplies. The box held a few liter-sized plastic packets. MacCauley looked at the pistol in Fallon's hand and gave a tiny smile.

"Why the pistol, Tomas?" he asked.

"Your messengers got a wee bit excited," Fallon answered dryly. "Given the circumstances, I thought it best."

MacCauley closed his eyes and leaned back in his chair away from the table. A large vein began to pound in his temple.

"Christ," he sighed.

"We didn't know what to expect," Johnny said defensively. "Yuh just said to bring 'im."

MacCauley grimaced. "I'm sorry," he said to Fallon. "We're having to make do these days."

Johnny flushed and started to speak, then bit his lip and looked away. His cheeks reddened.

"Get out," MacCauley said.

"Seamus," Ned began, then stopped as the flesh tightened across MacCauley's cheeks and the Belfast commandant for the PIRA stared stonily at him. "Yes sir," he said meekly. He grabbed Johnny by the arm. Johnny jerked his arm away. Ned stepped close to him.

"Don't be foacking crazy," he whispered hoarsely. He glanced white-eyed at the men standing impassively in the shadows.

Johnny stared defiantly at MacCauley, then his eyes blinked, and he turned and strode rapidly away into the darkness toward the door.

"Follow them," MacCauley said to the shadows behind him. One of the shadows moved around the rim of the pool of light and disappeared. Soon, a door slammed, echoing hollowly through the warehouse. MacCauley gestured to a ladder-backed chair across the table from him. Fallon shook his head.

"I won't be here that long," Fallon said. "I brought your dirty laundry back to you this time. But no more."

A tiny smile tugged at MacCauley's lips, but his eyes remained dead, frozen in the past like a statue. A rat scratched softly over a pile of scrap wood in the corner, his nails making a rasping sound in the silence. MacCauley gently rubbed the bridge of his nose between his eyes.

"The best are gone, Tomas," he said tiredly. "It's been too many years. But now, it might be over."

"Over?"

MacCauley nodded. He reached slowly into a briefcase beside his chair and took out a sheaf of papers held together by a large clamp. "We seem to have come to an agreement with most of the Protestants and the British," he said. He tossed the sheaf of paper in front of Fallon and pointed at it. "That will be released tomorrow. Gerry Adams and the others are going to support this fully. Of course," he added, "that bastard Ian Paisley and his riffraff aren't taking part in it, but what do you expect from a man with a pebble brain?"

Fallon leaned forward, glancing at the title: NORTHERN IRELAND PEACE AGREEMENT/DECLARATION OF SUPPORT. He shook his head and leaned back.

"We've been here before, Seamus," he said softly.

MacCauley rubbed his eyes and leaned back against his chair. Tired lines made his face seem gray and large pouches sagged the bruised flesh beneath his eyes. "I know. I know. But we have hopes that this time it will go through. The British prime minister, Tony Blair, is supporting it—"

"Means nothing," Fallon interrupted. "The Brits would support anything, now, that would get them out of Ulster. You know that. Read the *Manchester Guardian*. Latest polls show the people are tired of the 'Troubles' and willing to do anything to get out. Blair's a politician. He'd support the Devil himself if it would make him look good in the polls."

"Aye," MacCauley grunted. "There's that. But Mo Mowlam— the Northern Ireland secretary—is standing firm on releasing the prisoners despite what that bastard Lesley Rodgers, the chairman of the Police Federation, shouts. She's holding the line on that despite the Royal Ulster Constabulary protests. And," he emphasized, stabbing a blunt forefinger at Fallon, "the Taoiseach Bertie

Ahern is supporting the agreement as well and even David Trimble, the head of the Ulster Unionist Party, is supporting it."

"Trimble?" Fallon shook his head. "The Democratic Unionists won't stand for that. Not if Ian Paisley has anything to say about it and he will. Or his son. Doesn't matter. If this agreement goes through, the good Reverend Paisley will slip out of the limelight and that lying whoreson won't stand for that. That son of Satan should have been sent below to his father's realm a long time ago despite political repercussions."

"Ah, Tomas, Tomas," MacCauley sighed, shaking his head. "We knew that we wouldn't win this war with a gun. Eventually we had to come to the table. The gun was only a way of forcing the issue. And now we have it." He pointed again at the agreement. "Right there, lad. Right there. It's peace, Tomas. Is it so hard for you to accept?"

"Not hard at all, Seamus," Fallon said. "I don't think it will hold, though. There's been too much killing on both sides for it all to be forgotten at the snap of the fingers, a scribble of a pen."

"Nevertheless, there it is," MacCauley said. "And it goes out tomorrow. A cease-fire."

"I'm happy for you," Fallon said. He pushed the sheaf of papers back toward MacCauley, who shook his head.

"Keep them. They're yours, Tomas," he said. "Read it and see what you think."

"So you brought me here for this?" Fallon shook his head. "No, I don't think so. This could have waited until tomorrow. What is it?"

"We still need you," MacCauley said quietly.

Fallon shook his head. "No. I told you when I left the North: I'm finished."

"It wasn't your fault," MacCauley said softly. "It was just an accident. Accidents happen in war."

Shadows suddenly shifted, displacing light, and he saw again a bright red flashing burst from the automatic rifle in the soldier's hands as he sprinted across Shankill Road toward the darkness of an alley, his shadow dancing grotesquely on the walls of gutted buildings from the light of burning gasoline spilling from the overturned Saracen, and he laid the trigger back on the UZI sending bullets into the darkness after the soldier and the screams came back at him, screams from young voices that would never grow old.

"Tomas," MacCauley said gently.

Fallon blinked. The harsh light returned. He clenched his hands tightly in his lap to hide their trembling.

"We need you," MacCauley said again, quietly.

"No," Fallon said.

MacCauley stared at him for a long minute. A foghorn rolled on the river, a lonely sound in the night. He raised his hand. Another of the shadows stepped forward and placed a large manila folder in his hand then retreated back beyond the rim of light. MacCauley held it for a moment, then placed it in front of him and bent the silver prongs together, opened the envelope, and removed two photographs. He slid them across the table to Fallon.

He glanced at them. The first showed a young boy sprawled in the garbage of an alley, an empty bottle of cheap wine in the palm of his hand. The bones of his face had been broken and one eyeball had fallen from its socket and lay across his cheek. In the other, a young girl lay naked on an iron bed, her thin legs an obscene sprawl. Cigar burns covered her body. A hypodermic lay in her hand. Fallon looked up impassively at him, leaning back in his chair. MacCauley took another photograph from the envelope and slid it across the table.

Fallon stared at them. What was that Joyce said about pity?— The feeling which arrests the mind in the presence of whatsoever is grave and constant in human sufferings and unites it with the human sufferer— Appropriate.

"I have a dozen of these," MacCauley said quietly. "All drug victims and not one from a broken home."

Fallon frowned. The authorities were exceedingly harsh on anyone caught trying to smuggle drugs into the country and the penalties if one were caught with them were stiff. One had to be either arrogantly sure of one's own invulnerability or desperate enough for the money to be willing to gamble with one's life. Despite himself, Fallon felt his interest quicken, and he took a deep breath and held it. This is how it begins: the adrenaline push, the pulse quickening, the challenge. But in the end, it is always the same.

"Since when does Ireland have a drug problem?" Fallon asked.

MacCauley scrubbed his hands across his face. "It's been getting worse the past four years. First, among the children of the rich Protestants sent to school in England and the United States, but now, drug use is spreading into the Catholic neighborhoods. It seems someone is looking to establish a new market now that gun-running is in danger of no longer being lucrative. But"—he leaned forward—"up to now we've left it to the police and Gardai to solve."

"And now?"

"Now, it's become political." Fallon sat back, staring at Mac-Cauley expressionlessly. "The command thinks that it's time Sinn Fein and the Provisionals take a hand in stopping the drugs. If drug trafficking escalates as it seems to be doing, then Paisley and his supporters will use that against us. Especially"—he gestured at the packets—"if it can be traced to gun shipments. The guns are bad enough, given the cease-fire agreement—makes us look a bit hypocritical. What do we need guns for if we're not planning on using them? But the drugs"—he shook his head—"there's no romance in drugs. We'd lose the U.S. support as well as the Irish people."

"And if you stop it," Fallon interjected softly, "you can use it against them."

MacCauley nodded grudgingly. "Yes, there's that. It's become a big enough issue that whoever can bring an end to it will have political clout, you see."

"Oh, I see," Fallon said mildly. "Wouldn't it be nice if the Provos could succeed where the government has failed? Drugs tarnish the romantic imagery of the IRA in the eyes of the world. It isn't the drugs so much as the Provos and Sinn Fein trying to clean up the tawdry taint to their name, right? Show the world that we really aren't the thugs and gunmen that the Prods have been contending all these years, and all that, right?"

"You really can be a bastard, Fallon," he said.

Fallon ignored him. "It's the times, Seamus. It's the times."

Tiny muscles bunched and clinched along MacCauley's jaw. He stared into Fallon's eyes for a long moment, then took another photograph out of the envelope and slid it across the table to Fallon.

"Look," he said harshly. Fallon picked it up and held it for the light to fall across the glossy surface. It was a picture of a dead boy. His eyes were closed, dark hollows that made his cheekbones skeletal in the harsh light reflecting from the stainless steel of the morgue tray. His stomach had fallen below his rib cage, making a basket of flesh and bone. His throat had been cut, neatly, surgically, in a single brutal sweep.

"He was fished out of the Liffey this morning," MacCauley said, a strange clicking in his throat.

Fallon slid the photograph back to MacCauley and leaned back against the chair, waiting impassively. MacCauley picked up the photograph, stared at it for a long moment, then looked out into the darkness.

"My sister's boy," he said. Muscles bunched and knotted at the corners of his jaw. "He found out about this." He reached into the packing case and slapped a plastic pouch on the table between them. A tiny white cloud puffed up. "And let us know. So they killed him."

"Who?" Fallon asked.

"Whoever has been shipping the drugs into the country," Mac-Cauley said. He shook his head. "This peace agreement has brought a halt to arms shipments. Or we thought it would," he amended. "Fact is, we have stopped bringing in guns and ammunition for quite some time now, hoping that this agreement would go through. We didn't want to upset the cart, you see. Show of good faith and all that. But that has caused some, ah, economic shortfalls to some concerned parties. And now they are using the old routes to bring in drugs. And, I might add, some arms as well. We suspect INLA and the GDC." Fallon raised his eyebrows at mention of the latter group, but MacCauley ignored him and continued. "We intercepted a shipment of AK-47s. The drugs were inside the crates. Drugs are riskier, but the profit margin's higher and drugs don't normally take up as much room as the arms and ammunition did. We think this was a convenient shipment—the drugs and guns at once." His eyes held Fallon's: cold, hard, with angry lights glinting like hard frost deep within them. "But we really don't know who." He made a deprecating gesture. "We bought so many guns over the years from so many different people that it could be anyone who is looking to keep profit margins up."

"Economic standards must be maintained," Fallon murmured. "And drugs don't kill as many innocent as guns. Besides, drugs are quieter. Not a bad economic move. Lower overhead, higher profit margin."

MacCauley gave a curt nod. "Yes. Do you remember Seamus Twooly?" Fallon nodded. "Dom Flynn and Gerard Cassidy?"

Fallon's eyebrows raised. "Thugs all of them. I thought we let the British have them for the Piccadilly bombing in eighty-one when they robbed a bank without approval."

"Aye. The bank wasn't in on the plans. They took advantage of it for their own sake. We found out it was them only after a 'grasser' told the tale to the RUC boys. The board decided it would be in our best interest to cut them free."

"Why not eliminate them altogether?"

MacCauley gave a bleak smile. "Ah, politics, Tomas. Politics. And how would it look if people knew we were shopping our own for expedient's sake?"

"We've done it before. Remember Cassidy? Liam Drumm? and sure, you haven't forgotten your mate Richard O'Bannion? Remember the Conor Larkin affair and Lord Mountbatten's death up in Mullaghmore when Drumm and Cassidy and O'Bannion blew up Mountbatten's boat and killed him and his family? You killed O'Bannion yourself for his part in that one."*

"I remember," MacCauley said. "But in this case, the board thought it would be better if people saw Twooly and Flynn and Cassidy being dealt with by the law for the robbing of the bank. It was part of the plan to show the world that the PIRA was not a bunch of bloodthirsty terrorists, but an army fighting for Ireland's freedom and one willing to be bound by law."

"Murder excepted?"

MacCauley ignored the irony of Fallon's words and continued. "They escaped from the Isle of Wight prison six months ago. Since that time, they've started their own movement. They call themselves Gaelach Dearg Craobh—the GDC. They've got about twenty of the riffraff in with them; that's all. But 'tis a ruthless time they've been having ever since."

"The Gaelach Dearg Craobh? The Irish Red Branch? A nice touch that, bringing in Ireland's old history. Cúchulainn of Muirthemne and the Red Branch of Ulster. Nice appeal to nationalism," Fallon said.

*The Gombeen Man

MacCauley made a face. "Yes, and they even use the oath of Cúchulainn."

"A bit melodramatic, but effective," Fallon murmured.

"More than a bit," MacCauley said. His eyes bored into Fallon's. "I want them dead, Tomas."

"So that's it," Fallon said quietly. "It's personal." Relief swept over him, but it was short-lived. Even though MacCauley was personally involved that did not mean the council wouldn't approve his actions. Perhaps they already had. Who could know? There had been so many lies over the years the truth could only be known when it had become bitter vetch, so stagnant that the perfumes of all the lies in the world could not hide its stench. With a start, Fallon suddenly realized this had happened. The "Troubles" had passed from lies to truth and since becoming truth, they would never end. When the soul of a man is born in this country, he thought, the country holds it prisoner, keeps it from flying. The snares keeping it entrapped are nationality, language, and religion, all appearing under the commonality: cause. MacCauley's words broke in on his thoughts.

"You owe me, Fallon," he said softly. "I've kept the boys off you for years. There's them who wanted to put you down when you left."

"It would have been costly," Fallon murmured.

"A man can't watch his back forever. Not even you," he said. "You owe me."

"There's been enough killing," Fallon said.

"The drugs," MacCauley said quietly. "I want the bastards who did this."

"I'll think about it," Fallon said, rising.

"Fallon," he began.

"Two days," Fallon said.

"Not good enough," he said. "I have to be able to tell the boys you're back in." He looked away. "It's the deal, Tomas. Sorry, but there it is."

"Two days."

"They'll send someone after you," he said warningly. "They mean it this time."

Fallon stood and walked away from the table. Outside, it had begun to rain, a "soft night." Fallon opened the Judas gate and stepped out of the courtyard. The Cortina was gone. Fallon turned the collar up on his jacket and began to walk back toward the river. He felt cold and wretched and empty as he realized the one thing he feared had happened: the past had caught up with him.

3

THE HOMELY WOMAN NEATLY DRESSED IN A MAID'S UNIFORM
watched curiously through the rain-streaked window as a gleaming
black limousine slid neatly to the curb in front of No. 10 Downing
Street. An unsmiling man dressed in an overcoat over a somber
black suit opened the rear door and held an umbrella as Sir Edward
Bell carefully stepped out, positioning his well-polished shoes to
avoid the puddle directly beneath his door. He adjusted his hom-
burg and coat, tucked his briefcase beneath his arm, and hurried to
the entrance, his face a stern mask of frown lines.

The woman turned from the window, thoughtfully chewing
her lip.

"They arrived yet?" the cook asked from the stove. She tasted the
soup she was stirring and made a face, reaching for the rosemary.

"Oh, yes," the woman said. The cook grunted, carefully mea-
suring the rosemary into the pot in front of her.

"You'd better ready the tray," she said. "The PM will be ordering the tea directly."

The woman crossed to the table where the silver tea service
had been laid on a tray. Carefully, she took a small handful of
Darjeeling leaves, crushed them between her palms, and dropped
them into the tea pot. She took hot water from the stove and filled
the pot, firmly closing the lid to allow the tea to steep. She
glanced around: the cook was engrossed in gently stirring the

soup on the stove; the butler sipped from a mug as he read *The Times* propped against the condiment tray on the servants' table against the far wall. Swiftly, the woman took the silver sugar bowl from the tray and set it on the shelf above the service. She smiled secretly to herself: crude, but it might work.

The door opened as Bell neared, allowing him to step into the foyer. He paused, taking a deep breath, feeling the history of the building speaking from its old bricks stories of triumphs and tragedies and near-tragedies narrowly averting the making of Britain into a wasteland. He slipped from his overcoat, handing it to the man.

"The prime minister?" Bell asked.

"In the library, Sir Edward," the man stiffly answered, accepting the overcoat. He shook it gently, flicking the few drops of water from it and hanging it on a hook. "If you will follow me?"

He turned and led Bell to a door, discreetly knocked, then slid it open. "Sir Edward Bell," he announced quietly, then stood back, allowing Bell to enter.

"Thank you, John," the prime minister said, rising. He smoothed the fall of his coat, and automatically checked his care-fully combed dark brown hair before crossing to Bell and shaking his hand. "Nasty bit of weather. Sorry you had to come out in it. I suppose it couldn't wait."

"No, sir," Bell said stiffly. "Recent developments may give us a bit of leverage with that Irish cease-fire and a bit of consideration with economic sanctions on imports and exports to Ireland."

"What does this have to do with me?" the prime minister asked, motioning Bell to an overstuffed armchair in front of the fire. "Shouldn't that simply go through channels in your office? I'm afraid I don't see the urgency."

"Usually, sir, but this time, I'm afraid it's a matter of relation-ships with the Republic of Ireland. The European Economic Community conference scheduled next month has made the situation a bit, shall we say, 'delicate'?"

"Go on." The prime minister frowned, leaning back in his chair. He pushed the buzzer beside him.

In the kitchen, the butler glanced up at the wall, sighed, and folded his paper. He stood, shrugging into his coat. "Come along, now," he said to the woman. "It's time for tea."

The woman nodded, picking up the tray and following him from the kitchen.

Bell leaned forward toward the prime minister, carefully choosing his words. "The Republic of Ireland is planning on requesting higher tariffs on goods currently protected through export exchange agreements. That will allow the Republic to place higher taxes on goods being imported into the Republic. Now, that might be good for Ireland, but it would be very harmful for Britain's foreign trade office. We have a lot of exports to the Republic. And that would give the Sinn Fein boys a lever for nationalism: Buy Irish. We need permission to go into the Republic. A clandestine operation."

The door opened and the butler entered with a woman, her hair pulled severely tight in a bun. She wore no makeup. Bell fell silent as they laid the service. The prime minister frowned.

"The sugar?" he asked, a slight touch of annoyance in his voice. The butler glanced at the tray, then frowned at the woman. She looked flustered.

"I'm sorry, sir," she said. "I'll fetch it straight."

She left while the butler finished pouring the tea. He offered each a tray upon which four choices of biscuits had been arranged. Bell took a shortbread biscuit while the prime minister declined.

"That will be all," the prime minister said. The butler nodded and withdrew as the woman rushed in with the sugar bowl.

"I'm very sorry," she said. The prime minister waved her away, and she followed the butler from the room.

He closed the door gently behind them, then frowned at her. "We will have no more embarrassments like that, is this understood? In the future, check the service carefully before you bring it."

"Sorry, sir," the woman said, casting her eyes down. "It won't happen again."

"See that it doesn't," the butler said sternly. He took his watch from its vest pocket and checked the time, clucking to himself. "Go back to the kitchen and wait while I attend my rounds." He turned and walked down the corridor, disappearing into the back rooms.

The woman smiled at his back: a check on the maid's duties and the rooms right after tea. On schedule. It had not varied over the past six months since she had been given her position. She stepped closer to the door, leaning forward, listening.

"I'm afraid I don't see the difficulty," the prime minister said, spooning sugar into his tea. "Why not go through the Gardai? Why get involved in the Republic in the first place? Haven't we always dealt satisfactorily with them in the past?"

"Not entirely, sir," Bell said, sipping his tea. "Evidence has been lost in the past when a few crucial cases have come up that might have allowed us to requisition some of the assassins who fled over the border. I really don't wish to take a chance on this one because it has, er, 'international' implications."

"International implications?"

"Yes, sir. We received our information from the Mossad," Bell said, setting his tea aside. "One of their chaps apparently has managed to follow the back trail of arms one of the terrorist groups in Germany used. It is the same source—out of Boston via the Mediterranean—that used to supply arms to the PIRA. Rumor has it that the Boston source is adding drugs to its arms shipments to Ireland." He gave a wintry smile. "This, of course, puts us in debt to the Mossad. In the past, we would have simply gone in and destroyed the arms shipments. But drugs, well, that is something a bit more public. We might be able to use that as a lever in negotiations. With this new cease-fire and peace negotiations going on, we need to regain 'face' in the international area. I know"—he held up his hand at the prime minister's frown—"but we must be pragmatic about this, sir. If the peace accord goes through after this cease-fire, then the Sinn Fein boys are going to look like heroes. The Provos will have brought Ulster and Britain to their collective knees. But if we can break this drug-smuggling wide open, then we will receive a lot of favorable publicity from the press. And"—he paused to sip from his tea—"we still aren't finished with the arms smuggling, either."

"I thought the agreement was being held with the new accord," the prime minister said, frowning.

"Oh, it is with the Provos," Bell said. He gave another wintry smile. "But we have allowed this thing to drag on long enough over there that many splinter groups have formed. The INLA and the GDC—a new group, the Gaelach Dearg Craobh—means the Irish Red Branch—the Irish are so melodramatic—are a bit more fanatical than the Provos and the Sinn Fein *and* they don't agree with Gerry Adams and his boys. I'm afraid they are going to be holdouts in this affair. We think it's the GDC that is bringing in the new arms, but we can't be certain at this stage."

"I see," the prime minister said. He slowly sipped while he thought. "Go ahead with your plans, but be very careful that you don't violate Ireland's borders, if you can." His voice hardened. "I want that peace accord signed whatever it takes. If you have to go in and 'quietly' take care of the INLA and that new group—the GDC?—then do it, but do it quietly. The country has been fed up with the Troubles over there for years. Frankly, I wish one of those boys would have taken care of that Paisley fellow awhile back. We might have had things settled by now if that had happened. But we must work with what we have. Handle the guns quietly—we don't want to give the Protestants anything to use to stop the negotiations at this point. As for the drugs"—he furrowed his brow thoughtfully—"as soon as you get something, let me know so that we can arrange a press conference. We'll get as much mileage out of this as we can. Lord knows we could use some good publicity for a change."

"Yes, Prime Minister," Bell said politely.

"I do not mind operatives being sent into the Republic, but I do not want them to be, er, visible."

"I understand, sir," Bell said, rising. "We will probably have to bring in the Americans."

The prime minister frowned. "That might not be a bad idea. The president is sending a man to help with negotiations." He smiled. "He needs a cause to take the attention of the U.S. off his, ah, peccadillos. The Americans might be quite willing to help us out over there. Go ahead and contact them. Who's your counter?"

"Richard Wright, sir. In the Agency."

The prime minister pursed his lips disapprovingly. "Oh. *Those* boys. Well, can't be helped, I suppose. But keep me informed—especially if you must go into the Republic. I need time to prepare a denunciation of any charges that may be coming if our operatives are caught."

"Perhaps, sir," Bell said tactfully, "that might not be a bad thing to do after all. We might be able to dissuade the Republic from their plans to ask for a lifting of the limitations on import tariffs."

The prime minister frowned. "Isn't that blackmail?"

"Only if it works," Bell said smoothly. "Otherwise, we can fall back on the politics of the situation."

"Let me think about it," the prime minister said.

The woman slipped away from the door and hurried to the kitchen. The cook looked up at her arrival.

"His nibs a bit upset about the sugar bowl?" She grinned.

The woman made a face. "You know how he gets. Stuffy old starch." She crossed to the counter and folded napkins for a minute, then suddenly snapped her fingers. "I forgot to tell Timmy what time to pick me up tonight."

"Keep it short," the cook cautioned as the woman crossed to the telephone on the wall by the back door. "Don't let his nibs catch you. You know the rules about personal calls."

The woman waved her hand, lifted the receiver, and quickly dialed a number. "I'll only be half-a-sec. Hello! Tim? Mona. Listen, I won't get off until after eight tonight, okay? So let's forget the flicks and just grab a bite at the Silver Tassie. Isn't it tonight that Joey's playing the piano? Right. See you, then. Ta."

She hung up the receiver and smiled at the cook. "See?"

"You've got a real winner, there," the cook said. "Now, my man would 'ave ten minutes of questions. You better 'ang on to that 'un."

Mona smiled as she moved back to the counter, picking up another napkin to fold. Carefully, she lined up the edges of the linen, running her thumb down the crease to seat the fold. She hummed under her breath as she worked, letting her mind slip back fondly to the night before, and their frantic loving in the rooms above the pub off Grafton Street. She thought fleetingly back to their first meeting two months ago when Manchester United had played Leeds. A drink after the game in the Grafton Street pub and now—. She glanced up at her reflection in the window, dim against the raindrops. There had been others prettier in her group at the match, but he had chosen her. She had been surprised when he called her the next day and asked her to the cinema. An aunt had once said she might look like Virginia Woolf if she only wore her hair differently and used a touch of makeup, but Mona knew makeup could little change her bold nose and the flat planes of her face. Her legs, though, were finely shaped and rounded and although her breasts were a bit pendulous, Timmy had said they reminded him of fresh pears. She was grateful to him, and it was only a small thing he had asked of her.

THE MAN HUNG UP THE TELEPHONE AND POURED A GLASS OF whiskey from the bottle on his desk. He looked across the room at the man standing by the door. "Alert the boys," he said. "Mona's got something hot."

"I'll bet she has," the man coarsely sniggered, shrugging into his jacket. He pulled a scully cap low over his brow.

"None of that; none of that, now, or I'll be thumping your head a good one," said Tim Cahill, London liaison officer for the newly formed Gaelach Dearg Craobh. He waved the man out and leaned back in his chair, picking up his glass, sipping it. Now, what do you suppose the bastard's up to this time?

4

MORNING SUNLIGHT DANCED OFF THE WAVES IN THE BAY BELOW THE cottage on one of the Cooley Mountains called Long Woman's Grave outside Omeath, across Carlingford Lough from Warrenpoint in Northern Ireland. Over there, Fallon was a wanted man with a heavy price on his head. Here, in the South, the authorities pretended not to notice his presence. A ship from the British navy sat in the middle of the lough to prevent the forays of the Irish Republican Army, rumored to be rampant in the woods and villages between Omeath and Dundalk. Occasionally at night, the IRA or Provos would slip arms across the lough, landing at Rostrevor, a smaller town along the coast to the east.

Fallon stared at the sunlight shimmering on the bay and the British ship, wondering how soon before the ship was withdrawn, now that news of the cease-fire and treaty talks had been released from Stormont to mixed reviews of outrage and praise. He shook his head and strolled back toward his cottage. Not that it made a great difference, he reflected. "Black" Ian Paisley and his followers did not favor any democratic process that might make Ulster a part of united Ireland. The "reverend" had already been on the radio, fuming about the betrayal of Ulster. And on the other side there had been Bernadette Devlin McAliskey's vehement rejection of the peace talks, rapidly being called the Belfast Agreement or the Mitchell Agreement after the American George Mitchell who had chaired the talks. No, he decided, until the firebrands were quenched, there was little hope that peace would come to Ulster to stay despite the claims by the press.

Behind the cottage, carefully terraced gardens rose up to the pine trees. The gardens were bordered by color combinations of blues, white, cream, and silver. Tall delphiniums, well tended to flower twice in June and September, towered over blue saliras and daisies, agapanthus, and alpine thistles. Another border held plantings of red berberis, henchera palace purple, bronze phormium, roses, fennel, dahlia, the Bishop of Llondaff—all offset by creamy plumes of *Artemisia lactiflora* and *Macleya cordata*. At the back of the garden, an old iron arbor, blue verdigris, opened out onto a planting of foxglove, bluebells, musk mallow, lady's mantle, and slipper orchards along a wood-chip path leading into the trees.

Fallon paused, watching, remembering Homer's lines about Thetis, goddess of the silvery feet, when she came to comfort her son Achilles after his disagreement with Agamemnon:

> Gliding she rose and broke like mist from the inshore
> grey sea face, to sit down softly before him,
> her son in tears—

But Fallon had no tears with which to greet the sea nymphs; the time had long past since he had had tears. He could no longer remember the last time he had cried. Before university, he thought. A lifetime ago. When Mother was killed in an auto accident on N5 and Da died the following year from a stroke. But there have been no tears since. There has been no need for tears. The numbers of the dead themselves have been your tears. But why is there no feeling?

He turned and entered his cottage. Miss Sheba greeted him silently from her perch on the arm of his chair.

"Everything's all right," he told her. She grumbled deep in her throat then leaped lithely to the floor and walked regally to the tiny alcove and sat in front of the refrigerator, carefully curving her tail around her like an Egyptian statuette.

"Let me guess: you're hungry, right?"

She ignored him and stared at the refrigerator door. Fallon opened the door and removed a small bottle of cream. He poured some in a saucer and placed it on the floor for her. Then he opened a small tin of tuna, flaking it into her dish. He watched her eat daintily while he filled the kettle with cold water and placed it on the burner to boil.

"They want me back," he said to her. She paused and raised her head to stare at him with her sea green eyes.

"I know," he said. "But it's a bit different this time."

She made a disgruntled noise in her throat and returned to eat. The kettle whistled. He removed it from the burner and poured it over Darjeeling leaves, setting the pot aside to steep. He brought his cup and saucer from the table beside his chair and rinsed them at the tap.

He walked into the small bathroom he had added off the kitchen alcove and ran hot water into the lavatory bowl. He whipped up a quick lather and spread it evenly across his cheeks, staring at his face in the mirror. He noticed his thick black hair, liberally streaked with silver, curling over the collar of his shirt and made a mental note to visit the barber in Omeath. Tiny crow's-feet led out from the corners of his eyes—laugh lines, some would have called them, but it had been a long time since he had last laughed. The flesh beneath his chin was a bit soft, but it was still firm enough not to be jowly. He scraped the lather from his face, splashed on Bay Lime to tighten the skin, then returned to the kitchen and poured a cup of tea. It was nearly black. He tasted it: bitter, strong, good. He carried the cup and saucer back to his chair and placed it on the table. He fed a new brick of peat to the coals, then sat back and watched the tiny flames begin to curl and lick around the edges of the brick. He sipped, remembering.

Enough killing, he had said to MacCauley. He should have said too much killing; nearly twenty years' worth. He had been seventeen the first time and in his first year at University, living on the perimeter of the IRA, the fashionable sort of thing that young boys did to make themselves appear dashing and bold, to have an aura of mystic danger about them. It didn't matter that he was only a messenger, for that still made him a bit of a hero in the eyes of his classmates and the young ladies who followed his walk across campus with eager eyes. Only a messenger, delivering messages to MacCauley, when two members of the B-Specials broke into the room and, without thinking, he had grabbed Mac-Cauley's pistol from the table, the pistol butt sliding naturally into his hand, whirled and shot both the B-Specials between the eyes. As quick and clean a work as ever I've seen. You're a natural, lad, a natural, MacCauley had said, beaming, and his days as a messenger were over. How many had it been since? Too many to count and it really didn't matter, anyway. The first two had been two too many. Each person has a horror hidden within him he's better off not discovering for then he will have to live with that dark side of himself, trying to explain the horror of it over and over until he dies, an intoxicating horror simultaneously repulsive and addicting.

A car door slammed. Fallon slipped back from his reverie and rose, slipping the Baby Browning from his hiding place. Miss Sheba leaped to her place on the mantel, crouching, threatening growls rumbling from her chest.

A knock sounded on the door. He carefully slipped next to the door and peeked through the peephole bored through the heavy wood at the woman standing outside. She wore a bulky sweater in a fisherman's weave and a skirt the color of heather in bloom. Her auburn hair, lightly streaked with gray, had been gathered in back, exposing her broad forehead and high cheekbones. Her almond-shaped eyes had a slight slant to them, the irises emerald green, nose long and thin above a full, generous mouth.

"Tomas?" she called and impatiently knocked again. Fallon slipped the safety on the pistol and opened the door.

"Hello, Maeve. It's been a long time," he said, and stood aside to let Maeve Larkin enter.

"Yes, it has," she said, moving past him into the room. Her voice was low and warm, and he smelled the soap and a faint hint of spice she had used. He closed the door and followed her into the room. She stopped, staring curiously at Miss Sheba crouched on the mantle.

"A friend," he said. Maeve glanced at the pistol in his hand, and he stepped past her to place it back in its hiding place beneath the mantle. The cat yawned, her bright pink tongue curling back against the blackness of her mouth, and dropped from the mantle, pausing to give Maeve another close look, then walked regally down the short corridor toward the bedroom in back. Maeve laughed.

"I'm not so sure I made a good impression," she said.

"Miss Sheba's a hard one to please," he answered. "Tea?"

She nodded. "Please. A cup would do fine. There's a bit of chill to the air this morning. Spring is not quite here, I'm afraid."

He moved into the kitchenette as she looked approvingly around the room. She picked up the book lying beside the chair and glanced at the title. An eyebrow quirked.

"I didn't know you were a reader," she said as he emerged from the kitchenette, carrying a tray with cup and saucer and milk and sugar. He placed it on the small table. She stepped close to the bookshelves at the back of the room. "Dickens. Yeats. Beckett. Swift." She turned to look at him. "'Tis a strange man you are, Tomas."

He shrugged. A faint smile lifted his lips. "For a gunman, you're thinking?" He motioned to the chair and took one across from her.

"That's not what I was thinking," she said quickly, too quickly.

"No? Why not? It's what I'd be thinking."

She hesitated, then laughed, moving to the chair. "Well, maybe a bit." She sat, placed the book beside the tray, and lifted the saucer and cup. She ignored the milk and sugar, sipped, and nodded approvingly.

"You make a good cup, Tomas," she said.

"Thank you," he answered. "Most women don't like strong tea without sweetener."

"I'm not most women," she said.

"I know," he said. A long pause followed his words. The room seemed darker as he fleetingly remembered when she had been tortured in the interrogation cells at Castlereagh by the Royal Ulster Constabulary, who were after information she didn't know. No, one could say a lot about Maeve Larkin, but she was certainly not like other women. Any other woman would not have blown the balls off the man who had raped her. He cleared his throat.

"I've been reading about you lately. You've become a thorn in the Provos's side since Mullaghmore."

"That was awhile ago. Things were different then," she said, looking away from him.

"Have you heard from Con Edwards lately?" Fallon asked, mentioning the *Times* reporter who had discovered the identity of her torturer. For a time they had been lovers and together had discovered the traitor, the *gombeen* man, who had been responsible for the death of Lord Mountbatten and her husband, Conor Larkin, poet, professor, and one of the IRA's top gunmen in the early days before the Provos.

A wan smile touched her lips. "I think he's in Germany, now. He was in the Persian Gulf when that fiasco was brewing. He writes occasionally."

"Do you miss him?"

"I'm comfortable," she said evasively.

"Still alone?"

"Yes. And you?"

"I've got Miss Sheba," he said, nodding toward the corridor where she had disappeared.

"You must be lonely out here," she said.

"It's better that way. Safer, anyway."

"Another would provide an extra pair of eyes."

"And liability. What about you?" he said, changing the subject.

"Me?"

"How have things been with you? I read about your work occasionally."

"Slow," she said, then laughed. "No, it isn't going. Not well, anyway. I get so frustrated and depressed at times that I want to scream. There are times when I can go for weeks and not think about the British soldiers. I can pass them in the streets when I'm in Belfast and not even see them. Then I stop and tell myself that I'm beginning to become like the others and accept them, and the next time I see one, I must remind myself why they are here, and then I want to tell him, 'Why don't you get out of my country? There's nothing here for you but hatred.' But even then I know that damn few people anymore even realize they are there. Except the politicians and the old Provos. Without the British and the RUC, they would have no reason for living. And the young," she considered reflectively. "They would have no meaning to their lives if they didn't have war." She sighed heavily and glanced at Fallon. "Like you, Tomas. You need someone to take the place of what you have given up."

"Well, that may be all in the past, now, with the cease-fire," he said.

"Do you really think so?" she asked curiously.

"Not really. The Troubles have become a way of life, now. And there's too much hatred still there."

"And you don't want another to be with you?"

He shook his head and stared at the small fire playing on the coals. "Who could fit into my world?"

"You could go into others."

"No. I lost that right years ago. Probably around the time of Marie Wilson. When she was killed in that bomb blast at the civic center in Enniskillen back in eighty-seven, people like me ceased to be romantic."

"Were you involved in that?" she asked, her forehead wrinkling with sudden concern.

"All of us were whether we were there or not. There are no innocent people involved in the Troubles; all are guilty."

An awkward silence fell between them. They looked away, finishing their tea. Finally, Fallon asked if Maeve would like to take a walk. She quickly agreed and rose to carry their cups to the kitchen over his protest. She rinsed and stacked them neatly next to the porcelain sink and met him at the door. He slipped into a windcheater, checked the tiny automatic in the jacket pocket, and opened the door. Bright sunlight streamed into the room and they stepped out into its warmth. Fallon locked the door behind them and led her onto the narrow path that wound behind the cottage, leading up the mountain through the stand of trees. They walked close to each other, contented with the day and the heavy scents of wet wood and musty earth. A raven croaked at them and flew away, sunlight brilliant on his black wings. Tiny mice scampered in the underbrush.

"MacCauley sent you," Fallon said at last.

"Yes," she said. She slipped on the damp grass and he caught her arm, steadying her.

"But why did you come?" he asked. "I thought you were finished with us."

"The children. Whoever is bringing drugs into the country must be stopped. The Gardai doesn't seem to be able to do much about doing that. Sure, and I think you are needed, Tomas."

"He showed you the pictures." She nodded. He sighed. "Ah, well. What did I expect? The man is ruthless."

"What should I tell him? Will you do it, Tomas?"

"No. I'm through. What can we learn from more deaths?"

"Is that all?"

"No," he said quietly. "I'm afraid that if I go back in I won't want to come out again."

She walked to a fallen log and gingerly sat. She stared thoughtfully at him for a moment, then spoke. "I know you want no more of that kind of life, but sometimes we have to do unpleasant things. This is one of those times, Tomas."

"There are others who can be doing the job," Fallon answered. "Tell MacCauley to send one of them."

"He has," she answered. "Remember Joe Doherty?"

"The one who got away when some of the boys were ambushed by the Brits in Belfast? I think he was in the Na Fianna Eirann with me for a while."

"The same. He made it to America and was safe before Mac-Cauley contacted him in New York to be looking into some missing arms. It's the biggest loss since nineteen eighty-four, when the trawler *Marita Ann* and her arms shipment was captured. At that time, there wasn't a problem with drugs. Doherty agreed to look into it and a couple nights later, when he was serving drinks at Clancy's Bar, a couple of agents from the Federal Bureau of Investigation arrested him and sent him back to Ulster to stand trial for killing that Brit captain—what was his name? Ah, yes. Westmacott. Herbert Westmacott. But his brother stayed over there in America and MacCauley asked him to come in out of the cold. He did and three days later they found him floating in Boston harbor.

"Then MacCauley got another tip on the drugs and sent three of his people to Gibraltar to run a trace on the information. The

Special Air Service (SAS) gunned them down when they tried to cross the border into Spain. They were unarmed," she added.

"Anything else?"

"Yes." She hesitated, then her face hardened and she continued. "In February, a Brit soldier shot and killed a priest who was coming south over the border. He had information for MacCauley, but it died with him."

"I see," Fallon said slowly. "So, then. Someone has an arm into the network, I'm thinking. Another *gombeen* man." She nodded. "But I'm also thinking that MacCauley has others who can run the fox to ground."

"'Tis true he has others, but there's only one Tomas Fallon."

He shook his head. A look of pain swept over his face and disappeared. He turned to stare down into the lough. A tiny sailboat danced in the sparkling water, but far out on the horizon clouds were beginning to form. He watched the boat tack across the water.

"I know about the children, Tomas," she said softly. He shook his head.

"Ah, yes. The children." He turned to face her. "Everyone thinks it is the children. But the children are only a part of it. The truth of the matter is that I can see no end to it anymore. When we get rid of some of the bastards like Ian Paisley who hate only for the purpose of hating and make their fortunes from it, others just like them take their places. Paisley's son, for example. They're like clones, you understand? They mate and make another. There's simply no end to them. We're like mice in a revolving cage, running constantly and getting nowhere. Do you have any idea how many men I've killed?" She shook her head. A grim smile touched his lips. "Neither do I, but the figure doesn't matter. The number left hasn't changed. Others have taken their place who need killing just as badly."

"I'm sorry, Tomas," she said. "I didn't know."

He laughed. "No, you didn't. And I'm thinking you still don't." His eyes burned. "You see, there's nothing else left for me but the killing. That's the problem: I'm trying to feel again. So the answer is 'no,' Maeve."

She nodded and rose, brushing herself off. "A chroí. I understand. I'll try to explain it to MacCauley, but I'm not sure he'll understand."

"Oh, he'll understand," Fallon said. "You see, in that respect, we're all alike. The difference, though, is that MacCauley is afraid to step back and be nothing. And that is the real reason why he wants to find out who's bringing the drugs into the country. There may be a little politics about it all, but with the cease-fire on, now, why what is left for him? The drugs are only another battle, you see. Without the Troubles, we are nothing. And that is all we'll ever be. Do you understand?"

She nodded and, tucking her arm through his, turned to walk back down the mountain. The rain began to fall a little harder through the branches crossing the trail over their heads. Dark clouds scudded across the sky and when they emerged from the trees into the clearing, heavy whitecaps rolled across the gunmetal waters of Carlingford Lough, tossing the British warship at anchor in the middle of the bay. The air turned suddenly cool, and the wind began to sough through the trees, bending the blue and yellow meadow flowers and the purple heather. They hurried toward the back door of the cottage. A deep sadness filled her.

5

MISS SHEBA LANDED GENTLY UPON HIS CHEST, AWAKENING HIM. A low rumble vibrated from inside her. He sat up in bed and swung his legs over the edge. Miss Sheba leaped lightly to the floor and took two steps, crouching, facing the corridor. His hand automatically found the pistol on the nightstand beside his bed. He rose and glided on bare feet down the corridor to the main room. Gently, he touched the locks on the door; they were secure. He frowned. What had awakened Miss Sheba? He stood still, breathing quietly through opened mouth, listening to the sounds of the night: the gentle creaks as wood contracted, the hum of the small refrigerator. Then he heard that which didn't belong in the night: the rasp of cloth against the wall outside, the click of stone against stone, a soft curse. At least two of them, possibly more.

He moved swiftly across the room to the rear window, hesitated, then quietly unlocked it and slid it open. He stepped through onto the grass damp from the night dew and immediately dropped, squatting on his heels. His eyes probed the night, then he moved off rapidly through the moonless darkness, circling the house in a wide detour. He came upon them from behind. One fiddled with a shoe box against the wall outside his bedroom. The other two watched him as he worked. Fallon shook his head, sighed, then spoke.

"'Tis a nice soft night, but fair late to come a-calling, I'm thinking."

The two watchers spun around and fired into the darkness. Fallon fired back, deliberately holding his aim low. The two crumbled to the ground. One swore angrily while the other screamed.

"Mother of God!" the third exclaimed in a Belfast accent, holding his hands high overhead. "Be careful or we'll all go up."

"Ah, I'm dying! I'm dying!" one screamed. He began sobbing.

"Bastard."

Fallon moved silently beside them. "Turn around and face the wall. Hands against it; feet out: you know the routine." The third man promptly followed directions. Fallon could see his legs trembling in the darkness over the shoe box. He glanced at the other two on the ground. One had taken a bullet in the hip; the other held tightly to his thigh and swore softly.

"A doctor," the first moaned. A string of slobber ran from his mouth. Fallon ignored him and gathered their pistols. He laid them against the wall, well away from his prisoners.

"Who are you?" he asked the one with the leg wound. The man spat and stared defiantly at him.

"Foacker," he said. "Get it over with."

"Please," moaned the other man.

Fallon moved to the man spread-eagled against the wall. He placed the barrel of his pistol against the flesh behind the man's ear. The man flinched away, but Fallon pressed harder.

"What's in the box?" he asked softly. The man hesitated and Fallon increased the pressure with the pistol. "Now, then, I can always shoot you and look myself."

"Gelignite," the man muttered.

"Shut up," growled the man with the thigh wound.

"And?" Fallon prodded.

"Fulminate of mercury. It's touchy stuff."

Fallon nodded. "Who sent you?"

"UDF—the Ulster Defense," the one against the wall said.

"Foacker. Don't tell 'em nuthin', hear?"

"What difference does it make? Sure, he'll find out anyway," the other answered.

"How did you find me?" Fallon asked.

"Did yuh think yuh could hide forever? We have our ways."

"I've been out of it a long time. Why now?" Fallon asked. The man on the ground spat again.

"Not long enough," he growled. "Never long enough, Fallon. Did yuh think that we'd forget? Yuh left a lot of widows and wee ones over there. They've all got memories." He gave a short, ugly laugh. "Yuh don't retire from death, Fallon. Some things are never forgotten. And some things don't get covered with pieces of paper promising peace. There ain't no peace for the likes of you. Now, I've talked enough. Do it; get it over with."

"Take the others and go," Fallon said to the man against the wall. He stepped back and away as the other turned slowly in disbelief.

"You're letting us go?" Fallon remained silent. "Why?"

"There's been enough killing. Now, take them and go."

The man looked uncertainly at the two on the ground. "How? They have to be carried. I've only got two hands."

"That's your problem," Fallon said coldly.

"I can manage," the man with the leg wound said. He gritted his teeth and pushed himself to his feet. He gasped, hobbling painfully. His breath whistled between his teeth. He nodded at the other on the ground. "Help that poor bastard, and let's be going. We've foacked this one up, proper. There won't be much sympathy back home."

The other bent and lifted the man with the hip wound to his feet. He whimpered. The three began moving downhill away from the cottage.

"Just a minute," Fallon said. He stepped to the cottage wall, bent, and gingerly collected the shoe box. It was surprisingly heavy. He handed it to the man with the leg wound. "Be careful with that, won't you?"

"Shit," the other said, fumbling with it. He held it steadily in front of him. "I can't manage this and meself."

"You'd better. Now, leave!" Fallon said harshly.

"Sweet Mother," the unwounded man muttered. "For Christ's sakes, man!" Fallon lifted the pistol. "We're going, we're going."

The three shambled slowly down the hill. Fallon watched them as they moved through the gate. The man with the shoe box looked back at Fallon.

"Don't even think it," Fallon called. The man hesitated, then shrugged and began hobbling down after his partners. Fallon moved away from the house to watch their progress down the slope, feeling the familiar cold arms of the night embrace him. He shrugged irritably, fighting against the feeling. You are no more of the night, he told himself. You are through with this.

A sudden *thunk-thunk* disturbed his thoughts, and he glanced up at the night sky as a helicopter gunship on patrol suddenly flew over the mountain, its spotlight searching the ground. Fallon automatically fell flat beside the wall as the spotlight swept over the three men making their way down the mountain then back again. The helicopter hovered, then the spotlight swept away toward the cottage. The man carrying the shoe box stepped blindly into the night. A pebble rolled under the foot of his wounded leg. He stumbled. The shoe box slipped from his hands. A scream of sudden awareness sounded, then the night filled with a roar as the bomb exploded. Dirt and stones rained over Fallon. He heard glass breaking behind him. The helicopter veered away from the sudden flash of light and raced down the mountain, out over Carlingford Lough in a straight line for the border. Fallon swallowed painfully to equalize the sudden pressure against his eardrums, then cautiously rose to his feet. Down the mountain, a huge crater remained where three men had stood only moments before.

A heaviness descended upon Fallon, and he turned and walked inside the cottage. Miss Sheba met him, yowling, her fur standing on end. He bent and fondled her ears. She sniffed his hand, walked around him, then, satisfied that he was unharmed, jumped up on the mantel and turned to watch him. Fallon took a deep breath and went down the short corridor to the bedroom. He turned on the lights and dressed quickly in a black turtleneck and trousers. He sat on the bed to pull on a pair of black ankle boots, then stood and crossed to the wardrobe and reached in the back. He removed a black leather jacket and shrugged into it. Then he reached up on top of the wardrobe and took down a small case and placed it on the bed, opening it. Tiny lights flickered warmly back at him from the oiled dark blue finish of the CZ-52, an ugly weapon, yet beautiful in its ugliness, a reminder of what he had been. Memories slipped quickly by and he recalled the euphoria he'd first felt when the plump Ilich Sanchez had made him a gift of it in Paris after he had helped Sanchez escape arrest by the Défense de la Securité du Territoire (DST) after Sanchez had used the pistol to kill the traitor Michel Moukharbel who had betrayed him. The bullet that killed Moukharbel had passed through his body, the floorboards of the apartment, the ceiling of the apartment below, and a molded plastic table before embedding itself so deeply in the second set of floorboards that it could not be dug out by forensic experts. The attempt at arrest by Commissaire Jean Herranz had taken place in the Rue Toullier when Herranz had tried to arrest Sanchez in his girlfriend's apartment. Fallon had wounded Herranz with a bullet in the shoulder, allowing Sanchez to leap from the second-floor window onto the top of a truck parked in the alley. They lost little time in making their escape from Paris to Marseilles.

He lifted the weapon from its handmade case. The grip slid familiarly into his palm. The balance was heavy toward the barrel, and he automatically lifted a clip from the case and gently slid it home into the grip. The balance corrected itself perfectly. Automatically, his fingers grasped the slide and pulled it back, releasing it and sending a fat Tokarev 7.62-mm cartridge into the chamber. The cartridge had been hand loaded from a used casing by a friendly armorer in the Netherlands as had all of Fallon's ammunition—an old trick Sanchez had taught him: used casings reloaded were not admissible in any court since ballistic experts could not ascertain which weapon made specific scratchings on the casing. That made an automatic as safe as any revolver that retained fixed casings in its cylinder, giving the automatic user a three- or four-cartridge advantage over the revolver.

Fallon closed his eyes. Sanchez swam in front of his memory, short, fat, perspiration beading on his wide forehead above his too-close-set eyes. Again, he heard the words softly spoken and lightly Spanish-accented. It is the best weapon for an assassin, my friend, for there is none as powerful that can be fired as rapidly and as accurately. I hope it will serve you well when you return home. He handed Fallon a slip of paper. Memorize the name and address then destroy the paper. He will make you the cartridges you need if you tell him you are a friend of mine. His black eyes saddened as he gripped Fallon's forearms with strong fingers. I am afraid, my friend, that I have given you both a blessing and a curse, but this you will not understand until you are much older and less romantic. His voice had trailed off, disappearing in embarrassment as he recognized the melodramatic overtones of his words.

Fallon opened his eyes and looked down again at the pistol in his hands, seeing now a piece of metal coldly machined with precision settings. It was only a pistol, nothing more. Dimly, he heard the sirens of approaching Gardai cars. He laid the pistol back in its box and reached into the back of the wardrobe and removed a box containing a shoulder holster. He slid the pistol under his left arm and reached into the pistol box and dropped half-a-dozen clips into the side pocket. He slid open the drawer of the nightstand beside his bed and removed a thick wallet. He glanced through the large bills inside and slid it into the inside pocket of his jacket.

The sirens stopped. Fallon took a quick look around, then scooped up Miss Sheba and hurried down the corridor to the living room. He glanced out the window: revolving lights cast an eerie glow where the bomb had exploded. Figures moved like specters through the glow. One detached itself from the group and moved toward the cottage. Fallon grunted softly and crossed the living room in four quick strides. Gently, he lifted the latch of the back door and slipped out, firmly pressing the door until the latch caught. Then he turned and, carefully cuddling Miss Sheba in the crook of his arm, moved out into the darkness of the stand of trees behind the cottage.

6

COLD RAIN FELL LIGHTLY ON ALL OF BELFAST AND FOR THOSE WHO
lived in Belfast, the rain was generally all over Ireland, falling on
every part of the dark, central plain, the treeless hills of Sligo, and
the Bog of Allen, churning the waters of Carlingford Lough and
the river Shannon. The rain fell lightly too on the cemeteries
around Belfast where the bodies of soldiers lay among the bodies
of the innocent.

"Dobbie" O'Donnell moved down Bray Street from the corru-
gated-tin Peace Line, his hands jammed into the pockets of his
dirty khaki pants, his thin shoulders hunched up around his ears,
the collar of his anorak turned high to keep the rain from running
down his neck. His pointed nose glowed redly from the cold that
tightened the flesh over his cheekbones, leaving him ferret-faced.
The night was falling. Tiny bits of broken glass glittered like dia-
monds across the wet cobblestones while rats' eyes glared ruby
red from behind ash cans. He could smell the damp earth from the
window boxes used as tiny herb gardens. He shivered and softly
swore, hunching deeper into his coat. March was almost over and
the spring was coming. In a while, the moon would be rising, but
no moon would be seen in this gray twilight; only the pools of
blue-white light on the street from the street lamps. Faith, the
weather alone is enough to make a man tired without him having
to stump the streets looking for work that isn't there. You need a

holiday, he told himself. But there is little enough money for the odd pint or two and none for whiskey, so what chance is there for a holiday? He spat thick phlegm onto the street and stopped, gloomily looking about him. Everything looked dingy, dismal, scarred. Off the Lower Falls Road, dirty kids had been driven away from the cracked asphalt into tiny, tumbledown terraced houses. The shops on the main road were still open, but their owners had little hope of any business as they watched the rain through dirty windows covered with wire mesh. It really didn't matter, however: the green grocers had only a few potatoes and onions to sell, the tobacconists a bit more, but the florists waited patiently, lavish floral funeral wreaths standing on display just inside their doors. The West Belfast Social Security office also had wired windows covered with rubbish hurled at it by some of the twelve thousand unemployed it served. On its wall, someone had painted an advertisement for *An Phoblacht*, the Sinn Fein weekly newspaper. The roads and pavement were strewn with rubble.

He kicked angrily at a chunk of brick lying in the street, sending it skittering into the darkness where it struck an ash can. Rats squealed and scampered away from the sudden noise. Bloody rats! Bloody, bloody rats! A couple of pounds is all it would take and then you could be visiting your uncle in Donegal near Gortahock. And although the dark blue bilberries had not set on yet for the dance of Lughnasa celebrated during the beginning of the harvest season when the fields were golden with stands of wheat and the young people would go up into the hills of Beltany and Carn Tre-una before the priests stopped them (although a few still went deep into the hidden dales away from the stern eyes of the local fathers), there would be other dances now, spring dances, and the girls would still be as golden as the coming wheat and ready for planting. Ah, there was the place!

He stood in the middle of the street, closing his eyes, remembering. There is a field and a little river beside the stone cottage

with its thatched roof and there is also a road but the road is clean
and quiet and there is a big stone on the other side of the road and
a bird sits on the stone—

"Are you woolgathering, now, Dobbie? And here of all places
when the Prods could be picking your bones if you're not careful?"

He leaped and spun around, his stiff fingers scrambling in his
pocket for the flick-knife. He froze as a quiet chuckle came from
the black figure in front of him.

"Take your hands out empty, Dobbie," the figure said gently.
Dobbie swallowed painfully and slowly pulled his hands from his
pocket. The figure moved closer, and Dobbie heaved a sigh of
relief.

"Fallon. Yuh took a year off the back of me life," he complained.

"You need to relax more, Dobbie," Fallon said. "And keep your
voice down. The shadows have ears here."

"What are yuh doin' back in Belfast?" Dobbie asked, obediently
pitching his voice lower. "I thought yuh were through with the
boyos. There's a reward on your head to tempt all. And the peace
docket won't be taking that away any time soon."

Fallon smiled faintly, and Dobbie nervously shuffled his feet.
"Even you, Dobbie?"

Dobbie raised his hands, palms out, protesting, "Now, Fallon. I
didn't mean that. What manner of man would I be who'd turn a
friend? Haven't I always done right by yuh? Who warned yuh in
yer nest on Poole Street when Paisley's boys were only a block
away and closin' fast a few years ago?"

"I always wondered how they found me," Fallon said mildly.
"You wouldn't be having any notions in that direction?"

A chill ran down Dobbie's back. He shivered. His eyes slid
away from Fallon's face. "Times are hard, Fallon," he said defensively. "There are those who wouldn't do a thing like that are
forced to because there's no food for the table and their children
are crying from their empty bellies."

"You don't have any children, do you, now, Dobbie?" Fallon asked.

"No." Dobbie glanced away from Fallon's icy stare. He blustered. "Now, Fallon, yuh wouldn't be thinkin' I'd be droppin' the whisper on yuh? Even for five thousand quid?"

"Five thousand? My, the Prods must be getting desperate. Tell me, now, is the bastard Paisley putting this up out of his own good pocket? Or is it a bit of collective bargaining?"

"Eh?" Dobbie asked, wrinkling his brow in confusion.

"Who will be paying the thirty pieces of silver to the one with the Judas kiss?" Fallon said, slowly and clearly.

"Faith, when you speak like that I have little notion of what you're saying," Dobbie said.

"Who's paying the punt for my pound of flesh?"

"Oh." Dobbie's face cleared of confusion. "Anyone who appears at Sackville." He bared his yellow teeth in a ratlike grin. "Or anywhere an SAS man pretends to be one of us."

"Us?"

"You know," Dobbie winked and ducked his head, shuffling his feet nervously. A tic started high in his left cheek.

"Ah, yes. You're back in, then?" Fallon said solemnly. "Didn't I hear something about you being warned off by the boyos, and you promising to do the same to keep from walking on sticks?"

"Now, sure, and who would be telling the tale on something like that? When was I ever out?" Dobbie said. A flush stood out dark red from his cheekbones.

"Then you'll be knowing the presence of MacCauley?"

Dobbie looked away from him. "Ah. I don't know, Fallon. It's not like yuh were still one of us, yuh know? Not," he hastily added, "that I'm saying yer not, yuh understand. It's just that—just that—well, there's been a bit of talk," he ended lamely. Fallon stared at him. "Nothin' accusin' or anything, but, well, I, er—"

"Where?" Fallon asked quietly.

"Now, Fallon—"

"Where?"

Dobbie shrugged and wiped his runny nose with the back of his hand then scrubbed it clean along his pant leg. "The Briar and the Thrush. In the back room. He's there in the afternoons for who wants 'im. After that, I dunno," he said sullenly. "The man's become real suspicious of late." He tapped his forehead with a dirty forefinger. "The man's been talked to by the *aes sídhe,* some are saying."

"And since when have you been listening to the fairy folk, Dobbie?" Fallon asked. "Are you believing in them, now?"

Dobbie shrugged again, jamming his hands deep into his pockets. "A man must believe in something, and the priests have given us nothin' but promises of how great the next world will be. But that don't put a bit of bacon on the table for tae now, an' it don't put the jingle in the pocket for a pint now and then among a man's mates. I see nothin' different between the priests and the *aes síde.* What do you believe in, Fallon?" he asked, suddenly bold.

"*Lig Fáil,*" Fallon answered. "Only the past. The Briar and the Thrush? Off Glen Road?"

"He's there."

"One more thing, Dobbie. With the peace on and cease-fire called, who would be paying out the pound for my head, now?"

Dobbie shrugged. "The money's still up and there are those sayin' that it can be had from Paisley's Independent Orange Order and the 'Blackmen.' "

Fallon nodded. The Blackmen, members of the Royal Black Preceptory, an advanced Orange organization, were rabid about maintaining Ulster predominantly Protestant. Their marches were built on hate and they deliberately provoked the Catholics by pointedly marching through Catholic neighborhoods, taunting the residents with the Loyalist anthem "The Sash My Father Wore."

"Yuh have to remember, Fallon, that 'tisn't being a soldier yer wanted for; 'tis murder. There's no forgivin' that. Not yet."

Fallon nodded and turned away, heading into an alley branching off between two brownstones. Dobbie watched him go, his heart slowing its beating. He became aware that he was perspiring in the cold and cursed and wiped his forehead on the sleeve of his anorak. He sneezed and felt the cold beginning to settle in his eyes. Anger worked its way into his brain, and he kicked another broken brick into the darkness of the alley after Fallon.

"I'm not afraid of yuh, boyo!" he yelled. Echoes of his words came back to him from the alley darkness, and he shivered and hunched deeper into his anorak. "I'm not," he muttered, staring at the cracked toes of his shoes. "A hundred pounds is all it would take. A hundred foacking pounds, and this bloody whore of a city could kiss my bloody arse good-bye." Then he remembered the reward and stared half-fearfully into the alley as he slowly grew warm beneath the water-sogged anorak.

7

A LAYER OF SOOT NEARLY OBSCURED THE STAINED GLASS PANEL OF A thrush sitting on a briar set in the middle of the door. Fallon turned the knob and entered. A heavy odor of malt greeted him as he stood for a moment, letting his eyes adjust themselves to the dim. A long, mahogany bar, its surface scarred and dented, ran three-quarters the length of the room. A couple of tables and chairs stood scattered in the center of the room. Behind them were two high settles to provide the women who wanted it with a bit of privacy for their evening drink. A bench ran along the wall to the right, its surface polished gray from hundreds of bottoms covered with working corduroy. Behind the bar, a burly bartender rested brawny forearms upon the bar. His black hair was close-cropped, and he held a well-chewed stub of a dead cigar tightly clenched between yellowed teeth. A faint smile appeared at the corner of his lips and an eyebrow raised as Fallon caught his eye. Fallon nodded at him and glanced over the rest of the bar. Three crude men nursed pints of stout at the bar. At the opposite end stood four teenage boys wearing impressive suits and pointed Italian shoes with long, bulky, khaki coats hanging off their shoulders. The "mods," Fallon knew. He looked around for their opposite number, the "skinheads," who would be wearing Wrangler jackets, bleached jeans, and Doc Marten boots, or the "heavies," who wore leather and studs, but neither group was evident. Too early, he decided as he approached the bar. They would be searching for each other later. Funny. All the fighting going on and people look for even other reasons to fight and satisfy what they feel is an obligation. Or is it that the Troubles have become so familiar that it no longer feels like fighting? And now that the Troubles may be over, are the young looking for something to take their place?

"Hello, Willie," Fallon said, stopping in front of the bartender.

"Tomas," Willie acknowledged. "Been quite awhile since you were in here."

Fallon nodded. "Almost four years, I believe."

"Want a pint?"

Fallon shook his head. "No. MacCauley in back?"

Willie hesitated. "You're not wanted there."

A faint smile touched Fallon's lips. "Why?"

"You said it yourself: it's been four years. Times change."

"Times don't change, Willie, people change."

"Damn it, Tomas, you know the way of things."

"I do. Is MacCauley in back?"

"Tomas, I can't!"

"Aw, come on, Willie," one of the *bachlachs* said. "Since when do yuh give reasons to a wee one like this?" He gave Fallon an insolent grin. "Yuh got your answer, little man. Now, be off with yuh."

Willie took his cigar from his mouth and stared at the man. "Stay out of this, Dooley. You don't know what you're about," he said quietly.

"What's to know?" Dooley said. His beefy face crinkled in a suety smile, nearly burying his eyes. "Why, a good breeze would blow this one to his knees." He belched and turned and winked at his friends standing by his elbow.

"Dooley," Willie said warningly.

"Well, Willie, I'll just be takin' care of this little problem for you," Dooley said. He lazily reached out to grab Fallon then froze as Fallon moved his leather jacket open a fraction, exposing the pistol in its shoulder holster. His eyes stared flat and cold into Dooley's.

"Now, then. Was there something you were wanting?" Fallon said, his words falling softly in the sudden hush.

Dooley flushed and moved back away from Fallon, his fingers groping for his pint on the bar. His shoulders bunched tightly against his work shirt as he unsteadily lifted the glass to his lips, drinking deeply against the sudden shame.

"He's in back," Willie said nervously. He slipped the cigar back into his mouth then took it out again, holding it indecisively. Fallon nodded and crossed behind the *bachlachs* to the back door. He opened it and stepped through, softly closing it behind him.

"You damn fool!" Willie exploded. Spittle sprayed across the bar, covering Dooley who flinched away from it. "If it's suicide you're contemplating, be kind enough to do it in another's house." He nodded at the back door. "That one doesn't play your foolish games. He doesn't have to."

"Shut yer foacking mouth!" Dooley said thickly. His heavy hands opened and closed convulsively, the knuckles disappearing into the flesh. He glared at the others. "What are yuh all starin' at? Can't a man be havin' a drink in peace without others gawkin' at 'im?"

"Don't be blaming them for your troubles," Willie said.

Dooley pushed his empty glass across the bar. "Another," he ordered. Willie shook his head.

"I'm thinking not. The drink will be makin' a bigger fool of you."

Dooley made a strangling sound in his throat. Willie reached under the bar and brought up the sawed-off handle of a billiard cue. "Off with you," he said, pointing toward the door. "I'm not needing your custom in here."

"I'll be back," Dooley growled, making his way to the door.

"And I'll break your pate for the coming," Willie said, lifting the cue threateningly. "Stay your way."

Dooley swore long and fluently as he stepped through the door.

8

MacCauley looked up annoyed from the table where he was working as Fallon stepped into the room, closing the door behind him. His eyes widened.

"Fallon," he breathed.

"Don't say you weren't expecting me, Seamus," Fallon said easily. His glance flickered over the two others sitting at chairs away from the table then back to MacCauley.

MacCauley frowned. "Sure, now, and I wasn't. You made it plain when we met last."

"As did you," Fallon said. He stood casual, hip shot in front of the table, his left side toward MacCauley, his right hand casually holding his belt. Tension flared in the room. One of MacCauley's guards reached behind his back and Fallon's eyes leaped to his face. "Don't. You're not good enough," he said. The guard froze as MacCauley made a gesture of dismissal.

"Don't," he said. "He's right: you're not."

Fallon's gaze shifted back to MacCauley. A small smile lifted the corners of his lips, but his eyes remained bleak and hard. "The ones you sent weren't, either."

"But I didn't," MacCauley said flatly, levelly.

"And why would I be expecting you to say differently?" He shook his head. "Seamus, you never lied before. The words don't sit right with you, now."

"I'm not," MacCauley answered. "What happened?"

"They tried a bomb."

"And?"

"It left a big hole in the road."

"Jaysus," one of the men in the chairs breathed.

"They said they were UDF. I wondered if you had shopped me?" Fallon asked. "Who besides Maeve did you tell? For sure, no one else knew about Long Woman's Grave."

"The GDC," MacCauley said suddenly. "It has to be."

"And would they be having enough resources to use a gunship?"

"No, but whoever they told, would. You forget at times, Tomas: there's a goodly amount on your head, and the UDF or RUC, yes, even the SAS, would be liking to save themselves a jingle or two by taking care of you themselves. The Agreement doesn't forgive murders. It'll be time before they spell out what was murder and what was war."

"All war is murder," Fallon said absently. "But how would they know enough to use Maeve?"

"They had been around a long time before they were given to the RUC," MacCauley said. "It was no secret to anyone in the PIRA about Maeve. She's not exactly been silent, you know. They must have found out that we had contacted you and tried to take you out. Unless," he continued, "you told someone. You didn't, right?"

"No one," Fallon emphatically answered. His face tightened. "There could be no other way; you know that. It had to be you or someone who was in with you once like those bastards in the GDC."

MacCauley pursed his lips, nodding thoughtfully. He knew what Fallon was saying: everyone in the movement who had made it to the inner command had left his family, refusing all contact with them, deliberately cutting themselves away from those who could be used against them. In some cases, some family members had been seized by the Special Air Service (SAS) and tortured to reveal the whereabouts of their relatives known to be in the Provos, but they could tell nothing, and, in many cases, the Provos knew nothing of the difficulties their families were undergoing. It was better that way, much better. His own wife had been a victim of the inner rooms at Crumlin Jail and again at Castlereagh, dying hard when she couldn't make her captives believe she didn't know anything.

"I know," MacCauley said. "I apologize, Tomas. I thought you might have tried to go back."

Fallon smiled faintly. "Who would know me anymore?"

"That leaves the question of who knew how to find you," MacCauley answered. "I've told no one."

"What about Maeve?"

MacCauley's heavy eyebrows drew together in a frown. "What about her?"

"You told her," Fallon said pointedly.

MacCauley frowned. "When was this?"

"Four days ago. The others came that night after she was away."

"Tomas, I sent no one. No one," MacCauley said emphatically. He placed his hands flat on the table. "So—"

He never finished as the door suddenly crashed open behind Fallon. An RUC officer, armed with an Ingram submachine gun, charged through the open doorway, fanning out to the right, followed by his partner.

"Hands high!" he yelled. MacCauley froze. His bodyguards started to raise their hands. Fallon spun quickly, dropping to one knee, the CZ-52 slipping smoothly from its holster. He fired twice rapidly. The officers crashed back against the wall, their Ingrams slipping from nerveless fingers as twin black holes suddenly appeared in the middle of their foreheads. Fallon fired three more shots through the open doorway, the first catching a third officer in the stomach as he tried to come through.

"Back door! Quickly!" Fallon yelled. MacCauley's bodyguards galvanized into action, scooping Skorpion V2 61s from a small table behind MacCauley and leading the way through the back door. They leaped into the alley, swinging abreast of each other to face the street. The first fired a short burst, catching two RUC officers running into the alley. Fallon followed MacCauley as he sprinted down the alley, away from the street.

They wove their way through the warren of alleys away from the firing, working their way deeper into the Catholic neighborhood. They emerged into Fergus Lane and turned off into what appeared to be a cul-de-sac called Tuam's Circle although Fallon knew the house at No. 4 had a passage behind a cupboard in the back bedroom that led into a house fronting Donegal Road. Inside, MacCauley quickly pulled the curtains tightly closed then fell onto the couch, gasping for air, his face white from the efforts of the past hour. Fallon quickly satisfied himself that they were alone in the house, then took the chair facing the door. He took the CZ-52 from its holster, removed its clip, and reloaded it from loose bullets he took from his jacket pocket. MacCauley watched him while he caught his breath, then shook his head.

"Ah, Tomas. You haven't changed in spite of yourself. That was as efficient as ever! What have I been telling you? Look at yourself: sitting there without a thought as to what's happened while a bare hour ago the Prods nearly had a full bag: me and yourself."

Fallon slid the pistol back in its holster beneath his arm and leaned back against the chair. He eyed MacCauley impassively.

"It was only reaction: nothing more," he said. "But why would they be coming after you? The cease-fire's on."

"'Tis only a piece of paper for now. And there are those who would like to wrap up a bit of business before they're forced to live with it. But you, sure, and what did I tell you before? You can't help being what you are for all your fancy pretensions—your books and music and your hermitage on Long Woman's Grave—

none make you what you want to be!" He paused, eyeing Fallon closely. A sadness crept into his eyes. "Hate has created you, Tomas, as it has me. Too much hate. Now, it's all we've got left. Without it, what is there for us?"

A long silence fell between them. Dimly, Fallon heard traffic moving at the back of the house. The dream began pushing forward—bright red flashing bursts from the automatics. He shook his head, forcing the images away.

"It seems I have little choice, now, wouldn't you be saying?" he said at last. His words carried a hint of bitter irony with them, and MacCauley noticed it.

"No. And for that, I'm sorry, Tomas Fallon. More sorry than I can say. I wish that there was another way, but for people like you and me, there isn't. This is what we were made for and, God help us, there is nothing else that we can do. All the fine books and fine music in the world can't take away your gift with the gun, and all the fine philosophers and priests can't change the hate. D'yuh think He would have made us for something different? The curve of the plow handle won't fit your palm, nor will all the chalk-boards in the world make me a teacher. Yes," he said, noting Fallon's look of surprise, "it was that I was trained for. Can you see me on the strand near Inch picking up seashells and lecturing on them to rapt students? Neither can I. You were right: there has been enough killing, but there's more to come. Black Cromwell made certain of that when he marched his boys the length of Ireland and let his gallowglasses take what land and what women they wanted in payment for their services. It's a long history, Tomas, and the final chapter will probably never be written, for people have even longer memories and the ache and pain given to them will always be remembered. And"—he shrugged—"if they don't remember that, they'll remember what they are used to. The English may have created the monster, Fallon, but we have fed it, nurtured it, and released it."

"I can see where you would have been a good teacher, Seamus," Fallon said. "At least, a philosopher. But right now, there's the question of who has turned to the GDC. We need to work on that."

"I'll handle it," MacCauley said quickly. "You can start tracing the shipment."

"I think not. Little good it will do me to begin my run if I'm looking over my shoulder and wondering who's waiting for me at the end. No, first we find who's been telling the tale. And I think," he slowly added, his eyes narrowing into the future, "I may have someone who can help me there."

"Who?" MacCauley demanded. Fallon grinned crookedly. "Damn you, Fallon! You'll do as you're told."

"I don't work for you anymore, Seamus, remember?" Fallon said. "You've pushed me into this thing, but I don't work for you. I'll tell you when it's your help I'm needing."

"We can help," MacCauley insisted.

"And look where your fine help has gotten us," Fallon said acidly. "Had it not been for that I'd still be at Long Woman's Grave. You look for yourself. There's undoubtedly more than one who could have turned. You work from your end."

MacCauley eyed Fallon for a long moment, then said, "Tomas, I can't help you if I'm not in."

Fallon gave a grim laugh. "Seamus, I don't need the type of help you've given lately. Do me a favor: keep your help to yourself. Don't even be telling anyone that it's back in the fold I am. Things will be better that way, I'm thinking."

MacCauley flushed and started to speak angrily, but Fallon held up his hand, silencing him. "You can check on Maeve. I'm worried about her. You remember what happened to her back in the seventies when those RUC bastards caught her in Belfast. We almost lost her then."

A pained look fell over MacCauley's face as Fallon's words brought back half-forgotten memories. Maeve had been helping the American columnist Con Edwards do a series of articles on the Provos in Belfast when she, Edwards, and MacCauley's lieutenant and friend Dickie O'Bannion were captured by the RUC and SAS. O'Bannion had been a *gombeen*, an informer, and freed, while Maeve had been brutally and repeatedly raped in the basement of the interrogation center at Castlereagh. She had been freed by a Provo operation when the RUC tried to transfer her to the Women's Detention Center at Lisburn, but it had taken her a long time to learn how to shove the memory of her internment away.

"All right," he said slowly. "'Tis little help I'll be able to give you. The boyos won't cooperate with you. You'll be on your own. Completely. *But*," he emphasized, "you be certain to call if you need help. I'll be putting the boys out the minute you notify me."

"I'll be doing that," Fallon said. He stared out the window again, then said over his shoulder, "Are you aware of the works of Jung?" Fallon asked.

"I'm aware of them; not familiar with them," MacCauley answered. "I haven't had your type of university education."

Fallon smiled. "He speaks of something called 'synchronicity': events having a coincidence in time, and because of this a feeling of deeper motivation is involved."

"Oh?"

"Maybe it has something to do with 'predestination.' At least, on the surface, it seems as if it does. But does it? First, drugs appear. Second, you send for me. Third, Maeve contacts me on your behalf, although you don't know it. Fourth, well, that's personal. But, maybe there is something to Jung's theory. Or God's."

Fallon crossed to the window and peeked through the curtains to the street. "I always have been alone, Seamus. Even when I was with you. That's why I survived."

MacCauley nodded resignedly to the truth in Fallon's words and looked at the middle-aged man dressed in black carefully studying the street as he remembered the young Fallon who even in his teens had been made middle-aged by the times.

9

DOBBIE HUMMED AND STAGGERED ON THE SLIPPERY STONES AS HE turned off the concrete along Shankill Road into a narrow, twisting alley that led from the Protestant Shankill past the Peace Line into Catholic Clonard and the Falls. His head buzzed from the load of porter he had been taking on as he made his way up Townsend off Divis onto Shankill. It wouldn't do to take the quick way into Lower Falls off Divis for both Prod and Provo eyes watched those turnings. No, he had decided, far better to take Shankill and Brendan's Alley into Clonard and work one's way home by the puffin's flight rather than the crow's. Besides, there was no hurry; there never was a hurry anymore since the Orange Lodges had declared another hiring freeze upon the Catholics immediately on the heels of a survey by the London *Times* that revealed the majority of Britain's citizens in England favored withdrawing from Northern Ireland. A minister from Cornwall in the House of Commons had used *The Times* article to renew his demand for bringing British troops home, combining in his rhetoric the budget report of the cost of the "Troubles" to the English taxpayer: over £1 billion per year—money that could be put to better use in the welfare rolls.

He thought about the illegal pub, a shebeen nearly on the Line, that ignored licensing hours, its existence protected by Protestant and Catholic alike who found a use for such an establishment dur-

ing the "dry hours." Ah! 'tis good to have a watering place on the
way to a man's home after the thirsty business was over. A man
could build the Divil's own thirst when he was working with the
Prods.

He hawked and spat heavy phlegm. His foot slipped again off a
wet stone. He swore. God's heavy balls! Was there never no end
to the wetness this spring?

He paused in the middle of the alley, swaying slightly from the
drink. The words to the song he had been humming burst from
his throat:

> "In seventeen hundred and forty-four
> The fifth of December, I think 'twas no more
> At five in the morning, by most of the clocks,
> We rode from Kilruddery in search of a fox."

A window suddenly opened on the second floor of the brownstone on his left. Startled, he looked up and caught the contents
of a chamber pot full in his face.

"Gardee-goddamn-loo!" he strangled. His stomach heaved and
partly digested porter splattered the stones at his feet. He staggered to the wall and leaned weakly against the brownstone.

"Gawd," he said and froze as a chuckle answered him.

"Ah, now, Dobbie. 'Tis what you should expect when you don't
keep your mouth shut."

Dobbie peered fearfully into the darkness. "Who's there?" His
voice quivered.

"Have you forgotten your friends already, Dobbie? You must
have an easy time of it at confession. Or have you been remiss in
that too, now, Dobbie?"

"Fallon?" He swallowed and cringed as a figure moved out of
the shadows into the weak glow cast by a lamp over a door leading into a brownstone across from him.

"Yes," Fallon answered.

Dobbie swallowed and nervously laughed. "Yuh took ten years off my life. What are you sneaking around in the dark for?"

"Sometimes one can find things better in the dark, Dobbie. Nocturnal animals, for instance."

"Sure, and I wish I knew what you were talkin' about, Fallon." He laughed and gestured down the alley. "Come on to the pub. I'll buy yuh a drink and yuh can explain it to me."

He took a step away from the wall, trying to turn Fallon down the alley, but the dark figure remained still. He rubbed his hand across his mouth and wished that he could spit, but his mouth had suddenly gone dry. He could hear his tongue rubbing across the top of his mouth when he tried to make spit.

"Tell me, now, Dobbie," Fallon said conversationally. "When did you get the money? 'Twas only this morning you were putting the beggar's mark on me for the price of a pint. And now, you're flush? What good fortune has come your way? Did you find one of the wee people while you were poking around the back streets?"

"What'r yer sayin', Fallon? I was lucky to find an odders for a day, that's all."

"And where was this, Dobbie? This good fortune of yours, I mean?"

"Uh, over on Glen Road. Up in Turf Lodge. The gas company needed a few navvies. Picked up a couple of quid digging."

"A pick and shovel man? I didn't think it was your style, Dobbie."

"Anything's yer style when yer hungry," Dobbie said defensively.

"Even the tattle?"

Dobbie felt a sudden chill. "What are yuh sayin'?"

Fallon's voice went cold and flat. "I think you were visiting down at the station, Dobbie. I've been following you most of the evening. You've been treating the lads fair regular. The Swan, Cohan's, O'Malley's. Yuh haven't missed many. You manage very well on only a couple of quid."

"Fallon—" He tried to swallow and gagged against the dryness of his throat. "What—what are yuh doing?"

"You know what we do with *gombeen* men, don't you, Dobbie?"

"No," he whispered.

"Why did you do it, Dobbie?"

The words blurted from him before he could stop them. "I was hungry! Yuh ever been hungry, Fallon? No, I 'spect not. You've always been in with the boyos, and they know how to take care of the in-ones, right? The others, the soldiers like me, we starve. Or die. But not yous and the others like yous. Oh, now. Yer bellies don't growl and yer grates always 'as a fire lit in 'em." He suddenly became aware of his words. He turned away.

"Do it," he said thickly. "A little more blood will be nothing on yer hands, Fallon. Get on with it."

He closed his eyes, waiting for the bullet. He opened them after a long moment and took a quick glance over his shoulder: he was alone in the alley.

"Fallon?" The sound of water dripping answered him. He raised his voice. "Fallon! Where are you?" Silence followed his words. Hope flared within him, then died as he realized he would have to live with the death every day now from both sides: the boyos who surely knew he had turned the tale, and the Blackmen who hadn't gotten what they'd paid for. He stuck his hand in his pocket, feeling the crisp notes between his fingers. The fear grew within him, and suddenly he turned and ran through the alley, away from what would follow, toward nothing. Sobs broke from his chest. What was left? But he knew the answer to that. The fear was full upon him, a frightening thing compounded of his own terror and the intentions of the Provos and Prods. From which side would the bullet come? Mary, Mother of Christ! There's nothin left! Nothin! There never was! His lungs heaved for air. O my God! I am mortally sorry for having offended thee— He ran harder.

10

DEAR, DIRTY DUBLIN SPRAWLS UNDER A HEAVY SKY BETWEEN THE
purple and green mountains of County Wicklow and the compla-
cent hump of Howth Head to the north. The streets glower under
their black and gray mantle and are filled with spring shoppers
and the pubs with writers and artists, bankers and brokers, and
pirates and preachers, merchants and lawyers taking a break from
their duties at Four Courts, all satisfying their thirsts. Christ
Church Cathedral looms, a Gothic castle, casting its pinnacles
and flying buttresses to the gray clouds while the stark, bone
white columns of the Bank of Ireland look down College Green
opposite the long, gray façade of Trinity College.

Fallon sauntered through the gate in the gray stone wall and
across Trinity grounds, stepping easily in and out among groups
of students earnestly debating delicate points brought out by lec-
turers in morning tutorials. He felt a pang of loss as he recalled
similar mornings when he had once stood on the grounds of his
college in Belfast in hot debate over translations made of the
Ossianic Cycle fabricated by James MacPherson and the Ulster
Cycle and the Mythological Cycle of ancient Irish poetry. Those
days had seemed so real—the stark rooms and drafty halls, the
fleeting nights in the student pubs, the arguments, the first clumsy
courting and brief affairs born from the debates and casual meet-
ings over tea or the odd pint in the Commons. He recalled his first

minor triumph in academic circles: his translation of the combat of Ferdiand and Cúchulainn. Fragments rolled through his mind, and he paused to stare at the gray spires of the cathedral as the words charged out of the catacombs of dusty memory and rolled off his tongue:

"The roll of a chariot with fair silver yoke;
A great and brawny man topping o'er the heavy car
Rolling o'er Bri Ross and Brane, the swift path hastened
Past Old-oak Town's stump, bearing victory they speed!

"A cunning Hound who drives, a fair chief urging
A free hawk spiraling upwards, speeding
His steeds, brown and gray, towards the south!
Gore-colored, bloody Cua, sure to o'ertake us;
Chillingly aware—we know our vanity to hide the fear
Of defeat he will bring us from his charging car.

"Wail for him on the hill-cock who stood before the Hound
After I prophesied last year their meeting would come!
Beware the Hound from Emain Macha,
The Hound draped with all war colors,
The Hound from the Border,
The Hound from Badb Catha, the Battle Raven,
Terrible to behold. I have these prophecies from afar
And now I know them to come true as I can hear
Their chariots riding on the wind,
Swift and fast, riding to the sea."

He paused, shaking his head, suddenly aware of stares from a tiny group of students intently watching him. He shook his head, forcing the memory away, and turned and entered the library. Foolish man, living in the past glory, watch yourself, blend with the others, don't stand out. Ah, memory, tricking me with my youthful fancies. But he felt the loss as he felt the silence of the library around him, the smell of old books, the creaks of chairs, the soft shuffle of leather on stones, the quiet flipping of pages, the rustle of paper. He paused, letting his eyes adjust to the interior lighting. The noise of Dublin and Trinity seemed far away. The center of the library arched high overhead. Stacks ranged along the sides, their shelves filled with thousands of books. He breathed deeply as he moved through the library, inhaling the musty scent of knowledge. A slight smile lifted his lips at the queue of American tourists fidgeting impatiently as they waited for a brief glance at the glass-enclosed Book of Kells. One was using a book of travel photos to steady a copy of the London *Times* as he demonstrated his cruciverbalistic competence on the crossword.

Fallon slipped past the queue and worked his way up to the second level. He wove through the narrow aisles and found her perched on a stool, leaning over a reading table. He came up softly behind her and glanced over her shoulder at the print and recognized the Gaelic script. He spoke, translating as he read:

"They are gone, those heroes of royal birth
Who plundered no churches, and broke no trust,
'Tis weary for me to be living on earth
When they, oh Kincora, lie low in the dust!"

Maeve swung around at the sound of his voice. Her face mirrored surprise then broke into a wide grin. "Fallon. Well. I never thought the day would appear when I'd be seeing your company here!"

"Ah, well, Maeve. You know you should never be losing your faith in mysticism. Fate does strange things." He gave her a small grin as she slipped from her stool and kissed him on the cheek.

"Now, then. That's a reward that would bring old Brian back from his grave."

"On with you," she said affectionately. She leaned back on the stool, bracing herself with her hands on the table. The movement bunched her breasts against her purple heather-colored sweater. She wore a tan tweed skirt and penny loafers. Tiny lines appeared at the corners of her eyes and her hair had a few streaks of silver in it, but at a glance, one would say she was a coed instead of a lecturer in Celtic poetry—until one stared into her eyes and registered the pain and vulnerability touched with hardness in their depths.

"Now, then, what brings the hermit to Dublin town? Tiring of the solitary life?"

He shook his head. "You're mistaking me with my twin brother. He's the one who has forsaken this life for that of an eremitic. He's a Cistercian over in Kerry."

"A monk?"

"No. A priest. He had a parish in Ardoyne off Oldpark Road. In February seventy-one, the Second Battalion, Royal Anglians cordoned off Ardoyne and Clonard. They were looking for Sean MacStiofain and Seamus Twomey. Someone, probably a Prod from Shankill, told the searchers that they were attending Mass in my brother's church. They came to search the church, and when my brother tried to stop them from entering the sanctuary, they beat him. A woman tried to help him. They beat her too and dragged both out of the church and took them away to Castlereagh. She died there. My brother was released after six months. He had lost forty pounds, all of his teeth, and had to have a kidney removed. They never found MacStiofain or Twomey. They weren't even in Belfast, let alone Ardoyne. They were up in Derry."

"My God," Maeve said. Her face had grown white during Fallon's story, her lips a thin line stretched hard across her face. Twin bright spots of color highlighted her high cheekbones.

Fallon nodded. "We found out later that the Prods had known where MacStiofain and Twomey were all along. They used the rumor as an excuse to search the area, looking for arms and just generally harassing the Catholics. It's what you call 'politics.' We've had politics since the North was formed. There's been a one-party slate in the Stormont claiming to be for the people, but what did the Unionist regime ever offer the Nationalists?"

"I remember now: it was right after Ballymurphy. At first, the Royal Anglians wanted the PIRA to help maintain order after the police stopped their patrols. We didn't know that was only a ruse to identify the leaders."

"We lost a lot of good men shortly after that," he said.

"Was that when you joined?"

He grinned. "That's another story for another time. Who knew you were coming to see me?"

The question caught her off guard. She gave him a blank look. "What?"

"Our northern friends made a run on me shortly after you left," he said.

Anger flashed in her eyes. "And you think it was me?"

He shook his head. "No. But someone knew where you were going. They followed you."

She gave him a long, searching look. Finally, satisfied that he wasn't accusing her, she slowly answered him. "I didn't know where to find you. When MacCauley asked me to talk with you— what is it?" she asked as his face settled into a hard mask.

"MacCauley said he never sent you," he said softly. She frowned, twin lines appearing deeply between her brows. "When did he tell you?"

"He sent a man to me with his request," she answered. "But I didn't know how to find you so I sent word back to him through Michael John in Dobbin's—the pub on Stephen's Lane, you remember?"

He nodded. Dobbin's was a bistro that had begun catering to the tourist trade, which made it an ideal contact place for messages to be sent to the various brigade commanders and for money gathered in the States to be transferred to IRA contacts. Sometimes, the most obvious place was the best place to hide.

"Let me guess," he said. "The messenger didn't know where to find me either, right? And when you talked with Michael John, he told you, so MacCauley didn't have to be contacted. Neat. Very neat."

"The messenger wasn't sent by MacCauley, then?"

"No. Would you happen to know anything about the man?"

She wrinkled her brow, thinking. "Short—about my height—a face like a mouse except his nose twisted to one side, and nervous eyes. Brown hair, thin on top. A bit unkempt. Smelled of garlic. Bad teeth."

"You met him here? Your place? Where?"

"A note in my mail at the college. I was to meet him at Doheny and Nesbitt's. He gave me the message there after I stood him a pint."

"Doheny and Nesbitt's?"

"A pub on Lower Baggot Street. I got the feeling he was a regular there. For sure if the women didn't tease him as he took me to the back where the snugs waited."

"Did they call his name?" She shook her head.

"They did that. But I can't remember." The vowels grew long in her words as she slipped back into the country dialect. Briefly, he imagined her milking the cows, her skirt hiked up to bare golden calves, hands expertly working the udders.

"Try."

"Slattery," she said suddenly, the frown clearing from her face.

"'Slattery,' they said, 'is it a new *striapach* you'll be running, now. This one looks a twenty punter.' They were a callous lot, that bunch, and I had a feeling they held him a bare lift above the gutter."

A man passed their table, his eyes flickering over the titles of books piled on the table. They paused, waiting for him to work his way through the stacks away from them. A student at a table near them frowned at them and bent back to his work. Fallon stepped closer, murmuring.

"Not friends?"

She smiled, lowering her voice to a whisper. He leaned closer to hear, smelling the musk of her perfume, the hint of Pears soap. "Oh, no. Not friends. Not with one the likes of him."

"What about the men?"

"They ignored him." Her eyes turned hard. "Once along the road to Cork, I saw the lane littered with dead crows, shot from the fields. It was during the Lughnasa, and I remember thinking the crows had been well served for trying to reap the farmers' fields before they had been harvested. The men looked at him as a crow who had escaped the drive."

"And they thought you were one of his?"

She grimaced. "I got the feeling that no other woman would have been with him, and that being the case, why else should they treat me differently? It wasn't Maeve Larkin from Trinity they were seeing, but one of Badb's daughters who would lead them to their deaths if they followed her, but follow her they would—if out of sight of their wives."

"Sounds like the type of man the GDC would use."

She frowned. "The GDC?"

"Aye. A new group split off from the boyos. Scum all of them. They give themselves a grand name—Gaelach Dearg Craobh—to cover their dirty deeds. I think it's them."

"And MacCauley?"

"It's all we've got, then," Fallon said. "It's beginning to sound more and more like them. They are the only ones who would use a man like this Slattery."

"I see." \

"So, they knew him there?"

"So I believe."

"Then there it is I'll start."

"I'll come with you," she said, rising and smoothing her skirt behind her. The feminine gesture touched him, and for a moment, he felt the other world denied him: the world of woman and man, a terraced house opposite a park where the children could play. But, he remembered, the Ireland he had known that had made that all possible was gone forever, remaining only flickering images of a late-night film on television or on brochures sent out by Bord Failté for the tourists.

"I don't think so," he found himself saying.

"Fallon—"

"No. There's no need for you to come. I'll know him when I see him. Now, I'm not thinking you're not up to it, colleen," he said, staving off her angry objection. "'Tis well I know of your strength, and I've seen your courage. But there are those who will see the two of us together and recognize one by way of the other." He smiled to take the sting from his words. "You're too well known."

"You mean that you can work better without me," she said.

"In this case. Slattery knows you: he may not know me. I'm thinking alone the advantage is mine."

"You'll see me before you go after you find out?" she asked.

He hesitated. "If possible. A lot depends on Slattery. And others."

"I don't want to miss you, Fallon," she said.

"Is it flirting you are?" he asked, deliberately lengthening his brogue.

Her eyes twinkled and she said archly, "And if I am, what of it?"

"I'm afraid there's little left of the man for you," he said.

She began to gather her books, tucking them into neat piles, carefully sorting her notes. "How did it start?"

"For me?" She nodded. "It's a bit of romantic silliness."

"The dashing young man, I'll bet. Another Captain Lightfoot?"

"I was at Derry in October sixty-eight," he said quietly. She froze, then turned, slowly sitting on her stool, staring silently at him. "The Northern Ireland Civil Rights Association had planned a protest march against sectarian discrimination by the Unionist-controlled administration of Derry, who wanted to erase the city's Irish heritage. The councillors had installed gerrymandered electoral boundaries to maintain Protestant control. The RUC caught the marchers in a narrow street and cut off their escape while throwing one baton charge after the other at them between bursts from a water cannon. Eighty-eight people were injured and thirty-six arrested. Riots broke out across the city, and the Protestants turned to their guns, led by Paisley's followers.

"I wasn't on the march, but I was in the streets." He smiled, his lips twisting ironically. "You have to remember it was fashionable for students to form protest groups. I was at Queen's University and easily got caught up in the maelstrom of nationalism. Anyway, I remember being at the barricades when the Prods began shooting at us. We were unarmed except for bottles and stones. I dropped behind an overturned car. An old man lay in the open. He had a hole in the heel of one of his socks. Isn't that a strange thing to remember: a hole in one of his socks. What sort of historical anecdote is that? An old man with a hole in one of his socks and a pool of blood under his head. A priest crawled out to give him the last rites, and the Prods began shooting at him. He waved a large, white handkerchief at them, but it didn't make any difference: they kept shooting, but they weren't shooting to hit him. You understand? They made it into a game: taunting and teasing him, letting him live, but letting him know they could kill him whenever they wanted. His life belonged to them while he was in that street. They put a bullet through his handkerchief and shot all around him. They shot the old man again and again while the priest was administering the last rites. When he was finished, they bounced bullets off the paving stones around him while he crawled back behind the barricades." He gave a slight shrug. "I began running messages after that, becoming more and more involved. One day, I delivered a message to MacCauley. The RUC broke in on us. We managed to get away. And that is my story. I told you it was a bit romantic."

"How did you get away from the RUC?"

"They were very careless; I was not."

"I see," she slowly said. "And the legend of Fallon was born."

"Something like that. Take care of yourself." He leaned forward and kissed her cheek. "Watch yourself, now. And don't be taking any more messages from MacCauley. He wouldn't be sending them anyway. Wait until I sort this thing out."

"So you're back in," she said sadly.

"It's what you wanted, isn't it?" he asked.

"No," she answered. "But it's what was needed. I can't help but think it's a mistake we're making. You were out of it so long."

A crooked grin spread his lips but did not touch his eyes. "Is anybody ever out?"

She shook her head as she watched him go, Synge's words suddenly within her mind, and she knew then the loss of Pegeen Mike.

11

DOHENY & NESBITT'S WAS A DIRTY LITTLE PUB, THE BACK LINED WITH snugs where women were once restricted although Fallon could tell the rules had been relaxed. Three old women shared a bench around a small table. Three pints of dark Guinness stood half-full on its surface heavily scarred from years of thumping glasses. They nodded with jerky impatience as they spoke, each waiting for the other to be done before telling a larger tale than her predecessor. None bore the poised complacency that had become a myth with age. The oldest, the one with corded wattles along her throat, breathed sibilantly through her nose, fever spots the size of five pence high on her cheeks. Her narrow, flat chest pushed impatiently against the plain black material of her dress. A few younger women sat at tables farther in, their faces beginning to take on a doughy look and their waists thickening from their nightly Guinness. A couple eyed him speculatively as he crossed slowly to the bar, his eyes carefully scanning the drinkers.

"What'll it be?" the barkeep asked. His white shirt was stained at the armpits and the sleeves rolled up above his elbows, exposing thick forearms. His red mustache, ragged above pouched lips, looked wilted in the dim light. His eyes were flat and expressionless.

"Slattery?" Fallon said.

A man laughed from a table near him, and a young girl sitting with him leaned back in her chair, resting her arms along the back, her heavy breasts straining the buttons of her sweater.

"Now, then," she said. "You don't look the sort of man who would be needin' the likes of that one."

The man stopped laughing and leaned across the table. "Here, now, none of that, none of that. It's a shameless girl you're becoming, Sari, and we so close to an understanding, you might say."

"*You* might," she said. "But the words are your own and yours alone. I've made no understanding with anyone." She looked at Fallon, interest bold in her eyes. "But who knows what I might do?" she said meaningfully. She bit her full lower lip and looked suggestively at Fallon.

"What are you doing, Sari?" the man asked.

"Oh, do be quiet, there's a good lad," she said. The man glanced up at Fallon.

"What are you looking at?" he asked angrily. Fallon ignored him and looked again at the barkeep.

"Slattery?" he repeated. The barkeep took a dirty towel and slowly wiped the bar in front of him.

"Who wants to know?" he asked.

"I do," Fallon said.

"That doesn't tell me much."

"It tells you enough, I'm thinking."

The barkeep glanced into Fallon's eyes then glanced down at the bar and pretended to scrub at a spot on its mahogany surface.

"He comes in about one to cadge pints or a Paddy from anyone who'll stand him. Not many will."

"Where'll I find him now?" Fallon asked quietly.

"I'm no travel agency," the other complained. Fallon stared expressionlessly at him for a long moment. The barkeep shrugged. "He has a few girls standing corners in the Liberties— between St. Patrick's and the south bank of the Liffey? You might find him there, checking on them."

"Thank you," Fallon said politely and turned to go, but the man at the table bounced to his feet, barring his way.

"We have something to settle," he said.

"Teddy, leave it alone," the girl warned.

"Shut your gob," Teddy growled. He tilted his head back, looking down his nose at Fallon. "Well, bucky?"

"Listen to your friend," Fallon said. "Leave it alone."

"Would you listen to him, now," Teddy said in the sudden quiet of the room. He turned back to Fallon. "Give me a good reason why I shouldn't push your face in, now." He stretched with the arrogance of youth, secure in his own immortality.

"Because you couldn't," a voice said quietly from the back of the room.

The young man's head swiveled sharply at the intruder's words, an angry retort dying on his lips as a bulky man made his way up to stand in front of him. His black hair, thin on top, was combed straight back from a heavily scarred forehead. He was tall and solid with broad shoulders stretching the seams of his jacket and the ruddy cheeks of a drinker. His hands were huge and scarred, a pint of porter nearly invisible in one. Blue eyes twinkled at Fallon.

"Michael John." The young man swallowed. "Sure, now, and I didn't know 'twas a friend of yours I was speakin' to."

"Ah, Teddy. Now, what am I to do with you?"

The young man ducked his head, looking down at the floor. "I was only having a bit of fun," he said sullenly.

"No, lad, you wasn't. 'Twas a face you were puttin' on for yer cunny here," Michael John said, shaking his head sadly.

The girl gasped indignantly. "Did you hear what he called me? Did you, now? And you just stand there doing nothin' after I've been insulted by this—this—"

"Shut up, Sari. You don't know what yer sayin'," Teddy said quickly.

"I know when I've been insulted! Sweet Jaysus! What kind of

man are yuh? You who've been telling all about us havin' an understandin' an' all."

A sickly look came over Teddy's face. He pulled his head down between his shoulders and looked at Michael John.

"You see how it is," Teddy said.

"Ah, lad! It's a foolish man who lets a woman of this type push him into anything. Her toes have touched the ceiling for more than one man. Best you give this another thought before you do anything rash."

The girl squawked indignantly. "Did yuh hear that? Is there not a man in the room who will defend a lady's honor, then? A shame that the men of Ireland have come to this!"

Teddy drew back his fist and swung at Michael John. The big man caught the fist in his huge farmer's hand, squeezing it. Bones snapped. The young man yelped and pulled his hand back, cradling it with his other. Michael John looped an uppercut under the young man's chin, knocking him onto the woman's lap. His weight bore her back, and they tipped over, crashing to the floor, her dress flying up to cover them both. Fallon caught a glimpse of flimsy black knickers, white legs scissoring frantically in the air. A stream of profanity came shrilly from her lips.

"Ah, well. What can one expect from Irish womanhood," Michael John said. The room rang with hoarse laughter. Two men rushed forward to pull the unconscious Teddy off her and help restore her dignity. She gave Michael John a furious look then stormed out of the pub, her ears burning from mocking laughter. Michael John turned to Fallon.

"Well, now. 'Tis a long time since I've seen the likes of you. And where have you been keepin' yourself?" He poked a finger the size of a sausage at Fallon's hair. "Yer wearin' a bit of rime, now, where black used to be. But I don't think it's any wiser you've become or you wouldn't be socializing with the likes of these down here."

"It has been a long time, Michael John," Fallon answered, a grin tugging at the corners of his mouth. "And what brings you to this neighborhood? They throw you out of the others? Faith, it does a man good to know there are still some places maintaining a bit of dignity about them." He shook the big man's hand, carefully folding his thumb inside the grip to keep his hand from being crushed.

"Well, now, a mutual friend let on that you could use me services, knowing that such a wee one as yourself finds it hard to walk among the men." He glanced at the heap on the floor. "Not, though, that I think you'd have had much trouble with that one. Well, lad! Where are we off to?" He drained the glass in his hand and casually flipped the glass to the barkeep. He fumbled, then swore as the glass fell and broke on the bar. Michael John ignored him, draping a huge arm across Fallon's shoulders as they walked to the door. Fallon stiffened: the arm was as heavy as lead.

"Are you sure you're wantin' in on this, Michael John?" Fallon asked as they moved down the walk away from the pub. "I'm in alone, you know."

"Ah, well, now, how's that to be different from other times? We're always alone, ourselves. It's good to have someone watchin' yer back. Even you, Fallon, have no eyes in the back of yer head. An' Saint Columcille help me if I don't think yer gettin' slower in yer old age." He patted Fallon on the shoulder, unconsciously staggering the smaller man ahead a couple of paces. "Now, let's be off to wherever it is we're off to and find this Slattery who's been tellin' a few tales out of turn. I was tellin' himself just the other day—"

12

SLATTERY STOOD A HALF-BLOCK AWAY ON AN OFF-STREET IN THE
Liberties next to the dirty brick wall of a Dickensian tenement
while watching one of his two prostitutes work the johns. She was
a bit overweight, a roll of fat hanging on the waistline of her
short, tight skirt, her makeup not quite hiding the shopworn lines
around her eyes and cheekbones, but her breasts were huge and
still moved freely beneath her thin blouse. When night came, she
would still be good enough to land six or seven clients, but during
the day, she was a bit of an oddity and Slattery held little hope for
any success before dusk: her age was still too visible and worked
against her.

He sighed and leaned against the wall and pulled another cigarette from a pocket inside his jacket. The ground around his feet
was littered with stubs that he had smoked during his two-hour
vigil. He thought about Mackie, whose girls worked the southeast
corner of Merrion Square and thought about moving there since
Mackie's girls wouldn't show on the corner until late afternoon,
but he knew he wasn't strong enough to take the corner away
from Mackie. He lit the cigarette, expelling smoke with another
sigh. A dull pounding rose in his left temple from the last load of
porter he had taken on. He screwed his eyes shut against the
brightness of the gray day then opened them. The pain was still
there; a low, throbbing pain reminding him of his weakness. If he

had been strong enough, he would have had at least four more girls working for him and younger, too, than Rita, who was home with the flu today, and Sheena, who strutted the corner now in four-inch stiletto heels that made her breasts move like melons beneath the blouse. Gloomily, he watched yet another man side-step her advance and hurry away from her. He took a deep pull on the cigarette and leaned back against the brick building behind him. He closed his eyes and played his killing-time game, conjuring up a memory in which he played opposite Seka, the American porn queen. He rewrote the scenes daily in his mind. Smoke dribbled from his mouth as he pictured the two of them, naked, rolling in the shallow waters of the strand.

A sudden explosion jerked him awake. He stared at a ball of greasy black smoke boiling above the terraced houses across the street. He glanced quickly at Sheena, who also stared up at the smoke above her, her mouth hanging open, eyes squinted, the roll of fat beneath her chin quivering slightly.

"Ah, Slattery. Enjoying the death of more Brits and the bloody Protestants are yuh? Fine man. Fine man." He twisted his head violently to the left, narrowly throwing himself off-balance. A huge hand wrapped itself around his biceps, steadying him. "Now, lad, sure and it's something to get excited about, but, Jaysus, be keeping your pins under yuh, so."

He lifted his head. Blue eyes gazed cheerfully back into his own. A chill descended into his stomach. He swallowed, forcing indignation into his voice.

"And who the bloody hell are you to be giving words to another? Take yer foacking fingers off before I cut 'em off!" His voice rose shrilly at the end. The hand fell away. The big man's smile stretched across his battered face.

"Ah, well, now. Me name is Michael John, and this," he turned to the thin man beside him, "this is my friend. Yuh need know no more than that, I'm thinking."

Slattery stared into the slate gray eyes of the stranger. The thin man's black leather jacket gleamed softly with dampness. He wore his black hair cut short, revealing touches of gray. He stood relaxed, loosely balanced on the balls of his feet, his hands slightly curled at his sides. Slattery felt himself being drawn into the darkness behind the eyes and shivered. A thought struck like lightning behind the pain in his temple: *This is the one to fear.* He swallowed.

"And what's he to me?" he said gruffly, forcing his voice down a register. A slight smile flickered across the stranger's lips. Or had it? Slattery wasn't sure.

"It'll be worth your while," he said softly. Slattery strained to hear him.

"Aye, and isn't it I have heard that before? Foack off." He took a lungful of smoke and blew it into the air between them. A small tic started in his eyelid, and he silently swore.

"Ah, lad, 'tis an attitude yuh shouldn't be takin'," Michael John said regretfully. His arm stabbed out straight, his palm catching Slattery full in the chest, slamming him back against the wall. Slattery's cigarette flew from his fingers, and his mouth opened, gulping air like a fish out of water. His hands fumbled weakly against the brawny forearm pinning him against the wall.

"You talked with Maeve Larkin on MacCauley's behalf not long ago?" the thin man said. It wasn't a question, but Slattery treated it as such.

"And—and if I did, what interest is it of yours?" he gasped. Jaysus! Would he ever draw a breath?

"Who told you to go to Maeve Larkin?" the man asked, ignoring Slattery's question.

"MacCauley," he gasped. He drew a deep breath and forced himself to hold it. Michael John's arm suddenly flexed and slammed him harder against the wall. Large drops of rain struck his face painfully.

"Now, lad," Michael John said admonishingly. "Let's not be telling the tale. Answer the man's questions. He's a quiet man by nature is he, but, lad, don't be making him angry. No, you won't like him like that. It's a bad temper, he has."

"Foacking bastard," Slattery gasped. Michael John's hand flashed brutally across his face, rocking him. Bright lights flashed in Slattery's eyes; his nose began bleeding, and he could taste blood from his lips.

"Christ." He gagged, and swallowed the porter back down.

"'Tis a hard lesson to learn," Michael John said. "Now, answer the man's questions."

Slattery's hand dug into the pocket of his pea coat and rose with a flick-knife. He stabbed for Michael John's stomach, but the big man was too quick for him. The point stopped a bare inch from his belt. Michael John's eyes bored deeply into Slattery's, the smile slipping a bit from his lips. The muscles in his face tightened and his shoulder dipped sharply down. The bones in Slattery's hand shattered. He gave a sudden scream of pain and the knife clattered to the ground.

"A mistake," the quiet man said softly. "Now, don't be making another." He opened his leather jacket. Through pain-filled eyes, Slattery saw the CZ-52 nestled beneath his armpit. "Or, do you wish to be spending the rest of your miserable life walking on sticks?"

"Hey, what's goin' on?" a shrill voice sounded. A heavy-breasted woman grabbed Michael John's arm and tried to pull it free from Slattery's coat. Cheap perfume filled the air. Her eyes sparked angrily into Fallon's and Michael John's. Her makeup had been carelessly applied and old rice powder lay in the wrinkles around her eyes. She gave up tugging on Michael John's arm and backed away. She tried to kick him in the groin, her skirt sliding up thick thighs, revealing her nudity beneath. Michael John turned, catching the pointed toe of her shoe on his thigh. He grunted. Fallon sighed and stepped neatly around her, grabbed a flailing arm, and twisted it hard behind her.

"Ah, may God cut 'er balls!" she yelped. She filled her lungs to scream, but Michael John drove a fist into her stomach and the air exploded silently from her lungs. She sagged, forcing Fallon to use both arms to keep her from falling to the pavement.

"Enough," he said, casting a quick glance around. The rain began to fall. "In there." He nodded at an alley. "Before someone else decides to make our business his." Michael John nodded and propelled Slattery into the alley. He stumbled against a dustbin and nearly fell, but Michael John pushed him deeper into the alley, then around a dog-leg before hauling him up under an eave out of the downpour. Moments later, the woman slammed into the brick wall beside him. She gasped and slid down the wall of the terrace house, squatting precariously on her high heels. Her mascara had run, making her eyes mud puddles.

"Now, then, again the question," Fallon said, sliding in beside Michael John. The pistol magically appeared in his hand. He nudged Slattery's cheek with the barrel; it felt like ice and Slattery flinched away.

"They do marvelous surgery in the Royal Victoria Hospital now, repairing kneecaps. But then, they've had a lot of practice. But that's in Belfast, you know, although there's some that say Dublin surgeons can do the same. I doubt it; you'd have to go North, lad." He held the pistol so Slattery could see it. The pistol gleamed blackly in the cold, gray light. "This is a CZ-52. It was made in Czechoslovakia. A little man in the Netherlands supplies me with reloaded bullets from the Fiocchi plant in Italy. They travel over fifteen hundred feet per second. That's over four hundred twenty pounds. That means, my friend"—Slattery flinched away again as Fallon caressed his cheek with the pistol—"that if I should shoot you in the knee with one of these, it will blow the whole joint away. There's not a surgeon anywhere can rebuild

that. Do you understand what I'm saying, lad? I won't leave
enough of your knees for a surgeon to work with. You'll be a fine
sight, making your way on sticks. Maybe, they'll take your legs off
and you can push your way around on a little trolley and beg for
the odd shilling on street corners; for sure, no woman will have
you for a pimp then. What good would you be to her so?"

The woman looked up at Slattery. Her hair clung in a sodden
mess around her face like kelp and her makeup showed in
splotches like one of the Banshee. "Tell 'em," she said tiredly. "The
dirty bastards will no leave you alone 'til yuh do."

"Should I break an arm for you, Fallon?" Michael John said.
Slattery's face went white.

"Oh, Sweet Jesus and Mary and Joseph!" he whispered. "Is it
himself? *The* Fallon?" The front of his trousers suddenly became
damp. Fallon nodded. "They told me you were dead!"

Fallon shrugged. "They lied."

"'Tis true, then, what they say: you are the son of Finvarra—the
king of Daóne Sídh who rules the dead."

"Enough of this foolishness," Michael John growled. He
grabbed Slattery's right arm and bent it back. Slattery screamed
from pain.

"'Twas Anne Ryan who brought me the word!"

Fallon frowned and looked at Michael John, who shook his
head.

"And who might she be?" he asked.

"Tommy Coughlan's whoor," moaned Slattery. "Christ! Me
arm! It's broken!"

"Not yet," Michael John growled.

"Go on," Fallon gently prodded.

"He's the messenger for Flannery and Galvin," Slattery said.

"Michael Flannery? The head of NORAID?" Michael John
asked sharply. NORAID, the Irish Northern Aid, had been set up
in New York to solicit monies for the Provisional IRA. Publicly,

NORAID was sending money to Northern Ireland to help the victims of the Troubles, but much of the money found its way into the pockets of weapons dealers.

"Aye, that be the one," Slattery said.

"Why?" Fallon asked.

"Do yuh think me stupid? When those boys talk, I listen 'n' I ask no questions. I'm dead if not." Tears began to well up in his eyes. "Ah, please. Don't be telling where yuh heard that from. That's all I know. She got me at Doheny's. I don't know nuthin' else. Please."

"And where can we be finding this Anne Ryan?" Michael John asked.

"I don't know," Slattery said. Michael John pressed harder. A bone popped and Slattery screamed.

"I don't! By Mary and Brigid and me mother, I don't! Ask the Whistler over on Mount Street! He'll know."

"Whistler?" Fallon asked.

"The charley for the girls there," the woman said. "They give him a piece for keeping the watch against the Gardai." She looked at Michael John. "'E knows nothin' else. Can't yuh let 'im go, now?"

"Let him go," Fallon said quietly.

Michael John released him and stepped back. Slattery sank to the ground, holding his arm against his chest as tears streaked down his face. The woman reached out and pulled him to her, cradling his head between her huge breasts.

"There, now," she crooned. "Mother has you, now. It'll be all right." She looked up at Michael John and Fallon.

"Go away. You got what you wanted."

Fallon nodded and turned away into the rain, walking back toward Hogg's Lane. Michael John fell in beside him.

"Sure, now, and will you be leaving them like that?"

"Why not?" Fallon said. "'Tis sure they'll be telling no one what happened here. They'd be signing their own warrants."

"That's true, that's true," Michael John muttered. He wiped the water from his scarred forehead with his palm. "Jaysus, if I'm not needing a bit to build the fire in me belly again. Rain and more. You'd think God believes us to be fishes." Fallon grinned. "Well, now. Where's next?"

"Where else?" Fallon said. "Anne Ryan."

"Why not Tommy Coughlan? 'Tis a waste of time goin' to his cunny, I'm thinking."

"All life is a waste of time," Fallon said. "I don't have your faith in divine repopulation."

Michael John quickly crossed himself against the evil eye and followed Fallon from the alley. He felt troubled for he sensed a blackness about Fallon that he had never sensed before. Maybe it was because they had left Slattery and his whore alive when a few years back, a younger Fallon would not have hesitated to put a bullet in the head of each. He scratched his thick hair under his scully cap. Ah, Michael John! 'Tis only the darkness of the day and yer terrible thirst that's bringing on yer black thoughts— nothing that a wee dram couldn't cure.

He shook his head as they stepped from the alley out onto Hogg's Lane. But the blackness stayed with him.

13

It is a strange quirk of mankind that once independence is earned, man quickly moves to limit the independence of others. Ireland was no different from other new countries. Before Ireland's independence in 1921, one had little trouble finding prostitutes in the Monto District on Dublin's north side between O'Connell Street and Amiens Street Railway Station. But independence for Ireland brought about a sudden sense of propriety among the newly elite and demands were made on the newly created Gardai to stamp out prostitution. In a further demonstration of sudden piety, the city fathers quickly renamed Tyrone Street, running through the center of the district, Railway Street in an effort to stamp out the memory. But the prostitutes simply moved: some behind O'Connell Street itself, which quickly became famous for short romances; others to Fitzwilliam Street or Wilton Terrace.

Fallon and Michael John moved through the streets, past news agent shops and fish-and-chips takeaways, the ornate Edwardian building fronts of O'Connell Street with the colored lights of the hotels and cinemas falsely cheerful against the wide, wet, gray pavement gleaming red and blue against the steady stream of cars pouring from traffic light to traffic light. Down the middle of the street ran a median strip festooned with statues and ornate cast-iron streetlights. They moved out of O'Connell Street and into the narrow streets winding like a rabbit warren to the Royal

Canal. Here, the streets were dark and nearly empty, rain dancing like bits of broken glass on the stones.

The rain slowed to a drizzle and sudden scents of roasted coffee normally covered by coal smoke hovered over the street. The prostitutes began to emerge from the various pubs down the wide streets into which they had retired when the rain began to fall in earnest. The young charley known as "the Whistler" took his station at the Mount Street corner, lounging lazily against the church, ready to place two fingers in his mouth and utter a piercing whistle the moment a suspected Gardai began the walk down Wilton Terrace to Baggot Street Bridge over the Grand Canal. He eyed Fallon and Michael John suspiciously as they entered the street, hesitated, then placed his fingers into his mouth and gave his warning. The pair stopped and turned to him. He braced himself, putting a defiant look on his face as the smaller of the two approached him.

"You must be the Whistler, I'm thinking," he said. The young man grinned wolfishly, exposing large, yellow teeth.

"Sure, now, and what was yer clue?" he said cockily. The men exchanged bemused glances. The large man laughed.

"Well, now, that being the case, I have something to ask," the smaller one said, moving close to him. The Whistler shrugged and leaned insolently back against the wrought-iron fence. He pulled a cigarette from his pocket, lit it, and stuck it in the corner of his mouth. The smoke curled up and stung his eye, making it water, but he made no move to remove it. The men exchanged another look; the large man's grin grew wider.

"Ah, now, Fallon, wasn't I telling you this might happen?" He reached out and clapped the Whistler on the shoulder; the young man sagged, then quickly recovered. The gesture had been friendly, but his shoulder ached as if it had been punched.

"That you did, Michael John," Fallon said. He turned back to the Whistler. "Now, let's do it the easy way, shall we now?" He took a sudden step forward, nearly touching the young man. His hand moved, his fingers quickly flicking the cigarette away. The Whistler stiffened and tried to slide away to his right, but Michael John blocked him. His hands began to perspire. His mouth suddenly became dry. He tried to stare defiantly into Fallon's eyes, but they were lifeless, twin bits of black marble with silver glints in their depths. He looked away over Fallon's shoulder.

"I got nothin' to say to the Gardai," he mumbled.

"Gardai?" Michael John laughed, then leaned close to the Whistler, his breath like tiny explosions on the young man's cheek. "We ain't the Gardai, sonny boy. So you can forget the niceties by which they'd treat yuh. Would the Gardai be doing this?"

His big hand slapped the Whistler between his legs, grasping his testicles and squeezing hard. The Whistler's hands dropped down, trying to push Michael John's hand away, but the big man squeezed harder, lifting slightly, and the Whistler found himself on tiptoes.

"Now, be answering the man's questions, lad, or I'll throw you into Saint Stephen's cemetery without 'em. And, if you piss on me hand, I'll rip your dingus off and stuff it down yer throat. Now, do we have an understanding? Do we?"

He gave a gentle nudge with his fingers, and the Whistler felt his head bobbing frantically in agreement. Michael John turned to Fallon, smiling.

"See? See now? 'Twas only a wee misunderstanding. Nothing more."

"A subtle man, you are, Michael John," Fallon said. Michael John beamed.

"Now, lad, you see how it is? All I want is the answer to one question: Anne Ryan? Where is she?"

"Ah, Jaysus! Me ballocks is bustin'," the Whistler moaned.

"Anne Ryan?"

"Up Baggot Street. First right off. The Seven Bells." His eyes screwed shut from the pain. "Visitin' Black Jenny, she is. Oh, Christ! Leggo!"

"Let him go, Michael John," Fallon said. Michael John released his grip and stepped back. The Whistler sagged back against the rusty railing, his hands cradling his groin. "Now, it would be an easy thing for you to ring the Seven Bells and tell the fair Anne to be expecting two guests, but that would spoil the wee surprise, you understand? I would hate to come back and see you again. You understand?"

The Whistler nodded. Fallon took a punt from the pocket of his jacket and tucked it into the breast pocket of the Whistler's tweed coat.

"Now, off with you. Find the nearest pub and have a drink and forget us." The Whistler nodded and turned, shuffling painfully, bowlegged, up Mount Street toward Fitzwilliam. They watched him go, his feet splashing through the puddles between the paving stones.

"Do you think he'll call?" Michael John asked.

Fallon nodded. "Oh, yes. Once he's had a pint or two to help him remember how brave he is. But I think we have time."

They turned and hurried down Wilton Terrace. They passed groups of "dandy-dancers"—young men dressed in a curious mixture of stylishly cut, wide-lapeled jackets over double-pleated slacks and steel-toed Clark boots, who gave them arrogant looks that suggested territorial ownership. The canal water looked like tea with too much milk added. Rainwater trickled in icy runnels through the chinks in the cobblestone streets and alleys and the old brickwork sidewalks. The ancient stones of the buildings had turned black but the promising glow of pub lights shining through brightly colored lead-glass windows beckoned cheerfully to them. A door burst open on one and a man staggered out amid a publican's farewell and the tawdry smells of old porter and smoke.

They turned right onto Baggot Street and found a narrow alley shooting off to the right. It had once intended to be a street, but rapid building in the nineteenth century had stopped its progress. A plaque bolted to the brick wall high overhead named it Clifden Lane. They entered the lane, stepping carefully over the slick stones. An overflowing dustbin to their right was ripe with stinking garbage. Michael John wrinkled his nose.

"*Faugh!* 'Tis enough to turn good Guinness!" he muttered. His eyes narrowed in the dimness. "Fallon, I don't like this. Only one way in and out I can see. An' it's too quiet with the licensing hour upon us. 'Tisn't right, I'm saying."

"I know," Fallon said. His hand unbuttoned the leather jacket, letting it hang open. Michael John gave him a sideways glance and moved a few feet away from him. He pulled the door open to the Seven Bells and stepped aside to let Fallon enter first. The low susurrus of voices ceased and heads swiveled, silently considering them.

"God bless all here," Fallon said. Smoke hung heavily in the room, nearly masking the heavy odor of malt. The ceiling was low, heavy timbers exposed. The scarred mahogany bar stood like a peninsula at the far end of the room. A bench ran along the white plastered wall to his left. A small gas heater stood at its end to take the chill off the room, but it was too small to do an effective job for beneath the smoke and malt there was a hint of mold and decay. An old man in baggy clothes and a scully cap sat on the bench, his birdlike hands clutched around a glass of Guinness. Women sat with their coats on as if they were about to leave the small tables cluttered with their pints.

"Do you suppose it's a *ceilidh* they're holding in our honor?" Michael John murmured from behind him. Fallon gave an imperceptible shake of his head and crossed to the bar. The bartender swept a dirty towel across the sticky surface between them and looked questioningly at Fallon.

"Anne Ryan?" Fallon asked softly, his voice still loud in the room's quiet. "Black Jenny?"

The bartender's eyes flicked upward then quickly returned to Fallon's face.

"Never heard of them," he said in a voice raspy from years of drinking. His throat was stringy and his high cheekbones and bulbous nose red with broken veins. A large vein pulsed slowly on his forehead.

"Never mind," Fallon said, stepping away from the bar. He turned to the narrow stairway to the right of the bar.

"Hey! You canna go up there," the bartender piped.

"Of course we can," Michael John said, stepping behind Fallon as he mounted the stairs. "'Tis a simple matter of placing one foot before the other, you see." He demonstrated by placing his huge boot on the first step. It creaked in protest against his weight. The bartender shrugged and silently watched as they disappeared onto the landing above.

A door stood in front of them, the paint on its surface cracked and peeling, the smell of stale, cooked cabbage greeting them. Fallon stepped forward, turned the doorknob, and quickly entered. Two women looked up startled from their places at a plain wooden table. Before them were two cracked and chipped cups and saucers, a tea kettle to the right of the hefty one whose black hair bore evidences of a cheap wash and dye. The heavy flesh beneath her chin wobbled indignantly as she opened her mouth to speak.

"And who the bloody hell do you think you are?" she demanded. The younger one, a thin girl with platinum-bleached hair pulled back into a ponytail secured by a rubber band tightly wound close to her head, pushed back away from the table. Her hands dropped into her lap. The tops of her small breasts peeked whitely above her low-cut, dark green blouse. A tan leather skirt stopped halfway up her shapely thighs encased in net stockings like spider webs.

"Anne Ryan?" Fallon said, ignoring the large lady who pushed herself to her feet and started around the table toward them. Michael John stepped in front of her, grabbed her fleshy arm, spun her around and sat her in a broken armchair covered with a dirty red throw edged with green tassels. She grunted as she landed on the cushion. Springs squeaked loudly.

"Now, then, let the man say his piece," Michael John said. She started up from the armchair, only to sink back down as he waved a large admonishing finger beneath her nose.

"It's all right, Jenny," the thin girl said quietly. Her full lips pursed together then opened in a half-smile. "Yes, I'm Anne Ryan. And to what do we owe the pleasure of your company?" She crossed her legs, the skirt riding higher to show the tops of her stockings.

"I understand you've been looking for me," Fallon said. Her blue eyes narrowed. He cocked his head and smiled the smile that never touched his eyes. "The name's Fallon."

A fine eyebrow arched inquisitively. "And why would I be wanting to see you, Mr. Fallon?" she said, her voice low and throaty, carrying a suggestion of seduction in it.

"Suppose you tell me," he said, moving back against the wall to keep the full room in view.

"I'm not," she said, adding, "at least, I wasn't." The tips of her fingers began to play with the tops of her stockings. "But, then, maybe it's a mistake I've been making."

Fallon shook his head. "Oh? Well, now, the word is that you have been making it a point to find me."

"And whose word would that be?" she asked, her eyes holding his.

"Ah, now, lass, you know the game. 'Tis a question that won't be answered," he said. She studied him closely for a moment then relaxed and slid down in her chair, exposing more thigh. She gestured with her left hand.

"What the hell," she said. "Slattery, I know."

"And who sent you? The GDC?" She froze for a moment and Fallon nodded. "Then you know who they are."

She shook her head. "Never heard of them."

"I think not. Where do I find them?"

"Who knows?"

"I think you do," Michael John said. "An' if yer not quick about it, 'tis hurtin' yuh'll be."

She looked at Fallon for confirmation, but he remained impassive. She shrugged. "You see," she began, starting to rise. Her left hand casually gripped the hem of her skirt as if to tug it down, then suddenly jerked it up. Fallon had a sudden glimpse of sheer red, G-string panties and heavy dark pubic hair, then Michael John crashed into him, staggering him.

"Look out, Fallon!" he yelled, then grunted as the small automatic in her hand popped. He swung his hand, knocking the pistol away, then fell against Fallon, both crashing to the floor. The pistol clattered against the wall as she scooped her purse from the table and jumped through the doorway. Her heels clattered on the narrow steps as she raced down them.

"Sweet Mother-of-God!" Black Jenny gasped frantically crossing herself, ashen-faced. "He's dead for sure!" Her eyes rolled up into her head, exposing their whites, and she fell back against the chair. It groaned, then fell apart under her sudden weight.

Michael John moaned and rolled off Fallon, clutching his stomach. "Ah, shut yer bog, yuh ugly hag," he said through clenched teeth. His eyes caught Fallon's. "Away with yuh! Catch the bloody bitch!"

"Quit it," Fallon said. He kicked her ankle. She yelped, her eyes clicking open. She glared at him while she massaged her hurt. Fallon dropped to one knee to examine the wound: blood oozed from a tiny wound in his stomach. Michael John swore.

"If 'twas your belly, I'd say the same!" he snapped. "Go! 'Tis no grave matter. Catch the bleedin' whore! I'll be all right," he added as Fallon hesitated.

Fallon nodded and glanced at Black Jenny swearing softly under her breath as she rocked back and forth among the ruins of the chair, clutching her ankle in both hands. "Look after him. You don't want me back here!" he said icily. She started to direct her curses at him, then made the mistake of glancing into his eyes. She went pale beneath the heavy rice powder and shook her head, cringing back away from him. Fallon nodded and ran through the door and down the stairs.

"Here, now," the bartender blustered as Fallon leaped the last three stairs. "What's goin' on?"

"Call the ambulance! A man's been shot upstairs!" Fallon snapped. He started for the door, but drinkers had slammed their glasses down on tables at his words and rushed for the door. He waited impatiently as two men struggled to exit at the same time, then he slammed into them with his shoulder, sending them sprawling and cursing onto the cobblestones. Fallon leaped over them and sprinted to Baggot Street. He looked quickly both ways, but Anne Ryan had disappeared. Frustrated, he slammed his hand against the brick wall. An ululating siren sounded, nearing the street, and he turned, walking up toward St. Stephen's Green, moving slowly through the gathering crowd, losing himself in their anonymity.

14

MAEVE SHOOK THE RAIN FROM HER LONG, AUBURN HAIR AS SHE entered the Reading Room west of Old Library and glanced rue-fully at her reflection. You should have taken an umbrella to Berkeley Library. Even if you thought you could beat the rain. 'Tis no one's fault but your own.

She stiffened as a figure moved out of a dim recess and stepped in front of her, then relaxed as she recognized Fallon.

"Tomas!" she exclaimed, laughing shakily, relieved. "A fine start you gave me. What brings you here on such a dirty day? It'll give you a dose of pneumonia at no charge."

"Sorry, Maeve. But you know how 'tis. There are those who know about the two of us. Slattery showed that. I thought it best to be meeting you this way," he said, his face grave.

"You found him, then?" she asked, moving into the alcove with him. She shifted the heavy bag of books on her shoulder, and he reached out and lifted it from her, holding it easily in his left hand, she noticed, keeping the right one free. She became aware of the looseness in him, yet the constant awareness: the way his eyes flickered, constantly moving; the new lines in his face, tight-ening his cheekbones, his smile; the silver streaks in his hair; his slim hands, the hands of a concert pianist, and she remembered the time he'd once dropped onto a vacant piano bench in a pub near Sligo and brought the patrons to tears and joviality by running through traditional melodies, transposing scores on the spot to dictate mood change. And she smelled the nearness of him, the faint lime of his cologne, the damp leather, his maleness—a chill made her shiver.

"What's the matter?" he asked.

"Nothing," she answered, looking away from the directness of his question. "Did he tell you anything?"

"A name: Anne Ryan. Supposed to be the girlfriend of Tommy Coughlan."

"NORAID?" she said quickly, frowning. NORAID, the Irish Northern Aid Committee, had been established in America in 1970 with the approval of Daithi O'Conaill, a member of the governing board of the IRA, for raising funds to support the families of imprisoned IRA men. It had been established by three old IRA men who had fled to America in the twenties after the republican cause suffered defeat in the civil war: Michael Flannery, Jack McGowan, and Jack McCarthy. Originally, it had been linked with the Northern Aid Committee set up by Joe Cahill and Sean Keenan, leading IRA men. The Northern Aid Committee was replaced by the Green Cross, which was part of An Cumann Carbhrach, the organization for dependents of IRA prisoners. Although the monies were supposed to go to the families of the IRA men in prison, NORAID made no stipulations as to how the money was to be spent once it arrived in Ireland. Consequently, NORAID had come under close scrutiny by the Justice Department, which pressed it to register under the Foreign Agents Registration Act (FARA) as an agent of the IRA, and had been denounced by the British authorities as a money supplier to the IRA. After the hunger strikes of Bobby Sands and others who'd died in 1981, contributions to NORAID had swelled until nearly a quarter million dollars a year began finding its way to Ireland and IRA coffers, along with rumors of "special" shipments.

Fallon shrugged. "So I'm told. We tried to find her, but she got away. We almost had her, but she had a hideaway. She shot Michael John."

"Michael John? Is he bad hurt?" she asked, concern thick in her voice.

"He will be, I'm thinking. I had to leave him when I heard the Gardai coming, but he was awake and pushing me off. The bullet took him in the side, but went through. You'll check on him?"

"I will, of course. And yourself?"

"I'm all right. The bullet was for me. I must be getting old."

"Just a bit rusty."

"Perhaps. Do you know her friend? It's been awhile since I've been in and people like that change jobs rapidly."

"But he's with NORAID?"

She nodded. "It was Tommy Coughlan who brought the money NORAID gathered to help the good Reverend Ray Davey's work at Corrymeela for his family weeks—you know," she added at the quizzical look Fallon gave her. "Up by the Giant's Causeway where he started a retreat for both Catholics and Protestants whose families have been victims of the Troubles."

He shook his head. "Sorry. I thought that went under after Black Ian got himself elected to Parliament during the last gerrymandering of the Belfast districts," he answered, referring to the fundamentalist Protestant preacher who'd started his own Martyrs Memorial Free Presbyterian Church to preach his hatred of the Catholics. He had been a driving force in defeating all the attempts at reconciliation between the Protestant and Catholic political parties since denouncing the northern prime minister, Terence O'Neill, and leading mobs of cudgel-bearing Protestants against civil rights marchers. His venom-dripping denunciation of the Catholic marchers began the Protestant attacks on the Catholics and led to the fatal riots in 1969: Burntollet Bridge, the Bogside Battle in Derry, the Falls Road burnings, the Shankill Road killings.

"No, Corrymeela is still working, but money is getting scarce. There's not much in Ireland for that anymore. Not with unemployment hitting around fifteen percent." Her lips twisted ruefully. "I'm afraid Garret FitzGerald's 'new materialism' didn't work for us, and the Celtic tiger is really a little meow for most."

Fallon nodded. He glanced through the door as it swung open, admitting a harassed-looking lecturer wearing a damp robe. The rain fell in a torrent, glistening off the walks. The wind began to blow, battering the rain against the gray stone buildings, the chapel and dining hall opposite, until strips of mist seemed to form curtains around them. He was aware of the Fine Gael leader's theory that had drawn support from Donal Nevin, then assistant general secretary of the Irish Congress of Trade Unions. The sudden growth in Ireland's economy after it joined the European Economic Community in 1972 had swelled pocket books across the country, but with it came a heightened awareness of new luxury that could now be afforded and the gap between poverty and affluence suddenly widened. In the 1980s, growth suddenly tumbled as inflation rose rapidly to 18 percent, and those who had plunged into new luxuries suddenly found themselves again with less purchasing power and higher loan interests, and again the poor suffered as money began to be guarded and not given to the poor, who became even poorer. And now the pendulum was beginning to swing back for some. But the gap between the rich and the poor was simply getting larger and larger.

"So, NORAID is helping out there. Well, now, 'tis a fine change from guns," Fallon mused.

A frown darkened Maeve's face. "Sure, and that will never change. But what will they be sending over next, I'm wondering. There are those who like to watch the figures grow in their bank accounts and with the new cease-fire, why, what will they do now that one market has dried up? The Kerry route from Boston has been very good to some of the boyos for a long time, I'm thinking, and they may have found a new business with the drugs." She shook her head. "I can understand the want, but not the need."

"And how," Fallon asked, his lips turning up with the hint of a smile, "did you come to that?"

"Not so hard," she said dryly. "Sure, now, and have you forgotten I do a bit of work with the Cross Group? The mothers and wives there still have husbands and sons in the Protestant prisons and they have eyes and ears." She paused. "You know, Tomas, if you stop the drugs coming in, I wonder what they'll put out next, what with no more market for the guns."

Fallon nodded, remembering her involvement in the various peace movements after she'd shot the *gombeen* man who had betrayed her husband, Conor Larkin, and raped and sodomized her in the interrogation cells at Castlereagh after betraying her and Richard O'Bannion, the close friend and lieutenant of MacCauley. O'Bannion had been turned by the RUC and later killed by MacCauley. She had refused a marriage offer from the American correspondent Con Edwards after he'd helped Conar Larkin and MacCauley free her from the RUC when they had tried to transfer her to the woman's prison, and had immersed herself in efforts to bring peace to the war-torn North. But because her husband had been Conor Larkin, one of the Movement's legendary heroes, she still had contacts among the IRA men and Provos.

"Besides," she added, digging into the bag he held. "There's this." She came up with a copy of *An Phoblacht*, the IRA's newspaper. She folded it back to the second page and handed it to Fallon, pointing with a shapely forefinger at the story angrily deriding the security forces for the lack of arrests in the recent drug deaths of a young boy and girl. Fallon scanned it, shaking his head.

"There's no mention of Kerry here," he said.

She gestured impatiently. "I know. But the story *plus* the rumors coming through the Cross and the pub line say Kerry it was where the latest drugs came through."

"It's not much," Fallon said doubtfully, "but it's still more than we've got."

"You're off to Kerry, then?" Fallon nodded. She bit her lip, thinking. "Not much time, but I can still get Brendan Kennally—he's a soft heart—to cover my classes, I'm thinking."

"No," Fallon said gently. "You've done enough."

"But you have no one to watch your back now that Michael John is laid up," she protested.

"The game's beginning to be too ruthless; it's now playing the players. It's giving birth to people like the GDC."

"Then it *was* them."

He nodded. "I think so. Anne Ryan knew about them despite their low profile. There's no other way that she would."

"And now?"

" 'Tis time to do something about it, I'm thinking. There'll be no rest until I do."

"So, why are you back in it?" she asked. He shrugged.

"You're a romantic," she teased.

"No," he said suddenly sober. "Yeats was right: 'Romantic Ireland's dead and gone, / It's with O'Leary in the grave.'"

"Then why?"

"The truth?" She nodded. His eyes became lifeless. "There's nowhere else for me."

"You sound as if you're attending your own wake," she said.

"Perhaps I am," he said softly.

"I can't believe that, Tomas," she said.

He looked at her in silence for a moment, then said, "Maeve, darling, did you send Michael John after me?"

She lifted her chin, eyeing him levelly. "You said yourself it's been awhile since you were in. A man like you goes stale fast, Tomas, when he's not up against it constantly. I saw that with Conor."

"For that, I thank you, Maeve. But from here on, it's myself alone, understand?"

"Tomas—"

"Understand, Maeve? Anne Ryan was ready for us. She would have been gone if we'd been a half-hour later. There's a supergrass somewhere, I'm thinking. Did you call Michael John yourself?"

"No. I sent word. Oh, shit!" she said, slapping her forehead in disgust. Fallon slipped his arm around her shoulders.

"Now, don't be hard on yourself. You did what you thought was right. But from now on, let's keep things between the two of us."

"Where will you go in Kerry?" she asked.

"I still have a couple of friends there," he said.

"You'll keep in touch?"

He grinned, sudden lights dancing in his dark eyes. "Sure, and won't I be doing that. And, if you're needing someone, don't use the old line. Go to Dingle, the Half Door there on John Street, and tell them you're a friend of the Fallons. The ground's safe there. Even at Easter with all the tourists gone."

She stood on tiptoe and kissed him on the lips. Startled, he stepped back suddenly as if bee-stung. "Not allowed to kiss back?" she said, trying to make a joke of the sudden awkwardness between them.

"You'd be cheating yourself, Maeve," he said slowly.

"It's called being human," she said.

"Is it? I had quite forgotten."

"A fine-looking man like yourself? I find that hard to believe. Not a lover anywhere?"

"No," he said, half-turning from her. "Such things are for others."

"And what makes others different from you, Tomas?"

"About six hundred years," he said. "A man can't become what he's not, Maeve."

"No, but a man can change," she answered. "Anyone can change."

"No, some cannot, and that's the way of it."

She studied him for a long moment, then her face saddened. "Ah, Tomas. What has Ireland and her hate made of you?"

"What I am," he said simply. "There's never been room for anything else and now, now I think there's no room left anywhere but Ireland for a man like me."

"God be with you, Tomas," she said, taking her bookbag from him. She stepped out of the alcove. "Call me after Kerry."

He nodded and watched as she turned and walked briskly into the Reading Room, the leather heels of her shoes echoing with authority against the stone floor.

"Well, now," he said softly to himself. "What's this, then?"

He stood for a moment, feeling again the gentle pressure of her lips, then turned and left the building, hunkering deep within his leather jacket as the gray rain beat mercilessly upon him.

15

THE TIDE WAS OUT AND FALLON WALKED ALONG THE WET SAND,
inhaling deeply of the salt air and seaweed and kelp left on the
strand. Gulls wheeled overhead, splotches of white against the
lead gray sky, their raucous cries echoing in the crisp, afternoon
air. Tiny rails hopped along the wet sand between the puddles,
feeding on snails and bugs trapped in the hollows. It had been a
long and circumspect trip to Kerry from Dublin: by bus to Kil-
dare, then another bus to Wexford across the misty hills below
the blue Wicklow Mountains. From there, he rode his thumb
across the Knockmealdown Mountains to Kilkenny in the Batty-
howrd Hills. A farmer there had given him a ride to Cork in a
wheezing diesel truck loaded with cabbages, trailing past ascend-
ing pastures, glistening in the sun after the soft nights, strong
light falling flat upon stone. He took a bus for Tralee, but became
suspicious of two men riding a few seats behind him. He waited
until the last minute before the bus pulled out of Macroon, then
leaped out. The two tried to follow him, but he lost them in the
back streets. He took another detour past the twin hills known as
the Paps of Anu, crossed Macgillycuddy's Reeks on foot, nearly
falling in a gorge as he made his way blind over the Reeks by following the roll of a hill in the misty dark, and found a fisherman,
who had served with his grandfather in Dundee's Brigade, who
happily took him across Dingle Bay to Inch. From there, he made

his way through old IRA territory across the Slieve Mish Mountains to Castlegregary then north to the leeward side of Rough Point, the last leg proving the most hazardous, for the men and women of Kerry had been the fiercest fighters for Ireland's freedom and many there were who remembered the Fallons and had followed his own career with glee and would hear of nothing else but splitting a bottle or two at the local shebeen in his honor. He had been touched by their simplicity and honesty, taking nearly a week to cover the last leg of his trip, which could have been made in a few hours by automobile.

He breathed deeply, cleaning the past week from his system as he watched the thin old man walk into the surf, bend at the waist, and expertly cast a long line into the rolling, gunmetal sea. He played out line as he backed slowly from the water, his pants rolled up past knobby knees, exposing storklike legs with heavy varicose veins, the flesh pebbly blue from the cold, to a nest he'd made in the sand. He anchored the rod in a home-welded grip stand, then picked up another rod and waded out again into the sea. With one easy motion born of long practice, he cast the line far out into the swell. The cane rod flexed and made a graceful arch over the old man's head. At the top of its arch, the old man spat the conical weight out from between his lips. When the weight struck the trough between two waves, the old man raised the tip of his rod and slowly walked backward from the surf, keeping the line taut. He anchored the rod in a socket welded to angle iron driven deeply into the sand beside a gunnysack, then lowered himself onto a canvas stool, fished an old briar from the pocket of his oilskin jacket, and lit it with a kitchen match he struck with a thumbnail. His pale, watery eyes in his heavily seamed face never left the thrumming lines.

Behind him on the dunes well above the high tidemark sat a misshapen hut built of tar paper and old, mildewed canvas and odd-shaped driftwood weathered gray and oil tins cut and hammered flat overlapping each other like shingles. A rusted stovepipe, bent into a ninety-degree angle to keep out the rain, projected above the roof. A thin stream of gray smoke curled lazily from the pipe, spiraling upward into the mist until the heavy air flattened it into a slab. Driftwood had been pulled up into a pile beside the hut and an old axe had been buried into one of the logs to keep the edge clean. A makeshift drying rack had been made from poles and a wet net spread to dry over the center poles. A curragh lay top down next to the net and drying rack. It looked like a tinker's camp.

Fallon knew the old man had seen him approach, but the old man ignored him, concentrating on the fishing lines. Fallon felt a smile touching his lips.

"Catching anything besides the cold?" he asked. The old man pulled on his pipe then took the stem from between stumpy, yellowed teeth and scratched the salt-and-pepper bristle along his long jaw as he spoke.

"Sure, and if yuh were half the wise man yuh think yuh are, you'd be noticing the bag at me feet and how it twitches now and then before you made a fool of yourself with the question. Or did you now think it was one of the wee folk I'd caught, one of the Tuatha Dé Danann, and this is why I'm living in the fine castle back there?" He stabbed over his shoulder at the makeshift hut.

Fallon squatted on his heels beside the old man's chair. "How have yuh been, Uncle Dan?" he asked, slipping into the broad Kerry dialect.

"If I was any finer, I'd been dead long ago," the old man said querulously. The rod on his left suddenly dipped, and he quickly lifted it from the socket, striking hard in the same motion, then began reeling a struggling fish in through the surf. In moments, a young sea bass lay gasping on the sand in front of him. He cleaned the hook and carefully set it in the false eye near the handle before tightening the line and setting the pole back in the stand.

"Will you be staying for supper, now?" he asked, lifting the other rod from its socket and retrieving its line.

"If yuh've enough," Fallon asked.

"Always enough for family," Uncle Dan said, stripping the bait from the hook and setting the line. He handed the rod to Fallon and picked up the gunny sack, dropping the bass inside. With one hand, he collapsed the stool, nodded at the other rod in its stand, and said, "Be bringing the rods and stands, then, and we'll be after making us supper."

He turned toward the house, taking a couple of steps before stopping and saying gruffly over his shoulder, "'Tis good to see you again, Tomas." He walked to the hut, puffing furiously on his pipe, smoke trailing over his shoulder.

Fallon grinned, took the other rod from its stand, then awkwardly worked the stands back and forth until he could pull the anchor blades from their grip. He banged the stands together to free them from the clumps of sand clinging to the joints and walked up to the house. Uncle Dan had already cleaned the fish and started a fire with a block of peat beneath a grill lying across a square of stones. A wire screen, heavily larded, rested on top of the fire-blackened grill. He sat on the stool beside the fire, waiting.

"I wondered if I was going to have to take a trip down to help you," Uncle Dan said. "Knowing how soft yuh've become sittin' in your wee cottage on the hill."

"Did yuh think I'd been wantin' to get my hands dirty cleaning the supper? Sure, and me mother, God bless her, raised no foolish children," Fallon answered.

"There's some that would say different," Uncle Dan said gruffly. He plunged a liver-spotted hand into a bucket beside him and came up with a handful of wet wood chips. He tossed them on the fire, waited until they began to smoke, then carefully arranged the filets across the wire on the grill.

"Uncle Dan, Brian made his choice; I made mine," Fallon said quietly. "You have to respect that." Uncle Dan snorted and bit down upon the stem of his pipe. "Will you whisht, I'm saying?"

"Whisht yourself," Uncle Dan grumbled. "Your mother made sure one of yuh to be a priest." He looked at Fallon's dark hair. "Aye, and yer off-colored twin is better for it despite your mother's intentions, I'm thinking. A man making confession to you would feel the Devil's hand on his soul. But, now, I'm thinking that maybe yuh been feeling the pull of the cross for I've heard little of yer name these past few years. Nor seen more of yuh," he added, the consonants clicking in his throat.

"Well, you're seein' me now," Fallon said. He took a canvas stool from the side of the hut, placed it near his uncle, then sat, stretching his hands and legs out to the fire. He sighed. "Ah, but I'm destroyed walking."

"And why would you be walking when there're booses an' trains to be takin' the place of yer legs?" Uncle Dan asked, his eyes squinting against the smoke a sudden wind threw in his face.

"Now, you'd be knowing the why, Uncle Dan, if you'd put your mind to it. And who was it was telling me and my twin about his da, me grandda, nearly getting caught with Collins in his car but for the sake of a voice warning him? And himself going to Brandon as it were and refusing the ride in Collins's car, the same being ambushed and killed at Beal na mBlach in county Cork?" He made his voice quiver into a tenor. "'An', lad, there 'twas the Big Fellow himself covered with his sacred blood from the traitors' guns and the same with the others and 'is fine car with enough holes in it to create nests for wrens. An' me, on shank's mare, spared the time for bleedin' only for listenin' to the warnin' in me 'ed. 'Tis far better to keep to oneself an' be leg weary and tired rather than rested and dead.'"

A light lit in the depths of the old man's eyes, and he leaned forward, flipping the filets as he spoke. "So and well, there. There's those out seeking yuh? Gardai?"

Fallon nodded. "And some."

Uncle Dan reached behind him and lifted a glass quart measure around. Clear liquid moved in the glass. He unscrewed the lid and a raw, pungent smell of poteen crept out into the air. "Will you be havin' a jar?" he asked, looking at Fallon. He hooked two tin cups by his heel with a horny finger, handed one to Fallon, and poured without waiting for an answer. "Mind now, it ain't that fancy stuff yuh no doubt are used to drinkin', but it does the job. 'Tis from the Widow Killeen over in Brandon. She has a fine shebeen there and has her boy drop off a jar of poteen or two of her oldest run when he's making a trip to Stradbally." He winked. "Pegeen still knows how to keep the rough edges off it. The Gardai keep trying to close her shebeen, but the old girl's too foxy for 'em. She can see them comin' a mile before they're thinking about goin'!" He took a deep drink and smacked his lips. "A fine woman who's gettin' a bit lonely, I'm thinkin', and her man gone these past five years, and she the same time without Kerry-dancing in the clear nights of Lughnasa before the cold of winter."

"Ah, Uncle Dan, the Devil is with you, for sure!" Fallon said, taking a cautious sip and swallowing twice as the fiery liquid burned a path to his stomach. A warm glow spread throughout his body, and he sighed and waggled his feet at the fire.

"With all of us save one," Uncle Dan said, draining his cup. He refilled it and held the jar out to Fallon who shook his head, pulling back.

"Best one to keep a clear head, so," he said.

"That way, is it?" Uncle Dan said. He covered the jar and placed it at his heel within easy reach. He picked up two tin plates and slid the now golden brown filets equally upon them. Rain began to fall, and he rose, gripping his plate in one hand and balancing his cup upon the lid of the jar in his other. "It's becoming a shaky evening. Let's inside where 'tis dry."

Fallon rose and dutifully held the door for his uncle as the old man entered. He followed him inside, standing just inside the door and blinking as his eyes adjusted to the dimness. An oil stove stood on paving blocks in the corner and between him and the stove stood a badly chipped formica and chrome table and three chairs. A cot, covered with an old army sleeping bag, was tucked against one wall while its mate stood against the opposite. Clothes hung from nails hammered in walls. In one corner stood a green-painted cupboard. A coffee can filled with heavy fishhooks stood on a small table with spools of line and lead sinkers that had been molded in the socket of a pair of box-nosed pliers from cast-off tire weights. A basin and ewer rested on a washstand next to a bucket beneath a cracked shaving mirror hung from a nail. A strop hung next to the mirror and a cutthroat razor and mug and brush were neatly arranged next to the bowl. Uncle Dan nodded at them.

"Feel free to borrow my razor," he said. "But strop the blade clean when you've finished. I'm no potboy to be cleaning up after you, an' this is no boardinghouse." He sniffed. "An' yuh might be takin' a bar of soap down to the water. 'Tis a close fit in here an' one of us could use a proper wash."

"That I will, in time," Fallon said, crossing to the table to sit beside him. He suddenly discovered his hunger and bolted his food. Uncle Dan beamed and nodded with pleasure.

"'Tis fine to see yuh still enjoy an honest meal, now. I was afraid yuh might be thinkin' yuh was at the Grafton House grill."

"It'll do," Fallon said around a mouthful of fish. "And how have you been, Uncle Dan?"

"'How 'ave I been?' he's askin'! Sure, an' all this time he could've

been findin' that out for a five-pence card. But does the lad write
to the last of his family? Or even leave a call at the main house in
Tralee when I'm here fishin'? No, 'tis too busy he is with the fancies of the east. You're a shameful man, Tomas Fallon, to come to
a poor man's home and insult him with such proprieties! 'Tis good
yer father and mother 'ave been dead these past twenty years
rather than know how you've been treatin' your poor o' Uncle
Dan!" he added as an afterthought.

"You old phoney," Fallon said affectionately. "You have enough
money to live in fine fashion among the gentry yourself from Da's
business before he died. 'Tis of your own choosing you live out
here like a tinker on Rough Point, not from necessity. You've a
fine house in Tralee that the lawyers couldn't touch when the
business went down, and, I'm sure, knowing how you work the
figures in the trade, that you have a goodly sum set by to tide you
over in your waning years. Now, why would a man like you be
doin' that since there're no posters out on you?"

"But there is one on you, Tomas," he said quietly. "You're the
finest Kerry-dancer of all, but if I wasn't here, where would you go
when you needed a quiet place and someone to watch your back
while you drew a free breath for a minute or two? An' why
wouldn't that someone be me who has no family of his own?" He
cleared his voice in the silence between them. "Tomas, you know
you are my only heir, saving your brother Brian whose blood is
spoiled by his priesthood, and there're things you have to be
knowing." He pushed himself erect and hobbled across to the
cupboard. He opened the door and reached in the back, removing
a tin box. He shut the door and returned to the table, grimacing
against old pains as he lowered himself back into his chair. He
opened the box and removed a bank book. Fallon caught a quick
glimpse of a picture of his mother with a lock of golden hair
beneath the book before the lid closed. Uncle Dan handed the

book to Fallon. The legend *Suisse Credit* had been embossed on the blue cover. He opened it. His eyebrows lifted at the sum.

"There's also a fair amount on deposit in the Bank of Ireland in Dublin under my name, but yours is on the account too for anonymous draw and the Right of Survivorship against the time when you might need the odd punt or two and your name becoming a handicap." He held up his hand as Fallon tried to protest. "A savings and the death duties and all. Memorize the account numbers and the code. 'Tis the same at both banks: black rose. That's all you need to draw."

"Thank you, Uncle Dan," Fallon said. The old man waved the thanks away.

"'Tis nothing, 'tis nothing. Now, what is it that brings you to Kerry during the foul months when even American tourists stay at home or in Dublin?"

"Drugs," Fallon said quietly. The old man leaned forward, interest sparkling in his eyes as Fallon explained everything from the surprise visit sent by MacCauley to Michael John's wounding in Dublin, omitting only Maeve's kiss.

"I see," Uncle Dan said. "And what is it that brings you here, now?"

"Do you know anything about a group calling themselves Gaelach Dearg Craobh—the GDC?"

Uncle Dan's eyes narrowed. "And what would such a bunch of boyos be those?"

"The worst of the lot, Uncle Dan," Fallon said quietly. "Murderers all and murder for profit, it is. There's little done for the pride of Ireland despite their fancy name. But they know the ins and outs of the boyos. They were with them for a while until they stepped over themselves and then the board gave them to the Brits."

"Shopped their own, did they?" He shook his head. "That'd have never happened in the old days."

"I think it would. Serves as a better example than a bullet in the head and everyone wondering why. This way, people know them for what they were. Do you know anything about a recent run? A shipment of AK-47s came through Kerry not long ago. The drugs were in the crates. Did such a thing happen, now, and if so, who took it?"

The old man stared at him in silence for a long time. Gulls cried overhead and rain drummed on the roof of the hut, a quiet timpani soothingly augmented by the roll of the waves as the tide changed and began its creep up the strand toward the dunes and the hut safely standing above it in a clump of shore grass. Finally, he sighed and broke the long silence.

"Aye, I can see what you're askin' and except for family, I'd be driving you from me house with my stick. But, the truth is, one may have gone through off Brandon Point. A trawler came in and curraghs went out to meet it, taking crates across Tralee Bay to the point off Camp."

Fallon felt excitement growing within him. "And where did the mother ship come from and her name?"

"Boston, I hear. *Sibyl.* They've used her before. She fishes the banks for a month at a time. No one notices the odd day or two she's out."

"Tommy Coughlan?"

Uncle Dan's eyes lifted. He gesticulated wildly. "Ah, now, that darling's a mean one. Make no mistake about it. He wants to be more important than he is. He's an American out of Boston. His family is a heavy contributor to the cause and his father is a *bocóid* with the Silver Street Gang in South Boston. That's the only reason NORAID uses him. When the arms were coming across, he kept trying to go along, but the boyos didn't let him get out of Kerry. He kept trying, though."

"Anne Ryan?"

"You're really picking 'em now, Tomas. She's a little whore

who's fucked her way across Ireland. She's a Kerry girl; her da owned a pub somewhere around Dingle. When they were making the film *Ryan's Daughter* at Dunquin, she tried to get in the cast by sleeping with the film crew. Her da found out and belted her in front of his pub. She finally got in the films, I hear, but they aren't the films that play in theaters in Ireland, if you know what I mean. When her da died, she came back to sell the pub, and that's where she met Tommy Coughlan. He bought it and her with it." He shook his head. "That was a bad one, it was. Tommy Coughlan bought the pub from Anne, but it wasn't all hers to sell; part of it belonged to her brother, so. Coughlan tried to scare the brother off by having some bully boys beat the poor lad up, but the young man would have nothing of that. He filed a lawsuit against Coughlan and his sister."

The old man paused to have a drink. Fallon waited for a moment, then asked. "Well, so? What happened?"

The old man lifted rheumy eyes to peer out from beneath bushy eyebrows at Fallon. "Sure, and didn't he set fire to the cottage and burn it down with the brother inside? And making sure, he did, that no one would escape by rolling the brother's truck down to block the door?"

"And nothing could be proved by way of that?"

The old man shook his head again. "No. The truck apparently slipped its gear and when it slammed against the house, it knocked a lantern off the table. An accident, the authorities say, but those around here know differently. Anyway, Coughlan got the girl and the pub. It's turning a nice profit, now, it is, since there's no other to take the service away. Yes," he said to Fallon's raised eyebrow, "Coughlan took care of that too. After the brother was buried, he sent word around to the other pubs in the area that he wanted to buy in before other accidents could befall the lads. They sold."

"Would they be there, now?" Fallon asked, his pulse quickening.

"I doubt it. I'm thinking they're back in Boston, now. The boyos don't want him around any more than they can help it. Two years ago, he put a man in hospital for asking his whoor to dance. The boyos don't like that kind of attention."

"I see," Fallon said. He hunched over the table, using the tin cup half-filled with the widow's clear mead as a crystal ball. Well, now, you know who and where, now, but why? And the players, you know them too. But what is going on? Best stop thinking about it. You know there's nothing for you but to go to Boston from here. But how to get there? Your name and picture has a hallowed niche in Interpol's files.

"Will you be havin' another, Tomas?"

He looked up. Uncle Dan held the jar half across the table to him. He shook his head.

"Not right now, Uncle Dan. I still have some." He raised his cup. The old man snorted.

"Well, drink it doon. Or are you thinking of taking orders like your brother?"

"Oh, aye," Fallon said, swallowing the contents of his cup and holding it across the table. "As if the Church would have me." Slowly, he put the cup down on the table in front of him. His uncle gave him a quizzical look.

"What is it, lad?"

"Is Brian still at the monastery up near Ballintober?"

"No, lad. He's back in a parish not far from here. Dagdaskillen, it is. Why?"

"'Tis been a long time since we spoke. More than twenty years since Da died. I thought I'd pop around and chat him up."

Uncle Dan shook his head. "Good tolerance to you, Tomas. But I'm thinking it's little talkin' it's you'll do."

"One can only try," he said.

"Aye, that's true. But history is against you."

"History?"

The old man smiled faintly. "Listen."

Fallon obediently cocked his head, hearing the slow, sullen rumble of the waves on the sand, the wind gusting against the walls of the house. "What am I supposed to hear?"

"What are you hearing?"

"The wind. And the sea."

"The ancient sounds; the sounds of the Red Branch kings who had the most extraordinary warriors like Cúchulainn: unbeatable, yet doomed to die in battle after he killed his only son in a duel by the sea; the mighty warriors of Ulster whose druids told them they would rule forever. But then Saint Patrick came, and the Red Branch kings were no more. And now, their souls ride their chariots on the wind and the waves, crying for the Ireland that is now history. But, lad, Saint Patrick is history as are *his* followers, while the kings have their warriors back."

"Not very subtle, Uncle Dan," Fallon said.

"Ah, well. I tried. But, lad, when the warrior meets the man of God, he always loses. Always," he added emphatically. "Even in death, the priest wins: that's why there are so many martyrs. The warrior just becomes dust and his soul—" He gestured at the walls, shaking his head. "Brian will do you no good. He believes in Saint Patrick's ways, not Cúchulainn's."

"Sure, and I think the poteen is winning your tongue, Uncle." Fallon grinned.

The old man grinned back and poured again from the jar, topping Fallon's glass before he could stop him. "Aye, that may be. And do you remember what your da used to say?"

"*In vino veritas.* And Mother would pretend to be angry and say the only truth was that it gave him an excuse to have a jar with you."

"Ah, those were magic nights, they were," the old man said. "We solved a lot of problems those nights."

"But they came back in the mornings," Fallon said.

The old man sighed and took a drink, rolling the poteen around his tongue before swallowing. "That, me nephew, is why they call them 'politics.' The problem, you know, came with the Dev. Ah, but people loved him for his reputation made in the 'Rising' and the romance of being sentenced to death only to have it commuted in the nick of time. But De Valera was a shallow man for all of that. He had only a peasant's point of view, but the people didn't want him in that role so they made him a politician. The man had nothing but the name: no welfare program, no idea at all about international economics. So, he took whatever was thrown at him and paid nearly forty years of lip service to things he never understood. It was the Dev, you know, who really let the foreign money come in and buy up the country because they gave him funding for programs he thought he had to have but couldn't figure out how to get. And now, why we've got a new Irish Ascendancy beginning, and a social and economic system so solidly entrenched it'll take another Norman invasion to change it." He looked darkly at Fallon from under bushy brows. "At least, some of the boyos are seeing the problem: 'tis a new Dublin government we're needing to bring the bitch Britain to her knees; one that won't turn a blind eye to a well-turned Irish army. The whole world is sick over what's happening in the North, but there's no end to that. Although the Brits would dearly love to abandon the North because our friends in America won't bail out their economy until they resolve it. *But,* if a well-armed Dublin government takes a stand against Britain, well, then, that would bring the door closed on the Troubles in a hurry, leaving the dear Protestants to moan their miseries at the moon for all the good that would do them." He paused, sipping, then cocked an eye at Fallon. "And, while you are about this business, you be keeping in touch with your Uncle Dan, now. You can call at the main house in Tralee and leave a message if I'm not there. But someone's going to have to be watching over you, and you are needing someone to get in touch with, I'm thinkin'." His voice grew rough, and he thumbed a bit of water from his eyes. "Ah, but this talk is foul talk and surely we can lend the night better words."

He leaned down and pulled a battered tin box from beneath his bed. He opened it and pulled an accordion from it, slipping the collar around his neck and his hands through the ancient straps. "And now, enough of politics. Do you still have a voice with yuh, lad? A fine tenor if my memory serves me correct?"

"It's been awhile," Fallon said. "A long time."

"Then it's been too long. Do yuh ken 'The Rose of Tralee'?" He didn't wait for Fallon's answer, but broke into music. Fallon leaned back and lifted his chin, remembering the old verse. His voice rose, cracked and straining at first:

> *"Ballymullan's old castle stands lonely and hoary,*
> *Silently glassin' its shades in the lee,*
> *Tellin' in eloquent silence the story,*
> *That hangs 'round its walls in the Vale of Tralee."*

"Good," the old man grunted. "Now, the rest."

And the years fell away as Fallon closed his eyes, remembering his youth, spring wildflowers, the summer field work, and the dances of Lughnasa in the autumn. For a moment, his voice threatened to crack as he sang:

> *"The pale moon was rising above the green mountains*
> *The sun was declining beneath the blue sea—"*

When he finished, he opened his eyes, expecting his uncle to stop, but the old man was oblivious to him and swung into another song and another. Fallon gave up the present and allowed himself to journey back to times once forgotten, through "Slán le Máigh," "Kilkelly," and "Úna Bhán." "Slievenamon" rose with fighting spirit from the accordion followed by "The Two Travellers" and suddenly, the old man's own song "Roisin Dubh."

> *"There's black grief on the plains, and a mist on the hills*
> *There is fury on the mountains, and that is no wonder."*

And Fallon knew as he had always known that Ireland was not the land of the shamrock, but the land of the black rose. The land where for hundreds of years the people had been forced to speak in riddles and analogies and live lives of allusions; the land where the metaphor and simile became a way of survival after Cromwell's conquest had transferred all Catholic property to English hands following the siege of Drogheda when he ordered all three thousand of its defenders put to the sword and gave Catholic landowners the option of going "to hell or to Connaught," distributing three million acres of Irish land to his supporters; and, later, when three million Irish starved to death, the land where hundreds of years were spent looking for independence that had yet to be granted. Ah, yes, and the old patriot songs still burned, but for what end? Peace and freedom? Or eternal war? Fallon no longer knew. And as he sang his uncle's song, the melancholy settled on him again, and he found in the music, briefly, himself.

16

Time had passed Dagdaskillen many years ago, leaving a small, stone church built along Romanesque lines with stained glass windows so old the lead guards had been worn smooth by wind and storm; a pub, whose small doorway forced all to bow heads when entering, attached to a small store that doubled as a chemist's; and five houses fronting the narrow lane that snaked between stone walls. The church sat high on a hill above the town with a commanding view of the countryside. The churchyard was filled with tall headstones with faces worn smooth and narrow stone benches. One wall had a gate added to it to expand sanctified ground as death marched with time, demanding more space. A small cottage stood to the rear off the brow of the hill, a flagstone walk connecting it to the church through a tiny courtyard. An old oak tree, its trunk nearly a yard wide, stretched stark, leafless limbs over the cottage.

The day was gray and heavy, smelling damp of snow, and as Fallon watched, the door opened and his brother, wearing his cassock, stepped out, slipping the bolt to separate the door and closing the bottom half. The sight of his brother jolted Fallon: his face was thin and raw, painful lines finely drawn at the corners of his eyes, his lips downturned, laugh lines turned to grief. His hair seemed no longer to be reddish blond, but nearly white and cropped close to his head. He moved slowly up the walk toward the church, limping as though his hips pained him. Fallon waited until his brother was nearly level with him, then stepped in front of him. His brother stopped and raised his eyes. For a moment, they stared quizzically into Fallon's eyes, then cleared and became cool as he recognized his brother.

"Hello, Brian," Fallon said.

"Tomas. It's been a fair while," Brian said. He made no move to shake hands and a casual observer would have been hard-pressed to declare them brothers let alone twins: Fallon had thick, black hair sprinkled with silver and gray eyes that shined like silver when he was angry; Brian, blond with sharp blue eyes, seemed older by ten years. But a second look would reveal identical cheekbones and straight noses with a tiny hump in the middle, full lips, and wide foreheads. Brian's hands, however, were stubby-fingered, thick-nailed, and broad-palmed, a carpenter's hands; Fallon had the hands of a concert pianist: long-fingered, graceful, the half-moons clearly displayed beneath square-cut nails.

"I thought you were still with the Cistercians," Fallon said.

"No. That was only temporary." Brian looked away, across the land. "It was never meant to be permanent. But at the time, I needed sanctuary, and they gave it to me. For that, I'm grateful. Have you had breakfast?" He motioned behind him toward the cottage.

"I could eat," Fallon said. Brian nodded and, turning, retraced his steps to the cottage.

"You're looking well," Fallon said, following.

"As well as can be, considering," Brian answered. He opened the door, courteously stepping aside to allow Fallon to enter first.

Fallon ducked his head, stepping through the doorway. His eyes flickered around the room. The cottage was neat and clean, the walls newly whitewashed. A fireplace stood to his left next to a small corridor running down the front to the bedroom. The room in front opened wide and had been spartan furnished with a table and two hard-backed chairs. The table was bare except for a small crystal bowl containing a carefully dried red rose that looked almost black resting upon a bed of dried sphagnum moss. Along the back ran a bookshelf filled with books to an inglenook outfitted as a kitchenette.

"Still an aesthetic, I see," Fallon said.

A slight smile lifted Brian's lips. "I'll get your tea," he said, moving into the nook. He filled the kettle with water and placed it on a hot plate, then took leaves from a tiny canister, carefully crushed them between his palms, and dropped them into a Belleek teapot Tomas recognized as having been their mother's. Brian set out cups and saucers on the table and motioned Fallon to a seat. He placed a pot of honey and a loaf of thick, black bread in front of him and a butter plate with a heavy-bladed knife lying across its lips.

"Do you take anything with it?" he asked solicitously.

Fallon shook his head. "I take it black."

Brian nodded. An awkward silence grew between them while they waited for the kettle to boil.

"So." Brian looked startled as his voice broke the silence. "How have you been? I haven't heard much about you these past few years."

"I've been keeping to myself at the cottage outside Omeath. Remember it? Long Woman's Grave?"

"Ah, yes," Brian said, clasping his hands together, relief on his face. "Is it still alone on the mountain?"

"It is and will be," Fallon said. "I bought the land up to it."

"Oh? And the woods; are they still the same?"

"Full of fairies and wee people," Tomas answered.

"Good. Good!" Brian exclaimed, clapping his hands. "And Father Lanigan, is he still at the church there?"

"Retired in a cottage nearby. We play chess on Wednesday after he returns from Vespers. He's keeping Miss Sheba for me. My cat," he said to Brian's questioning eyebrows.

"Not married, then?"

"Ah, 'tis not a life for a woman to be having," Fallon answered.

"It's a life you've chosen!" Brian said sharply, then started and rubbed his hand across his forehead. "Ah. Sorry. I'm sorry. I should not have said that. A man's life is his own."

"As long as he doesn't step out of the shadow of God? You still put limits on forgiveness and living, then?"

"I said I was sorry."

"Aye, but meaning it is another thing. It doesn't matter if man believes in God, only that God believes in man. I've never understood why you can't understand that, you being His spokesman and all."

They glared at each other, each clutching tight fists in front of them, lips stretched tautly. Then Brian drew a deep, shaky breath.

"Aye, Tomas." He grinned crookedly. "The past is always with us in the present. You'd think times would change a man."

"A man is his past," Fallon said. "He can be nothing more." The kettle whistled, and Brian moved thankfully toward it. He busied himself preparing the tea and brought it to the table. He placed a plate of shortbread between them and sat. He carefully poured the tea then sat back.

"It *is* good to see you, Tomas, after all these years," he said.

"Yes," Fallon said. He sipped his tea. "What brought you out of the monastery?"

"The monastery was never meant to be a solution, only an answer. Here"—he gestured around him—"there are those who need me, and I can help them. And yourself?"

"The same," Tomas said.

Brian sighed. "I was hoping—" He stopped and gestured in dismissal. "No, that won't do. I don't want to fight anymore."

"We both do what we can. You help people with their spiritual lives, and I help with their lives now. Or tried to," he amended. He finished his tea and neatly placed the cup back in its saucer.

"*Tried* to?" Brian leaned back in his chair, looking appraisingly at his brother. "Do you mean to say you're finished with that life? Is that why I read no more of the terrible Fallon?"

"I thought so," Fallon answered. "But something's happened. I'm needed."

Brian shook his head. "*Your* need, you mean. You and your friends in the Provos."

"You're wrong."

"Am I?" He leaned across the table, clasping his hands as if he were praying on an altar. "The problem with the IRA today is there is no longer any aristocracy to rise up against, yet the IRA keeps insisting one exists. Revolutions are traditionally fought between peasants and nobility, but in Ireland, one can no longer define social classes or a conflict arising from industrialization. Ireland does not have an industrially defined history. Therefore, no neo-Marxist terms can be used to define the Troubles. Oh, I know about the hiring freezes the Protestants levy against the Catholics, but the people are the same. Yeats is right: 'Romantic Ireland's dead and gone.'"

"You're right," Fallon said. "But Ireland has never been one to bury her past deeply. She keeps it around like an old bitch the last of her litter when she needs someone to pull at her dry dugs once in a while to remind her she's alive. We have always been a people to live in the past. But the present will no longer allow us to do that." He gave an ironic smile. "I'm like the last of the litter kept around to push out into the streets when people feel the need to remember the past."

"What are you rebelling against then?"

"Ourselves. People are trying to keep the revolution alive so they will become tragic heroes. We are becoming victims of our own history because there are no heroes anymore; only old men and young people born old."

"Then it is time for you to get out, Tomas," Brian said quietly.

"This time, it's different," Fallon answered.

"What's different about killing?" Brian said.

"Drugs," Fallon said. "Someone is running drugs into Ireland along the old gun routes."

"Jesus, Mary, and Joseph," Brian said, leaning back in his chair and crossing himself. "So, it's come down to this, has it? And that makes what you're doing all right?" He shook his head. "That's why we have the Gardai. Let them handle it."

"It isn't that easy," Fallon said. "The Gardai can't do what needs to be done."

"Isn't it?" Brian fired back. "Or don't you want it to be for all your fine words?"

"At least I'm doing something. You aren't willing to be a part of your own life."

"What's that supposed to mean?"

"You know bloody well what it means! After Mother was killed what did you do but lift your Christ-pious eyes to heaven, exclaim 'God's will' and go back to your church!"

"Her death was an accident!"

"She was hit by a truck filled with British soldiers coming back from a drunk at Warrenpoint and the bloody bastards left her lying in the ditch! Or have you forgotten that, too?"

Brian averted his eyes from his brother's fury. "It's been a long time since then. Thirty years. It's a long time to carry hate, Tomas. Let her rest."

"I have," Fallon said, slumping back against his chair. He rose and walked to the door and swung the half-door open, breathing deeply of the crisp air. His brother watched him calming himself.

"At least, I've tried," he said, his back to his brother.

"Why did you stop?" Brian asked.

"There had been enough killing," he answered darkly. He turned back to Brian. "There'll always be Lennie Murphys who kidnap and torture Catholics, and there'll always be Orangemen meeting and making their mystical mutterings and giving their secret handshakes and winks. And there'll always be bastards like Ian Paisley. They've been here for six hundred years, and they'll be here for six hundred more. We are only fighting now because we were born to it and don't know what else to do."

"So. You have no hope then for the cease-fire or possible peace accord."

It was a statement, not a question, but Fallon answered it the same. "No, no hope. It's only a matter of time. There's been too much killing and not enough."

"So stop," Brian said. Fallon shook his head. "Ah, the drugs."

"They're going to the children," he said quietly. "I guess we haven't given them much, have we: killing or drugs. Not a very good world we have built for all our rhetoric, is it?"

"I heard about what happened in Belfast," Brian said. "I won't say those children's deaths weren't your fault: they were. But they were also the fault of everyone who has been a part of this mess. Ireland always eats her children."

"Maybe," Fallon said.

"It's people like you, though, who are helping to create the Irish Problem," Brian continued. Fallon arched an eyebrow in question. Brian nodded. "Oh, yes. You see, outside of Ireland, in America, for example, the Irish have made a decent name for themselves. They helped to settle that country, build it, make it a symbol of hope for others. They did the dirty work, at first, digging ditches and canals, laying railroads, fighting wars. But now they are in all the professions. Yes, the priesthood, but they are lawyers and politicians, doctors and dentists, even the police forces are mainly Irish. The Irish are holding society and order together. They are staving off anarchy. But here, in Ireland, they are destroying what they have built in other countries. Today, the most famous Irishman in the world is the uneducated paddy or *squaddie* who leaves a bomb in a car near a restaurant where innocent people are killed, or the one who kills a politician. We are rapidly becoming a race of murderers, Tomas. A race of murderers. Is that how you want your people to be remembered?"

"I would like my people to be remembered as being free," Fallon said quietly. "Wouldn't you?"

Brian let a long moment go, then said, "What brings you here, so?"

"I need to get to Boston," Fallon said quietly. Brian looked up at him quizzically. "Tomas Fallon can't get there. But Brian Fallon can."

Brian's face whitened. His lips thinned. "No," he whispered.

"It's time you did something, Brian," Fallon said. "You have pretended to be innocent too long. No one can be innocent in Ireland anymore. Everyone must have a piece of the blame. Collective guilt. When they let partition stand, everyone became guilty of the future. It's time for you to pay your dues."

"I've done nothing," Brian said.

"Haven't you?" Fallon turned away from the door. "Have you forgotten what happened to you and that woman in Belfast? Do you remember Crumlin Jail and Castlereagh? Have you forgotten the beatings and the smell of your own blood pouring from your mouth and what they did to you when you begged for mercy? Tell me, Brian: Why did the woman die and you go free? It wasn't because you're a priest. Priests mean nothing to Protestants; they never have. Once they even put a bounty on priests, remember? The same as for a wolf. So, why did you go free and the woman die, Brian? Why?"

"You don't know," Brian whispered.

"Oh, yes, I do," Fallon said. "You shopped her, didn't you, Brian? You told them what they wanted to hear to save yourself, didn't you? That was bad enough, but you told them a lie, Brian. The woman died, and you went free because of a lie."

"You can't know that!" he shouted wildly. His eyes screwed shut against the memory.

"Yes, I can," Fallon said wearily. He felt empty, hollow. He poured a cup of cold tea and drank it, trying to rinse the words away. "I even know the name of the man you told it to. He's dead now." He looked at his brother sitting hunched over in the straight-back chair, his hands clasped tightly in his cassock between his knees. "It's what I do, Brian," he said. "It's what I do. You can't sit and watch life in Ireland from a safe distance in your fine house, insulated by your collar and the confessional. And no priest has the right to damn himself; that right belongs to the God he believes in."

Brian rose and crossed to the door. He glanced at his brother, his eyes haunted with personal demons, then he stepped through the door without speaking and climbed the flagstone path to the church. Fallon watched him enter the church, then crossed to the nook and put a kettle of fresh water on the hot plate. The air of the room suddenly chilled him, and he crossed to the door, bolting the halves together. He crossed to the bookshelves, selected a well-worn copy of Yeats's *The Wind Among the Reeds* and settled himself at the table. The book fell open at "The Moods" and he read the opening line, "Time drops in decay" and thought about his brother reading these lines and remembering the decaying time he had spent in Castlereagh. Were the lines a form of penance? Had Brian been able to shove Castlereagh to the back of his mind?

The kettle sang on the hot plate, and he hastily rose and prepared a fresh pot of tea, carrying it back to the table. He seated himself, picked up the book, and tried to read the lines with his brother's eyes. The words were there, but he could not comprehend them with his brother's pain. He concentrated harder and slowly felt his own identity slip away into a gray, impalpable world. Dimly, he heard Niamh calling from the fairy world— *Away, come away*—and a cold wind seemed to brush against his cheek as he lost himself in story and verse.

THE DAY HAD GROWN DARK, AND HE HAD LIGHTED A LAMP WHEN
the door opened. He looked up as Brian entered the room, a light
dusting of a sudden spring snow on his shoulders. His eyes looked
red from weeping, his face gray and hollowed. He crossed to the
fireplace and lit the peat block on the grate. He crossed to the
bookshelf as Fallon stared into the flames. Something fell into his
lap. He looked down and picked up a passport with the Vatican
seal on it. He looked up at his brother.

"I spent five years at the Vatican before Belfast as one of the
secretaries for His Holiness," Brian said. He pointed at the passport. "The name 'Fallon' might still be called up on computer on
an Irish passport, but not on one with the Vatican seal: that's automatic diplomatic immunity."

Fallon opened the passport and looked at the black-and-white
photo of a younger Brian, his face free from pain. "You'll have to
change your hair," Brian said. Then he moved quickly down the
corridor and gently closed the bedroom door behind him.

Fallon watched the flames until the room became warm then
rose and crossed to the window and looked out. It had begun to
snow harder. He opened the door and left the cottage, latching
the door behind him. He walked up the path to the church and
turned to gaze out across the land. He watched the flakes, silver
and dark, falling across the land, and thought about his journey
westward. What was that the old people used to say? The next
parish over is America. But the songs will be the same, of rebellion
and cunning, and wishes for the romantic past. He turned the collar of his jacket up and moved out away from the church, feeling
the coldness of the flakes against his cheek as he walked down the
lane. The snow was rapidly covering the hills and falling hard
against the church and beginning to gather upon the headstones
and monuments in the churchyard, upon the living and the dead.

PART TWO ◆ America

17

His stomach burned, and for the fourth time that night, Central Intelligence Agency Director of Special Operations Richard Wright reached for the large bottle of Maalox in his bottom desk drawer. He unscrewed the cap and took a large swallow, grimacing at the chalky taste. He blotted the residue from his lips with his handkerchief, then leaned back in his leather chair, closing his eyes while he waited for the burning to ease, pressing his fingers against his slightly swelling paunch beneath his striped tie. Tired lines ran across his forehead, angling down toward his cheekbones. Sagging pouches beneath his eyes completed the basset hound look except for the nimbus of gray hair.

Christ! he thought. What a mess! Why can't anything be easy in this business? First, there was that affair in Argentina when our man was discovered passing information to the courier from the embassy, then there was that nasty bit when the Peru boys caught our man with some members of the Shining Path. Oh, yes, let's not forget Von Wettering getting caught in Germany and Ellis in Zaire. And now, just when those bog-jumpers are putting an end to the Troubles we have—he shuffled the papers on his desk, searching. At last, he found it and glanced at the synopsis. He winced—Mairead Duffy, shot and killed while she was driving with her fiancé to her parents' farmhouse. He pulled the pictures from the file and glanced at them. In one of the pictures, a

Catholic priest knelt beside the naked, blood-soaked, and spread-eagled body of one of the soldiers.

He tossed the pictures back in the file and leaned back in his chair. So far, there hadn't been any retaliation. But what the hell is the Gaelach Dearg Craobh going to do about it? A romantic bunch of bastards, I'll give them that. Seems like every other Irishman has his own organization. His stomach suddenly flared up, and he shook his head. Ah, Christ! He massaged his temples slowly, trying to relax, focusing upon the night before. Helen from Vassar, the perfect wife for an alcoholic senior senator from Mississippi. But his mind would not slip from the problems, would not focus on the hidden apartment in Georgetown with a separate entrance inside the garage near *The Exorcist* stairs, would not focus on the hennaed hair, pendulous breasts, wide hips, and butterfly tattoo on the inside of her left thigh. The words were there, but the images lost.

He rose and went to the window and looked out. From the seventh floor, he could just see over the hillcrest into the Potomac Valley now that winter had stripped the leaves from the trees. From the road, the building was pretty invisible. The parking lots had been carefully placed among the trees as had the hemisphere-shaped briefing theater. Spare flakes of snow fell against the pale stone of the building. Normally, he would have enjoyed the view for the grounds looked the best in late winter. But not today. He sighed and returned to his desk and sat.

In front of him lay a neatly typed report in an oversized envelope marked for his attention only after the alpha-numeric code stamped in block figures. The envelope was edged in red—a color easy to spot that meant it could not be left out on desks overnight but had to be secured when not in use. He rubbed his temples and leaned forward to again read the report, painstakingly searching for something, anything, that would suggest things were not as serious as he thought. Given the Middle East crises with that damn Saddam, the Afghanistan powder keg, Somalia. Hell, all those bloody African states that change their names after their monthly coups—and the growing tensions in Central America— it would be nice if he could receive good news for once. But he knew that would seldom happen: the DSO was not created for good news. This one, he thought sourly, could be as bad as they come. It was a reminder of one of the few rash moves he had made over the past twenty-odd years, the type of move one made out of exasperation when one's career seemed stalemated.

His career had been going nowhere on the National Security Council where he had been the Russian expert under Henry Kissinger and Zbigniew Brzezinski, who were being handicapped by all the religious nuts Reagan was bringing in. He remembered the frustration of Caspar Weinberger, who ran up against Sen. Jesse Helms while trying to name his staff to the National Security Council. Helms had vetoed all of Weinberger's nominees because he had wanted to name his own people to the council. Finally, a compromise was worked out whereby Weinberger could name his deputy, but Helms got to fill in the next five tiers on the list—which he promptly did with religious zealots and politically pure young men who had little, if any, training for intelligence work. Disgruntled, Wright had transferred back to the Central Intelligence Agency where he promptly became the director of special operations, burning under the interoffice joke that Operations would feel better if Dickie could at least have supervised two or three people for an hour before becoming DSO. Not even his Kissinger imitations had taken away the sting of the reminder that he had never been a field man.

He rubbed his face hard with both hands, but the memory stayed with him. That had been the source of his rash move, an attempt to become "one of the boys." He closed his eyes, remembering—

He was clearing old back files after his recent move back to the

CIA when he stumbled over a report dating back to his Saigon days when the CIA had run money through the Nugan Hand Bank in Australia to buy the opium crop of the war lords in Cambodia, Burma, and Laos in return for their raids on North Vietnamese outposts. Some of the opium had been funneled back into Vietnam to the Montagnards in return for making guerrilla raids into North Vietnam. That had been before the war lords began to make demands, bringing about the attempted destruction of the Golden Triangle by special task squads that failed desperately when the war lords, led by Khun Sa, the Triangle's biggest opium overlord, captured them at Chung Dao near the upper northeast corner of Thailand and contemptuously held them for ransom.

According to the records, there was still a sizeable account in the Nugan Hand Bank that had been established by the Bechtel Corporation on behalf of George Shultz, who had been involved with them before moving into office as Ronald Reagan's secretary of state. The germ of an idea began to tingle—wasn't the Nugan Hand Bank in trouble? Ah, yes, an article in *The Wall Street Journal* had predicted the futures of banks in foreign countries for overseas investors. What was it? Yes! The article had recalled the early Sunday morning when a police sergeant and a constable were patrolling a lonely stretch of highway ninety miles from Sydney, Australia, and spotted a Mercedes's parking lights on an old road off in the woods. Where was that article? He frowned, concentrating. Bit by bit, the article began to emerge in his mind—something, something—investigating, they'd found the body of Frank Nugan, chairman of a group of companies affiliated with the private banking concerns of Nugan Hand, Ltd. He was slumped across the front seat of the car in a puddle of blood. They'd searched his pockets, finding the business card of William Colby, U.S. director of central intelligence, and on the back of the card was a trip itinerary for Colby in Asia—what else? He frowned, then remembered: a Bible on the floor with a meat pie wrapper interleaved at page 252. Colby's name, and U.S. Rep. Bob Wilson of California, the ranking Republican on the House Armed Services Committee, scribbled on the wrapper.

A smile crept across his face. He swung his chair around to the computer terminal by his desk, entered his code, waiting impatiently for clearance. When it came, he pulled up Special Accounts, verifying the Nugan Hand account. A little over two million dollars. The last account query had been in the early seventies. Unbelievable that the account had been forgotten that long, but when Richard Nixon had pulled the troops out of Vietnam, several accounts established in other banks in Singapore, Bangkok, and Japan had had to be hastily closed and the paper trail burned. Briefly, he wondered how many other accounts lay idle in other banks, then pushed the thought aside. He signed off the special accounts, but staying in the finance files, called up the names of retired field men. Slowly, he rolled through the list, looking for a familiar name. He grunted with satisfaction as KENTON, SIMON flashed in white caps against the blue background of his computer screen. Kenton. Just the man for what he had in mind. One of the veterans who had been forced out of the Agency after Vietnam by those anxiously erasing records of operations from the threat of investigations. Kenton had been a rogue who would have given the Agency a black eye if his work in Vietnam had come to the attention of the new, antiwar boys looking for new causes to crusade against. Kenton had been pensioned off with a large retirement bonus that had allowed him to buy a bait and tackle shop in Key West. An appropriate place if he remembered the whispers about Kenton at Duong Van "Big" Minh's soirees at the old French house on Plantation Road, where young male homosexuals were in plentiful supply along with a few "special" girls supplied by Dinh My Linh, the uncontested queen of Saigon's bar girls.

Acting on a hunch, Wright transferred the money to a numbered account at Suisse National. Within hours of the transfer, Wright's telephone rang. He recognized the voice of retired rear admiral Earl "Buddy" Yates, who had been chief of staff for strategic planning for U.S forces in Asia and the Pacific.

"Dickie? Any truth to Nugan's death?" the retired admiral gruffly asked.

"All I know is what I read in the newspapers," Wright joked.

"Knock it off," Yates growled. "Was the Company involved?"

"You know I can't confirm or deny that," Wright replied. He could hear the heavy breathing of Yates on the other end of the line.

"What about the files?" he asked.

"I know nothing about them," Wright answered.

"You know what I like best about you, Dickie?" Yates said. "Your directness and constant help to old friends."

"I know nothing about any files at the Nugan Hand offices," Wright said. "Nothing has come across my desk at all. I only read about Frank Nugan's death in a recap of a story in today's *Wall Street Journal*."

"Could you find out?"

"No."

Yates swore and hung up. Wright later found out that Yates had immediately flown out to Sydney from his home in Virginia Beach. Together, he and Nugan Hand's vice-chairman, Michael Hand, a highly decorated Special Forces officer and former U.S. intelligence operator who flew in from London, gathered a few friends who cooperated after Hand threatened to arrange to have their wives cut apart, and spent a late night at the Nugan Hand offices, ransacking the files. They shredded hundreds of files and packed others in a carton and carried them to a butcher shop owned by Robert W. Gehring, a former U.S. army sergeant who had served in Vietnam.

A few months later, on April 11, 1980, to be exact, Wright remembered, Nugan Hand went into liquidation. He waited while liquidators in Sydney, Hong Kong, and the Cayman Islands investigated the company, searching for assets that had disappeared, leaving the company with such a large debt that it was barely able to pay 1 percent on the outstanding claims. The New South Wales attorney general's office issued a warrant for Hand's arrest. Investigators managed to trace him through Fiji and Vancouver before he disappeared.

Wright waited patiently as the investigation wore on. An Australian newspaper, *The National Times*, petitioned the Federal Bureau of Investigation under the U.S. Freedom of Information Act for its files on Nugan Hand. The FBI sent seventy-one pages, but the majority of them had been blacked out with the notation "B-1," indicating that the requested material was too sensitive to U.S. foreign policy to be released. The FBI claimed that it had already sent copies of the full 151-page file to the Australian Security Intelligence Organization (ASIO), a secret counterspy group that had a history of working closely with the CIA. ASIO refused to comment on whether the files had been received or not. With ASIO's refusal to cooperate, Wright breathed a little easier and contacted Simon Kenton, arranging to meet the former CIA man in Atlanta.

When Kenton walked into the restaurant of the Hilton in Atlanta, he was casually dressed in a sports jacket and open-necked sport shirt, a sharp crease carefully pressed into his trousers, his shoes highly polished. He was thinner than the last Agency file photo, his white hair fashionably longer, his face the color of burnt mahogany. Cold blue eyes quickly checked the room before he crossed and sat in the corner booth with Wright.

"So, how's the spook business?" he asked, flagging down a passing waiter. He ordered a double Jack Daniel's on the rocks. Wright shook his head at the waiter's inquiring glance, pointing to his half-filled glass of soda water and lime twist.

"As usual," Wright answered. He remained quiet while the waiter returned with Kenton's drink.

"I see that son of a bitch Colby is scrambling to protect his ass. Do you think Reig and Priest will keep him on after this Nugan Hand affair blows over?" Kenton asked. Wright permitted himself a small smile.

"It's good to see you are still keeping your hand in, Simon," he said. Kenton shrugged.

"I do my best. It's hard retiring," he added, his voice tinged with bitterness.

"I can imagine," Wright said softly.

"Hey, what about Red Jansen, the station chief in Bangkok? What happened to him?"

"Would you like to, um, 'unretire,' Simon?" Wright asked quietly.

Kenton sat back against the vinyl-covered booth, his eyes narrowing as he raised his glass, sipping the whiskey.

"Now?" he asked, setting the glass back on its paper coaster. "You know why I was drummed out. Why does the Company suddenly want me back? It can't be a change of heart; it doesn't have a heart."

"The offer is unofficial," Wright said, emphasizing the word. Kenton gave a short laugh.

"That sensitive, huh? Something happens and the old boys deny ever hearing about me, right?" He shook his head. "Man, it must really be a son of a bitch."

"Let's just say 'covert operation.' Are you interested?"

"How much? And don't give me the standard revenue crap. If it's as heavy as it must be, you're going to have to make it very worth my while."

"Fifty thousand."

"Dollars?"

Wright nodded. Kenton shook his head.

"Uh-uh. Pounds. Deposited in my account in Grand Cayman. *Before*," he emphasized, his eyes burning in the tan of his face.

"Very well," Wright said calmly.

"Maybe I should have asked for more."

"Don't get greedy. There are others who can take your place."

"I doubt it," Kenton said, raising his glass again. "Otherwise, you would have used them, right?"

"I'm a bit surprised that you didn't want to think about it," Wright said, ignoring the question.

"Have you ever been in the fish and bait business?" Kenton asked sourly. "It's extremely boring."

"I've never been to Key West," Wright said.

"You wouldn't like it," Kenton answered. "You never did attend any of Minh's parties, did you? Now, what's this all about?"

"It's really very simple," Wright said. "I want you to open up the old Mhadi Factory in Egypt, retool it to handle AK-47s, and establish a line through to the rebels in Afghanistan. That's all." He lifted his glass of soda water, sipping delicately as he watched the stunned expression on Kenton's face slowly turn to glee.

"You bastard," Kenton breathed. "You're running a rogue operation, aren't you? Why AK-47s? That may take some major retooling."

"Some of those weapons are going to be captured," Wright replied. "The Soviets will think some of the bloc countries are playing games with them. They'll accuse each other—"

"—and we will be in an excellent position to reap intelligence data from the confusion," Kenton finished for him. "Cute."

"I think so," Wright said modestly. "But we'll also have political leverage against the Soviets once we discover their smuggling lines—especially if we branch out into Africa in light of the recent UN hands-off decision."

"One thing: I need to know the markings and some serial numbers that I can run in succession. And they'll have to be realistic."

Wright removed a sheet of paper from an inside pocket of his jacket and slid it across to him. Kenton picked it up, unfolded it, and read it.

"Those are samples of the symbols and end numbers used by factories in Romania, Hungary, Yugoslavia, and Czechoslovakia. They will deny the numbers, of course, but they will correspond in succession to shipments of AK-47s they made to the Soviet Union. Alternate the runs with the various markings about every hundred or so. We don't want to point the finger at any one country."

"Makes sense," Kenton said. "But this isn't going to be cheap. Where do I get the funds?"

"From this account at Suisse National." Wright slid a small piece of paper over to him. "The exchange code is 'revelation.' You can only transfer funds, however, on the second Tuesday and third Wednesday of any single month except if the two days come back-to-back, and then you will have to use the fourth Wednesday. If you need to get in touch with me, call this number in Zurich. Leave a dead number with the answering machine, alternating the numbers plus or minus the number you want me to return your call to. If the day you are calling is an even date use plus; negative on the odd dates. I'll get back to you as soon as possible, but under no circumstances use the same number twice and change it immediately if I don't return your call within ten hours."

"Got it." Kenton picked up his glass, draining it. He gestured for another, then considered Wright silently for a moment before saying, "What are you getting out of this?"

"That's none of your concern," he said, finishing his soda water. The ice cubes rattled against the sides of the glass as he placed it precisely upon his coaster. "Was there anything else?"

"Do you have any restrictions on how I get the arms into Afghanistan?"

"No. Just get them there. Anything else?" He slid to the edge of the booth, suddenly anxious to be gone.

"No," Kenton said. He took the drink the waiter brought him.

"Then, good luck," Wright said, standing. He laid a ten-dollar bill on the table to cover their drinks, automatically checked his tie and the set of his jacket, nodded at Kenton, and left, glancing at his watch. He really should have brought Helen with him. Maybe next time.

He blinked, bringing himself back to the present.

"And that was your first mistake; you should have been more curious about the route Kenton set up into Afghanistan," he said softly to himself, staring at the report in front of him. A dull throb settled behind one eye.

Everything had been fine until Reagan and that blasted Oliver North had to bungle the affair with the Iranians. We damn near got caught in the backlash of that one. Fortunately, Kenton was quick enough to dismantle the supply route and dump the weapons remaining into the Red Sea before the Senate Investigating Committee got their teeth into the whole picture. My God! He closed his eyes and gently massaged the ache, trying to keep it from spreading. What had made Kenton go through both Iran and Israel? One would have been good enough! Those deserts are large enough to hide anyone in—even from NSA's satellites since I managed to get the routes and times off the satellite passes to Kenton. Fortunately, we could have discounted Soviet claims had we been caught since the weapons were all AK-47s, but the risk, the risk! At least, the Egyptians had kept their collective mouths shut, but why wouldn't they? Their economy certainly didn't suffer, but, damnit, Kenton should have known the risks!

He leaned forward and punched the intercom on his desk,

growling, "Gladys, get in touch with Dave and ask him to come to my office as soon as he can."

"Yes, Mr. Wright," came the metallic answer. He clicked off the intercom and rose, placing his hands on his hips, arching his back to ease the ache in his lower back. He glanced at the clock, grimacing at the time; he had been at his desk for five solid hours, working his way through that field report that had become Charybdis, sucking him down with her whirling eddies. He had to be careful; that long experience had taught him. The first thing was to openly question it with his DOC, Division Commander.

The door opened and Dave Kelly walked in, looking fresh and unruffled in his double-breasted charcoal pinstripe. A canary yellow handkerchief matching his tie (carefully tied in a Windsor knot, Wright noticed: he was suspicious of men with Windsor knots: they suggested vanity) peeped discreetly from the breast pocket of his suit. The cuffs of his shirt showed a precise three-quarter inch below his jacket sleeves. Black onyx gleamed from his cufflinks as he carefully hitched up the leg of each trouser to preserve the crease before seating himself. He looked inquisitively at Wright, his features calm and guarded. Wright admired his composure. He picked up the report and handed it to him.

"Have you seen this?" he asked. Kelly glanced at the red lettering on the folder.

"It's marked for you only," he pointed out.

"Which means there're only about ten copies of this floating around instead of the usual twenty," Wright said sourly. Kelly shrugged, and opened the report, scanning the synopsis. Secrets were rarely sacrosanct in the upper division of the CIA as knowledge was both power and protection, and there was a wild scramble in all offices to remain discreetly aware of everything that went across the director's desk. He finished quickly, then glanced up at Wright, his eyebrow lifting questioningly.

Too quickly, Wright thought with satisfaction. You have seen it. Aloud he said, "Do you know anything about it?"

"No," Kelly said slowly. Wright could see his mind working feverishly behind his pose of studied calm. "This is a new one on me. Who's running it?"

He looked up as Wright spread his hands. "I don't know. But it must have been going on for a long time. It isn't yours?"

"No," Kelly said, quickly adding, "That means we have a rogue somewhere."

"Looks that way," Wright said. He pointed at the report. He belched gently, tasting the Maalox again. "We have a bit of a problem with the dead Mossad agent. He was killed with a nine-millimeter at the Connecticut Avenue Club in Washington. Sam Waterston in homicide got the call. He had the Israeli embassy notified of the death of one of its citizens. They were at the scene within thirty minutes. That made him suspicious, and he held the man's personal effects back until he had had a chance to go through them. The Israeli embassy has been pulling a lot of favors in, trying to get Waterston to hand over the agent's personal effects. They've even lodged a formal complaint with the State Department, but since the man's name doesn't appear on any lists of those granted diplomatic immunity, Waterston's managed to hold out against the pressure. When he found the list of the AK-47s in the man's personal effects, he called us. A field agent was dispatched to the hotel. He brought the man's personal effects here and gave them to Research to process."

"How did we find out he was Mossad?"

"This photo, taken in 1978 in Berlin. The man he's with is Solomon Ben-Gurion—the head of Special Assignments for the Mossad. He was listed in the photo identification as Leon Jablon-ski. But in this photo of him again with Ben-Gurion at the El Al airline counter in London he's listed as Hasim Rasheen."

"Do we know who he is?"

"A pretty good idea," Wright said grimly. "We think he's Jacob Manel—a cousin to Amos Manel, the defense purchasing mission officer who was wounded in September 1982 by members of the Lebanese Armed Revolutionary Faction. According to our files, he managed to infiltrate the Rote Zora in Frankfurt am Main—the anti-Zionist, fascism, imperialism—all the isms except their own—you know." Kelly nodded and Wright continued. "This is the hardest group to get into since it is composed of many cells with less than ten members per cell. It does have contacts, however, with the Irish National Liberation Army and the Provisional Irish Republican Army. And, we think, the new GDC."

"Hence, the tie-in with the Irish message," Kelly prompted. He shook his head. "But the cease-fire has put an end to that, hasn't it?"

"Maybe. We don't know that yet. But we believe he's the one who warned us of the RZ's attempt to bomb a U.S. military train in August 1987. We managed to siderail that train, but in the confusion, a freight train slipped through and detonated the bomb at Hedemlenden before we could reach the bomb to dismantle it. Since that time, he's been pretty silent."

"Until now. What was he doing at the Connecticut Avenue Club?"

Wright shrugged. "We don't know, and the Israelis are playing this one tight-lipped." He hesitated, then added, "The Rote Zora seems to be concerned with decentralized terrorism. The Rote Armee Fraktion might be trying to recruit them, but I don't think they'll have much success. Although RZ has worked with the RAF before, it normally tries to keep separate. The members seem to prefer the anonymity of their individual cells."

"Are they tied into any of the Palestinian terrorists?" Kelly asked.

"Probably. We think some of the members were trained by some of Sabri al-Banna's people in the Abu Nidal Organization after it moved from Syria to Libya. Since ANO sponsors many training camps in the Libyan desert, they would have come in contact as well with the Hezbollah people and the DFLP—the Democratic Front for the Liberation of Palestine."

"And all of these have links with Ireland. Or had," he amended.

"Maybe they still do. The INLA and GDC are relatively small, we estimate the membership at less than twenty each. They seem to be a bit more reactionary than the Provos—the Provisional Irish Republican Army—one can expect that from Marxists, you are aware—but INLA did collaborate on occasion with the Provos. Still, they are more fanatical and may still be looking for arms to carry on the fight. There is a lot of discontent over there about the accord, you know. Gerry Adams is hard-pressed to keep all the splinter groups in line. They object to anything other than total surrender by the Protestants and Britain, and Ian Paisley's group and others like him are holding fast on their no-surrender line as well. So we could expect the INLA or this GDC to be still looking for arms to carry on the fight."

Kelly shook his head. "I don't know," he said doubtfully. "It would be a question of purse strings. Even the Provos had a hard time occasionally getting weapons and they have been tied in directly with NORAID in the U.S. for a long time. Where would INLA and GDC get the monies?"

"There is evidence of their contacts with the RZ and the French Direct Action—AD—group. Our people in Britain say that the explosives to have been used in INLA's plot to bomb the Chelsea Barracks in London in 1985 were supplied by the AD people. Incidentally, our British friends suggest Manel may have been the source of the tip that allowed the British enough time to stop the terrorists. INLA's leaders—Dominic McGlinchey, Gerard Steenson, and Thomas Cassidy—were all killed in 1987. Harry Flynn was arrested in France in eighty-six. They're small, but extremely brutal, and that has caused a bit of tension with the Provos." He ran his hand through his hair. "But they're nothing compared with this new group the Terrorist Section has turned up: the Gaelach Dearg Craobh, the GDC. I take it their name means the Irish Red Branch. It's supposed to reflect back in Irish history to the days of the ancient heroes. There's nothing heroic about them, however. They're even more of a bunch of thugs than the PIRA."

"Are they connected to any of the other terrorist groups?"

Wright nodded. "We have to suspect so. They seem to be able to get in and out of situations with relative ease. And they have money. Where that's coming from is anybody's guess."

"NORAID?"

"Maybe. But if so, it's being done on the quiet. Since NORAID had to register under the Foreign Agents Registration Act with the Justice Department, we have been able to keep reasonable tabs on them. The only trouble is that some of those bleeding heart liberals with the ACLU keep the Justice Department tied up in courts every time they try to review NORAID's records by claiming that FARA is in violation of the First Amendment. Consequently, we really don't have the entire picture. They *could* be siphoning off funds to splinter groups such as INLA and GDC without our knowledge. Or the Provos, for that matter. It's a bit of a mess. The money, however, is not the question. The question is where would they get the weapons?"

"What about Gerry Adams and Martin McGuinness? Could they be in the picture somewhere? Maybe playing both ends against the middle? Adams has played both sides of the coin before. Back in 1972 he was pretty hardlined. He's worn the guerrilla jacket as well as his Bond Street—or is it Grafton?—jackets."

Wright nodded. "Possibly. But Seamus MacCauley supervised the reorganization of the Provos into cells—Active Service Units—in 1977 after a few informers helped the authorities to round up some of the leaders. These cells are similar to the RZ—compartmentalized with members knowing only each other and the immediate commander. The reorganization helped to eliminate the number of informers—*gombeens* and supergrasses—so we are having a difficult time keeping our files current. Incidentally, the Provos have received large amounts of money from the government of Libya. We know two million British pounds were given by Libya to the Provos. You remember that five tons of Libyan weapons were intercepted off the coast of Ireland in 1973—the British got Joe Cahill then too—and in November 1987 another shipment from Libya was confiscated off the French coast."

"So the Mossad agent could have been eliminated by any one of these groups," Kelly stated flatly.

"I'm afraid so," Wright sighed. "The internetwork between those groups is such that they pass on requests for such favors." He glanced at the report and shook his head. "You know, even though Manel appears to be Mossad, he could even be a member of the Israeli terrorist group that calls itself the 'Wrath of God.'"

Kelly grimaced. "Rather dramatic."

Wright nodded. "Most guerrillas seem to be highly romantic. They see themselves like Charlemagne's paladins, out to save the world. They don't realize that the world is no longer a romantic place; that's why we don't have heroes—just dogmatic clerks and computer experts."

"In a way, it's a shame," Kelly said, clucking his tongue.

"Perhaps. But see if you can find out anything, will you? Don't do anything until you get back to me. We might be able to salvage something out of this, ah, indiscretion."

Kelly nodded, rising. He pointed at the report. "Shall I take it with me?"

Wright shook his head. "Leave it. I'll have Gladys make a copy for you." Kelly turned to the door. Wright's voice stopped him. "Oh, by the way, congratulate that young research assistant—

what's his name?" He picked up the report, opening it. "Peter Robinson. Perhaps a move to covert operations?"

Kelly frowned. What Robinson had put together wasn't so much research as it had been luck. What do you have in mind? Aloud, he said, "Good idea. We could use another man in the Terrorist Section. I'll get right on it."

"Good," Wright said as Kelly opened the door and left, leaving Wright behind, studying the document. The move would place Robinson close to him. Should the young man uncover more, Wright would be there to ride over anything that might implicate him. Power has its advantages. But how did this become knowledge?

He opened the report again, his eyes skipping over the now-familiar words and phrases. Apparently, this Robinson had caught multifeeds from one of their agents who had managed to infiltrate the Mossad and a freelance operative in Ireland, both concerned with a shipment of AK-47s that had gone astray somewhere. Two seemingly routine messages that together created a puzzle. One report of a shipment of AK-47s disappearing was explainable, but two reports of shipments disappearing showing up simultaneously suggested a route. But what had made Robinson put out an "all search" command through Central's computer? Idle speculation? Curiosity? And how in the world had he uncovered the route to Afghanistan? That had been closed for three years now, along with the Mhadi factory. You had been careful to keep data out of the computer, so how did it manage to get there?

He gnawed his lower lip as he crossed to the window behind his desk and stood, staring out onto the barren December landscape. Somewhere, you have made a mistake, but where? How? You even used a retired agent in Kenton. An idea tickled the edges of thought, and he crossed to his computer and sat, carefully working his way through a series of offices to cover his own computer trail. Finally, satisfied that he had by-passed computer monitoring, he moved into Finance, frowning when a command leaped onto his screen, demanding clearance. His own would have given him immediate access, but would also immediately register him as the query initiator. He opened the file on his desk, found Robinson's clearance, and typed it in, asking the computer for a reconnect. Immediately, the computer pulled up Kenton's bank file. He scrolled through the data, then stopped as the name of a Cairo bank flashed onto the screen.

Clever. After the death of the Mossad agent, Robinson must have run a routine check on agent involvement in the Middle East and the bank records of a retired agent came up, showing money transfers from Suisse National to Grand Cayman to Cairo. Why the bloody hell hadn't Kenton run a direct transfer to a dummy account in Cairo?

The answer came to him as he split the screen image, comparing the records of Kenton's account in the Grand Cayman bank to his account in the Cairo bank. Twenty thousand transferred from Suisse National to Grand Cayman, but the next transfer from Grand Cayman to Cairo was for only seventeen thousand. Rapidly, he compared the other transfers. In every instance, Kenton had left a few thousand in his Grand Cayman account.

I'll be damned! The bastard was skimming. No wonder he ran the money through his account in Grand Cayman. What better way to hide his little side action? And who would think to check the records of retired agents? Hell, even I didn't know we had a constant monitor on past agents. I wonder which of my predecessors set that up? So, Robinson has the bank account of a retired agent in Cairo, a munitions factory in Egypt, and two separate accounts of shipments of AK-47s disappearing—no, that's too sketchy.

He pulled out of the Finance section and typed in a query on Robinson's research, again using Robinson's own code. When the information blinked on his screen, he stared in disbelief. Kenton had used Faud Ahkkam as one of his runners. Jesus! The same man who is currently being used by the Agency in Iran to monitor Saddam Hussein's military buildup in defiance of United Nations sanctions! Although Ahkkam was only the odd assignment contract man, the recent Mideast conflict had grown enough that the Agency needed all the Arabic-speaking men it could get.

But Ahkkam is little more than a bandit who raids indiscriminately back and forth across the various borders; first in Iran, then Afghanistan or Lebanon. Boundaries mean nothing to him or his band of renegades.

Wright picked up a paper clip from his desk and began to absentmindedly play with it. At least now he knew how Robinson had stumbled onto the old operation. He hadn't come through the financial records first; he had found an active operation and through routine file checks had come across enough oddities to put together the scenario he suggested in his report. Rotten luck. That's all it was: Kenton's selection of Ahkkam a couple of years previously and Ahkkam's selection again. But the question is, how had those AK-47s come to be stored in an Israeli warehouse?

18

A LONG TIME HAD PASSED SINCE THEIR MEETING IN ATLANTA, BUT Kenton looked the same with his outdated attire of sports coat and open-necked sports shirt. Wright had remembered their last meeting and had carefully chosen Flo's Place on Chesapeake Bay precisely for that reason: one wasn't regulated to a tie as in most places in Washington, D.C., yet a tie was not out of place in Flo's, which catered to everyone. And, he thought as Kenton stood inside the door, letting his eyes adjust to the dimness, people respect each other's business. Kenton spotted him sitting in the corner booth in the back and carefully made his way through the tables to him. Wright had chosen the booth for its high backs which helped isolate its occupants from the rest of the room.

"Your call surprised me," Kenton said. A waiter materialized at his elbow and placed a glass dark with Jack Daniel's in front of him and disappeared. Kenton took a sip and grinned. "You remembered. I'm touched."

Wright grunted and waved the compliment away. "We have a problem."

"Oh?" Kenton said. He took another sip, then placed the glass on the scarred table in front of him. He folded his hands and sat, waiting.

"Your route from Egypt to Afghanistan has been uncovered by a researcher at the Agency," Wright said bluntly. Kenton took another small sip and placed his drink squarely back on the coaster. Wright admired his steadiness.

"How?" he asked calmly.

"You used Ahkkam. Why the hell did you choose him?" he asked, suddenly furious.

"Take it easy," Kenton said. "I used him because I knew him. Shit. He's not even Agency. I thought he was safe, then. Not many would ever dream of using someone with his reputation. What better recommendation was there? You," he added pointedly, "were the one in a hurry. I didn't have time to develop a sanitized route."

"What about the AK-47s?"

A guarded look dropped over Kenton's eyes. "What about them?"

"I thought you dropped all of the last run in the Red Sea. At least that was what you told me."

"I did," he said calmly, picking up his drink, sipping. His eyes watched warily.

"Don't pull that crap on me," Wright said softly. "They've turned up. In Ireland, of all places. And with a shipment of drugs inside them as well."

He shrugged. "I wouldn't worry about it. You're covered. No one knows about your involvement in this and I went through Blackie Cassidy in Boston. Blackie won't say anything. He's solid."

"Blackie Cassidy? Jesus Christ," Wright said wearily. "You went through him?"

"What's wrong with Cassidy? Shit, his brother's the president of Lockwell University, for Christ sakes."

"And Blackie is working with the FBI—the Federal Bureau of Investigation," Wright said, leaning over the table. "You really fuck up in spades, don't you, Kenton?"

"You're wrong," Kenton said. He placed the glass down on the table in front of him and his hands on either side of it. "Cassidy's solid. He's been shipping arms and money over to Ireland for years."

"Yeah, the Irish Mafia of South Boston," Wright said scornfully. "The Silver Street Gang. All honor and green sashes and all that. The man has been a loanshark and narcotics runner for a long time and why do you think the FBI hasn't come down on him? He's been informing on the others and letting the government take care of his dirty work. He turned when he went to Alcatraz for bank robbery. Oh, he's solid all right, you idiot. And now we have a few crates of AK-47s that were supposed to have been destroyed."

"How do you know they're ours?" Kenton asked. He took another drink then played idly with the glass, making damp circles on the tabletop. Wright watched him with annoyance.

"The Mossad conveniently kept a record of the serial numbers. But you know all this, don't you?" he said suddenly.

A grin split Kenton's thin lips. "Can't put one over on you, can I, Dickie? Yes, I know it."

Tiny muscles bunched along Wright's jaw. "What's going on?"

Kenton made an elaborate gesture with his hands. "It was the last shipment before I shut down the factory. Ahkkam had picked up the rifles from the boat at the coast. He was taking his usual route through Waddi Quruum when he stumbled upon an Israeli raiding party. In the fight that followed, he was forced to abandon the shipment in order to get away. The Israelis took it back to their home base. From there, it went to the Mossad warehouse in Tel Aviv."

"Why didn't you tell me about all this?" Wright said. He could feel tiny beads of perspiration forming on his forehead.

"So you could do what? Worry? Look at you: you're doing that now, and there's not a thing at all to worry about. We knew some of those weapons were going to fall into Russian hands, didn't we? What the hell? The whole idea of the exercise was to make certain those weapons could not be traced back to us. And they can't."

"*They* can't," Wright said gratingly, leaning forward. "But the serial numbers might match those you should have dumped. And then the Mossad or someone will be able to trace them back to the factory. Jesus!" He leaned back, fumbling his handkerchief out of his pocket. He blotted his forehead.

"Don't you think I knew that?" Kenton asked, his eyes dancing with dangerous lights. "Hell, that was the crack. That was why I went along with it—the rush."

"And the money was good," Wright added viciously. "Especially when you had the opportunity to pay yourself a few dividends."

"You found that, huh?" Kenton said, shaking his head admiringly. "I've gotta hand it to you—you run a close tab."

"I expected it," Wright said coldly. "That's automatically written into operations—graft."

"I wish I had known that in Vietnam," Kenton complained. "I would have skimmed more."

"I'm sure you would have. But let's get back to the subject at hand, shall we? We've got drugs and AK-47s about to screw up the cease-fire in Ireland, and if that happens there's going to be a hard investigation into where they came from. I know that you were careful, but there's always one thing that isn't covered. Always one thing."

"Oh, that." Kenton picked up his glass and took a large swallow. "Don't worry. I took care of it."

"You—took care—of it?"

"Right. I thought those weapons might surface sometime, so I bought a little insurance." He gave Wright a smug smile, the flesh drawing tightly over his cheekbones, creating a death's head. His pupils were tiny black ice surrounded by frosty blue, startling against the deep tan of his face.

"What was that?"

"I put an, ah, 'acquaintance' on retainer," he said. "It doesn't matter where or who. He's expensive, but worthwhile. And he handles the shipment at the other end." He made an expansive gesture, nearly knocking his glass over, and laughed.

"So where are the guns now?" Wright asked. Kenton gave him a long, slow wink.

"I really don't know," he said vaguely. "It doesn't matter."

"Oh, Christ," Wright muttered.

Kenton laughed and wagged a forefinger at Wright. "Now, that's information that might be worth a penny or two, wouldn't you think? Who was it who said 'knowledge was power'?"

"Many people. Keats claimed it could make a man a god," Wright said.

"Like Jupiter?"

"More like Janus," Wright said dryly. "Huxley said a little knowledge could be dangerous. Personally, I think he was probably more right than Keats."

"My, that could almost be construed as a threat," Kenton said mockingly, leaning back against his seat.

"Threats are useless if made from a position of weakness," Wright said.

"You would do well to remember that," Kenton said. His smile remained fixed, but there seemed to be more tooth than humor to it.

"Positions are tenuous things," Wright said. "Like buildings on sand. A little tremor can bring them down. Would you like to know who has those guns now?"

Kenton straightened and lifted his glass, saluting Wright. "I have a hunch you're about to tell me."

"Don't be so damn melodramatic," Wright said irritably.

"You're the director," Kenton pointed out.

Wright permitted himself a wintry smile. "It seems the IRA has decided that it is going to clean up its own house. You know how they are: romantic and mercurial. With the peace accord proposed, they are going to suddenly show that they aren't thugs and gangsters or terrorists. They need respectability now. So what the Irish police haven't been able to do, they will."

"That might explain that murdered Jew in the Connecticut Avenue Club, wouldn't it?" Kenton said. Wright's eyes narrowed. "How did you know about that?"

"I saw the story in the *Post*. It makes sense, though, doesn't it?"

"I'm not sure," said Wright. He chewed on his lower lip, frowning at the wall behind Kenton. "The question is: what was he doing in the United States? If he was trailing the arms, why wouldn't he be with them?"

"Maybe he was," Kenton said, casually lifting his glass. The ice cubes rattled against his teeth as he finished the whiskey. He replaced the glass. A waiter appeared at his elbow, whisking away the empty glass. Kenton nodded at his question of another.

"I don't think so. It's a long way from Israel to the United States. Why not go the usual way through Sardinia and Marseilles? Or even a more direct route on a tanker going back to Bantry Bay after collecting crude from Kuwait? Those tankers cut through the Suez; it would be far easier to arrange a transfer there—and safer. Shipments from the U.S. are more suspect than from other countries. We have more Irish than Ireland—or at least those who want to be Irish for a moment or two."

Kenton shrugged. He leaned back as the waiter appeared and placed a fresh glass of whiskey in front of him. He took the five from Kenton's fingers and nodded his thanks as Kenton waved away the change. "I really don't see the problem. Let them look. They'll stumble around a little then go back home."

"No, I don't think so," Wright said drily. "It's my understanding that they pulled one of their top guns out of retirement and have turned him loose."

Kenton laughed. "So we have a bog-trotter running around waving his pistol and all? For Christ's sakes, Dickie, you really think one like that can match up against the Agency? Turn your dogs loose on him. Invent some story or other and go after him. Hell, you're Special Ops. You can pull in the people you need." He laughed and drank from his glass. "I don't see where it's any business of mine. I'm out of it."

"No," Wright said softly, leaning across the table. "Not this time. No games. You know the routine; you were part of it long enough. Or don't you remember the camp at An Thoc?"

"That was a long time ago," Kenton said quietly. His eyes burned into Wright's.

"Yes, it was," Wright said. "But there is no statute of limitations for crimes against humanity. Simon Wiesenthal has been proving that for almost fifty years now. Remember Eichmann in Argentina? The Butcher of Lyons?" His mouth curled with distaste. "You really had a unique way of getting information, Simon."

"I don't think the Agency would like that to be leaked out. Might prove to be a bit embarrassing to them," Kenton said quietly.

"Maybe. But do you really want to take that chance?"

Kenton glared at Wright, but the DSO stared back calmly, his eyes hard and unyielding. At last, Kenton looked down at the glass of whiskey in front of him. "What do you want?" he asked.

"That's simple," Wright said calmly. "You said that I had access to the, ah, 'special people,' and you are right. I have access to you, Simon. You are the special person I'm going to activate. And you will arrange for this loose cannon to be, ah, disposed of. Right?"

"Yes," Kenton said sullenly.

Wright nodded. "Good. Now, is there anything else I should know about? I don't want any more surprises. I don't like surprises," he added slowly, emphatically. "Any more AKs unaccounted for?"

"No," Kenton said suddenly.

"Good," Wright said. He slid from the booth, carefully set his coat, touched his tie, and walked away without looking back.

Kenton watched the door swing softly shut behind Wright. He drained the glass of whiskey and rattled the cubes impatiently until the waiter appeared. He handed the glass to him and said, "A double." The waiter silently took the glass and slipped away.

Anger burned in Kenton's throat, threatening to gag him. He swallowed and reached across the table and picked up the glass of soda Gates had barely touched. He drank deeply, then took a deep breath, willing himself to be calm. There will be another time. A stab of pain centered above his eyebrows, clamping his head in an iron vise. A mirage floated in his peripheral vision. His lips clenched into tight white lines. He squeezed his eyes shut. Tiny yellow flames exploded behind his eyelids. Oh, Christ! There will be a time—there will be a time—

19

THE SNOW THAT HAD BEEN THREATENING THE SEABOARD FOR THE past few days finally began to fall. Wright looked out at the thick flakes floating down. Although he hated winter and considered Easter a bit of a bore as well, he had to admit it would be a relief from the leaden days that normally made the countryside with its dead grasses and black trees stretching bare branches to the lowering clouds seem like a Picasso nightmare. But late snows were the worst. At least he had a bit of vacation coming with a visit to his sister and her family in Chicago. That was the way to celebrate Easter: a brief visit with a family for three or four days, then one could leave the yelling children and whining mothers. Again, he felt the satisfaction of a bachelor's life. He thought about Helen and the apartment in Georgetown she shared with her alcoholic husband the senior senator from Mississippi, and the time they would have together after her husband entered Bethesda for his yearly drying out over the spring break. A discreet knock disturbed his thoughts.

"Enter," he called. The door opened and shut, and he sighed and turned to face Tom Loudon, Operations Officer—Terrorist Section. "Yes?"

"Sorry to disturb you, sir," Loudon said. He was carefully dressed in a three-piece suit, pin-striped charcoal, with a pearl gray tie carefully tied in an overhand knot. His Vandyke beard was carefully trimmed, his hair conservatively cut. He looked like a successful broker.

"What is it?" Wright took his chair behind his desk. Loudon laid a folder with a black slash across it in front of him. He opened the folder and stared at the photo of a young man with unfashionable long hair dressed in a black leather jacket. He held a pistol in his hand and was looking over his shoulder at the photographer. The bricks of the building behind him were vague blurs. Telephoto lens, he automatically registered. Maybe mid-seventies when taken.

"Who is he?" he asked.

"Tomas Fallon," Loudon said. "Probably the best gunman the IRA has. We hear from London that this is the man the IRA has sent to find where the drugs and the shipment of AK-47s came from. This is the only suspected photo of him. It was taken in 1969 during the Battle of the Bogside in Londonderry after the Apprentice Boys' March by an SAS photographer. At least, we think it is him."

"No school photos? Anything more recent?"

Loudon shook his head. "No. Everything seems to have disappeared. I'm afraid we really know very little about him. His mother was apparently killed by the British in an automobile accident, and his father died shortly after from a stroke. He has a twin brother who is a priest, and an uncle who lost his fortune when Northern Ireland opened its doors to overseas industry. His factory couldn't compete, and he lost a bundle when he underwrote a British tanker that came apart in the North Sea, spilling crude over half of the Baltic Coast. The environmentalists ate him up and his partners—all British—left him holding the bag. He's a recluse now, lives most of the time in a shack on the Kerry coast although he does maintain a home in Tralee. Spends his time fishing."

"No one else?"

"No one. Fallon seems to be the personal boy of Seamus Mac-Cauley, the Belfast Brigade commander."

"He's not a boy any longer if this was taken in 1969. That's over twenty years ago. Any other known contacts?"

"There is a suspected one: Maeve Larkin, a professor at Trinity College. The widow of an old IRA gunman, one Conor Larkin who also taught at Trinity—a specialist in the Ulster Cycle. She took over his position after he was killed during a shoot-out on the Manchester docks while stopping an assassination attempt on Lord Mountbatten. She had been arrested earlier on a trumped-up charge—you know how those courts are: they have suspended human rights—and Conor Larkin helped break her away from the convoy taking her out of Castlereagh. We believe MacCauley and Fallon were in on that as well."

Wright took the second photo from the file and looked at Maeve Larkin. Her hair fell loosely to her shoulders. Her forehead was wide, nose straight, mouth maybe a little too wide, but not really noticeably so. "Very pretty. A widow?"

"She was over thirty years younger than her husband."

"Strange." He took the third photo from the folder. He looked very familiar. He looked up to at Loudon.

"Con Edwards. A reporter for the *Times*. He's here in the States for now, getting a special award from the Press Club for his series of stories about that mess in Somalia. Normally, he's one of the overseas men for the *Times*."

"What's he doing with these people?"

"We think he might have been involved as well with freeing the Larkin woman. When she was arrested, the British soldiers pulled him in too. They tried to cover up their mistake by forcing him to sign a disclaimer, but word leaked out. Strange that he hasn't written anything about what happened there."

"Strange, indeed," Wright muttered. He fanned the pictures out on the desk in front of him and studied them. "Where's Fallon now?"

"We don't know," Loudon said. Wright looked up, frowning irritably. He shrugged. "Sorry. That's all the British could tell us other than he's believed to be headed to the United States. We've alerted Immigration to double-check all passports from Ireland, and triple-check all flights from there."

"He won't be dumb enough to come that way if this is the best photo you've got of him in twenty years. A man like that is a very careful man."

"Everybody makes mistakes," Loudon said.

Wright pretended not to hear. He pulled the last two photos from the file. One was an old man staring defiantly into the lens, a briar clamped tightly between his teeth.

"His uncle?" Loudon nodded. Wright looked at the last photo. A young, blond priest smiled pleasantly. His cheeks were ruddy, his eyes crinkling at the corners. He wore a white surplice, his hand raised as if blessing the photographer.

"His brother," Loudon said. "I'm afraid it isn't much."

"What about his brother?" Wright asked.

"What?"

"His brother. He's a priest, yes, but what else do we know about him. Is he IRA too?"

"No, the opposite, in fact. He was with the peace marchers at Londonderry and worked with several other protest groups in Belfast. He was arrested along with a woman of his church when the Ulster Defense Regiment broke into the sanctuary of his church while searching for guns and he tried to stop them. I gather they gave him a rather rough time in the Crumlin Jail and later in Castlereagh. The pope protested, and they had to release him to avoid diplomatic embarrassment."

"The pope himself?"

"That is my understanding. Seems as if Father Fallon—Monsignor, now—was an emissary for the Vatican for a few years before returning to Ireland at his request. That was just before the peace march in Londonderry. He had his choice of churches, according to our reports, and took one on Falls Road. Very strange. It's almost as if he was trying to be a martyr."

"Or trying to atone for something. Doing penance."

Loudon shrugged. "Perhaps. But he's not there now. After his release, he went to a Cistercian monastery for a couple of years and now is the priest of a small church in a rural village somewhere in the backwaters. He seems to be trying to lose himself."

"Lose himself?" Wright echoed absently, staring at the priest's photo.

"Why else do a hundred-and-eighty-degree turn with his life?"

A glimmer of an idea flitted across Wright's mind on bat wings. His eyes disfocused as he stared at the photo, willing the thought back. The photo swam in his sight, the edges blurring, darkening.

"I think," he said suddenly, "that Fallon will be coming in on his brother's passport."

"We'll get him then," Loudon said. "I'll alert Immigration—"

"It won't do any good," Wright said. He smiled and shook his head admiringly. "If I'm not mistaken, he'll be traveling on his brother's Vatican passport. Probably from Paris or maybe even Rome. He's probably here by now. He strikes me as the sort who wouldn't procrastinate."

"Christ. Where now?" London muttered.

"I think a watch should be put on this man," Wright said, picking up the photo of Con Edwards.

"I don't know," Loudon said doubtfully. "He has a lot of choices to choose from among the Irish sympathizers."

"He won't go to them, yet. He strikes me as a loner. That's the only way he could have lasted this long. He's used to making his own way."

"I'll check with Immigration and see if a Father Fallon has come through." Loudon turned to leave.

"And put a watch on Edwards," Wright called. London paused. "Should we notify the FBI? We're on their turf."

Wright shook his head. "No, not just yet. Let's keep it to ourselves. If anything comes of it, then we can let them in on it. But for now, let's just keep it between the two of us."

"What about Kelly? He's Operations."

"No, the fewer, the better. Like you said: technically, this belongs to the FBI. Send one man from here up to New York on the shuttle. I don't want the New York office in on it, either. If Kelly comes in on this, then the Operations staff is notified and the FBI. Formalities, you know." He grinned sourly. "Best keep it between the two of us and the one you send. Have him report directly to you as the case officer. Understand?"

"Yes sir," Loudon said. Case officer! This was far better than the routine of the data bank.

"Move your things from your cubicle to"—Wright pulled open a tray on his desk, glancing at the office roster taped to its surface"—310-A. It's in the Arab section, but it's private. I'll inform the section chief to be expecting you. Anything else?"

"No sir," Loudon said, excitement shining in his eyes. He left, closing the door softly behind him. He moved through the outer office into the corridor, imagining the looks on the faces of his former coworkers in the data bank as he cleared his desk and files. Too bad you can't tell them, but if you use a cart, they'll know you've been promoted.

Wright rose and crossed to the window, staring out at the snow gathering in soft drifts on the ground. He would have to cancel his sister's invitation, but he had no regrets about that. He had already sent his packages. He frowned. Had he sent his last quarter's tax estimation in? He was sure he had, along with the last of his tithing pledge to the First Baptist Church in Alexandria.

Helen, on the other hand—he sighed. Maybe, with luck, he could still make his promise to Helen.

He turned and went back to his desk. He sat, rubbed his eyes, then opened a folder there and read:

NAME: Cassidy, James J.
AGE: 67
DOB: 9-3-29
HEIGHT: 5'8"
WEIGHT: 155
HAIR: White
EYES: Blue
ALIAS: Blackie Cassidy
Alcatraz. Bank Robbery. Linked to several murders but nothing proven. Armed and dangerous. Prefers knives.

His eyes skipped down to the synopsis.

For more than 20 years, Cassidy has been the reputed "Don" of New England's Irish Mafia. He is a throwback to the gangsters of the thirties: quick-witted, hot-tempered, ruthless. After his release from Alcatraz where he spent nine years for bank robbery, he established his empire in South Boston. He works out of the back of a liquor store on the edge of South Boston. He has been working with the FBI to bring down the Italian Mafia but while doing so, he quietly built up his association called the Silver Street Gang. His business is built around loan-sharking and narcotics. He was regarded as untouchable due to his FBI association until he and his associates Stephen "The Rifleman" Flynn and Joseph "Big Joe" Coughlan tried to extort money from a local tavern owner, Tim Connolly. Connolly went to the FBI who were forced into building a case against the "Don of South

Boston." He is believed to be traveling with a woman named Mary Dunne who has been charged with harboring a fugitive. Rumor has it Cassidy has made his way to Ireland and is hiding out in a location set up by his brother William Cassidy, former Mass. State Rep. and presently president of Lockwell University.

He closed the file and leaned back in his chair, staring at the ceiling. Interesting. One bad brother, one good. Cain and Abel. And the good brother takes care of the bad despite the consequences. Things are getting curiouser and curiouser. If the IRA supposedly has Cassidy, then surely they know where the guns and drugs came from. So why send Fallon?

20

SIMON KENTON SWORE AS THE TELEPHONE RANG SHRILLY INCHES from his ear, driving a nail deeply into his pounding skull. He rolled away from the naked young black man curled on the bed, sleeping with his back to Kenton. He reached for the telephone, growling, "This better be damn good!"

He recognized the voice on the other end and quickly sat up in bed, swinging his legs over the side. "Yes?... Fallon? You're sure about that? I know you should know, but are you sure he's here in the States? New York, I've got it. Keep me informed."

He hung up the telephone and sat, rubbing his temples hard, trying to stop the drumming. A slim, black arm snaked around his neck, gently pulling him backward. He pushed away and sat up.

"Not now," he snapped. He rubbed his face and rose and went to the small kitchenette and poured a glass of water. He opened the small refrigerator under the cabinet and removed an ice cube tray, dumping the cubes in the sink. He dropped a handful into the glass of water, then ran cold water over the ice cubes, filling the sink before he pushed his face into the water, feeling the cold take away the headache and ease the throbbing behind his eyes. He dried his face on a small hand towel, then went to the desk and sat naked in his chair, pulling the telephone to him. He dialed a number and listened to the ring as he checked the calendar: an odd date. He mentally subtracted a number from his own, then gave that number to the answering machine when it picked up. He hung up the telephone and lit a cigarette, waiting. The return call came in three minutes and he smiled thinly to himself as he picked up the telephone.

"You are very prompt," he said. "Now, listen. I have heard that Fallon is in the States. Never mind. I told you I had my own people. It will be expensive. Face it: we are both the hunted ones for that man. But you are the anonymous one. It won't take long before he discovers me. It's my neck on the line, but I have a couple of bolt-holes. Do you? Yes, you could say this is blackmail. I'll take care of him, but I have no intention of being impractical about the situation. A hundred thousand dollars and expenses. I don't travel cheaply. Yes, you could get a cheaper freelancer but I'm the best you have if you want to avoid the Agency. The others might be a bit more careless and that would be risky. They would take your money, make one run at him, and then leave or make excuses as to why it couldn't be done. You want the best, you pay. I don't care where you get it. You want the job done you will have to come up with the money somewhere. Actually, it isn't all that hard. As a former employee, you can write off my fees under the consultant accounts. Do you want me after him or not? Very well. Use the Cayman Island account. Half now, half when I'm finished."

He hung up the telephone and drew a deep breath. He reached for another cigarette, then glanced in the mirror and saw the young black man staring at him.

"I forgot about you," he said.

The black man smiled. "A hundred thousand dollars? We can have a lot of fun with that."

"You heard?"

"Everything," the black man said. "Now, come here."

Kenton shook his head regretfully and rose. He walked naked back to the bed. The man smiled lazily at him as Kenton sat on the edge of the bed. When he reached for him, Kenton struck him hard in the throat with the edge of his hand, crushing the young man's windpipe.

"I'm sorry," he said softly. He reached out and tenderly stroked the young man's forehead with the palm of his hand as he choked to death.

"No loose ends," he murmured.

He rose and leisurely walked into the bathroom and turned the shower spray on cold. He waited for a moment then stepped inside, gasping as the cold water stung him, making his flesh glow. He stood a long time in the shower, letting the water beat over him, driving the hangover from him. Then he toweled dry and dressed in a jogging suit and left, carefully locking the door behind him.

After four blocks, his heart hammered hard against his chest and he gasped for breath. Sweat ran freely from his forehead, but he forced himself to breathe deeply and regularly, ignoring the tiny black dots dancing at the edge of his vision. He ran two miles, then let himself back into his apartment. He stripped naked and did a hundred push-ups and a hundred sit-ups. He went back into the shower, then slipped beside the corpse of the young black man, rolled on his shoulder away from it, and slept deeply.

He awoke at midnight, yawned, stretched, and carefully dressed in black sneakers and running suit. He stepped out onto the balcony and looked down into the alley, carefully studying the darkness. Satisfied, he went back to the bedroom, collected the black man, and carried him out to the balcony. He took one more look, then lifted the body and threw it over the edge. He listened to it land and watched carefully to see if anyone came down the alley. Satisfied that no one had seen him or the body, he went downstairs and into the alley. He picked the broken body up in a fireman's carry and went down to the end of the alley where a Dumpster filled with garbage stood. He opened the Dumpster, heaved the body up into it, then climbed in after it, burying it deeply in the middle.

He climbed out of the Dumpster and out of the alley and started jogging toward the park a mile away. He returned after an hour, sweating heavily, but feeling refreshed. He glanced down the alley but it was still deserted. Then he entered his building and took the elevator to his apartment. He let himself in and quickly showered, then seated himself at his desk with a glass of orange juice and reached for the telephone.

It was time to begin the hunt.

21

SIX HUNDRED MILES AWAY, A SLEEPY TOMMY COUGHLAN, REACHING for the telephone, rolled away from the naked Anne Ryan. She mumbled in protest and tried to slide next to his warmth. He cursed and pushed her away. She grumbled sleepily and rolled away, curling into a ball, clutching her pillow between her legs.

"Yeah," he said into the telephone. "Who?—What the hell do you want? Do you know what time it is? I don't care if—Who?—Who the hell is he?—Well, let him come. My father will—Fuck him! And you! I'm not afraid of any half-assed bog-trotter—Shit—Okay, but I can handle him—I'm listening—Fuck off."

He slammed the telephone back in its cradle and pulled a cigarette from a crumbled packet on the nightstand beside the telephone. He lit it, coughing the first lungful out in a dirty, gray cloud. Tears came to his eyes. He picked up the glass holding a half-inch of whiskey and drained it, gagging it down, waiting until the burning ball hit his stomach. He sighed, and drew again, more cautiously this time, on the cigarette, half-inhaling it, then blowing it out. He felt light-headed, and then the room leaped into crystal focus.

"Who was that?" Anne asked sleepily from behind him.

"Someone calling for my own good, he said," Coughlan answered, coughing. "Why do all the calls late at night have to be for my own good?"

Anne sat up, ignoring the covers that slipped from her cone-shaped breasts. She reached across and took the cigarette from him, drew deeply on it, and eased the smoke from her lungs. "Do you have any more of that whiskey, now?" she asked.

He reached down beside the bed and pulled up a bottle of Southern Comfort, poured a couple of inches in the glass she handed him, and another inch in his own. She drank it down and leaned back against the headboard.

"Well, then, and what was the call?"

"Oh, you know," he said, staring hungrily at her naked breasts. "It seems a man called 'Fallon' is in the country looking for me."

"And—" she prompted, sipping from her glass.

"He's been sent by the boys," Coughlan said. He reached out, touching her breasts gently.

"Jesus," she said. "Fallon."

"Just another piece of shit looking to make a name for himself," Coughlan said.

"No, 'e isn't just another 'piece of shit,'" she said. She brushed his hands away. "You really are a dumb fuck."

Coughlan's eyes narrowed. "You watch yourself. You just watch your fucking mouth."

"You don't even know who Fallon is, do you?" she taunted him. "You really don't."

He flushed under her sarcasm. "Who is he, some sort of super-man, I suppose? Another of those legends you people in the old country like to make out of ordinary men?"

"Fallon is special," she said. "He's a legend, yes, he is, but he's more so than you know."

"So, what the fuck does that mean to me? I'm 'Big Joe' Coughlan's son. I do what I please, when I please, and if I tell a bog-trotter to jump, he jumps. Do you understand me?"

She laughed. "There's a whole world out there who cares less about your father and even less about you. People like Fallon. He would step on you like a cockroach and there's nothing you or your father could do about it, so."

A red haze drifted over his eyes. In fury, he struck out at her, his palm cracking loudly against her cheek. She gasped, then leaped forward, her teeth locking hard on his shoulder. He howled and tried to pull her loose, then they were snarling and twisting on the bed like cats, the telephone call forgotten in the sudden moments of their lust.

SHE LAY IN BED BESIDE HIM, CHAIN-SMOKING KING-SIZE FILTER CIGA-rettes until gentle snores bubbled from him. Then she rose and quietly slipped out of the bedroom into the living room. She picked up the telephone and dialed and waited impatiently, studying her naked self mirrored in the glass of the sliding door leading out onto the balcony above Fifth Avenue. Central Park was black outside the window but she could see the bright lights of New York City stretching away on the other side of the park.

"Hello?—It's me.—Yes. He's asleep. Have you heard about Fallon, now? He's in the country.—Very well.—Yes, I know him. He came for me in Ireland. I was lucky to get away.—An accident. It doesn't matter how." She sighed heavily. "All right, I'll watch him, but it's gonna cost you. And I need a pistol. Small. A twenty-two caliber with hollow points. A garter holster. I didn't bring mine through customs. Too risky. I'll take tea at Tavern on the Green. Leave the package for me there.—Yes."

She hung up and took a cigarette from the packet lying on the table. She lit it and strolled to the window, looking out over the city. She glanced at the bedroom and grimaced. The son wasn't the father, that was certain. And her flesh tingled as she remembered the slow lovemaking of the father who willingly deposited weekly checks in her bank account in Dublin for her services as his son's bodyguard. And the fool son thought it was his charm that kept her by his side. She laughed silently and finished her cigarette. She crossed to the bedroom and quietly let herself back in. She slid into bed. He rolled away from her. She smiled and yawned and stretched luxuriously. The satin sheets slid along her naked flesh, exciting her. Too bad he was asleep, she reflected. He really wasn't such a bad lover. Almost made the job a pleasure, in fact. But he would only be the occasional one-nighter if it wasn't for his father. And, she reminded herself, his father's deep pockets.

22

NEARLY TWO THOUSAND MILES AWAY, SEAMUS MACCAULEY LOOKED
up warily as the door opened in the back room of the safe house in
Wilton Terrace. He relaxed as he recognized one of his bodyguards. "Yes?"

"We got word that Fallon is in the States," the burly man said.

"The States?" MacCauley shook his head admiringly. "Now,
how do you suppose he managed that?"

"I don't know," the man said. "Do you have any word for our
people there?"

"Tell them to look for him," MacCauley said tersely. "Tell them
whatever he wants."

"They ain't going to like that," the man warned.

"Oh, I think they will," MacCauley said. A grim laugh burst from
him. "I don't think that Fallon would like it if they did otherwise."

The man nodded and left, closing the door behind him. Mac-
Cauley looked at the door for a long moment, thinking. Then he
pulled the telephone from it and dialed a number. He waited as
the call clicked through overseas operators.

"We may have a problem," he said when someone picked up
the call on the other end. "The Washington boys know about Fallon—No, don't tell him, but watch his back. If you can," he
amended. "And tell your people to be careful."

He hung up and stared at the peeling wallpaper. He sighed. He hoped Fallon wouldn't need the backup. The young Fallon wouldn't have, but who knew how much of an edge a man like Fallon lost when he was inactive for almost four years? Better to put two cats in the bush for the bird than one and hope for the best.

23

GEORGE PRZYBLSKI TOOK THE PROFFERED PASSPORT FROM THE PRIEST in front of him and glanced at it. From the Vatican: diplomatic immunity. He flipped it open, staring at the picture of the young priest inside, comparing it to the man in front of him. There was a resemblance, to be sure, but the picture was an old one and showed a young priest full of hope and spirit. The man in front of him seemed *stolid*, he thought, that was the word. It was a good word, useful in many situations. The man in front of him was stolid, one who had seen more misery in the human spirit than the young priest in the photograph.

"This is an old photograph, Father," he said.

The priest gave him a small smile. "Not so old, my son. A lot has happened since then and now."

"I see." He frowned. He should call in his supervisor; there was enough discrepancy about the photograph that he would be justified. Then a young child tugged at the priest's coat and the priest looked down and smiled, and Przyblski saw the priest behind the photograph and flicked the page, stamping it hard. He handed it back to the priest.

"Welcome to the United States, Father," he said gruffly. The priest took the passport from him, sketching a blessing with his forefinger. He picked up a case by his side. "What do you have there, Father?"

"A communion set, my son," the priest said. "For after the confessional, you see."

"Welcome, Father," Przyblski said. The priest sketched another blessing.

"Thank you, my son," he said, and moved out away from the immigration station. Przyblski watched him go, then sighed and turned to the next person in line, a harried-looking dowager, her hair slipping in damp ringlets down the side of her face, mascara in clumps on her eyelashes. He sighed again, reaching for her passport. At least he would have one thing to tell his wife about his job. It wasn't every day that an Immigration official checked through a monsignor from the Vatican.

24

THE DOOR TO THE SACRISTY OPENED. MSGR. BRIAN FALLON LOOKED up from his knees where he had been praying. He recognized the man and sighed impatiently. "Yes? What can I do for you?" he asked.

The man shut the door behind him and crossed to Brian, pulling out a chair and sitting. He bent and took Brian's hands in his own. "We have been worried about you, lately, my son," he said.

Brian withdrew his hands and sat back on his heels, looking up at him. His face seemed strange in this light, less forgiving, stern, foreboding, almost, dare he say it? Satanic. He shook his head. "Stop it. You're not being funny," he said.

"Oh?" The man chuckled and leaned back. "Have you thoroughly lost your sense of humor?"

"What do you want?" Brian asked again.

"Where is your Vatican passport?" the man asked.

"It took you long enough to figure it out," Brian said.

"You should have told us," the man murmured.

"Why? It doesn't concern you. Besides, he *is* my brother, you know. One has certain obligations to one's family."

The man's eyes came flat and cold down to his own and Brian felt a faint coldness brush over him. "One cannot pick one's family, but he does pick his friends," he said. "The question is, which do you value the most?"

"Perhaps it is not 'which' but 'what'?" Brian said, looking away from the man's frozen eyes.

The man chuckled. "Ah. A question in metaphysics. Very well. Let us look at relativity. You do understand relativity, don't you? Of course you do," he continued without giving Brian a chance to answer. "A man with your education understands the relative relationship of God to modern man and modern man to God, right?"

"That is something He needs to explain to us," Brian answered. "Why shouldn't we put the same demand on Him that He places upon us? He demands that we be holy; why isn't He?"

The man smiled faintly. "Questioning your faith, now, are you, Monsignor?"

"Not at all," Brian said. He turned and looked at the seated figure. "You see, it is He who condemns us, but it is also He who furnishes us with the temptations to condemn us. Is this a benevolent God? Or has He taken sides in this island we call home? Does he really have a love for His children? I don't think so. I don't think so."

"Faulty logic. But logical." He leaned forward and took Brian's chin in his hand, twisting hard so the priest had to stare into his face.

"But if you are not ready to meet Him so you can ask Him yourself, you will keep us informed about other happenings with your brother, won't you?"

"And if I don't? What then? Will you kill me?"

"No," the man said, patting Brian's cheek. "No, that we won't do. The trouble with priests is they all want to be martyrs. But a martyr is also a holy person. Are you truly a holy person, my son?" he asked mockingly. "And what if your flock discovered what really happened in Crumlin Jail? What then? Hm?"

Brian looked away and the man laughed quietly, releasing his grip on the priest's chin. "Yes. I thought not. Well, we all have our own private little hells, don't we? I've often wondered: the closer one comes to God does he also come equally close to Lucifer? And if so, which is the sin? And to whom does he owe the greater allegiance: to his fellowman or to God?"

The man laughed quietly and rose and walked to one of the stained glass windows, admiring it. Brian stood up and quietly took the man's seat. He stared up at the crucifix carved out of blackthorn hanging on the bare, whitewashed wall. Tears came to his eyes and he tried to say an act of contrition, but the words froze on his lips.

"What do you want?" he whispered.

"Your help," the man answered. "And we want you to remember what happened in Castlereagh. You do, don't you?" Brian nodded silently. "There's a good lad." The man came back and patted his knee. Brian flinched. "Now, have you heard from your brother?"

"Yes," he answered softly.

"And do you know where your brother is?"

"No. Not exactly."

"Oh, we know about the United States. And your passport. It came through on the international check. We monitor all diplomatic travel, you know. But we think you could find out for us, couldn't you?"

"I don't know."

The man's face hardened. "Try."

Brian nodded and rose and left the sacristy, making his way along the path to the cottage. The man followed him, closing the door softly behind him. Brian reached for the telephone, dialed a number, waited a moment, then said, "Uncle Dan? It's Brian. Yes. I wonder—"

The man smiled and crossed to Brian and softly massaged his neck.

25

BLACKIE CASSIDY SHOOK HIS HEAD IN IRRITATION AS THE TELEPHONE rang. He looked up, wating for Mary Dunne to answer it. She put down her book and crossed the room and picked it up.

"Yes," she said. "Who's calling?—One moment." She covered the mouthpiece of the telephone. "It's our friend in Belfast. Do you want to take it?"

"No," Blackie said. He heaved himself up and walked heavily across the room. "But I'd better take it." He took the telephone from her. "Get me a drink." He waited until she walked from the room, then he lifted the receiver and said, "Well?—Whatta yuh mean the shipment's gone? What happened?—MacCauley? Who the fuck's he?—Provo commander? What the hell does he—They what?—Let me get this straight. The boyos are a bit upset because we brought over a taste along with the AKs? That was part of the deal, goddamnit. The GDC gets the AKs and we get the sugar. They look one way, we look the other, and everybody gets what everybody wants. The risk is mine.—No, damnit.—They did what?—One man?—Shit. What are you worried about? What's one man against my boys back in South Boston? I'll turn Coughlan on him—Yeah. Keep me informed."

He hung up and took the glass Mary brought to him. He took a loud swallow then exhaled deeply, savoring the aftertaste of the Irish whiskey.

"What's up?" Mary asked him quietly. "Trouble?"

"Nothing that we can't handle," he growled. He took another sip of the whiskey. "Get Coughlan on the line. We need to put the boys onto a little problem before it develops into something bigger." She turned wordlessly to the telephone. "Then go shopping for a bit." She looked at him. "I have a call I gotta make privately."

"Jim—"

"Some things, darling, you don't get to know," he said quietly. "Some things nobody else gets to know. Not even Billy."

Like Simon Kenton, he thought, and went off to refill his glass while she completed the call.

26

WILLIAM CASSIDY LOOKED UP IN IRRITATION AS THE DOOR TO HIS walnut-panelled office opened. His head ached from looking over the large sheets of budget figures for Lockwell University and the snow rattling against the panes of the French windows had become an irritation.

"Yes, Edwards?" he asked testily, recognizing his butler.

"A gentleman to see you, sir," Edwards said. "He wouldn't give his name."

"Billy knows me quite well," a familiar voice said from behind him, and Cassidy sighed in exasperation as Joe Coughlan shouldered his way into the room, followed by Stephen "The Rifleman" Flynn. Edwards's eyes flared for a moment, then a veil dropped over them. He glanced at Cassidy.

"Shall I remove them, sir?" he asked.

Flynn snorted and walked over to a hunt table against the wall under a Remington painting. He lifted a bottle of single malt Scotch, poured a tumbler half-full and brought it back to Coughlan. He smiled at Edwards. "I don't think you would like to do that," he said.

Edwards's eyes crinkled a bit at the corners and he glanced at Cassidy. "Sir?"

"No, Edwards. Would you bring coffee, please? I'll be all right," Cassidy added as Edwards hesitated.

The butler nodded and left and Coughlan nodded toward the doorway. "Pretty cocky, ain't he?"

"He can afford to be," Cassidy said. He glanced at Flynn. "He would have ripped your head off if you pushed him. You're a lucky man."

"Right," Flynn said, looking unconvinced.

Cassidy smiled faintly. "Have it your way. Just don't push him." He looked at Coughlan with distaste. "Well? What brings you here?"

"I come on behalf of your brother," Coughlan said. He drank the Scotch and placed the glass on the edge of Cassidy's desk.

"Then you may leave," Cassidy said. "My brother goes his way and I go mine."

"Uh-huh," Coughlan said. "But we have a small problem that needs dealing with."

"And you can't deal with it?" Cassidy asked, leaning back in his chair. He smiled. "What good are you, then, Coughlan?"

Coughlan laughed and shook his finger at Cassidy. "Very good. Quick. That's what made you such a success as a representative, isn't it? I can deal with it—or should I say him—but I came to warn you that Blackie says we gotta loose cannon running around over here from Ireland."

Cassidy frowned. "And what does that have to do with me?"

Coughlan shrugged. "Nothing. Unless he comes here looking for Blackie."

"I thought Blackie was in Ireland," Cassidy said. "Last I heard he and that Dunne woman were in Cong in Ireland."

"Well," Coughlan said, shaking his hand back and forth. "Maybe, maybe not. You would know more about that now, wouldn't you?"

Cassidy stared silently at him and Coughlan laughed. "Yeah, I can see you know. So don't sit there like you're king of the shit pile. You're wading in it as deep as we are. Look"—his face tightened as he leaned over the desk—"I didn't wanna come out here on a goddamned night like this to warn you about this crazy Irishman running around over here, but Blackie insisted that I do so. I guess he figures he owes you and his sister something. I don't know why. But there you have it. Watch your back."

"You're too kind," Cassidy said quietly. He looked up as Edwards entered the room, carefully balancing a tray with a silver coffeepot and three Beleek cups and saucers. He placed it on the hunt table beside the bottles and poured a cup of coffee and carried it to Cassidy. "Thank you, Edwards," he said. He looked up at Coughlan and Flynn. "Would either of you care for a cup of coffee?"

"No," Coughlan said abruptly. "I wanna get back to South Boston before this shit gets any deeper. Come on, Flynn."

"I thought you were in jail, Mr. Flynn," Cassidy said. "Murder, wasn't it?"

"Well," Flynn said, spreading his hands. "You know how it is. Gotta have a witness or something. Habeas corpus. Get it?" He laughed.

"Can it," Coughlan growled, heading for the door.

"Show them out, Edwards," Cassidy said.

The butler nodded and followed the pair out, discreetly closing the door behind him. Cassidy leaned back in his chair and sipped the coffee. He rolled the French roast over his tongue approvingly and studied the fire flickering in the fireplace across the room.

"Goddamnit, Blackie," he said tiredly. "What have you dragged me into this time?"

27

THE PRIME MINISTER LOOKED UP IN ANNOYANCE AS SIR EDWARD BELL was ushered into his office. His head ached from trying to make sense of the large report in front of him on the upcoming European Economic Committee, and he was in little mood to play cloak-and-dagger games with Bell.

"Yes, Sir Edward? You stressed urgency with your call."

"That I did, sir," Bell replied. He glanced over his shoulder, waiting until the PM's secretary closed the door behind him.

"Well?" the PM asked impatiently.

"I'm afraid I have bad news, sir," Bell said. "We believe that there is an IRA agent on your staff. Or," he amended, "should I say, a GDC agent? The splinter group from the IRA?"

The prime minister sagged back against his chair. "Who?"

Bell shook his head. "That, sir, we don't know. We got word from our American cousins of their suspicions."

"Oh." The PM sniffed. "The Americans. They see spies in their breakfast cereal. Is that all?"

"Perhaps it would be better, sir, if we did as well. Remember Philby and Burgess? A suspicious mind might have stopped that little bit before it got so far out of hand."

The PM scratched the backs of his hands as he contemplated Bell's words. At last, he nodded. "Perhaps you're right. Do we know who?"

"A fair idea, sir," Bell said. "Ever since we got word, we have been monitoring your staff. There is a young maid whom we believe to be the one."

"Mona? I thought you vetted her," the PM said.

"We did, sir. But apparently we didn't go back far enough."

"What do you propose?"

"She'll have to be taken in for, ah, questioning, sir."

The PM winced. "And?"

"I would imagine there is something under the Official Secrets Act that we will be able to use on her."

"Do what has to be done," the PM said. He pulled his chair up closer to his desk as Bell turned and left. Christ! What all had she gotten?

MONA CROSSED THE KITCHEN TO THE TELEPHONE. THE COOK raised her eyes and shook her head.

"You've been making that a regular habit," she warned. "You need to be talking a bit more in the morning about your schedule rather than making it up as you go along. You know the rules."

"I'll only be half-a-sec," Mona said, picking up the telephone. She quickly dialed a number, waited a minute, then said, "Sorry, hon, but I'll be a bit late again tonight. His nibs is having a couple over for a table of bridge and I'm on. Do you want to go out for fish and chips instead? Okay. Ta."

She hung up the telephone and turned around. A tall man dressed in a tweed suit stood in front of her. Another in a black suit stared coldly at her from behind her. She felt her heart leap in her chest.

TIM CAHILL HUNG UP THE TELEPHONE AND DRUMMED HIS FINGERS on the table in the rear of the Black Dog. What did Mona have now? It's been a short time since the last call and—

The door broke open and three men stepped inside, pistols leveled at him.

"Tim Cahill?" the leader said.

Cahill didn't answer, but slipped his pistol from under his sweater and rose, firing. A hail of bullets took him in the chest, throwing him back against the wall. He fell in a crumpled heap on the floor.

WRIGHT PULLED A FILE FOLDER FROM HIS DESK DRAWER. HE OPENED it and began to pore over it. The GDC had drawn only three sheets of paper. Most of the information had been sent over by Sir Edward Bell as a way of saying thank you for the information Wright had volunteered earlier in the week. Most of the report, he noticed sourly, was pure speculation. But that was something that he was used to: most of the reports that crossed his desk of a similar nature were the result of speculation.

"The Gaelach Dearg Craobh (GDC) appears to be a small, cellular group that uses terrorist tactics for its own profit and gain," he read. "It blankets its activities under the guise of nationalism, hence the dramatic name for itself. It is attached to the Irish Republican Socialist Party (IRSP), a political splinter group of the Official Irish Republican Army (OIRA). The group apparently was formed by Seamus Twooly, Dom Flynn, and Gerard Cassidy, all three former members of the Provisional Irish Republican Army (PIRA). It is our understanding that the three were turned over to the British by the central committee of the IRA, however, when they began to design their own operations without clearance. These operations, however, were not political targets in so much as they were targets of materialistic opportunity. The IRSP is currently denying its connection with the GDC although its newspaper, *The Starry Plough*, still reports their operations when of a military nature.

"In the past few months since its creation, the GDC has been condemned by the PIRA for its March assassination of leading British Conservative Party member Anthony Powell in Great Britain. This action shocked the British authorities since Powell has been highly critical of Britain's involvement in Northern Ireland. Since that time, the GDC has not made any political operations, contenting itself with banks, kidnappings, and train robberies both in Ulster and the Republic of Ireland and Great Britain. Rumors have come to our attention of recent involvement in drug activities within the Republic and Ulster as well.

"There appears to be evidence of GDC contacts with the West German Revolutionary Cells (RZ) and the French Direct Action (AD) groups. From this association, the GDC has emerged as a brutal and unpredictable organization. Its funding appears to be through several Irish sympathizers in the United States and, it is believed, through the Irish Northern Aid Committee (NORAID) {National Headquarters: 273 East 194 Street, Bronx, New York}. We believe this group to also be connected to Joe Coughlan. Coughlan is reportedly the lieutenant of the Irish mob headed by James 'Blackie' Cassidy in Boston and, in addition to supplying arms to the PIRA on a semi-regular basis, runs a numbers racket, prostitution, protection, labor unions, and other diverse criminal activities in Boston. Following a confrontation with the Salvatore family, other organized crime has stayed out of Boston. There is no indication at all that Coughlan/Cassidy is in the drug trade, however. His involvement with the GDC is apparently only through his connection with NORAID. There is no evidence of his direct support of this group."

But where, then, would the GDC be getting its drugs? he thought. He tapped his forefinger on the file thoughtfully. And why is the information on them so sketchy? We should have quite a file on them by now.

28

NEW YORK WAS FAST FILLING WITH WHITE POWDER AS FAT FLAKES floated thickly through the barren trees of Central Park, between narrow passages separating towering piles of brick and stone, covering cracked concrete and asphalt, burying animosity with it and creating a fairy city. Stately, plump Con Edwards slowly slipped his way on wet leather soles down Seventh Avenue from celebrating what he could not remember at O'Grady's on Eighth Avenue. The backs of his calves ached. Did I really dance a jig with pretty Molly, the daughter of him who owns the bar? He seemed to be having a bit of trouble disfocusing the disfocus into which his eyes slipped when he relaxed his concentration as he weaved his way gently along the way, counting the doors he passed, some with cheerful lights flashing in celebration of the Easter season that reminded him of Christmas. God! but I love the Christmas season with garlands leaping across the street and the store windows bedecked with trains and dolls and basketball hoops and Red Ryder BB guns and runny-nosed children pressing as close to the frosty panes as they can get, trying to osmosistise their tiny bodies through the double-thick panes into the wonderlands spread before them.

Yes, Christmas was the season he liked with everyone filled with bonhomie, but the day posted a dismal last on his list of days for never did he feel so alone as he did on that day when he rambled around his empty apartment in whatever part of the world he was in or the *Times* apartment on Seventh Avenue it kept for its reporters they called in for conferences or, in his case, an award, a prestigious award, the Horace Greeley Award given once every five years to the top newsman selected by his peers. It was the third time he had used the apartment for an award: the two others had been for Pulitzers. Each had been a time to renew old acquaintances, and this time had been no different. Easter may not have had the joy of Christmas attached to it, but at least he had the chance to visit old friends and that did make it seem a bit less lonely. Oh, the hell with it. Holidays pretty much meant loneliness, regardless of when they came.

He shook his head sadly and remembered back to when he had stood in as godfather to young Molly, the daughter of O'Grady— he hummed a quick few bars of the song—and she had baptized the priest with a sudden wet diaper. And he remembered how O'Grady had laughed when he'd tried to back away from being the godfather as he wasn't Catholic. Ah, man, what the priest doesn't know won't hurt 'im, and it isn't the religion that's so important, it's the man! A carefully kept secret it was too not only from the priest but from pretty Molly's mother, who held a reverence sure to get her sainthood for the Church and its maze of bewildering tracts. He and pretty Molly's father had spent many happy hours late at night after closing time in himself's bar, cramming for the examination by the priest who was skeptical that the *Times*'s "Man on the Scene" who often wrote in such heretical prose was a member of the church. But they had carried it off— indeed they had, and now pretty Molly was eighteen and a woman, and suddenly the Jameson's left him and he felt more alone than he had in years.

He found the brownstone and moved up the stairs to the foyer. His numb fingers punched in the security code and the door opened.

"Con?"

He paused, frowning as memory tried to wash over the Jameson's fog in his mind; then Ireland came flooding back, and he turned, squinting into the shadows.

"Maeve?" He took a step, then a shadow separated itself from the others and moved into the light. For a moment, he was afraid, for she seemed no different from when last he had seen her on the bleak slopes of the cemetery on the English shore where they had buried her husband, Conor Larkin, among the graves of the Irish dead who had flown their native land and now lay silent in rank and file, staring out across the gray Irish Sea toward their homeland. His throat caught, then he saw the tiny differences time had made on her: faint gray lines in her auburn hair, tiny wrinkles set in the corners of her almond-shaped eyes, her high cheekbones softer, her lips fuller, a roll of soft flesh beneath her chin. Yet her skin was still translucent and beneath her spring coat, he could still make out the peasant's body shivering: wide shoulders, pear-shaped breasts—had her middle thickened? he couldn't be sure—still, nothing kept a man from noticing everything about her at once.

"It's been awhile, Con," she said. Her emerald green eyes drew him to her. He swallowed convulsively against his suddenly dry throat.

"Almost fifteen years. You stopped writing," he blurted out, then mentally kicked himself for his abruptness.

"You didn't. Maybe less than before, but once a month 'tis sure I'd be that a letter from my dear friend Con Edwards would find its way to my box."

"Friend?"

"Con—don't, please," she said, looking away out to the dark street. The spring snow had increased, the romantic imagery of Frost gone, the flakes falling purposefully now with a savage intensity, falling obliquely through the thin light from the street lamp. Con followed her look, thinking, it's falling all over the seaboard, out covering Long Island and Poughkeepsie, up the coast to Boston and Back Bay and Marblehead, Thoreau's woods, and Emerson's house, and the Concord Bridge that arched the flood. For once, the forecasters had been right: the snow is falling on every New England stone-edged field and pine-covered mountain, every cemetery with its garden of headstones and crooked crosses—

"I'm sorry," he said, jerking himself back from maudlin maundering.

"Thank you," she said.

They stood awkwardly for a moment, then Edwards made a gesture toward the interior of the brownstone.

"Would you care to come up?" The words felt formal and stiff upon his lips. "In, I mean—"

"Yes, I would," she said, suddenly shivering. She smiled brightly, trying to put the awkwardness behind them. "And if there's a drop around the place not bespoken for, I'd be beholden to you for a taste—for medicinal purposes, you understand? I wasn't expecting this snow when I left home. And wouldn't you know they closed Kennedy just after my plane landed—"

He laughed, remembering fondly the good times they had known, deliberately suppressing the ugliness: their sudden arrest by the British and RUC, the long days and even longer nights in the cells at Castlereagh, their love, the bitterness of her marriage to Conor Larkin, falling in love again, the tiny mole in the small of her back—but the memories were still there at the edge of his thoughts and, he sensed, hers.

"And how is Michael John?" he asked, opening the door and stepping aside for her to enter first. "Is he still as irascible as ever?"

"'Irascible'? A fine man you are with the words. Yes, he's fine. Although," she added, stepping through the doorway, leaving faint traces of heather wafting gently over him, "it'll be a while before he can enjoy the odd jar. Hospital is funny about that with gunshot wounds, you know."

"Gunshot? Christ! What happened?" he asked, stopping in the doorway.

"Not here," she said, glancing around. "'Tis best told in one's own rooms."

"Right. Right. Ah, yes, of course," he said, hurrying past to lead her up the stairs to the second-floor apartment. He fumbled with the key, swearing softly at his fingers made thick from cold and drink, then threw open the door and flicked the switch. Maeve stepped through the doorway and paused inside the vestibule, surveying the room. In front of her, the living room opened onto a bay window, cushions covering the seat. A sofa and coffee table faced a Victorian fireplace. Two overstuffed chairs shared a reading light and table in a nook next to the kitchen on the left. A short hallway to the right led to two bedrooms.

"Nice, Con. Yours?"

"No. It belongs to the *Times*. They loan it out to the out-of-town staff when they are called in on conference." He took their coats, carefully shook the water from them, and hung them in the closet.

"Congratulations on your award," she said, moving into the living room. She glanced at the fireplace, noting it had been converted to gas.

"You heard about that? How did you find me?" he asked, following her. He turned on the gas and punched the ignitor twice before it caught. Warmth began to spread out into the room.

"I called the paper to see where you were, and they told me," she answered.

"Of course. Stupid of me," he said, moving toward the kitchen. "But what made you think I would be in the States? I wrote you last from Munich." He disappeared around the corner. She heard a cupboard open and shut, the rattling of ice, the clink of glass.

"I read the story about you in the paper. It said you were here for the award ceremonies at the Press Club."

"I forgot about that," he said, emerging from the kitchen. He carried two glasses filled with ice and a bottle of Bushmill's to the sofa, placing them on the coffee table. They sat, reaching simultaneously for their glasses.

"*Slainté*," she said, raising her glass. He tipped his against hers, and they drank. She sat her glass on the table and leaned back against the sofa, closing her eyes for a moment. Tired circles showed beneath her eyes, and the firelight made the fine lines around her eyes and lips stand out against the ivory of her skin.

Con leaned forward to splash more Bushmill's into their glasses. "What brings you to New York?" he asked. "Surely not to find me. You had no way of knowing I would be in the States. And what is this about Michael John?"

She opened her eyes, rolling her head against the back of the sofa, considering. His face seemed haggard, the jowl line thickening. His eyes were bright, almost luminescent in the heavy tan he had brought back with him. His nose twisted to one side from having been broken sometime in the past. His lips were tight, the lower one fuller than its partner. His hair was still full, but thinning and unruly as always. His fingers, short and stubby, clutched the glass in a wide, thick palm, the hands of a dockworker or farmer, not the hands of a writer. He had a paunch, but it seemed more a deep belly rise than fat. And she remembered the gentleness of his arms and quickly took her mind away from memory.

"Still the questions, Con. All right. We have a bit of a problem back home, and I'm afraid it's spilling over the waters to here," she said.

He set the glass on the table beside hers and sat back, his eyes holding hers, watchful, probing. "Go on."

"Well, it really is a twofold problem. First, you know about the cease-fire"—he nodded—"and, as you can probably guess, not everyone is happy about it. That damn Paisley's the worst, but the other side has its own, too. They brought in a shipment of guns after the cease-fire had been reached."

"Christ," he murmured. "After all the deaths, they want more?"

"Complete surrender, not negotiations. It's the Gaelach Dearg Craobh—the Irish Red Branch—the GDC. A bit melodramatic, but"—she shrugged—"it reminds people of their heritage. Mac-Cauley and the others in the Provos want to stop any more ship-ments before Paisley and others like him get hold of the news and use it to destroy any possibility of a peace accord. But that's not all: it seems that drugs are beginning to be easier to get and the Gardai's stumped," she said. "So, in a gesture of good will to the Republic, the boyos have decided to take a hand. Again, our old friend MacCauley."

"I see." He rubbed his hand across his forehead as if trying to erase cobwebs. "Pretty smart. Stop the guns before the information falls on the wrong side of the negotiating table and show that the boyos really are wonderful people by stopping the drug shipments that have baffled the Republic's police. Both functional and good public relations at the same time. And the drugs are coming from here? A bit odd, that. I would think they'd come in from the East. It would be much simpler to bring them in that way instead of from the States. And a lot less risk in having the shipment stopped."

She shrugged. "One goes where one can. And it's not so risky. Dummy runs were often set up so the police would stop looking for the real ones."

"That still doesn't explain why you're here. Or about Michael John," Edwards said.

"MacCauley turned Tomas Fallon loose on it."

"Fallon! Here in New York?" A chill seemed to enter the room as he remembered the black leather-clad youth lounging against the doorway, an UZI dangling from his long, thin fingers, the age in his eyes.

"Yes, but he's outside the pale. It was the only way," she added, heading off his next question. "There's no way to tell whose fingers are dirty."

"I see. So he's alone?"

"He had Michael John, but a bullet laid him out. He's in hospital. Oh, he'll be all right, but he's out of the picture now. Yes, Fallon's alone."

"And so you are taking Michael John's place," he said.

She nodded. "'Tis something that can't be done alone."

"Is that it?"

"I don't know what you mean," she said, her brow furrowing.

"I think you do. He's another Conor Larkin. A bit younger, but there's no difference between them. What is there about men like that that you can't shake?"

She refused to meet his eyes. "It's what we all are. It's Ireland."

"Nonsense. They're not rebels anymore. They're only gunmen, killers who are using the past for committing atrocities. People like them try to justify today by making the past virtuous, but that doesn't work. The past served a purpose then, but not now. You can't keep reinventing the past for today. That's the business of tyrants and dictators. The days of the romantic gunman belong to the historians. They don't even make good films anymore because people have learned how to distinguish between necessity and brutality. You're an intelligent woman: surely, you can see that."

"Do you know the story about Sweeney?" she asked.

He made an impatient gesture. "The madman. Sure. Yeats and Eliot."

"One is fair and the other bigoted. But 'tis no matter. It isn't the story of a madman; it's the story of all the Irish.

> "Amocht is fúar, an snechta
> fodeachta is búan no bhocta,
> nidom neirt isin deabuidh
> im geilt romgeophuin gorta."

"You've lost me," he said, shaking his head.

"That's usually the case with Americans arrogant enough to think they can understand the Irish."

"Or the Irish arrogant enough to think that others are incapable of understanding them," he flashed in return. "I don't speak Irish or Gaelic. Ninety-five percent of the world doesn't. Does that make you elite or out of step?"

"Sorry. Sorry," she said hastily. "I was out of line. I don't know why I did that. Habit, I guess."

"There're a lot of habits that should be broken," he answered stiffly. "So you want to tell me what that was all about?"

"The whole key is poverty—poverty forever—and Sweeney, wanting to flee across the crowded sea, but he cannot for he's in tattered rags in the cold snow."

"I don't quite think that I'm most Americans anymore than you're most Irish," he said testily, still a bit angry. "It's still reinventing the past whenever it's convenient to do so."

"Perhaps I'd better go." She made to rise, but he stretched out his hand, stopping her and shaking his head ruefully.

"Please stay. I'm sorry. We should talk about something else. I'm a bit garrulous. The drink does that to a man, you know. Isn't that what you Irish say? The devil has him by the throat?"

She stared into his eyes, seeing the old hurt struggling within him. "Are you sure?" she asked. "I don't want the past between us."

He shook his head. "There's nothing we can do about that. It'll always be there. But what we can do is go forward."

"Con, it is an obligation," she said.

"No, it isn't. But you are too close to it to see it differently. Are you in love with him?"

The sudden question stunned her, and she leaned back away from it. "Lord, no," she said shakily. "Sure, but there're a few years between us for that to be."

A half-smile tugged at his lips. He leaned forward to collect his glass. "There're not that many, Maeve. The years matter only to those who let them. They are only a convenience, not an excuse. Why did you come here? Fallon?"

"You're the only one he knows in New York," she said. "He'll get in touch with you."

Edwards laughed and drained his glass. He swallowed twice, convulsively, against the liquor's burn. "I'm not the best-loved among your friends, Maeve. Or have you forgotten the night in Mullaghmore when I brought the British in? You weren't very pleased and neither were your friends who thought me only a little better than Liam Drumm."

And briefly the painful memory came back to her. Ah, yes, my beauty, and weren't you something all stretched out on the table for me and my mates (whispering, whispering, chewing her world up into granules), you weren't too proud then, my beauty, and the Brits coming in to save them with MacCauley and Fallon suddenly behind to keep the Brits from interfering and Con slowly explaining who could I go to and the pistol bucking in my hand as Liam Drumm screamed and held himself, begging, begging—

"You could never be a Liam Drumm," she said, forcing the memory away.

"No? Then why didn't you come with me? I was offering marriage, you know."

"Sure, and it's for the asking that I'm thanking you. But it wasn't the time, Con. Not then."

"How about now?"

She caught her breath, then forced a laugh. "It's a gentleman you are, Con Edwards. There's no mistaking that. After all these years—"

"Would you?" he interrupted.

She leaned forward and picked up her glass, draining it. She shook her head, avoiding his eyes, staring into the fire. "It seems the time is still not right."

"Will it ever be?" His words seemed thicker, now, but she knew it wasn't the whiskey making them so. For a moment, she felt the word "yes" forming itself in her throat. It would be good—very good—and why are you being so foolish with a man who loves you so? But she swallowed the word.

"I don't know," she said softly. She stared into the fire away from him, unwilling to look at the hurt she knew was there upon his face. The fire was warm on her and the whiskey warm inside her, yet she felt a coldness that couldn't be touched by either fire or whiskey, and she recognized that coldness over which she had no control, the coldness that was a part of the life of each Irish man and woman, a part of their heritage, a cataloguing of years and names and dates: Cromwell, William of Orange, gallowglasses, white boys, *gombeen* men, the rising—all of it summed up in two words: Sinn Fein: ourselves alone.

He cleared his throat, and she heard the gurgle of the Bushmill's being poured into their glasses.

"I have a bit of time coming; is there anything I can do for you?" he asked gruffly.

"Thank you, Con. Thank you for that." She took his hand, squeezing.

"Ah, go on with you," he said in a terrible Irish accent. She smiled.

"Friends?"

"For now."

They drank, and he rose and went to the kitchen for more ice, saying, "Now, then: tell me everything, and let's see what we've got."

Relieved to have the awkwardness behind them, she began.

29

FALLON WATCHED AS MAEVE MET CON EDWARDS OUTSIDE HIS door, and waited until the door closed behind them before emerging from the shadows across the street and walking west back toward the Cistercian hospice. The street lamps cast a soft nimbus through the snow now falling heavily, thick, wet flakes that covered the roofs of cars and streets and sidewalks with an eiderdown quilt. Lights flickered cheerfully through the bay windows of the houses he passed. Faint strains of music reached out to him, calling cheerfully a celebration of the season of hope to which he silently uttered the cry, *Abba! Adonai!* and felt the loneliness of the night falling upon his black-coated shoulders. His hair, now bleached blond—almost white—showed beneath the fedora with its brim down-turned, and his priestly collar glowed from beneath his chin. Under his arm the CZ-52 nestled comfortably, having been dismantled and smuggled over in pieces beneath a communion set, the bottom carefully lined with thin lead sheeting to foil airport scanners. An old friend he encountered at Dillon's in Dingle had carefully altered the case for him, remarking at the time the silliness of it all as weapons were cheap to be had in America and the risk of discovery not worth the chance. But the security of familiarity had prompted Fallon to insist, and he had bought a dozen bottles of Harp beer as they adjourned to the man's cottage off Inch Strand where the man had his shop filled with a Herbert lathe, a Myford, and a Boley watchmaker's lathe next to a Boxford shaper and Senior milling machine. The job took nine bottles, two for Fallon and seven for the worker, the last causing him to squint against the tubular light as he carefully reglued the red velvet back into place over the altered communion box.

The trip over had been relaxing except for a middle-aged, mousy Iowa schoolteacher who had worriedly confessed her sins from her Irish fling. Fallon was amazed at the number of men she had slept with, the last a ménage à quatre on the eve of her departure, leaving him amused enough to give absolution in the quiet of the evening in the front section of the Aer Lingus airplane. It would do no harm for he was sure it would be a repeated confession under more formal circumstances for the schoolteacher struck him as one who would repeat the confession several times for reassurance and reminder of the time she had had away from the strictures of her profession.

Customs had been easy; a quick question and chalk marks on the sides of his luggage—one suitcase and the communion case—for a priest seemed to have an unreserved immunity from question of wrongdoing, the collar serving as an emblem of sanctity for the layman.

A door flung open from a bar across the street startled him in the quiet of the night, and he stepped quickly next to a lamppost as two men staggered out into the snowy night, arm in arm, their voices harmonizing despite the season in affirmation of the joy of Christmas with chestnuts roasting on an open fire and Jack Frost nipping at their collective noses in nostalgic remembrance of Christmas past. Behind them the light from the bar threw a yellow path of welcome out onto the snow as music flew through the door after them and soared out into the night. The mullioned window of the bar had been hung with tiny red and white lights and green shamrocks lightly frosted with half-moons of artificial snow for St. Patrick's Day. He watched the singers stagger down the street. A shadow moved in a doorway. He frowned. He had sensed something behind him since leaving Edwards's apartment. You're getting old, he chided himself.

On impulse, Fallon stepped out into the street and crossed to the bar. Over the door in bas-relief lettering he read: BRENNAN'S. Brian Boru's harp had been painted in gold gilt on the glass of the door. He turned the knob, opened the door, and went inside the warmth. A group of men stood around the lower end of the bar, pints in their fists, faces reddened from drink, lustily singing to the accompaniment of a piano played by a young blind man. Two women sat quietly at a small table nearby, glasses of sherry in front of them, patiently waiting, tolerating with good humor their husbands' participation in the songfest.

The bartender smiled cheerfully at Fallon as he approached the bar. "Happy Easter, Father," he said.

"A bit early for that, isn't it, now?" Fallon asked. The bartender's eyebrows lifted.

"From Ireland?" Fallon nodded. The bartender extended his hand across the bar. "Welcome, welcome. I'm Brennan." Fallon shook his hand.

"Father Fallon," he said. He gestured at the shining copper fixtures. "Your place?"

"Such as it is," Brennan said modestly, but Fallon heard the pride in his voice. "What'll you have?"

"Bushmill's, if it's no bother," Fallon said. "And a large one against the cold, if you please."

"A clear pleasure," Brennan answered. With deft motions, he placed a thick-bottomed tumbler on the bar and filled it with a practiced twist of his wrist. He waved away Fallon's money. "Your money's no good in here," he said. "A priest drinks free in Brennan's, and one from the old land doubly so. Where are you from?"

"County Kerry," Fallon said, sipping the whiskey. "And many thanks. And you?"

Brennan made a face. "From Brooklyn. Third generation." He leaned forward, speaking conspiratorially, proudly. "My grandfather came from Cobh after the 'Rising' failed. He was with them, you know. Killed a black-and-tan with that." He turned and proudly pointed to an old chrome Webley and blackthorn shillelagh with a rawhide wriststrap mounted on a walnut board hanging above the back mirror.

"And a good man, he was," Fallon said. He pointed to his glass. "Would you be joining me in a drink to him and his friends of the Easter Rising?"

Brennan beamed and produced another glass from beneath the bar, twisting a large dollop of whiskey into the glass. "And proud I am to lift one with you," he said.

They lifted their glasses and drank. Brennan immediately refilled them, lifting his and intoning, "May you die in Ireland."

"Aye, but by Jesus and Mary not for a while, yet," Fallon answered. Brennan laughed, sputtering into his drink.

"You're the strangest priest I've ever met, Father," he said, recovering from his laughter. The piano player rolled into "The Bells of St. Mary's" and the singers briefly buried their noses in their pints before breaking into song.

"We all do our part," Fallon answered.

Brennan winked, and leaned over the bar, lowering his voice. "We all do. Some of the Sons of Erin gather a fund twice a year for the cause, you know, Father. We may live here, but our hearts are there." He thumped his chest proudly. "And I'm the one who collects it all."

"And what do you do with it, then? Surely, you're not sending it to the Provos. 'Tis a bad lot they are, and more to come that doesn't need help from here, I'm thinking. The day for that is gone; what is left must come from the government. Although," he added, "'tis a failing that appeals to a lot of Irishmen."

Brennan smiled and shook his head. "We give it to NORAID. I

figure there're others for that. You know, the hotheads who do their talking with a drink in their fists." His face clouded for an instant. "Most of them are in Blackie Cassidy's Silver Street Gang up in South Boston. But I don't think they'd be a match for the old ones." He looked up reverently at the pistol on the wall. "I'm sure my grandfather would agree. For all his part in the 'Rising,' he felt for the people more."

"NORAID? Michael Flannery and Martin Galvin? You've met them, then?" Fallon asked.

"Oh, sure," Brennan said offhandedly. He refilled their glasses. "There's not an Irish bar in all New York that hasn't. But I don't do business with them. I turn everything over to Tommy Coughlan who does the collections for them. He comes down from Boston to collect from us." He pointed at a large bowl half-filled with paper money and coins. A sign pasted on the glass showed a picture of a child with hungry eyes and the legend SAVE THE CHILDREN. "It's the one good thing Cassidy's people do—when they're not bilking people out of their lottery winnings or trying to sell their peculiar insurance—you know," he said to Fallon's raised eyebrow, "the guarantee that nothing will happen to your business if you take out a policy with them."

"I see. Well, now, isn't this a convenience, though?" Fallon said. "I have a wee bit of business with them. Would you be knowing how I might get in touch with them? Some of us are trying to raise a little money for the orphans. We'd like to help expand Reverend Ray Davey's work up at Corrymeela. Have you heard about it, now?"

Brennan shook his head, twin lines of disapproval appearing between his eyes. "A Protestant? Those who are causing our Troubles?"

Fallon smiled faintly. *Our* Troubles, is it? A common affliction among the Americans who want to be Irish.

"But a good man, nevertheless," Fallon said. "There are victims on both sides and so far, the Protestants are the only ones who are doing much of anything on such a grand scale for the children who are victims of the Troubles."

"I see," Brennan said, a smile breaking across his beefy face. He winked. "It would be helpful in the 'negotiations' if the good people can point to a similar operation run by priests. Is that the figuring? Especially now with the cease-fire?"

Fallon let a small smile play on his lips. "You see the good of it all, then?"

"Oh, I do." The other laughed. "For a moment, there, you had me worried, Father. But now I can see that you're one of us after all."

"Then you'll put me in touch with Coughlan?"

"I'll do better than that. I've got his number. You're welcome to it," Brennan said. He crossed to the cash register at the back of the bar. He reached beneath the register and removed a small black book. He opened it, found the number, and copied it onto a cocktail napkin. He returned the book to its resting place and crossed back to Fallon, handing him the napkin.

"I hope this helps you," he said. He reached into his pocket and removed a large number of bills held together by a money clip in the shape of a claddagh. He peeled two off and handed them to Fallon. "And here," he said roughly, "is a bit to help you along the way, Father."

Fallon looked down at the two hundred-dollar bills. "'Tis a good heart you have, Mr. Brennan. And that I'll tell all." He slipped the bills into his pocket and lifted his glass to Brennan.

"May the saints guard you," he said. He drained the glass.

"It's nothing," Brennan said, embarrassed. "The season makes us maudlin."

"True. A glorious season; a glorious season," Fallon said. The piano player finished "The Bells of St. Mary's." Fallon nodded in his direction. "Would he be knowing 'The Kilruddery Hunt'?"

"Billy!" Brennan shouted. "Give us 'The Kilruddery Hunt'! My son," he said aside to Fallon.

The young man turned blind eyes in their direction. "Sorry, Dad. I don't know that one."

"Ah, well," Fallon said, picking up his fresh glass of whiskey and moving to the piano. "Give us room, and I'll let you hear."

The young man slid over as Fallon sat beside him. Brennan patted his son on his shoulder, saying, "We're blessed tonight, Billy. This is Father Fallon from County Kerry."

"Pleased to meet you, Father," Billy said.

"Likewise," Fallon answered. He ran his fingers over the keys, moving through a brief introduction and into the runs of the song, lifting his voice in tenor,

> "In seventeen hundred and forty-four,
> The fifth of December, I think 'twas no more."

The others gathered eagerly around him, listening intently to the man from Ireland who brought an official song with him, concentrating on the words, watching the slim fingers glide over the keys, endeavoring to bring themselves closer to their imagined heaven in the old country in the shadow of the song. And Fallon played on, repeating the song twice until they had the words before surrendering the keys to blind Billy, who stumbled through it once before remembering F-sharp and playing it faultlessly while Fallon led the others through the lyrics, linking a mystical bond through himself to them, an apostolic succession to what they called their Fatherland though none had been begetted there and none would visit, remembering it only in nostalgic verse because it had become fashionable and would remain a fashionable fraud in the safety of their land from the reality of the land they fatuously claimed as their own.

30

Simon Kenton took a deep breath and stepped out of the doorway and casually followed Fallon down the street from Edwards's apartment. He watched as he entered Brennan's then shook his head in mock derision as he saw the tail pause beside the window, look inside the bar, then slip away and enter a diner down the street. He glanced around for a backup and, seeing none, sighed heavily. Wright's boys needed further lessons in the basics. No wonder the Agency was in such a hell of a state.

He slipped back inside a darkened doorway and settled himself into his warm overcoat, thankful that he had two pairs of woolen socks on under his heavy brogans and light silk long underwear to help hold in the heat. He was warm and content except for his face and he pulled his scarf up, tying it across like a bandana, and flipped his collar up around his ears. He was comfortable—as comfortable, that is, as he was able to get. The rest of the cold he ignored by reflecting on what he had learned so far from picking up Fallon. That it was Fallon, he was certain, despite the priestly disguise and blond hair. Elementary for those used to looking past the general façade and he was quite used to that. Clever, though the customs folks should have picked up on it sooner. Priests are seldom questioned—especially those using Vatican diplomatic passports. Minor officials are usually unwilling to chance raising international outrage over diplomatic immunity. During the Cold

War years that had caused a lot of headaches in the Russian House.

A tiny smile flickered over his thin lips. Of course that had little to do with his old department, which had carte blanche with those dealings until the altruists of the Reagan administration came to power and later the new Democrats, who pried their way into areas that didn't concern them, questioning each tiny detail of government business that was best left alone. He frowned. A lot of good agents resigned in disgust over that. And a lot of departments had been closed in the name of "streamlining" the budget in order to keep prying eyes from probing too deeply into Company business. He sighed. And that flooded the market with too many mercenaries willing to freelance for various governments.

Enough, he told himself. Where has Fallon been hiding himself? There're no shortage of Catholic churches and parish houses around the city. He could be in any one of them. You can't take him here; too risky. You need some place where he repeats himself. Where you can set up ahead of time and wait.

He sighed and shifted his feet slightly, slouching into a corner away from the occasional wind that whipped coldly down the street, dancing a white cloud ahead of it. That there was such a place Fallon frequented, he was certain. All men were creatures of habit even if they tried not to be. And that was the weakness of everyone. Even yourself, he reminded himself. Although what it is, I don't know. And if you stay in the business long enough, you will be in the same situation and someone will find you and someone will kill you. Either that, or someone will get lucky and stumble upon you by accident. The two enemies of an agent: habit and chance. Neither one could be fully guarded against. But that in itself was invigorating. Like having the sword of Damocles hanging over your head on a slender thread. Sooner or later it would drop. It was the "when" that was fascinating.

He heard the strains of "The Kilruddery Hunt" roll out of the pub and his lip curled with distaste. The Irish and their damned sentimental airs. Always carrying their nationalism on their arms like a badge of honor. But that too was predictable. His pulse quickened. Perhaps that was Fallon's weakness? The pub was not so much a watering hole as it was a social gathering. Now if he could only find where he was staying, perhaps there was a pub within easy distance of his room. And if so, then that could be where he could dispense with the great and mystical Mr. Fallon. Poison slipped into the pint? The ice pick up under the shoulderblade? Or simply a bullet as he walked out of the pub half-blinded from the pub's lights into the dark street?

He bent to his task, brow furrowing in thought.

31

THE HARSH NOTES OF THE TELEPHONE JERKED TOMMY COUGHLAN awake, pawing his way over the top of the sleeping Anne to pull the insistent instrument from its cradle. She protested crossly and curled away from him as he growled sleepily into it.

"This better be damn good." A dull ache began throbbing in his left temple; his mouth tasted harsh and fierce from the bourbon drunk the night before. Hangovers were bad enough in the morning after a full night's sleep, let alone—he glanced at the clock on the table beside the telephone—when one had been asleep only four hours.

A quiet chuckle answered his words. "Ah, now, Mr. Coughlan. Sure, 'tis not inconveniencing you, I am, but there's a wee problem that we need to be discussing. A matter of a certain agreement made between two parties and here we have someone ignoring that agreement. A sad thing that is. And there's the matter of an additional shipment that's also not wanted. Now it's come to my attention that you may be the one who would be able to help me resolve all that. Do you ken what I'm saying, now?"

"Who the hell is this?" Coughlan demanded. "And what the fuck you doin' callin' me in the middle of the night?"

"I would like to meet you say tomorrow evening at eight by the clock at O'Grady's on Eighth Street."

"Fuck you," Coughlan snarled.

"It isn't a request," Fallon said quietly. "Be there, Mr. Coughlan. I don't want to come looking for you." He abruptly hung up.

A cold chill ran across Coughlan's flesh. He stared stupidly at the receiver for a minute before slamming it down. Anne moaned in protest and rolled over, staring at him. She ran a hand down his naked back. He shrugged irritably and reached for the crumpled packet of cigarettes on the nightstand beside the bed. He fished one from the packet and jabbed it into his mouth, lighting it and drawing acrid smoke deep into his lungs. He coughed, expelling smoke in tiny gasps.

"What is it?" Anne asked.

"Some fucking bastard telling me to meet him at O'Grady's. Me! Tommy Coughlan! As if I'm a fucking glazier's boy to be running here and there for putty and nails!"

"Who was it?" she asked, sliding up in bed. The sheet fell away, exposing her breasts, large dark nipples like plums. She took the cigarette from his fingers, drew on it, and handed it back.

"Some fucking bog-trotter," he grumbled. "As if I'm supposed to jump to his orders. Fuck him."

"Fallon," she said.

He paused, squinting through the smoke at her. "You think?"

"It sounds like him."

"Fuck him."

"A lot have tried. What are you going to do?"

"Nothing."

"That'll only bring him here," she said. "You don't know what he's like."

"And you do, I suppose?"

"It was him and another who caught me at Black Jenny's place. I was lucky to get away. Not many do."

"He's that good, you think?"

"I know he's that good. He has to be to have been around as long as he has. Especially in Belfast."

"Belfast?"

"He's MacCauley's boy; I told you that before."

"The Provo?" She nodded, watching as his face screwed up, searching memory. Then his face relaxed as memory dawned. "*That* Fallon we got the call about before? I'm supposed to be worried about someone like that? Someone swipes the milk from a Prod's doorstep and they're singing fucking songs about him that night."

"He's real enough," she said. "And he's called you. You'll have to do something about him if you don't want him here, I'm telling you. He's not one of your jolly boys who'll be doing the weekend business. They don't even say his name loudly in Belfast but that he might hear."

"This ain't fucking Belfast," he snarled.

She eyed him thoughtfully for a moment, then said, "Let me tell you a bit about this Fallon—"

"I don't wanna hear no more," he said, covering his ears. "I'll send some of Daddy's boys from the docks to make the meet at O'Grady's. After he gets out of the hospital, he'll be all too glad to catch the boat back to old Ireland."

"You'd better make it a lot of boys, then, and not ones you'll be needin' again, I'm thinkin'."

"Nobody's that good," he said.

"Eight wasn't enough when they surprised him in Falls Road one day. And sure, didn't the Royal Fusiliers send eight new black coffins back home after he was done?"

"Careless."

"You're a stupid man," she replied. She swung her legs out of bed and walked to the bathroom. "Send your men, but don't be planning anything more for them after." She closed the door to the bathroom. He waited until he heard the water running, then picked up the telephone and dialed a number from memory.

"He's called," he said when the telephone was picked up on the other end. "He wants to meet me tomorrow night at O'Grady's. I'm sending a couple of men instead." He listened for a moment, then hung up the telephone. He reached for the bottle of bourbon on the floor beside the bed and took a dirty glass from the nightstand. He drank, shuddered, poured another and drank again.

And now, bucko, we'll just see how fuckin' good you are—if there's anything left of you after my boys are finished.

32

FALLON STOOD ACROSS THE STREET FROM O'GRADY'S, HIS HANDS shoved deep into the pockets of the overcoat loaned him by a kindly priest at the Cistercian hostel after he heard Fallon was going out that night. It was a good coat, heavy and lined and the pockets deep enough to hold his pistol in the right-hand one. His fingers curled around the butt, his thumb on the hammer and rear sight to prevent snagging if he should have to remove it in a hurry.

Warm light sent a cheerful glow through the windows of O'Grady's, spilling out through the panes decorated with green-sprayed shamrocks. Fallon smelled the fecund odor of garbage from the overflowing cans in the alley behind him over the cold and wet air. Faint strains of music carried across the dirty slush to him from the bar, and he recognized the cheerful notes of Brendan Grace singing "I sell apples and oranges..." and he hummed softly to himself the tune of "Biddy Mulligan" as he waited patiently in the dark mouth of the alley. He moved his feet, gently working his toes to keep them warm in the thin leather shoes. The fedora's brim had been pulled low to keep the wind from tearing his eyes. The priest's collar glowed softly beneath his chin.

He watched as two men rounded the corner at the end of the block and started casually toward the bar. He glanced to the other end and noticed another pair walking toward the first pair. They wore black watch caps pulled down over their ears and heavy coats and steel-toed boots. His eyes narrowed: they were out of place in the neighborhood; they belonged in a working-class area close to the docks. He watched as they met in front of the door. The first pair went inside while the other two lounged on either side of the door. One of them eased his hand out of his pocket, and Fallon caught the glint of metal as he tucked it behind him. A small grin touched the corners of Fallon's lips. The others came out. The taller one shook his head at the other two. They huddled together, and Fallon stepped out of the shadows, crossing the street toward them. One stiffened and nudged the man next to him as he noticed Fallon's approach. Then he saw the collar and relaxed. The second one nodded as Fallon walked up to him.

"Good evening, Father," he said, the nasal vowels marking him from Brooklyn. Rheum dripped from his nose, and he wiped it away with the back of his hand. His face was mottled blue from the cold, and Fallon smelled raw whiskey rising from him as he came to a stop five feet away, slightly turning his left side to them and signing the cross with his left hand to draw their attention as he slipped the pistol from his pocket with the other.

"May Saint Brigid and Mary and Joseph be with you," he said. They stiffened at the sound of his voice and slowly began to move apart. Hands crept toward pockets, but Fallon watched the one in front of him who had taken something metal from his pocket. "Sure, and 'tis a cold evening to be standing outside in the foulness when there's cheer and warmth inside. Now, why would four fine fellows like yourselves be wasting your time on the sidewalk when you could be leaning your elbows on the bar inside and having a drop of the hardest? Would one of you be Tommy Coughlan?"

"Fallon," the one in front said.

"Yes," Fallon said. He swung the pistol up and shot him in the kneecap. He cursed as he fell to the ground, a hammerless revolver flying from his fingers as he tried to break his fall, then the pain hit, and he screamed and tried to hug his knee to him, then screamed again as the broken bones ground together.

"Shit!" another yelled, and tried to jerk a pistol from his coat. Fallon's bullet caught him in the shoulder, breaking it. He spun backward and fell, falling onto his wounded side. He rolled over and vomit streaked from his mouth.

Coolly, Fallon swung the pistol to another. The man threw up his hands, and Fallon dropped the barrel and pulled the trigger, blowing the man's kneecap out the back of his knee. The man fell, cracking his head against the concrete; he lay still as blood began seeping down the cracks in the sidewalk to the gutter.

The last man freed his pistol and fired a wild shot that ricocheted off the brick building across the street and sang down the alley. Then he turned and began running down the street as fast as he could. Fallon raised the pistol as if on a firing line. The man felt a powerful blow as the bullet slammed into his spine, knocking him forward flat on the pavement. He stared, dazed at the rough concrete inches in front of his eyes. He opened his mouth, then the light faded, and he died, wondering what he was doing on the ground.

A low moan came from the man lying in a pool of vomit and blood at Fallon's feet. Slowly, he rolled onto his side, curling himself into a fetal ball. Fallon knelt on one knee beside him.

"Tommy Coughlan?" he asked.

Sweat beaded the man's face, and he squeezed his eyes tightly shut against the pain beginning to build out of the shock of the bullet. Fallon gripped him hard by the shoulder, shaking him.

"Coughlan?" he asked again.

The man opened his eyes, staring into Fallon's. "Jesus," he whispered. "I'm shot."

"Yes. Coughlan, now. Which was he?"

The man shook his head, gasping against the pain the movement caused him. "Not here. He sent us. Ah, God!"

Fallon shook him again. "Where'll I find him?"

"Boston. Now," he gasped. A trickle of saliva slowly fell like a spider's filament from the corner of his mouth to the gray concrete.

"Where?" Fallon demanded.

"Don't know—Timmy O'Brien, maybe—" His eyes glazed, and the man fainted.

The door burst open behind Fallon as people squeezed out of the bar.

"Jesus Christ!" someone said in an awed voice.

"It's a priest!"

"He's got a gun!"

"Call the cops!"

A woman screamed.

A bullet snapped past Fallon's ear and broke the glass window of the pub. Fallon rolled quickly on his toes, spinning away from the man, glancing behind him. He caught a slight movement in a doorway and reflexively threw himself backward, flat on the pavement as another bullet snapped over him. He fired three times rapidly at the doorway as he rose quickly to his feet and ran across the street into the black alley.

"Get him!" someone shouted.

"Fuck that! He's got a gun!"

"A priest!"

Fallon ran deeper into the alley, the darkness comfortable around him, making his way through the alley, then another, feeling the familiarity of being home.

But who had fired those shots?

33

KENTON SWORE AND DUCKED BACK INTO THE DOORWAY AS FALLON'S shots chipped the brick and ricocheted down the street away from him. He glanced back out as Fallon raced across the street and into the alley. He sighed and carefully slipped the silenced .32 Walther inside his coat. He slipped his hand inside his coat pocket and touched the .25-cal. pistol he kept for emergencies there, sliding the safety on and off. When he had seen Fallon move against the thugs—he frowned, wondering who had sent them and why—the gamble had suggested itself One of those accidents that had suddenly fallen his way. Just bad luck that his first shot had missed.

He shook his head admiringly. Fallon was quick. One of the quickest he had seen. A warm feeling crept over him and he smiled in the darkness. Any doubts he had had about the worthiness of Fallon as an opponent were gone. He could understand now how the man had lasted so long in such a risky business. He had a natural feel for it. Like he had, Kenton admitted. He had no doubts about his own ability: any who did were quickly dead. Confidence was necessary and to find another one with the same ruthlessness to be that confident was exhilarating.

He turned and slipped quietly out of the doorway, walking back away from the pub. Only a fool would follow Fallon down that alley. He had tried and lost. And he had lost his chance at

catching Fallon at the Cistercian house where he had been staying. Only a fool would return there and Fallon was obviously too
good to be that foolish. But he would need a bolt-hole and
Edwards's place was the obvious place to go. There or Brennan's,
and another pub was too obvious. Yes, it would be Edwards's
apartment. Man was a creature of habit. At least it was a worthy
gamble.

He found a telephone booth and stepped inside. He dropped a
quarter in the slot, then dialed a number, waited for the the line to
clear, then tapped in four more numbers. He whistled softly as he
waited. He spoke quickly, giving the telephone number he was
calling from and disconnected the call, pretending to talk while
he waited for the call back.

34

WILLIAM CASSIDY HAD NOT BEEN ASLEEP LONG WHEN THE TELE-
phone rang beside his bed. He rolled over and groggily lifted it.
"Hello?" he said. He coughed and repeated himself.

"Billy? That you?"

He sat up in bed and turned on the bed light. "Blackie?" He
glanced at the clock: 4:00 A.M. "Do you have any idea what time
it is?"

"Yeah, I keep forgetting that." Blackie chuckled. "But you
always were an early riser."

William closed his eyes. "What do you want, Blackie?" he asked
tiredly.

"Now is that any way to greet me? After all I've done for you?"

"And what is that?" William asked.

"How soon they forget."

"Coughlan came to see me. Is that what you called about? If so,
he gave me the warning. I appreciate it and good night."

"Knock it off, Billy!" Blackie said sharply. "This is serious."

William sighed. "Everything is serious with you, Blackie. And if
it isn't serious, you make it serious. I'm tired of this. It seems I'm
always pulling you out of one scrape after the other. Remember
when you tried to stiff Donohue with those jukeboxes in his tavern down in Quincy? He went to the FBI over that."

"And the FBI got what they wanted," Blackie snapped.

"As did you," William snapped back. "You managed to work that informant routine fairly well to your advantage. The FBI's arrested most of your competition."

"Is there a point to all of this?"

"Yes," William said. "Leave me alone. I'm through. I have my own life to lead and it isn't as part of Blackie Cassidy's Silver Street Gang."

Silence grew and William listened to the seashell echo of the ether as he waited for Blackie to answer. He closed his eyes, picturing his brother seething, the red slowly gathering in his neck then surging upward in a rush to infuse his face. His eyes would bulge and a large vein would pound in his forehead and—

"William, you goddamn do what I tell you, hear? I don't have the time to argue with you. Who knows if your line ain't tapped. Remember what happened in the past when you wouldn't listen to me?"

Automatically William's fingers touched the scar beneath his pajama top where Blackie's knife had sliced him when they were children and he wouldn't give Blackie the money he had collected from selling empty pop bottles when his brother had demanded it. He had been saving for a year to buy a bicycle and Blackie, five years older, had had a date with Rosie O'Neill, the neighborhood nymph. Eight stitches had been needed to close that, but Blackie got the money and Rosie that night.

"I remember," he said wearily. "What is it you want?"

"That's better." A quiet chuckle came down the line. "Not as much has changed since South Boston as you think, has it, Billy?"

"No," he said quietly.

"I want you to get in touch with a man named Simon Kenton and tell him that I want this loose cannon running around over there stopped. Don't call Coughlan and tell him. From what I hear, this Fallon may do a good job of upsetting the balance of things before Coughlan gets lucky. And some things Coughlan doesn't need to know. Understand?"

"Yes."

"Now you do this, Billy," he said, his voice dropping and tightening. "I don't want to have to come back there and do it myself. Understand?"

"How do I get in touch with this Simon Kenton?"

"That's better. Hey, when this is all over, why don't you come on over here and we'll tour around a little? Okay?" Blackie said, and William pictured the shark's smile spreading across his brother's predatory features.

William hung up the telephone after Blackie's instructions and stared at it for a long minute, then rose and dressed in his robe and padded silently downstairs to his study. He went to his desk and sat, thumbing through his address book for the NORAID number and Martin Galvin. He dialed the number, and when a sleepy voice answered, said, "Martin?—William Cassidy.—I'm sorry to disturb you at this hour, but something has come up. I need to get in touch with the Provo Belfast commander. Can you help me?"

As he waited he opened a drawer and removed a telephone directory. He found the number for the Federal Bureau of Investigation under GOVERNMENT, FEDERAL.

"Yes?—Thank you, Martin—No, I don't know when he'll get back.—Certainly. I would be happy to tell him for you.—Thanks."

He hung up and stared at the number he had written on his desk pad for a long minute. Then he sighed and punched in the numbers for an overseas call.

35

THE CONTINUAL BUZZING WORKED ITS WAY THROUGH THE THICK cotton of sleep, jarring Con Edwards awake. He groped for the alarm, punching blindly in the dark at its "OFF" button, swearing when he realized it was the door and not the alarm. He rose in the dark and groped his way through the bedroom, pulling on his robe as he went. He stubbed his toe painfully against the jamb, swore again, and flipped the light switch on in the living room as he hobbled to the door. He opened the intercom and growled, "Who the hell is this?"

A quiet laugh answered him. "Now, is that any way to be greeting old friends?" a soft voice asked. "'Tis most happy you are to be seeing me, I'm thinking."

"Fallon?"

"Sure, and there's a good many by that name, and me alone and shivering on your doorstep without so much as a by-your-leave or invitation to enter and share a jar."

Edwards pushed the electric release on the door. "Second floor. The front apartment facing the street," he said. He flipped off the intercom switch and vigorously rubbed his hands through his hair. He hurried into the bathroom and rinsed the thick taste of the night from his mouth with mouthwash, and went into the kitchen and turned on the drip coffee machine he'd made ready only a few hours before. He glanced at the wall clock: 2:00 A.M.

Christ! The bloody Irish have no awareness of time. He started for the bedroom, then changed directions in mid-stride at the soft knock at his door. He checked the safety chain, then opened the door a crack.

A blond-haired priest smiled back at him. He blinked in confusion.

"Yes, it's me," the priest said. Edwards hurriedly closed the door and slipped the chain free, opening it again and standing aside as Fallon entered. Edwards shut the door, locked it, and stood for a moment with his back against it, considering the man in front of him.

"You've changed," he said. "More than the hair and the clothes, I mean."

Tired lines radiated finely from the corners of Fallon's eyes and mouth. His cheeks seemed sunken, gray, and dark half-moons rested under his eyes. His hair showed colors of straw and silver and a faint streak of black where the bleach had not quite reached and had been closely cropped, but it was something in his eyes looking back at him that Edwards first noticed. There was a depth, a meaning there, that he did not remember.

"Time does it to all of us," Fallon said. He stood close to the wall, away from the windows. "Are you alone?"

"Maeve's here," Edwards answered. Fallon glanced automatically at the bedroom door standing open. "No, not that one." Edwards gestured at the second door. "There."

Fallon nodded, checking the rest of the apartment.

"You don't seem surprised."

"I saw her," Fallon said.

"When?"

"Two days ago. I was watching your place when she came," he answered.

"How did you find me?" Con asked.

"I called the *Times*. Doors open for a priest, you know."

"Speaking of which," Con began, but Fallon interrupted. "Is that coffee I'm smelling?"

"Sorry. I'm forgetting my hostly duties. Would you like some?" He moved toward the kitchen. "It'll just take a minute."

"And a bit of whiskey to give it courage, if you can manage," Fallon answered. He crossed to the couch and gratefully lowered himself onto it, feeling the day wash over him again. He closed his eyes, gently massaging them with the balls of his fingers.

"Tomas?"

He opened his eyes. Maeve stood uncertainly in the door to her room, clutching a green robe close about her neck. Her hair fell in rumpled waves to her shoulders. Her face gleamed almost translucent. Tiny lines appeared between her eyebrows.

"Now, were you expecting another?" he asked. Con appeared in the kitchen doorway at the sound of their voices.

"I'm making coffee," he said. "Would you like a cup?"

"Please," she said. "Plain." He nodded and went back into the kitchen. She turned to Fallon, crossing and sitting beside him on the couch. "I think I see how you got in. Your brother's passport."

"Yes."

"I wondered how you would work that."

His forehead wrinkled. "And Michael John. How is he?"

"Fine. The Gardai are not amused with the tale he's been telling them. They know him from their files," she added.

"And MacCauley?"

"Mad. Like Sweeney. You're making a lot of waves, Tomas."

"There's no help for it," he said softly. "'Tis a dirty business that wants a bit of cleaning."

Edwards appeared from the kitchen, gingerly carrying a tray on which he had placed three cups in their saucers, a pot of coffee, and a bottle of Bushmill's. He placed the tray on the coffee table in front of the couch, then took a chair opposite them. Fallon eyed the bottle.

"A northern whiskey, but the better of the two. You're a man of distinction," he said with satisfaction.

"Maeve filled me in on some of the happenings," Con said, ignoring Fallon. He reached out and poured a dollop of the whiskey into his and Fallon's cups before adding the coffee. He filled Maeve's cup with coffee and handed it to her, then took his and leaned back in his chair, sipping.

Fallon nodded, taking his saucer and cup from the tray. "It's been difficult."

Con's eyebrows raised. "Trouble?"

"A bit. A very foolish man sent a few men to speak with me in his place."

"And?"

"They had nothing to say I wanted to hear."

"Who was it?" Maeve asked. She took a tiny sip from her cup.

"Tommy Coughlan," Fallon answered. "I found his number by accident and rang him up. We were to meet at O'Grady's." He looked at Edwards. "Would you be knowing it?"

"Yes. Good friends," Con said. He placed his cup and saucer back on the table. "What happened?" he asked quietly.

Fallon sighed and took a drink before answering. "Coughlan sent some of his boys instead. I don't think they wanted to talk."

"Was there a shooting?" Maeve asked.

"Unfortunately," Fallon answered. He caught the sudden look on Con's face. "It was outside the bar," he added.

Relief showed on his face, and Con leaned forward, asking, "Anyone killed?"

"Yes."

"Were you seen?"

"That's why I came here. They'll be looking for a priest, now— an *Irish* priest," he added meaningfully. "It won't take them long to figure out, I'm sure."

"Interpol," Maeve said thoughtfully.

"And others," Con said sourly. "Don't sell our police short: they have a lot of files available to them through the wonderful world of computers." He looked at Maeve. "Eventually, they'll put it all together after they run everything through the network. The British will share what they have on you and me. That business in Ireland a few years back will still be in the files somewhere. I don't think we have much time."

"Especially since you saw fit to bring them in," she said pointedly. Fallon held up his hand. "Peace, peace. Your sharp tongue will get us nowhere, Maeve. How much time do we have?" he asked Edwards.

Con frowned and picked up his cup. He filled it with whiskey, ignoring the coffee. He took a large drink, shuddered, and said, "Not more than a couple of days. We're okay tonight and tomorrow, I think. The next day would be a gamble." He looked critically at Fallon's clothes. "We'll have to get you out of those."

"I'll go out in the morning," Maeve said. "Give me your sizes."

"Good," Fallon answered. He finished his coffee and looked at Con. "And there's something you can do too if you're willing. I know I'm putting a lot upon you, but—" He shrugged, letting his voice trail off.

"I'll help," Con said. He gestured toward Maeve. "For her sake, though. I don't want you to get the wrong idea, Fallon."

"I won't," Fallon said calmly. "And I know. 'Tisn't much I'm asking: just an address or two to a telephone number."

"Good. As long as we're straight. I'll get you some blankets. You can use the couch." He rose and disappeared into his bedroom.

"A bit brusque," Fallon said.

"It isn't his fight, Tomas," Maeve said.

"No, it isn't. I'm beginning to wonder to whom it belongs." He lifted the bottle of whiskey and dribbled some into his cup, adding coffee.

"I know," Maeve answered. "The old ways are fast disappearing."

"If they're still there at all," Fallon said.

He glanced at her. A sense of vulnerability passed between them, isolating them, making them islands lying outside the disorder and irrational knowledge of their world and the august destiny begun by a few so many years before on the steps of the Dublin General Post Office, and they felt the loneliness of the years between them. She rose and left without speaking for her room, gently closing the door behind her. Fallon looked up and saw Edwards standing in the doorway to his bedroom, watching, holding blankets and a pillow. Silently, he crossed and placed them on the couch beside Fallon.

"Thank you," Fallon said. Edwards made a gesture of dismissal.

"Sleep tight," he said. He looked at Maeve's closed door, the muscles bunching along his jawline. He started to speak, then gave Fallon a wan smile and turned back to his bedroom.

Fallon waited until he saw the light turn out in Con's room. Then he crossed to the telephone and picked it up, dialing an international number. He waited, listening to the clicks through the ether, then the telephone was picked up on the other end.

"Uncle Dan? 'Tis Tomas here.—I'm staying with Con Edwards here in New York.—No, you don't know him, but he's a friend of sorts from the past.—With Maeve Larkin during that bloody business up at Mullaghmore years back.—Yes, that one. I'll be here awhile. Have you heard anything from MacCauley or the boyos making the runs?—No new shipments have been coming through, now?—'Tis good, 'tis good. If you hear anything, call me here." He read off the number then hung up and returned to the couch and his coffee.

He sat a moment, considering what had just transpired. Con Edwards and Maeve Nolan-Larkin. There's a bit of awkwardness there that had not been there before. Perhaps it is the past remembrances of what they had once been. But I think it runs deeper.

His brow furrowed in thought, then suddenly, unbidden, lines from an old eighth-century poem appeared in his mind:

> —and the soul of Cúchulainn appeared
> To thrice fifty queens, who had loved
> The Hound of Ulster and had combed
> His three-hued hair with golden threads
> With their hands, to them appeared
> His soul, floating in his phantom chariot
> Over Emain Macha to the lead-gray sea,
> And as he rode the war chariot, he chanted
> A mystic song whose silver notes wove
> Thrice through the air above their heads,
> Filling them with knowing dread
> Of the Day of Christ coming soon,
> Followed by the black Day of Doom.

And a great sadness fell upon him as he knew himself and what he had become to be the third man.

36

LOUDON KNOCKED EXCITEDLY TWICE ON WRIGHT'S DOOR BEFORE opening it and entering. Wright lifted his eyes from the file he had been reading. His eyebrows rose at the break in protocol as Loudon crossed the expanse from the door, a newspaper thrust out in front of him.

"We've got word from New York," he exclaimed. Wright took the paper from his trembling fingers, settled his glasses, and glanced at its contents. "You were right: he came in on his brother's passport. Our man on Edwards's apartment picked him up a day ago. He followed Fallon to Brennan's—a known IRA haunt from the early twenties when IRA gunmen made it their rendezvous in New York. De Valera used it himself when he came over on a funding jaunt after being released from British jails."

"What happened there?" Wright asked, scanning the story outlined with a heavy black marker. Loudon made a face.

"Fallon began to play the piano in the pub. It looked like he was locked in until closing time so our man took the opportunity to slip away and phone in. When he returned, Fallon was gone."

"Jesus Christ," Wright muttered. His knuckles grew white around the newspaper.

"I put two other men on," Loudon rushed. "I put a watch on

Brennan's, one on O'Grady's—another Irish hangout—and sent our original back to Edwards's apartment. Fallon surfaced at O'Grady's in that shooting"—he pointed at the story in Wright's hands—"and we followed him back to Edwards's place. He's there now. Or at least he was"—he glanced at the watch on his wrist—"fifteen minutes ago."

"Put another man on him," Wright ordered. He slid open a desk drawer at his elbow and slipped the paper inside. "Draw from the new people. Maybe we can use this as a training ground."

"Should I go through Operations?" Loudon asked.

Wright shook his head. "No need to bother them. Besides"—he gave Loudon a tiny smile—"I want to keep this unofficial. Otherwise, our friends in the FBI will have to be notified and they tend to get a bit upset when they think we've been working in their bailiwick. I'd just as soon keep the Justice Department out of this as long as possible."

"Yes sir," Loudon said. He turned and left, gently closing the door behind him. He strode purposefully down the corridor to his office, a tiny cubicle without a window, and entered. He removed his jacket and carefully draped it over the back of his chair before seating himself before the computer. He signed on, typing his Level Ten password in to access Records, and brought up the roster of the newest officers. He selected one and imported his file to the New York office, encoding special instructions over the director's authority. He waited until the clearance signal was returned, then backed out of the file. He frowned as a message flashed on the screen: FILE WORKING. His fingers danced across the keyboard again. His frown deepened as FILE COPIED appeared on his screen moments before it closed.

A virus?

He opened SYSTEMS and double-clicked to make sure the virus

check was on. It was, and he sat for a moment, drumming his fingers on the keypad. A nagging doubt worked in his mind. His fingers danced across the keys again, coding and encoding, searching for what had kept the file from closing for thirty seconds.

37

FALLON WAS IN THE BATHROOM, SHAVING WITH EDWARDS'S RAZOR when the doorbell buzzed. He crossed to the intercom by the front door and pushed the button.

"Yes?" he said.

"A Special Delivery letter for Mr. Edwards," a tinny voice answered.

"Place it in the box," Fallon said.

"Someone's gotta sign for it," the voice came back.

"Mr. Edwards is not here at the moment," Fallon said.

"That's okay. Anyone can sign for it. Will you let me in?"

Fallon pushed the OPEN button and returned to the bathroom. He finished shaving and wiped the excess lather from his jaw before the knock came at the door. He crossed back to the front door as he slipped into his shirt and looked through the peephole. The mailman stood on the other side, his beefy face red from the climb up the stairs. Fallon opened the door.

"Here you are," the postman said, extending a letter. Fallon took it and the proffered pen.

"Sign the chit on the back and give it to me, would you?"

Fallon turned the letter over: the back was bare. He looked questioningly at the postman. A smile split the thick lips as his hand came out of the mailbag, gripping a silenced pistol.

"Inside," he said. He took a step forward, forcing Fallon back.

He stepped through the doorway, heeling the door shut behind him. "Keep your hands away from your side."

"Who are you?" Fallon asked, obeying.

"Doesn't really matter, does it?" the man said. He grinned and raised his pistol.

"I'd like to know," Fallon said, his mind racing, searching for a way out as the barrel loomed large in front of his eyes. He tensed his muscles, watching the man's finger.

The door opened to the postman's left.

"Who is it, Fallon?" Maeve asked, yawning and moving into the living room. The postman's eyes flickered toward her. Fallon took a quick step to his left and buried his foot in the postman's groin. His knees buckled as his face turned white. Fallon reached out and grabbed the pistol, bending the man's hand backward. A tiny *plop!* sounded just before the man's finger broke in the trigger guard. Glass shattered behind Fallon. The man yelped in pain just before Fallon whipped the pistol against his jaw. His eyes went glassy, and he fell to the floor, curling into a fetal ball, his hands cupped between his legs.

"Are you all right?" he asked. Maeve nodded, her eyes wide, sleep vanished.

"Who is he?" she asked. She gripped the collar of her robe tightly about her neck.

"Sure, and I doubt he's the postman he claimed," Fallon said, dropping to one knee beside the man. He ran his hands rapidly over the unconscious form, searching for weapons. He found a tiny automatic in an ankle holster and a large knife in the right-hand pocket. He checked the man's pockets, uncovering a return ticket on a flight to Miami, a roll of peppermint candies, a small packet of tissues, a money clip containing four hundred dollars in fifties, and a small notepad with a tiny gold pen in a leather loop at its side. Fallon smiled.

"A professional," he said, gesturing at the contents of the man's pockets. "No identification."

"Professional?" Maeve frowned. "You mean one of the boyos from NORAID?"

Fallon shrugged. "Perhaps. But I doubt it. There'd be no reason for them not to have a wallet or identification. That is the act of a government man."

"British?"

"Maybe," Fallon said thoughtfully. "The SAS is turning out men with careful attention to their dialects from their language school in Surrey. Why they would want an agent here, though? I have my doubts."

"But why would the Americans send a man after you? And how would they know where to look?"

"Perhaps they're doing a favor for their darling cousins across the pond. As to knowing where to look, perhaps it's not me they're watching, but yourself."

"Me?" She frowned, perplexed. Then her face cleared and she made a disgusted sound deep in her throat. "Of course. They would still have the records of Castlereagh, wouldn't they? When Con and I were arrested together in Belfast? The bloody Brits and their German cousins have always been keepers of records." She crossed the room to the kitchen and opened the refrigerator, removing a carton of orange juice and poured a glass for herself. She drank, watching Fallon tie the man's hands and feet together with the man's belt, snubbing them squarely, tightly, so that the flesh puffed out over leather. His hands would throb painfully upon being freed.

A key turned in the lock and Edwards entered, swinging the door shut behind him. He froze, staring at the trussed man on the floor.

"What—" His brow furrowed as he looked questioningly from Maeve to Fallon.

"A bit of a nuisance," Fallon said. He rose, nudging the figure with his foot. "The postman cometh from the dead letter office. You can roll over now." He nudged harder with his foot.

The man grunted and rolled to his side. Pain pulled the corners of his lips down. He curled forward, grimacing against sudden, remembered pain.

"It'll all be over in a minute," Fallon said. "It only seems to take forever. Of course," he added, "time is somewhat relative." He picked up the pistol, pulling the slide back slightly. A brass cartridge gleamed coldly. He knelt beside the man and pressed the barrel against the man's cheek. The man stared back unblinking.

"Ah, yes," Fallon said. He shook his head. "You're being very foolish, but 'tis what I would expect from one like yourself."

"Do you know who he is?" Edwards asked.

"No, but I know what he is," Fallon said softly. "Don't look like that, my friend. Even people like us have a place in this world. Remember: no actions are bad in themselves—even murder can be justified."

"Murder? Never!" Edwards said.

Fallon shook his head. "This from a man whose country built the atomic bomb? Man cannot build the world on morality for morality is like tidal sands: forever changing on the whim of the current. *"L'homme sait que le monde n'est pas à l'échelle humaine; et il voudrait qu'il le fût."*

He pressed the barrel against the man's knee. "He knows I won't kill him because then he could tell me nothing. Right?" The man blinked. *"But,"* Fallon emphasized, "pain can be permanent. You understand?"

"For Christ's sake, Fallon!" Edwards blurted, starting forward. Maeve reached out and stopped him.

"He really doesn't want me to do this," Fallon said conversationally. "Blood is so difficult to clean up. But you would know that, wouldn't you?"

The man sighed. "Coughlan," he said sullenly.

Fallon looked sharply at Edwards. "And your instructions?"

"To kill you." The man nodded at Maeve and Edwards. "And them."

"I see. And for whom do you work?"

"I just told you."

"No, you told us who sent you, not your employer."

"I work alone," he said defensively.

"I think not." Fallon jabbed him in the knee with the pistol. "It's your choice."

"I freelance, now," the man insisted, wincing away.

"But before, you used to work for the government, right?" The man's eyes flickered. "I thought so."

"The government?" Edwards asked. "British?"

Fallon looked down at the man and raised his eyebrows. The man closed his eyes and shook his head.

"Yes," Fallon said, rising. "Well, it doesn't really matter, does it? All governments are brothers when favors are owed or willing to be bartered. What did you find out?"

Edwards looked warningly at the man on the floor.

"Oh, that. It doesn't matter," Fallon said. "After I'm gone, you simply wait a few hours, then call the police and report a burglar you've happened to surprise when you suddenly returned home. No need to explain further. You bashed him with this," Fallon picked up a lamp and smashed it on the floor next to the man. "And that is all there is to it. Your apartment, an intruder, voilà."

"And no bump upon his head," Maeve said. Fallon nodded approvingly at her.

"You're remembering the way of things," he said. He stepped over the figure, turning the pistol in his hand. The man tried to kick, but Fallon neatly sidestepped and brought the pistol down against the man's head. He sighed and went limp. Fallon fingered the bump rapidly rising on the man's head and nodded in satisfaction. "Ah, that will do nicely, it will. I'll be leaving him with you," he said to Edwards. "Sorry, but there's nothing for it. He may protest, but little good it'll be doing him. When you call the police, it would be well done if you had a few of your peers standing by to keep him from being lost in the shuffle, if you follow my drift."

"What now?" Maeve asked.

"To Boston," Fallon answered. "That's where I'll be finding Tommy Coughlan, I'm thinking."

"I'll come with you," Maeve said. She drained her glass in one long swallow and placed it upon the drainboard. She started across the room toward her bedroom.

Edwards started. "Maeve," he began, then stopped when she turned to look questioningly at him.

"I'll be careful," she said, looking fondly at him. "But 'tis something I have to do, Con. You must understand this."

"Understand what?" Con said. "That you are chasing your own death?"

"'Tis a common Irish ailment," she replied, trying to pass off the bitterness with a joke.

"The gods only allow one to pursue death so long before they grant the finding of it. Even Irish gods eventually lose patience with mortals who insist upon playing games with them."

"Ah, perhaps," she said, the smile becoming tight upon her lips. "But you know how we are: Up the Republic!" She glanced at Fallon. "I'll only be a moment." She turned again for the door.

"No," Fallon said. She stopped, turning toward him.

"No? But who will be watching your back?" she asked. "The time has come, Tomas, to talk of these things."

"I'll manage," he said.

"But why?" she asked, her face mirroring her concern.

A tiny smile tipped the corners of his lips. "If it is yourself they're watching, then 'tis you they'll be following. Besides," he added, "'tis easier to hide one than two."

Maeve frowned. "And more dangerous. Who'll watch your back?"

Fallon shrugged. "The same one who's been doing it these thirty years past. The old captain himself."

"You heard what he said," Maeve replied, nodding at Edwards. "You can only mount your chariot so many times."

"What else is there for me? The answer remains the same: no." He turned to Edwards. "And did you find anything for me?"

Edwards reached into his pocket, removed a folded piece of paper, and handed it to Fallon. "A friend of mine owes me a favor. The library did the rest."

"Library?" Fallon asked, unfolding the paper.

"The public library lists NORAID offices in both Boston and New York. I couldn't find anything on Tommy Coughlan there, but I went to the *Times* office. I checked in the morgue and found a bit on Tommy's father. He's a lieutenant with Blackie Cassidy's Silver Street Gang in South Boston. Blackie has a brother who is the new president of Lockwell University in Massachusetts. I don't know if there is a connection there, but he is his brother."

"There could be," Fallon said. "Brothers still remain close despite what one does."

"I wouldn't know," Edwards said. "I don't have one. Or a sister. Anyway, I checked with one of the crime reporters at the *Times* bureau in Boston. Seems like there's a rumor of the FBI giving Blackie carte blanche for little favors he does them. One judge has even demanded an FBI report on Blackie and now it seems he has quietly disappeared." Edwards gave Fallon a hard grin. "Supposedly your boys back in Ireland are taking care of him for favors he did them in the past, running guns, the story goes."

Fallon's eyebrows rose. "Which boys? There're quite a few of them anymore."

Edwards shrugged. "Don't know." He glanced at Maeve. "You know it's all the same to us. We aren't used to revolutionary fine hair-splitting. One terrorist group—sorry, 'army'—in the same country is the same as another to us here in America. When we fought our revolution, we only needed one army. I guess it was a form of united nationalism that seems to have slipped out of favor with revolutionaries anymore."

"It's a start, though," Fallon said. "Shouldn't be too hard to trace down. I'll pass the word along and see what happens." He glanced at Maeve. "You too? Between the two of us maybe we can get some answers."

She nodded. "I'll go through the Dublin folks."

"Fine," Fallon said. He looked back at Edwards. "What else?"

"I've got what addresses we had on the Coughlans and Blackie's brother, William, if you want them."

"I'll take them," Fallon said. "Although I don't think his brother is going to be any use to us. I could talk to him, I suppose, but something tells me that wouldn't help me much. The Coughlans, though, interest me greatly."

"All right. And I have the information on that telephone number you gave me. It's for an Anne Ryan. My friend has a friend with the telephone company."

Fallon looked at Maeve. "Isn't love grand?"

"The bastard put the phone in her name to stop people from finding him. Clever. He didn't know about the reverse directory."

"I wonder why he didn't get an unlisted number?" Edwards said.

"Safer this way," Fallon answered. "Lots of people have friends with the telephone company, I would expect. This way, one must know what one is looking for or have the number. This the right address?" Edwards nodded. "Then I guess this is it?"

"You won't reconsider?" Maeve asked.

"New tricks for old dogs? I don't think so," Fallon said. He looked at Edwards. "If I can get a shirt and tie from you? They'll be looking for the good Reverend Father so it's time for putting him to rest, I'm thinking."

"Of course," Edwards said, relief suddenly shining from his eyes.

"An old one, now," Fallon called after him. "Nothing to be dragging the attention."

He turned to Maeve as Edwards disappeared down the short hall into his bedroom. "Not exactly broken up about my leaving, would you say?"

"Are you doing this because of him and myself?" she asked quietly.

"Well, now, that would take some thinking on my part, wouldn't you say?" Fallon said. Lights danced in his eyes. Maeve slowly nodded.

"You're feeling the old days pressing back, aren't you?"

"I can't be what I'm not," Fallon said.

"Jesus Christ! You sound like Conor did before they killed him on the docks!" she said vehemently.

"Your husband was a good man, Maeve."

"That's not what I meant."

"I know. It's good of you to care, Maeve, but the yesterdays are gone. Days only come once and after that they are only shadows of what was once splendid happiness. I tried to be someone else, but I cannot. *Dis altier visum.* I am only what I have become and there's no use to pretending to anything more."

"That offers little hope for you."

"The time of man's want is always midnight. I spent the majority of my youth fleeing Crumlin Road Jail and sending its wardens to hell. There really is no place for me. Can't you see that, Maeve? Not anymore. The world is tired of our little problems in Ireland. Romantic Ireland is dying a long overdue death. When the shadows of the past come flickering into the present, I breathe a sigh of relief because I have one more chance. This," he gestured at the unconscious man on the floor, "is an anodyne; it halts forward movement for a while. Without it, the future holds only oblivion."

"To be a hero, right?" she said sarcastically.

"No, to know that I am still alive; nothing more," he answered.

"And if the peace accord goes through now that the cease-fire's on? What if it is all over? What then is left for Tomas Fallon?"

"Oblivion," he said.

The door shut behind them and Edwards appeared, holding a clean white shirt and a black knit tie in front of him. "I'm afraid I don't have much to go with your black suit. Will this do?"

"Perfect," Fallon said. "I could be anybody."

38

SIMON KENTON MOVED SLOWLY THROUGH THE CROWD AT GRAND Central Station. He smiled to himself as he noticed for the third time the Agency man and his backup: one standing close to the newsstand by the foyer, pretending to read a newspaper, the other across the room beside the men's room, pretending to sweep the floor, tipping anyone by not straying far from his cart. He decided the one at the newsstand must be the control officer: he was older and held the cleaner job. Kenton had smelled the spice cologne he'd used when he had stopped at the newsstand to buy a copy of *The New Yorker* that he now carried beneath his arm.

In the old days before Wright, both of you would have been reassigned to a desk outside of field operations, he thought.

He stepped around an old man shuffling among the crowd, carrying a sign proclaiming him to be a veteran and one of the homeless. Kenton felt a flash of irritation and pressed his arm hard against his side, feeling the weight of the pistol in its holster beneath his armpit.

Why didn't the police move those bums out? It isn't right that people should have to put up with them. A veteran too.

His step slowed as he contemplated turning back to the man and confronting him, but he remembered the confrontation he'd had in the park in Miami a few days before, leaving the man bleeding and broken on the ground just before a police cruiser had slowly turned the corner.

Careless, too careless of you.

His step paused as a man in a black suit carrying a black over-coat over his arm crossed his path in front of him. He frowned. What is there about the man's suit? He slipped behind the man, staying twenty feet away. The man stepped up to a window to buy a ticket, and Kenton used the opportunity to set his briefcase down and take *The New Yorker* from beneath his arm. He opened it and studied the college photograph of Tomas Fallon.

It could be him. The cheekbones are high enough and, if one added gray streaks in the hair and a few wrinkles—. The man's face, though, the expression, something, something—. He swore softly at the uselessness of the thirty-year-old photograph. The suit! Of course! The cut is all wrong!

He smiled and tucked the magazine back under his arm, picked up his briefcase, and moved to the vacant window next to the man, pretending to fumble for his wallet.

"A ticket to Boston, please," Fallon said.

Kenton smiled in satisfaction. No mistaking that accent. "Boston," he said, sliding a fifty-dollar bill under the glass to the ticket man. He waited impatiently while the man slowly counted out his change and slipped it back under the window along with his ticket. He turned away from the window and looked quickly over the crowd, searching for the man in the black suit. Then he found him, moving toward the tracks. Good. Maybe we can make it look like an accident.

He took a step, then was brought up short as the homeless man stepped in front of him.

"Get out of my way," he said rudely. He started to push past the man, and suddenly a tiny light sparkled and he stepped back quickly in reflex. He caught a glimpse of the needle and deflected it with *The New Yorker*, stepping in close and jabbing stiffened fingers quickly just beneath the man's breastbone. The man gagged and slumped and the needle slipped from his fingers. Kenton grabbed the man's collar and pretended to be trying to hold him up as he forced him to the ground. He quickly scooped the needle up and, hiding his movement with his body, forced it in under the man's arm. The man's eyes widened in shock and realization. He tried to push away, but his arms refused to cooperate.

"Hey, buddy! You all right?" Kenton exclaimed. He felt for a pulse.

The man opened his mouth and tried to speak, but no sound came from his throat. A sheen of perspiration broke out on his forehead and his throat swelled against his collar. He gasped, strangling. Kenton obligingly loosened his collar. He smelled sour wine on the old man's clothes. Then he leaned close and whispered in the old man's ear.

"Did Wright send you?"

The old man's lips moved. His eyes blinked, then rolled up to expose the whites. He gave a slight nod. "After—"

"Fallon? After Fallon?"

A hiss slipped from the man's lips and he lay still. A tiny smile showed beneath the stubble on Kenton's face.

"What's going on here?"

Kenton glanced up at the policeman standing over him. He stood up and away and gestured down at the old man.

"Christ! I think he's having a heart attack!" he exclaimed. "I don't know what to do!"

The policeman grunted, then knelt beside the old man. Kenton glanced around the crowd slowly gathering. He forced himself to look past Fallon, swearing softly to himself. Now Fallon had seen him and would remember him if he saw him again. He would have to be careful.

Slowly he edged his way back into the crowd and away as the policeman forced two fingers into the man's mouth. He clamped hard on the old man's tongue, firmly anchoring it to his front teeth. A fist thumped against the old man's chest followed by sharp, rhythmic jolts, and then the policeman spat in distaste and clamped his mouth tightly on the old man's.

Kenton rapidly left the terminal and ran around to the other side, entering by the other door. He paused, removing his top coat and draping it over his arm. He tossed *The New Yorker* into a trash can and entered the men's room. He made his way to the line of sinks and bent to wash his hands, his eyes casting around. He saw the line of toilet stalls and a man's feet, trousers down around his shoes, his briefcase on the bathroom floor next to the adjoining stall's wall. Kenton slipped into the stall, cast a quick look around. It would be chancy. He pushed the door closed and stood up on the toilet, slipping the silenced .32 pistol from beneath his arm. He looked over the stall and quickly fired one shot into the man's startled face. He grabbed the man's overcoat hanging on the hook behind the door and quickly stepped down. He pulled the briefcase from under the stall, hung his own over-coat on the hook of his own door, and removed the pistol from its pocket and stepped outside, brushing himself down.

Two businessmen entered, arguing among themselves. They ignored him as he crossed to the line of sinks and again washed his hands. He casually dried them, feeling the adrenaline sing through him. Close, very close. But that was part of the game. He strolled outside, pleased with himself, shrugging into the man's overcoat. He carried the briefcase with him. The overcoat was too big but not noticeably so. It would do. He smiled to himself and made his way toward the tracks. Fallon had the luck of the Irish with him. Kenton wouldn't be able to make a run at him now. It would be too chancy. He would have to wait until Boston. But there was really no timetable he had to keep. Not now. Not after Wright's little fiasco. He would take care of Wright as a favor to himself. But first Fallon.

FALLON WATCHED CURIOUSLY AS THE POLICEMAN WORKED FRANTI-
cally to revive the old man. He frowned as he saw the well-
dressed man who had caught the old man quietly work his way
backward through the crowd beginning to gather. When he
reached the back of the crowd, he paused for a moment, then
turned and rapidly walked away, leaving the terminal. Unusual.
Normally one stood around to see what happened next. Although
many wouldn't want to get involved, there was a certain morbid
curiosity that kept them around such a situation. Human nature.
But this—. Fallon frowned and looked swiftly around the terminal. His eyes locked with a man lounging by one of the news-
stands. The man immediately dropped his eyes to the newspaper
in his hands. A familiar coldness settled over Fallon, and suddenly
he became aware of the crowd around him, the hint of dust in the
air, stale sweat and old clothes; perfumes and colognes. The light
brightened, and he saw everything with a sharp clarity. His eyes
flitted around the room, cataloguing and dismissing the people.
There should be another one. He could be a lone wolf, but it was
unlikely. His eyes trailed over the custodian slowly sweeping
toward him, dragging his cart with him after every couple of
steps.

Fallon glanced behind him; the platform was fairly clear. A
young woman, neatly dressed, stood waiting patiently a few yards
away at a ticket office, glancing at her watch, then the entry to the
tracks. But she didn't pay attention to the crowd gathering around
the old man. Beyond her, a group of young blacks stood chatter-
ing noisily. Fallon looked back. The man with the newspaper was
slowly moving down the far side of the room, holding the paper
in front of him as if engrossed in an article, but Fallon could tell
from the set of his shoulders, the sense of tautness about him, that
he was pretending. Fallon slipped on the overcoat, freeing his
arms. The custodian kept sweeping toward him. Fallon glanced

impatiently at his watch, shook his head, then moved off sharply across the room, placing a travel group with a huge pile of baggage between him and the custodian. He angled toward the bank of telephones, drawing a line that would intersect with the other man. He slipped the CZ from its shoulder holster and held it negligently in the folds of the coat beside his leg.

The man slowed and stopped as Fallon drew near. Casually, he folded the newspaper back. Fallon spun and took three quick steps, placing himself close to the man. He smiled broadly and jammed the pistol hard against the man's ribs, shielding his action from the room with his body. He clasped the man on the shoulder, holding him like a good friend. The man stiffened, but did not move.

"Well, then," Fallon said loudly. "'Tis glad I am that I found you. I've been looking all over for you to say good-bye."

"Who are you?" the man asked. Fallon shook his head.

"Wrong answer, boyo," he said quietly, keeping the smile. "I know who you are, and you know who I am and what this is jamming your ribs. Otherwise, you would have pulled away from me, now, like the good and innocent man you claim to be, you see?"

"Um," the man answered. Fallon felt the man's muscles tense and squeezed his shoulder hard.

"You'll never make it," he said softly.

Tiny muscles bunched in angry protest at the corners of the man's jaw, then relaxed. "What now?"

"Better. The man with the broom—one of yours?" He nodded. "Good. Any others?" The man hesitated, and Fallon jabbed him hard with the pistol. The man gasped. "I'm known for my kind and gentle nature, but you are beginning to irritate me. Where are the others?"

"Outside," he gasped. "The bum on the ground. The woman in brown tweed at the ticket office. That's all." Fallon jabbed him again. "Yes, that's all."

"Call the woman over. Careful, now."

Fallon turned to watch as the man gestured. At first, the woman ignored him. "Again," Fallon murmured. The woman frowned. Fallon nudged the man with his pistol. He gestured angrily. The woman shifted her shoulder bag from her left shoulder to her right as she started across the room toward them, slowing as she crossed in front of the broom man. Fallon saw her lips move fractionally. The broom man gave a bare nod, put his broom back into the cart, and moved behind it, fiddling with the cleaning bottles on top. Fallon gave the woman a small smile as she stopped in front of them. She slipped her hand into her shoulder bag, and Fallon leaned back, showing the pistol to her.

"Remove your hand. Slowly, now," he said. She slid her hand from the shoulder bag, casually resting it on top. "Set your bag on the papers there and remove your coat."

"Why?" she asked.

"Because I have a pistol, and I don't think your broom man is that good a shot across a crowded room, do you?"

She set her bag on the counter and shrugged out of her coat, draping it over her arms. Beneath the coat, she wore a soft pink blouse that matched the color of the heather in the coat's thread. She gave Fallon a toothy smile. "Now what?"

Fallon nudged the man beside her. "Rip her blouse off."

"What?" The man half-turned, but Fallon rammed the barrel of the pistol hard against his ribs.

"Do it, or I'll shoot your knees off," he said, stepping behind him. "Are you wanting to spend the rest of your life on sticks, so?"

The man took a deep breath and reached out with both hands, seizing the collar of the woman's blouse and ripping it in two. The woman staggered forward, and Fallon savagely shoved the man into her.

"Scream," he said sharply. He raised his own voice. "Hey!"

The man and woman fell in a tangle of arms and legs. The woman screamed. A florid-faced man passing by shouted, "What the hell?" dropped his bags, and tried to pull the man off the woman. The man rose to one knee, then the woman's thrashing heels caught him, throwing him off-balance against the florid man's legs. They fell into a heap. The woman screamed again as a crowd gathered around them. A policeman shouted, pushing his way through the crowd. Fallon slipped unnoticed behind the newsstand. He moved casually around the edge of the crowd until he came to the broom man, standing on tiptoes, trying to see over the heads of the crowd. Fallon slid the CZ-52 back into its shoulder holster under his arm. He picked an aerosol can of cleaning liquid and sprayed its contents into the man's eyes. Quickly, he dropped the can into the refuse bag on the cart and stepped away as the man howled and dug his knuckles into his eyes. A few close to him turned from the crowd to help, solicitously leading him to the men's room.

Fallon walked rapidly away, back to the track where the Boston train waited. He stepped aboard and moved down the aisle of the car, searching for a seat. He found an empty one next to a young man scowling at a tattered copy of Plato's *Republic* and dropped in beside him. He jostled the young man, who gave him an annoyed look and slid closer to the window. He slid the book bag on the floor closer to the wall with his foot.

"Sorry," Fallon muttered. The boy nodded, keeping his eyes upon his book. Fallon glanced past him out the window, checking the landing: it was clear, and he leaned back against the seat, sighing deeply as the train pulled slowly away from the terminal. He closed his eyes, willing rest.

He didn't notice Kenton slip into a seat at the other end of the train, twisting himself so he could keep Fallon's reflection in the window across the aisle. He settled himself patiently to wait. He had missed the time at the tracks, but then there would be another time. All one needed was patience. He sighed happily, content with the game.

39

WRIGHT TURNED FROM THE WINDOW IN HIS OFFICE AS THE DOOR opened behind him and Kelly walked in, his brow a thundercloud, his eyes angry flashes. He slapped a sheet of paper on Wright's desk.

"What is this?" he asked.

Wright picked up the paper, scanning it. "It looks like a fouled mission," he said.

"I know that," Kelly answered testily. "What I don't know is who authorized it."

"Actually, I did," Wright said, seating himself behind his desk. He placed the paper in the exact center of the blotting pad on his desk and folded his hands over it.

"I see," Kelly said, taken aback. "May I ask why you went outside of Operations? This should have been coordinated through my office. Was it for the British?"

"The British have been trying to catch Fallon for nearly twenty years," Wright said. He glanced down at the paper, a smile quivering at the corners of his mouth. "Well, it seems he's made a fool of our people too. One arrested for an assault upon a woman— one of ours, I presume?" Kelly gave a curt nod. "And the third man taken to the hospital with burned eyes?"

"Superficial inflammation. Painful, but no permanent damage," Kelly said. "It's almost like he *knew* we'd be there."

Wright laid the paper back on his desk and frowned, lowering his brow and looking up from under busy brows in imitation of Henry Kissinger. "Zere is alvays zat expect-ta-tion, of course, zince a man zuch as zis vun vould be alvays expecting zuch dings to happen," he growled gutterly. "Ze Great Man, Herr Doktor, to me zaid zis himzelf vhen ve vere flying back from ze conference in Paris und he began pacing up and down ze aisle in ze airplane, muttering 'I am ze greatest man in ze vorld und I cannot use my own bathrooms'."

"Very good," Kelly said. "You do that well."

"Thank you," Wright said. He leaned back in his chair and stared impassively at Kelly. "I've wondered about you for quite some time now, Dave. Too many operations have gone wrong over the past eighteen months. We have been severely embarrassed several times in the press when we should have been totally anonymous. Isolated incidents that only a few had complete knowledge of, tiny incidents leaked to certain people who had no way of knowing without being deliberately told. Only someone with intimate knowledge would have been capable of putting entire stories together for the outside world. How long have you been with the GDC?"

"Me?" Kelly asked, shocked.

"Oh yes," Wright said softly. "You." The door opened and two men stepped in behind Kelly. He glanced at them, then turned back to Wright. He stared impassively at Wright.

"You're wrong," he said flatly.

"Am I?" Wright opened the tray of his desk and removed a sheet of paper, sliding it across the desk toward him.

"What?" Kelly picked up the paper, frowning. "What's this?"

"A read-out from your computer."

"You ran a frame-search on my computer?"

"Don't be obvious, Dave, it doesn't become you. You've never been obvious before; even when you were being tolerant, you were never obvious. Of course I did."

"But this isn't mine. I never made those operational codes," Kelly said, tossing the paper back on the desk.

"No? Well, let's see what it does," Wright said. He raised his hands, ticking off the points as he named them. "*I* was the one running the show on Fallon. *You* tapped into my man's computer to find out what we were doing. Of course, I had to have a reason for doing this. And I did." His eyes held Kelly's: cold, impassionate. "I found out about a little rogue operation being run in Afghanistan by someone from inside the organization. Someone who had access to the files of retired agents. And who had knowledge of the Nugan Bank. Not many have been around long enough to be able to know all that. There's myself, of course, and—well, you." He smiled disarmingly at Kelly. "I knew it wasn't me," he said smoothly. "That leaves just you. Oh, I suppose there would have been a couple of others somewhere in the agency, but it would have taken someone who had the access and someone high enough up to slip through the coding blocks. That eliminates a lot of people. And, when I ran that check on you"—he nudged the paper on his desk with his forefinger—"why wouldn't you know that your computer comes up in the figuration. There's the contact with Simon Kenton, the transfer of monies from the old Nugan Hand accounts, the setup of the arms factory in Egypt—"

"And all by you," Kelly said quietly. "You tapped into my computer and ran the show through my data bank, didn't you?"

"But it's all from your computer account. A pity," Wright said, shaking his head. "You forgot about the 'mousetrap' we had built within the system, didn't you? Too bad. The question is, why did you do it? I hope it was something more than just money."

"Pretty good," Kelly said. He nodded at the men standing impassively by the door. "Of course, you know that you can't use them. What have you planned? A heart attack?" Wright's eyebrows raised fractionally. Kelly gave a grim smile. "Yes, probably.

It doesn't matter. The fact is that you don't dare take that chance. I could be working for another agency, right? Like the Justice Department?" He shook his head. "No, the best you can do is to push me out. You can't take the chance that an investigation— and there would be one—might fall back on you. Did you think to erase all the 'mirrors'? I wouldn't want to gamble on that. No, the safe thing is simply to drum me out of the service, right?"

"And why is that?" Wright asked.

"Because you don't know what I may have found out up to now. The best you can hope for is to try and obliterate everything. Which," he added, catching the flicker in Wright's eyes, "you've already done. If not, you will have done by the time I get back to my people. Whoever you think they are."

"Justice," Wright said with distaste. "You have to be with Justice."

Kelly smiled and spread his hands. "Speculation. Pure speculation."

"Of course it is. Everything we do is on speculation. You are being rather tiresome, Dave. I told you I didn't like you when you were obvious," Wright admonished. "The thing that bothered me the most, though, was when strange events began to happen in Australia with the Nugan Hand Bank and the sudden death of Frank Nugan. The Nugan Hand Bank was ticketed for my immediate attention. After all, we used to route the monies we used to buy the opium shipments of the war lords in Burma and Cambodia through the Nugan Hand Bank in return for which the war lords raided the North Vietnamese villages and stores. This was an extremely sensitive operation, for if the public ever found out about it, heads would have rolled beginning with the president's. Consequently, only a few were involved in it." He paused, watching Kelly for a moment before continuing. "You were one of those few, Dave."

"As were you," Kelly interrupted. "And a few others."

"But none who have had any access to the files," Wright said.

"*And*, only one field man who made all the arrangements for the Afghan run: Simon Kenton."

"Why would I contact Kenton?" Kelly asked.

"I don't think you did," Wright said. "I think he contacted you. He had the key to where the extra guns were being stored after he closed down the Egyptian factory. You had the sales references he needed."

"Why me?"

"Because you were on the Terrorist Desk before you moved to Director of Operations. Is that where you became a member of the GDC? You don't have to answer; it's obvious. I imagine that Ireland isn't the only place where illegal arms could be shipped. I wouldn't have suspected you but for Fallon. I wondered why he was making a run in New York. After all, wouldn't the IRA know where the shipment was coming from? But Fallon refused to use the IRA's people. I wondered why, and this made me start looking through our own files. I stumbled across this"—he tapped the paper again—"when I checked the mousetrap."

"A fascinating story, but it's only a story," Kelly said. He shook his head. "You can't use it."

"Of course I can," Wright said. "I can use anything. I'm the director."

"The press would crucify you."

"On that you are right. But then you would be brought up on trial too, wouldn't you, Dave? And the Justice Department would have to admit to spying on a sister organization. I don't think they would like that, would they, Dave? So I'm going to have you taken immediately from here and all your credentials stripped. Everything will be changed, Dave, by the time you get to your car telephone. It's not all that hard—simple code exchanges, you know. And I'm reassigning all your staff as we speak. A pity. You were quite good in your own way." He looked at the two men standing impassively behind Kelly. "Very quietly, please. Don't even let him go back to collect his hat and coat. Straight to his car." He glanced at Kelly. "I do hope you have your car keys in your pocket, Dave. Otherwise it will be a long and cold walk off the grounds."

"You son of a bitch," Kelly said quietly.

"You don't have them? Very well." He glanced again at the two men. "Take him in a car to the Jefferson Memorial and drop him there." He smiled at Kelly. "I'll arrange to have your car delivered to your house, Dave. The keys will be left in it. We are, after all, civilized, aren't we?"

Kelly turned and walked silently to the door. He paused while the two men opened it. He stared back at Wright.

"Good-bye, Dave," Wright murmured.

Kelly turned and stepped through the door. The two men followed him, softly closing the door behind them.

He sighed and leaned back in his chair, smiling softly to himself. It had been a hard plan to put together, but his instincts had been right. Kelly made a good Judas goat. His Irish background fit the situation perfectly. He looked up in annoyance as the door opened and Loudon entered.

"Is it—" Loudon asked softly.

"Yes," Wright said. "I think we will be having an opening soon in the DO's office. Not as director, you understand. That would raise too many questions. But, I think, a substantial place."

"And Fallon?" Loudon asked.

"I'm afraid Mr. Fallon will have to be eliminated," Wright said. "One mustn't take too many chances. Take care of it, please."

Loudon nodded and stepped back out of the office. Wright grinned at the ceiling, tapping his fingertips on the desk. *I wonder if the good senator from Mississippi has been released from Bethesda?* A smile of anticipation crept over his face. He leaned forward and picked up his telephone, dialing.

40

THE GRAY WAS LOWERING WHEN FALLON FINALLY EMERGED FROM the maze of tiny side streets behind Kenmore Square and between Commonwealth Avenue and the Charles River. For a while, he had been lost around the Boston Public Garden among the tree-lined streets with gaslights on the street poles and the brick side-walks that made him think of Belfast. He got his bearings at Trinity Church and Copley Square and found his way through the commercial center down Washington Street toward North End and Faneuil Hall. He noticed how the buildings seemed to be taking on a seedy look between Beacon Hill and the North End, especially around the Prudential Plaza and Kenmore. The Boston College students loudly shouting at each other made him think fleetingly of Queens University, but he pushed those thoughts away as he made his way into Quincy Market. He had tried the address for the NORAID offices on Washington Street, but the door was locked and no light shined through the pebble glass of the door. He had debated for a moment about slipping the lock for the door was old and cracked and a good quarter-inch gap appeared between the door and its frame, but reason told him he would find little in the office to warrant the gamble of being dis-covered. Instead, he elected to try Tommy Coughlan's address on Milk Street.

He moved easily through the crowd, slipping between couples

with a polite "excuse me" and deftly sidestepping the defiant ones. Out of habit, he checked his back in the windows that he passed, looking for faces that reappeared in his wake. Halfway through the market, he caught the man in the gray fedora with its brim pulled low slipping in behind an unshaven man with a face like a ferret who slipped away as the man in the fedora passed him. He frowned. It could be a mistake. Then he shook his head. Lad, you've been watching so long that you might be seeing snakes for snails.

He stopped suddenly and reversed his steps, sliding into one door of a bakery, then out the other, crossing to the other corridor paralleling the one he'd left. He turned back in his original direction, checking his back in the reflection of a window piled high with reduced-priced clothing. Ferret-face was back.

A grim smile crossed his lips. Then again, boyo, sometimes snakes are snakes. I wonder who they are?

He plunged ahead, lengthening his stride. He emerged on Clinton, a side street running parallel to the market. He stepped into a shop on the corner of Commercial and bought a Boston College sweatshirt as he pondered his next move. When he emerged from the shop, he glanced casually back toward the market. Fedora pretended interest in a display of canned goods while Ferret-face lounged in the doorway of a cigar shop, talking up a young woman wearing too much makeup and too tight a sweater. Fallon smiled thinly and slipped a button on his coat, letting it fall loosely around his hips. A door opened at the end of the block, letting a burst of music spill out into the street. His ears pricked at the familiar notes of "Glen Swilly." He stepped out of the doorway and made his way down to the bar and paused, reading its name above the door: The Black Rose. He glanced quickly down the street: his two followers had moved up toward him. Fedora's hand was in the pocket of his overcoat. Ferret-face, across the street from him, had his hand behind his back.

Fallon turned, opened the door, and entered. A wave of sound struck him—skirling pipes and guitar, a flute, and an accordion—as the singer, a long-haired youth, moaned into a microphone a quarter-inch from his lips:

> *"No more at ball or harvest home my violin I will play,*
> *No more I'll dance the Irish Reel among the girls so gay;*
> *I've left my violin behind that was so dear to me,*
> *'Twill keep my place when I am gone, far far from Glen*
> *Swilly."*

Fallon wove his way through the crowd to a small table at the back of the room where a middle-aged dwarf sat alone, his foot tapping time to the music, a half-empty pint of Guinness in front of him next to a small glass bearing Paddy's logo.

"Would you mind if I joined you?" Fallon asked.

The man looked up, sweeping Fallon with startling blue eyes. "Over recently, are you? And from Kerry? Or is it Cork?" He gestured at a place beside him on the bench.

"You have a good ear," Fallon said, sliding onto the bench. He placed the package containing the Boston College sweatshirt next to him. "'Tis only a few days now."

"A-huh," the dwarf said, eyeing him shrewdly. "And I suppose you've lost your papers between there and here too, is it?"

"Ah, but there you're wrong. 'Tis only hasty judgment of the kind a Donegal man would be making that drove you to say such things." He motioned at the waitress. "Will you be having another?"

The dwarf laughed and reached for his glass, draining it. "Sure, and for a man fresh off, you must have a golden pocket with you. Yes, I'll have another, and here's my hand upon it. They call me Billy O'Toole."

"Fallon." He shook the dwarf's hand, surprised at the strength in it. The dwarf cocked an eyebrow, waiting. Fallon ignored him, giving his attention to the waitress, ordering a round for Billy and a Bushmill's for himself. Billy laughed.

"Well, one name's as good as another, Fallon. What are you about?"

"Visiting. Just visiting," Fallon said.

"You found the right place, then," Billy said, winking sagely. "We have a lot of 'visitors' in here most nights."

Fallon noticed the catch in his voice and turned his attention to Billy. The dwarf nodded. "Oh, yes." He waved his hand over the room. "Most all here." He fell silent as the waitress appeared out of the crowd and placed their order in front of them and departed, swinging her hips through the crowd. "She is."

"Her, now, you say," Fallon said.

"Been here two months, she has, slipping across from Canada. No papers. But she knew enough to come here."

"What's so special about here?" Fallon asked. He tasted his drink and put it aside.

"Not many there is who would be drinking that stuff. The North is well-hated here."

"Politics is politics and whiskey is whiskey," Fallon answered.

The dwarf laughed. "Sure, and it's a Kerry man you are. A Cork man would swallow any swill as long as it came from the Republic. A Kerry man's nondiscerning."

"As it may be. This place?" Fallon prodded gently.

The dwarf gave him another wink. "Been here awhile the owner has, but he came over the hard way. Rumor has it he killed one of Craig's boys and had to be making himself scarce. That was before the Provos, you know."

"I know," Fallon said. He took a tiny sip from his glass and put it down. He glanced at the door and stiffened as Fedora walked in

followed moments later by Ferret-face. They stood on the periph-
ery of the crowd, scanning the faces, searching for him. Billy
noticed the sudden tension in his shoulders.

"Yes," he said dryly. "I can see that you do. Do you know
them?"

"No," Fallon said.

"And you're not wanting to make their acquaintance, I'm
thinking?"

Fallon shook his head. Fedora noticed him and brushed his
nose with the knuckle of his forefinger. Ferret-face caught the gesture and stood on tiptoes, craning his neck. His face tightened as
he found Fallon. Slowly, they began to work their way through
the crowd.

"You'd better leave," Fallon said. He moved his coat back. Billy
glimpsed the holstered pistol.

"Now, don't be doing anything rash," he said somberly. He slid
from the booth and skipped his way nimbly through the crowd of
drinkers to the bar. He stepped behind it, motioning to one of the
bartenders. The man slid down the bar and bent to hear the dwarf.

The crowd broke into applause as the band finished the set and
the players carefully stacked their instruments for a break. Fedora
and Ferret-face paused while the crowd milled around them as
several shouted for the band to continue playing. An idea worked
its way into Fallon's mind. He pulled his coat over the pistol and
slid from the booth. In four quick strides, he sprang onto the
raised platform the band had been using for a stage and sat down
behind the piano.

"Here, now!" a voice cried from the smoke.

Fallon ignored him and let his fingers run over the keys, select-
ing rhythm and chord. Quickly, he built a driving bass and swung
into a rollicking version of "The Muskerry Sportsman." Sound
from the crowd dwindled as he slipped from eighths into six-

teenths, and then someone began to clap and another picked up the beat.

"Ah, Duhallow maids! Duhallow!" someone cried. Fallon flashed a grin at the audience, noting Fedora and Ferret-face as they were pressed back against the bar by the crowd turning its attention to the stage. A bartender tapped Fedora on the shoulder. Fedora jerked his shoulder away and irritably shook his head. The bartender said something else. Again, Fedora shook his head. The bartender pointed toward the door. Fedora shrugged and waved two fingers. The bartender slid two dripping glasses filled with black Guinness in front of them. Reluctantly, they took the glasses, sipping.

Fallon shifted his attention as someone leaped onto the stage beside him. A long-haired youth smiled at him, nodded, and sat behind the drums. His foot found the bass pedal, and he began beating on the tom-tom. Another figure joined them and the eerie wail of the pipes sounded an octave above Fallon's treble, and he passed the melody up, providing counterpoint to the pipes' skirling. The crowd picked up the beat, and Fallon risked another glance at Fedora and Ferret-face. Their glasses were half-empty, their faces slack. Fedora turned to the bartender and started to speak. His partner suddenly collapsed. Fedora turned to grab him, and his legs folded, pitching him forward over Ferret-face. The sudden movement caught someone's attention and laughter spilled out into the room.

Fallon quickly moved into the final bars and brought the song to a close. He stepped from behind the piano, nodded at the crowd's applause, and held his hands up, palms out, against their demand for more. The lead singer stepped back up on the stage and grinned at Fallon.

"If you want to sit in, you're more than welcome," he said. "'Tis a fine hand you have, and Ryan can always use a break." He nodded at another young man who joined them. Ryan held out his hand. Fallon took it.

"I'll be glad to have another one if you want to take the set," he said. Teeth flashed whitely from his curly black beard.

"You're too kind," Fallon said. "But my fingers need resting and me throat's purely parched."

"I know the feeling," the drummer said. He waved his sticks at Fallon. "Johnny Reardon. And you're welcome." Fallon waved and stepped from the stage amid groans of disappointment from the crowd. He made his way back to his table, pausing as someone leaped from a chair to seize his hand. Some patted him enthusiastically on the back and demanded whatever he was drinking be sent to his table.

The dwarf waited for him as he slid behind the table. "Full of surprises, now, aren't you?" He grinned as Fallon glanced over at the bar. "They'll be taken down to the docks and left to sleep it off. A slight addition to their Guinness, and they'll have the head like a smithy's anvil to remind them of it in the morning. Relax," he said, pressing Fallon's arm as he made to rise. "There's no one else about. The boys have made sure of that."

"The boys?"

The dwarf nodded. "Oh, yes. Friends have taken care to check outside and about. You're quite safe, for the moment," he added.

"Who are you?" Fallon asked.

"Now, I told you that a bit ago." Billy grinned.

"No, you didn't," Fallon said. "You were expecting me, weren't you? How? And why?"

Billy toyed with the glass in front of him for a long moment, then sighed and looked up at Fallon. "Do you know what it's like to be someone like me?" He laughed, but there was no humor in his laughter. "Ah, of course you don't. How could you?" He shook his head. "Being a dwarf is a joke to many. No one takes you seriously, you see. You're just a little man to them; one who is *tolerated* and bought drinks. But is there a place for one like me with them? No. Eventually, you become like a piece of furniture: there, but not there, you follow me?" Fallon nodded. "And so, word is passed among the 'big boys' around you and you catch little things that they don't think you're catching. Because you're not real, you see. You're only a freak of nature, and who takes freaks seriously? That's how I knew you were coming, Fallon. I heard. That simple. I heard."

"And from whom did you hear these tales, Billy?" Fallon asked.

The dwarf grinned. "Ah, now. Sure, and you can guess that, can't you? The word's out on you, Fallon. Out by those who have reason to want you dead."

"The Gaelach Dearg Craobh," Fallon said.

Billy nodded. "Oh, yes. Those are the ones. And others."

"You know what they are?" Fallon asked.

"I know who belongs to them," Billy said. "That's enough. There's no good there, Fallon. No good at all."

"But how did you know enough to find me here?"

Billy laughed. "It was a guess. I'm here most nights. It's where all like you end up."

"But I knew nothing of this place until I walked through the door."

Billy shrugged. "It doesn't matter. There's no place else you could go in Boston. All end up here. You would have found it; of that, I was sure. It was just a matter of waiting."

"But the question is: how did you know I was coming to Boston?"

"The word," Billy said, tapping himself on the side of the nose. "The word came down. 'Tis a good price on your head, now, Fallon. And the O'Briens have been put on it to find you and collect it."

"But, how—"

Their waitress materialized at their table and began unloading drinks from her heavily weighted tray. She flashed a smile at Fallon, her nose wrinkling. She had a dash of freckles across her cheeks, her hair gathered in a long, honey-blond ponytail and secured with a rubber band. A pang of emptiness swept through Fallon.

"You'll be awhile at those," she said, her vowels long in a Belfast accent.

"That I will," Fallon said ruefully. "Tell me, now: isn't there a good man or two around to be helping me out?"

She laughed and swung her head saucily. "There's men about, no doubt of that. But none as good as you, I'm thinking," she added archly, smiling.

"And what do such men call you?" he asked.

Dimples widened in her cheeks. "Pegeen," she answered, cocking her head. "When I let them."

"And when do you let them?"

"Usually after two." She nodded and left. Billy sighed and reached for one of the glasses.

"This is beginning to sound like one of those bad movies with Charles Boyer," he said, raising the glass to his mouth.

"You're too young to have known Charles Boyer. Did you find out who they were?"

"*Algiers.* Hedy Lamarr. Unfortunately, she kept her clothes on so we missed her fine acting talent. Yes. They belong to the O'Brien family." He finished the glass, smacked his lips, and reached for another. "There might be something to the separation of state and distiller after all."

"Who are the O'Briens?" Fallon asked.

The dwarf sighed and placed the glass in front of him. "I've heard about a Fallon from the North. A cold man, they say. One with no nerves."

"Is that what you've been hearing?"

Billy nodded. His fingers still toyed with the glass. "Something of a legend, they say. But, of course, I could be wrong, for what would such a man as this Fallon be wanting here when there's plenty for him to be doing in his own bailiwick? Besides, the trouble with legends is they're too often the result of someone's communion with too many jars."

"There is that," Fallon agreed. He picked up a glass, tasted it, and set it back down. "Who are the O'Briens?"

"Now, that's a puzzle," Billy continued. "What would such a man as this be wanting with scum like these who deal in people's miseries?"

"Drugs?" Fallon asked, pitching his voice low.

Billy nodded, sighed, and raised his glass. "The worst of the lot. The enforcers of Blackie Cassidy's Silver Street Gang. And those are ones we could surely do without." He drank and stared moodily across the room at the band. "Why are you here, Fallon?"

Fallon studied him for a moment. "I think you already know that, don't you, Billy?"

"Yes, I suppose I do." He fell silent for a long time. Fallon leaned back in his chair, waiting, giving him the time to sort his thoughts.

"You don't want to mess in this, Fallon," he said at last. "These people are too powerful. Not the O'Briens, necessarily; they're just those to whom the others parcel out the jobs. You may have been fighting the Brits for a few years, now, but the Brits have rules they play by. These boys have no rules and long arms. They're not a country; they have their own world and governments owe allegiance to them."

"Ah, well. We'll just have to make do, won't we?"

"Don Quixote is only a story, man!" Billy said sharply. "There's no truth to him at all."

"Maybe there should have been," Fallon answered. "Now, will you be telling me what I'm asking?"

Billy leaned back against the wall and sighed. "The O'Briens work for the Coughlan family who are with Blackie Cassidy. They get the dirty work to do. Like you."

"Coughlan." Fallon grinned and reached for his glass. "So. Tommy Coughlan has a bit of muscle behind him."

"Do you know Tommy Coughlan?" Billy asked, surprised.

"Not really. What can you tell me about him?"

"Ah, he's a mean one, he is. A mean one. Spoiled by his mother who is an O'Brien herself. The darling of her eye, and his father, Joe. But he's not got his father's mind, if you follow me."

"A bit thick?"

Billy nodded. "More than a bit. His da's been bailing him out of one fix after another. Tried to get him into some of the better schools, Exeter, that type, you know, but Tommy managed to get himself thrown out of each one and his da's money wasn't enough to put the fix in there. So, he's given little odd jobs to be doing here and there to earn a bit of money and make him think he's one of the crowd, but his da pays him more than the job's worth so everyone knows him for a joke. When he gets into trouble, he whines to his da, who hands out the job to the O'Briens to take care of. He lost a lot of money once to a bookie here in town who refused to take his action until he paid on the account. Tommy told his da and the bookie went out of business. Some say he went to Costa Rica for his health. Some say he went to Jamaica. I think he went off India Wharf. He left too many open accounts behind to be anywhere else."

"I think I'm getting a picture of Tommy Coughlan. Anything else?"

Billy nodded. "Used to be a regular whips and chains boy, but not lately. Word is he has a bit of a quince from the old land who can give him all he wants."

"Anne Ryan?"

Billy looked surprised. "Ah, lad. You know more than you let on. Yes, that be the one." He reached for another glass; his words were coming thicker now. "Now, I have a question: What do you want scum like that for, Fallon?"

"Ah, now, that's something best left out of your ears. If a man were looking for Joe Coughlan, where would he be finding him?"

Billy shook his head. "In Back Bay. He's a place off Beck Road. Be careful, Fallon. Be real careful. Joe has a real fondness for his boy and a long, long arm. A lot of people owe him favors that they would be happy if he collected on."

"I'll keep that in mind," Fallon said, rising. Billy caught his arm.

"But that doesn't mean that there aren't those around who wouldn't be looking to do Joe Coughlan a turn or two. Especially if it fell upon his son. Remember that, Fallon. There are people here if you need them."

"Thank you, my friend," Fallon said, gently pulling his arm free. He gestured at the drinks remaining on his table. "Now, would you be doing me a favor?"

Billy eyed him closely a minute, then glanced at the table and gave a short bark of laughter. "Ah, well. 'Tis a man's job ahead of me tonight."

Fallon laughed and turned to leave, bumping into Pegeen. He looked down into green eyes. Tiny lights danced within their depths. The crowd pushed them against each other, and suddenly he was conscious of her breasts pushing against his chest.

"Now, and where do you think you are going? The night still has legs on it, it does," she said, grinning at him.

"Well, now, the night may be young, but I'm feeling my age. And there's a place to stay I have to be finding before it gets much older or it's a bench in the park I'll be sleeping upon."

"Now, that would be a terrible thing for a man like you to be doing, so," she said. He felt her fingers in his pocket. He reached up and captured her hand before she could withdraw it. "I have a wee place on Hull Street twelve blocks north near the playground. Not much, but it has a couch that you're welcome to. I'll be off at two, but there's no sense in waitin' around for that. The key's in your pocket if you're wantin' to be getting a bit of a kip while I finish up here."

"Ah, 'tis a fine lass you are," Fallon said, gently removing her hand. He felt the key in his pocket and made to take it out. "But I'm not what you're thinking I am."

"And I'm not what you're thinking I am," she flashed back. Angry lights appeared in her eyes. "'Tis only a favor I'm doing; nothing more."

Fallon held her eyes for a long moment, then slowly nodded. "Then it's for the favor that I'm thanking you, Pegeen. And I'll be waiting for you."

A smile crossed her face. "Sure, and who else would you be waiting for?" she asked saucily. She moved away, back to the bar, where she gathered a tray of drinks and made her way through the crowd. Fallon watched her for a moment, then slipped through the crowd out into the night. A fog was rolling in across from the harbor, leaving tendrils of clammy mist upon his cheek.

"So, then, we have you now, Tommy Coughlan," he murmured. And he heard the distant skirling of the pipes and from afar, the ancient clamor of warriors riding their chariots to the sea. He shook himself and moved off through the fog, working his way north to Hull Street.

41

THE ROOM IN THE HOUSE IN THE BACK BAY WAS HIGH, AND DISCREET lights made the walnut panels glow with warmth. But there was no warmth in the glare Joe Coughlan directed at his son sitting uneasily in the leather chair across from him. He rose and went to the hunt table upon which an array of bottles had been placed. He poured a large whiskey in a Waterford glass and drank half of it before turning back to his son.

"So. You fucked this up royally," he growled. "Shit. You'd think I was used to you fucking everything up by now."

Tommy stirred in his chair and tried to meet his father's angry eyes, but failed. He looked at the flickering flames in the fireplace then at the Irish decorations scattered throughout the room. "What would you have done?" he blustered. "I sent some boys after him. Who'd a thought anybody'd be that good?"

"Christ," the senior Coughlan said. He closed his eyes and rubbed them with his thumb and forefinger, then opened them and stared at Tommy. "Christ. What in hell did you think he was? Some two-bit numbers runner? Some wino fucker we send around to bag the whoors?"

"I thought he was another one of those *squaddies* that keep showing up on the doorstep," Tommy said defensively.

"What? Jesus Christ! The man's been workin' for the boys for twenty-some years and the Brits chasin' him all that time and you thought he was one of the *squaddies?* Ah, Christ." He gulped his drink down and poured another and crossed behind his desk, a large oaken affair that had once belong to Oliver Wendell Holmes and sat in a chair supposedly one of James Madison's. He absently rubbed his hands over the leather of the chair. He breathed deeply, composing himself, then sighed and leaned forward, speaking softly. "Tommy, you've gotta learn to think and not with your cock! Think! Common sense should've told you that this guy was something special. An' failin' that, why didn't you talk with some of the boys? Hell, some of the boys, *you* should have known about Fallon. You've run enough money to them in Ireland for the NORAID folks."

"Nobody talks to the messenger, Dad." Tommy sulked. "That's all I am to them—a fuckin' messenger. There's no fuckin' reason at all to take the money to Ireland then bring it back again to buy guns from us. A fuckin' idiot can do that. I know you made up the job for me. Hell, why wouldn't they just buy the guns and ship them over from here? Why the extra trip?"

Joe closed his eyes, mentally counting, then opened them and looked at his son. "Again, think. The boys over there have to see the money. Telling them's not enough. Then they know they got it and they know they can spend it. You gotta learn stuff like this, Tommy. You can't just tell people what they got; you gotta show them. People are suspicious. They want to see for themselves. And we want them to know that we ain't screwing them."

"We could be anyway," Tommy said sullenly.

Joe looked at him closely. "Tommy, if you've been skimming from the money when you take it over there, you're playing a game that ain't a game to them. They don't care who the fuck you are. They think you've been skimming some of that money, they'll kneecap you. And there ain't a goddamn thing I can do about it."

"Big Joe Coughlan afraid of a bunch of bog-jumpers?"

"Tommy, those people don't care about Big Joe Coughlan and

they don't care about Blackie Cassidy and they don't care about anything but what they're doing. There are people who you just can't fuck with and that don't mean you ain't tougher than them. There are people who just keep comin' at you no matter how many times you beat them down. And those are the people who scare me, Tommy, because they just don't give a fuck and they don't have nothing that you can do to them to make them scared."

"Be a cold day in hell—" he began, but Joe shook his head and held up his hand.

"Tommy, you're just as dumb as that fuckin' wall. You gotta learn about people. You gotta learn when you can skim and when you keep your fuckin' hands in your pocket. As soon as you show me you know that, I'll move you in. I told you that."

"Joe Coughlan's boy: a fuckin' messenger. Who takes him seriously?"

"Nobody," Joe said. "You haven't earned it. You want respect, you've gotta earn it."

"Who don't respect me?" Tommy said. "I take care of those."

"Beatin' up whoors and pimps don't get you the respect you need," Joe said patiently. "That kinda respect you get from those who believe in you."

"Believe what?"

"What the fuck you want them to," Joe said. "Now, look what you got us into. We got a fuckin' loose cannon roamin' around the streets thanks to that fuckin' Cassidy who wants to move drugs into Ireland. Okay. Fine. But those people we were selling the guns to before the cease-fire don't like drugs. Blackie don't listen and now I got this fucker running here and there looking for us and I don't want him to find us." He took a deep breath. "So, now, I think you'd better tell me why this Fallon's lookin' for you."

"How the fuck should I know?" Tommy said. His eyes avoided his father's glare. He stared sullenly at the fire. A log cracked and fell. A grandfather clock next to the door tolled a Westminster chime.

"Okay, Tommy. I'm gonna help yuh, but I gotta know why," Joe said. "If you've done something to fuck over the Provos and those people—"

"Joe Coughlan's afraid of a bunch of ragtag guys pretendin' to be an army?" Tommy sneered. "I can't believe that."

"Tommy—you didn't hear a fuckin' thing I said, did you?" his father roared, smashing his hand on the table.

"I'll take care of it!" Tommy shouted back. "Just stay the fuck out of my business and let me handle it my own way, okay?"

They glared at each other for a long minute, then Joe sighed and opened his hands. "Okay. It's yours. But don't use any of the dockworkers anymore. It don't look good when you go to them. Use some of the boys from South Side. O'Farrell's there."

"What about the O'Briens?" Tommy asked. "Why not them?"

Joe's eyebrows raised. "Because I'm giving you the O'Farrells, that's why. I got other things for the O'Briens. I don't wanna pull them off. O'Farrell's lot is free at the moment. They should be enough. At least," he added, "they ain't dockworkers."

Tommy flushed and started to say something, then bit his lip. He rose, straightening the gold chains around his neck, pulling the cuffs of his silk shirt out the sleeves of his Brooks Brothers jacket to expose the gold cufflinks. "Okay. The O'Farrells it is."

He walked to the door and opened it.

"Tommy," his father called. He paused and turned around. "Be careful. You've underestimated this Fallon once; don't do it again."

"I'll take care of it!" Tommy snapped. He stepped through the doorway, pulling the door closed sharply behind him.

Joe waited for a long minute, thinking, remembering. He had started out on the docks as a dockworker thirty years ago for sixty-seven cents an hour, feeding his mother and four sisters with his wages. Then, one day, one of O'Ryan's mob had tried to lean on him and he had broken the man's arm and collarbone. He'd taken the man back to Jimmy O'Ryan at Terkel's Café and shoved him into the booth across from O'Ryan. O'Ryan had looked at the man then at Coughlan.

You got balls, kid.

And you got bums working for you.

Strong talk.

There's the proof. I could've killed 'im.

Why didn't you?

For what? You'd only send others.

You want his job, then.

I'm whole; he ain't.

It had been the beginning of Coughlan's rise through the ranks. Ten years later after O'Ryan died, Coughlan froze out O'Ryan's sons and took control of South Boston. Five years later, he had his thumb in almost every pie in the area except for the Italians, who wisely left him alone after trying once to take South Boston away from him. They had sent one of the Salvatore family after him. That had been close. He had been coming out of O'Leary's place over on Green Street when the man made his try. He would have succeeded too only Flynn had been there and put a bullet between the man's eyes. He remembered the look Flynn had given him then.

You need a good man around.

I thought I had them. Assholes!

You didn't.

You looking for work?

Always. But I don't come cheap.

A hundred a week suit you?

That's what you pay the others and look what nearly happened to you.

You got a point.

The dagos gotta word for what you need.

What's that?

Consigliori. That means—

I know what the fuck it means.

Well?

It looks like you gotta job. But don't ever use a fucking Italian word like that around me. Find something else to call yourself.

What about *garda cosanta?*

What's that?

Like a bodyguard. Only something more. It's Irish.

Irish, huh? Keep it.

And Flynn had been worth every penny. He had sent the Salvatore man's testicles wrapped in a jewel box from Tiffany's back to the family. There'd been talk of war, then, but cooler heads prevailed and an "understanding" was made between them. Coughlan would stay in Boston and leave the rest of the States to them. It had been enough, and after Blackie Cassidy asked him to come in with him, he had grown very wealthy over the years. Boston was the Silver Street Gang, but he knew that Blackie's hold on Boston was a tenuous one and others were watching, waiting for the same opportunity that he had waited for before moving in and taking everything he had built.

He sighed and leaned forward, touching the button on the intercom on his desk. "Get in here," he growled, and flicked the intercom off, leaning back in his chair, scowling at the ceiling.

The door opened and a slim, dark man entered. He crossed silently to the desk and waited patiently. At last, Joe looked at him. His eyes were black bits in his slim, white face. He looked almost skeletal. His cheeks were sunken and his lips one thin line.

"Well?" Joe asked. "What did you find out, Flynn?"

"Tommy's in deep," Flynn answered, his voice raspy. "I don't know what he has done but somehow he gave some of the boys over there a line they can follow back here to the States." Flynn shook his head. "What do you want?"

"I gave him the O'Farrells, but I don't think they're gonna be enough to stop this Fallon."

"Fallon?"

Joe heard the note in his voice and looked closely at Flynn. "You know him?"

"Yeah. Of him, that's certain. Saw him once when I went over to see MacCauley to set up the running for Cassidy. Remember? He'd be older now, but he had to be good to be that young and that close to MacCauley. Then," he shrugged. "You know. You hear things. The Brits gotta reward on his head and word is double that if someone can put a hit on him."

"The Brits? They got the SAS and they put out a hit on a guy?"

"He's that good, Joe."

"Jesus. Better than the British government? Shit." Joe drummed his fingers on the desktop, thinking. "So that's what Tommy's up against. Question is, why him?"

Flynn shrugged. "Who knows? Probably got to drinking in one of the pubs over there and let his mouth run before he put his brain in gear. What you want to do?"

"We got any idea where Fallon's at?"

"No, but it won't be hard to find out."

Joe chewed his lip, considering his options. At last, he looked at Flynn. "This is all Blackie's fuckin' fault. I tried to tell him drugs into Ireland's bad. Bad. Guns we can explain away and make a bit of money off. Makes us look good, but fuckin' drugs is something else. That's dirty to those guys. We can get away with it here 'cause those college kids don't think there's nothin' wrong with usin' 'em. Here, people think drugs ain't so bad. But in Ireland, shit, we're askin' for trouble. And," he added resignedly, "looks like that's what we got."

"Word has it that we ain't exactly popular with the Provos."

"Yeah." Joe drummed his fingers again, then leaned back in his chair, rolling his glass of whiskey between thick palms. "Watch Tommy. I don't want him hurt. He's going after Fallon."

"Joe, you know the kid ain't good enough for that," Flynn said quietly.

"I know, I know. Like I said: I gave him the O'Farrells to work with. They'll help. Jesus. What is that kid thinkin'?"

"He's trying to make himself into you, Joe, you know that."

"Yeah, but he ain't gonna make it, is he?" Joe looked around the room and shook his head. "All my life I work to build this, thinkin' I'm gonna leave it to Tommy." He looked up at Flynn. "He's gonna need help to hold it together, Flynn."

The man nodded. "And that may not be enough. He's not strong enough."

"I know. I know," Joe said, burying his nose in his glass of whiskey. "Christ."

"What do you want me to do?" Flynn asked.

"Alert the O'Briens," Joe said.

"I already did that," Flynn said.

"You did? Who the fuck told yuh to do that?" For a moment, Joe glared at Flynn, his knuckles growing white around the Waterford glass. Then he relaxed and nodded. "No, you were right. It's best that we have the O'Briens in on it."

"Anyone particular I should give it to?"

"Let the O'Briens figure it out," Joe said. "And maybe Tommy will get it done."

"Do you believe that, Joe?"

Joe gave him a long look. "No, I don't. But I wanna believe it. Now, go. Wait a minute. Maybe you'd better alert the O'Briens for backup. Hell, what was the Brit price on him?"

Flynn nodded. "Five thousand."

"Double it," Joe said. "Double it and turn it out on the streets. For that price, we might as well have Boston declare war on Fallon."

"It's safer," Flynn agreed. He turned and left the room, gently closing the door behind him.

Joe turned and looked into the fire. For one brief moment, he thought he saw his son's face outlined in the coals, and a cold chill ran over him despite the heat of the room, and he drank deeply of the whiskey against what could be an omen. A cold breeze fluttered against the back of his neck and a voice mockingly said, "Ah, a drop of the hardest on a day like this is surely one of God's blessings."

He whirled, slopping the whiskey over onto his hand. He cursed and pulled his handkerchief from his breast pocket, wiping his hand as he eyed his visitor lounging just inside the French windows.

"I don't know who the fuck you are, but you just put a nail in your coffin," he snarled, reaching for a button on his intercom. The stranger lifted his pistol, and Joe froze.

"The name's Fallon," the stranger said. "And you could be calling your secretary or the lad who just left, but the meeting will not be that long for the taking of notes."

"What do you want?" Joe said, narrowly eyeing the pistol. It was, he decided, one of the ugliest pistols he had ever seen, black and deadly.

"For now, a moment of your time. We have a wee problem with someone who's running arms and drugs into Ireland. The arms were welcome and may be once again, but not now. As for the drugs"—he shook his head—"now they are never to come across our borders. I presume it was just a case of misunderstanding. Or maybe one of your lads is going into business for himself. Your boy, Tommy, has come to our attention as—a possible tout for the business. We'd like you to have a wee talk with him."

"I don't know what you're talking about," Joe said.

Fallon sighed. "Now, let's not be pretending what we're not, shall we? You are Joe Coughlan, and you or your people once received money from NORAID to help the families of those poor Irish soldiers interned by the Prods and the Brits in Northern Ireland. Your son is, shall we say, the bag-boy for Martin Galvin—we suspect he's been skimming a bit of money off the top, but that's another point for later—and he brings the money over to Ireland. We send it back with our order. Except we stopped that with the cease-fire. Maybe a shipment just came through because it was too late to stop. A possibility, I suppose, but someone has picked up a nasty habit lately of bringing drugs along with the shipment. Drugs like heroin, you know. We don't like that, Joe. We appreciate your help and all, but we don't want the drugs in Ireland. Put a stop to it. Halter your boy, Joe."

"You march into my house and give me, Joe Coughlan, orders?" Joe said. His neck swelled against his collar. "Now you listen to me, Fallon."

"No, you listen, Joe," Fallon said. The syllables clicked against each other like ball bearings. "We're telling you to pull your son in check. Or I shall do it for you. And if I do it, it will be permanent. You understand? We're giving you this as a warning because you have been good to us as you have been good to yourself by, what is it, Joe? Fifteen percent? That we can tolerate, knowing you have business expenses and all—I wouldn't let it get any higher, though—but the drugs are out. This is not negotiable, you understand."

"You can go to hell," Joe Coughlan said. "Now get out."

"That's your last word on the matter?"

"You heard me."

Fallon sighed. "I thought that was what you'd say when I saw what a fine house you're living in. You know, it's a house like the landlords used to live in whenever they'd visit their estates in Ireland. They made fine fires. You've come a long way, Joe. Too bad you have forgotten your history."

He turned and stepped through the French windows and was

gone before Joe realized he was going. He turned to the desk and savagely jabbed the button on his intercom. "Flynn! Goddamnit! Get in here now!"

The door flew open and Flynn glided into the room, pistol in hand, his head swiveling rapidly back and forth.

"What is it?"

Joe pointed at the open windows. "That bastard Fallon was just here. What kind of security do we have around this dump, anyway? He could have been some dago, and I'd be dead!"

Flynn quickly crossed to the windows and stepped through them into the night. Joe shook his head and grabbed his glass and went back to the hunt table. He filled the glass with whiskey and turned as Flynn entered.

"He didn't kill the guards," he said. He shook his head. "The man must be like fog. He avoided the sensors, everything. What'd he want?"

"He was from the boys in Ireland," Joe said. "He told me to stop Tommy from running the dope along with the gun shipments."

"Uh-oh. So they haven't made the connection to Blackie, yet. They think Tommy's wildcatting the drugs along with the arms shipment. That could work to our advantage, Joe. Tommy could be a stalking-horse."

"No!" Joe said abruptly. "We ain't gonna risk Tommy's skin in this."

"Maybe you'd better think again about that, Joe," Flynn said. "If this guy is as good as this, he could make a lot of trouble. We could put a big screen around him and let Fallon walk into it. Be easier than looking for him. Let him come to us."

"No," Coughlan said. "Just get the bastard."

"What about Tommy?"

"What about him?" Joe asked belligerently. His eyes locked with Flynn's for a long moment. At last, the thin man sighed and shook his head.

"All right, Joe. It's a mistake, but I'll put the boys on him. Should I warn Tommy?"

Joe thought a minute, then shook his head. "No. Tommy started this. Let's see if he can finish it. This might be just what's needed. Sort of a training ground, d'yuh know what I mean?"

"I know what you mean, but it could get very expensive," he warned.

"Hell, what's money but to be spent?"

"I wasn't talking about money," Flynn said as he crossed to the door. He left, softly shutting the door behind him.

Joe turned and looked into the fire as he sipped his whiskey. He thought about Flynn's words. He rose and went to his desk. He opened a drawer and removed a small address book. It took him a minute to find the number. He lifted the receiver and called the international operator.

42

FALLON CAME AWAKE, LISTENING IN THE DARK. THE TAPPING CAME again at the door. He rolled easily from the bed, the CZ fitting smoothly into his hand. He crossed the darkened studio apartment, moving silently on the balls of his feet. He reached for the key in the lock, soundlessly turning it to unlock the door.

"Fallon?" Pegeen whispered. She tapped again on the door. Fallon gently turned the knob, then quickly opened the door, flattening himself against the jamb. He glanced quickly out into the hallway: she was alone. He relaxed and flicked the light switch on beside his shoulder.

She blinked in the sudden light, her eyes suddenly growing wide at the pistol in his hand. "What?" she said in confusion. Fallon reached out and gently pulled her into the room, closing the door and locking it behind her. He glanced at the cheap clock on the wall: 3:00 A.M.

"You made good time," he said.

"What—what are you doing with that?" she asked, staring at the pistol.

"Well now, it seemed a good idea at the time," he said, trying for a smile.

"Oh God," she moaned. She dropped into a straight-backed kitchen chair, her hands dangling between her legs. "You're one of them, aren't you? One of the boyos from home?"

"You didn't know?" Fallon asked quietly. He moved to the bureau beside the bed and slipped the CZ back into its holster. He slipped the harness around his shoulders, then turned, facing her. She shook her head.

"Sure, and if I didn't think you were one like me: new here, looking for a place to belong." She shook her head. "You played the piano like a professional; what was I to think?"

"What's left from a one-time dream," he said. "In another life when I was at university."

"I thought I'd left all that behind," she said numbly. "And here I am with it following me." She looked around the cheap, one-room apartment. The furniture was simple; a bed tucked against a wall, four wooden chairs to a plain kitchen table next to a counter that formed a tiny kitchenette, large pillows around the room in place of chairs, raw pine boards separated by old bricks serving as bookshelves against one side of the room, a small stereo cassette player on one of the shelves next to several cassettes of pop music.

"And in my own home, nevertheless." She gave a rueful laugh. "Ah well. Wasn't I the silly one to be looking for a new start?"

"What's wrong with that?" Fallon asked, moving beside her. He touched her arm; she pulled away.

"Don't," she said. "Don't."

"All right." He moved across the room from her, sitting on the bed.

Tears filled her eyes. She blinked them away, turning from him. "Who are you here for?"

"What makes you think I'm here for anyone?" he asked.

"Don't be making me out as stupid!" she said, tossing her head. She sniffed and took a tissue from the pocket of her coat, blowing her nose. "What would bring a man like you here? Unless you're running from someone? But that's not right, is it? You're not a man for running."

"No," he said. "It isn't."

"Then you're here for someone. Why couldn't you just leave things over there?"

"And what about yourself, Pegeen?" he asked.

She laughed. "Oh yes. What about me?"

"You're no stranger to this," he said. "Belfast, right? If I was to guess, I would guess Divis."

"And you'd be wrong. The Short Strand. At least, it was. Until the bloody Ulster Volunteer Force came through on a retaliation run. They chose the Shilling and Crown where Mum and Da were having a pint with friends on Internment Night. The bonfires were ready, huge stacks of wood, some two or three stories high, ready for the torch and Mum and Da had gone in for a pint before midnight when all would be set on. It was then the bloody UVF bastards decided to have their own little fire: a firebomb."

"And you?"

"Me? I was workin' the tables at the Europa. I didn't know what had happened until I returned home after midnight when the fires had burnt out—it was safer to travel the streets, you know? The neighbors were kind enough to tell me."

"And you came here? Looking for what?"

"A new life," she said. "What does anybody come here for? I wanted away from it all. Away from the killing and the hate. And you follow me. Oh, I don't mean that literally—"

"I know," he said quietly.

"It's just that I thought I'd left it all behind me, so." She sighed and rose and went to the sink. She drew a glass of water, drinking it down. She slumped back against the sink, hugging herself. "Who are you?"

"Just a man with a dirty job," he said quietly. "You don't want to know."

"You've done this before, haven't you?" He nodded. "Fallon. Fallon—" Her eyes widened. "Jaysus," she breathed. "I thought you were dead."

A tiny smile played across his lips.

"Me da used to tell us the tales about you."

"A long time ago," he said.

"It seems near enough," she said.

"Yes, you're right," he said. "It will always be near enough."

She gave him a curious look. "Funny. Somehow, it doesn't seem like you belong to your reputation. I get the feeling that you'd rather be somebody else."

"Wouldn't we all?"

She shook her head, shrugging her coat from her shoulders and draping it over the back of one of the kitchen chairs. "No, it's something else."

"I'd better go," he said, rising. He shrugged into the shoulder harness and reached for his coat, but she stepped forward, taking it from him.

"You really don't like this, do you? Your eyes," she said suddenly. He remained quiet, looking at her, watching as she frowned, puzzling over the situation. Then her face cleared and slowly she nodded. "I remember now: you disappeared, didn't you? There are those who thought you were dead. What happened?"

"Time happened; I grew older."

"And—" she prompted.

"And Belfast didn't; it remained the same. Neighborhoods drawn up into camps, each besieging the other. But nothing changed. New faces came and went; new graves were dug and fresh bodies put in them, but nothing changed. We would shoot some of theirs, and they would shoot some of ours. Mothers would cry, and fathers would stand at bars with pints in their fists cursing the sons of other fathers. Then more graves would be dug and more bodies made to fill them. It was enough."

"And now?" She nodded at the gun under his arm. "Do you really think it will end until you throw that away?"

"No," he said. "But it's gone too far too long for me to be without it."

"And why are you here?"

"There has been one change," he said. "Drugs." Her eyes widened. "Someone's running drugs into the country."

"And you're here to stop that?"

"Yes."

"Just you?"

"Yes."

"You're a poor romantic fool," she said. "One man."

He smiled and reached for his coat. She pulled it away from him and hung it on the back of another chair. He looked into her eyes. "Are you sure?"

She nodded. "Yes. There's no escaping it, I'm thinking."

"No," he said. "There isn't."

"Hold me, Fallon?" she said. "That's all. Just hold me? For a while?"

"Yes," he said. He opened his arms, and she stepped into them. She winced as her cheek struck the butt of the pistol beneath his arm. He shrugged out of the harness and tossed the pistol on top of the bureau, then hugged her to his chest. He smelled the smoke of the bar in her hair and beneath it, a clean fresh scent like lavender. And he felt the sadness of both.

43

THE SMELL OF BACON WOKE FALLON. HE SWUNG FROM THE BED AND looked across the room at Pegeen standing in the small kitchenette. She smiled back at him.

"Good morning," she said. "How'd you sleep?"

"Ah well, well," he said. He stood and stretched the night knots from his muscles.

"Hungry?"

"I could eat," he said. He grinned at her. "You're moving around bright and early this morning."

"A person has to eat," she said defensively, then grinned again. "It'll be a minute or two. I laid out the towels and such for you in there." She nodded at the bathroom off the hallway. "You'll have to use my razor, but there's a new toothbrush on the counter for you."

"You've the heart of an angel," Fallon said.

"Get on with you," she said, turning away from him and busying herself at the pan. Twin bright spots of pink appeared in her cheeks. Fallon laughed and walked into the bathroom.

He emerged minutes later, his hair wet, a bit of soap below his ear, twin nicks across his left cheek. "Can I use your phone? I need to call my Uncle Dan. I'll reverse the charges."

She nodded, and he picked up the telephone and quickly made the arrangements. She handed him a piece of bacon while he waited. He wolfed it down, tasting the sugar of the cure in the meat.

"Uncle Dan?—Yes, it's me. I'm in Boston now. A different number." He read it off. "Yes, another 'friend' I guess you could say— No, a girl—a woman," he hastily corrected as she threatened to throw the spatula at him. He grinned back at her. She stuck her tongue out and began preparing the plates. "Yes, Uncle Dan. A fine colleen from home. Pegeen's her name—'Tis enough for you, you old reprobate. Any word from MacCauley?—Anywhere else?—Watch yourself, Uncle Dan. We had a bit of trouble at Con Edwards's place in New York. They might trace me back to you.—You take care."

He hung up and moved to the counter where Pegeen waited with the plates laid out. He picked up the glass of fresh orange juice and drank it down.

"Your uncle? In Ireland?"

He nodded, picking up the plates and carrying them to the table. "Yes. All I've got save my brother. He's a priest," he added.

"Now isn't that something. One brother damning the souls and another trying to save them."

"I suppose so," he said soberly. "But Uncle Dan's all we've got left other than a few odd second cousins here and there. He's retired now, but at one time, he ran as fine a shipping firm as you could want."

"What happened?" she asked, sliding onto the chair he held for her. He moved to the other side of the table, sitting.

"When the Republic opened its doors to foreign trade, they left out the import-export sanctions that would protect the Irish business. A lot of them folded in the open market. They couldn't compete. Uncle Dan, was one of them. He went bankrupt, but before he did, he managed to pull a lot of his capital out of the business. Now he spends most of his time fishing. Keeps him busy, you know."

"He must feel badly about that," she said, buttering the toast. She handed a slice to him. He nodded his thanks.

"Oh, I expect he did at first. I really don't know as I was spending most of my time in Belfast then. But he's an old man now, and it's good that he can do pretty much what he wants."

"And yourself? What about yourself?" she asked. She kept her eyes on her plate.

"I've been out of it for a while. A few years, yes," he said as she looked up in surprise at him. "When my da died, he left my brother and myself fairly well off. Enough to keep me in the family cottage near Warrenspoint. Do you know the place?"

She nodded. "Yes. We used to go down to the hotel there on vacation when I was a girl. Oh, it was grand times, it was. The sun, the sea."

"Ah well. The hotel's gone now. A bomb." A frown clouded her face, and he quickly moved on. "Do you remember the mountains to the south?" She nodded. "Well, the one long one is called Long Woman's Grave. I have a small cottage there I share with Miss Sheba. My cat," he said as she arched an eyebrow. "Although I don't know who belongs to whom."

"And what do you do there, Tomas Fallon?" she asked, pouring the coffee.

"I read and tend my flowers and play the piano and on Wednesday after Vespers, I go down the side of the mountain to the home of a priest and play a game or two of chess."

"It sounds lonely," she said.

"It is," he said. "But that's what is left for me."

"It's what's left for all of us," she answered.

"Yes," he said. "For all from the North."

"Will you stay?"

"Do you want me to?"

"I think so," she said. "Besides, you gave your uncle my number."

"I did that," he said, grinning. "Sorry. I should have asked first."

"It's all right. And what are you up to and about today?"

"I think you know," he said quietly, the laugh lines disappearing from his face. His eyes lost their warmth, and she bowed her head over her coffee.

"Yes I do."

They finished their breakfast in silence, the early happiness of the morning a distant memory.

44

Tommy Coughlan moved exaltedly down India Well toward the wharf where the *Sibyl* lay tied. He remembered the talk with his father the night before and played the talk back in his mind, substituting the things he should have said for the things he'd said.

Just a fucking messenger. Shit. What would he think if he knew that I had been skimming, and that skimming bought a couple of pubs in the old country and a few other things as well? Little Tommy ain't as fucking dumb as he thinks! Maybe you should have told him.

But he shivered as he thought what admitting to skimming would have meant to his father. It wasn't so much stealing from the bog-trotters that would have brought his father's anger down upon him but the thought that he was stealing from his father. And Blackie Cassidy.

A cold sweat broke out as he thought about what Blackie would do to him if he found out that Tommy Coughlan had been taking money from his shipments. He didn't worry about NORAID or the boyos. Shit, not one of them would dare do anything to Joe Coughlan's boy.

He remembered the telephone call that morning and laughed out loud as he thought about Fallon's words to him.

That sonofabitch doesn't know who he's messing with. The O'Farrells will find him, sure. And if not them, the O'Briens.

Because, Daddy, I know that you'll put the O'Briens behind me. You always have.

He emerged on the wharf and walked down to the *Sibyl*. He swung himself aboard and carefully picked his way across the deck to the cabin, ducking his head to enter. The captain, an Aran Islander who had fled the bleak shores and even bleaker life, looked up as he entered.

"The best morning to you," he said. Coughlan smiled at him.

"Well, Captain, will we be having another run coming up?"

"Aye. The guns will be waitin' off the Banks for us. And yourself, will you be sending aboard a supercargo?"

"That I will, that I will." Coughlan took a silver flask from his coat pocket and unscrewed the cap. He offered it to the captain, who shook his head. Coughlan shrugged and drank deeply before replacing the cap and the flask back into his pocket.

"You'll have to have it aboard this evening," the captain said. "We'll be catching the late tide. We won't be able to wait."

"That might be kind of tight," Tommy said.

The captain shook his head regretfully. "I've got my orders from your father. I've got to clear Deer Island Light by midnight."

Tommy's eyes narrowed. "I can have the stuff here by nine."

"That'll be too late. I have to catch the turn," the captain said. "The boat will be waiting for us with the guns. Best if you have it here by five so we can get it stowed. We'll be hard-pressed at that," he added.

"You'll wait if I tell you," Coughlan said evenly. The captain's eyes narrowed.

"We have a rendezvous," he said. "I can't be missing that one."

"I'll get the shipment here when I do," Coughlan said tightly. Anger sparked from his eyes. The captain took a step back, his face setting into a cold mask. "Do what I tell you, now."

"It's Blackie Cassidy's boat," the captain said quietly.

"And it's Blackie Cassidy's supercargo that you'll be taking on board when I get it here."

The captain shook his head. "I think not. You can explain it to Blackie if you want. Me, I'm getting the guns over there when he says. It's your ass that'll be wanting, not mine. I keep the ship's schedule. It's your job to get the shipment here on time. Have it here by six. We sail on the tide."

"Goddamn it," Tommy said roughly. His hand slipped inside his coat, then froze as the captain looked over his shoulder.

"Good morning, Sean. Would you be helpin' Mr. Coughlan ashore, now? I think he'll be going."

Tommy glanced over his shoulder. The first mate stood shortly behind him, big and brawny, his face cold and impassive above his heavy beard. He swallowed his anger and pushed his way past and out of the cabin. Outside he drew a deep breath then turned and shouted back down into the cabin.

"You be waiting for me, hear, Captain? Or there'll be someone else sailing this boat on its next trip!"

The captain appeared in the doorway. Tommy's face burned as he recognized the contempt in the captain's eyes. "I hear you," he said. "And I'm telling you that we sail on the tide. Now run along and make your arrangements." He turned away from Tommy and went back into the cabin.

Tommy seethed as he climbed back onto the wharf and began walking rapidly away. His ears burned with shame. He composed again the words he should have said in his head.

45

FALLON STOOD ON MILK STREET ACROSS FROM THE ADDRESS BILLY had given him in the Black Rose the night before. He watched carefully, but noticed only one man standing in the foyer of the address, reading a paper, stamping his feet now and then against the cold.

Fallon smiled thinly as he moved down the street, crossing over to come back from the east. The man watched him as he approached. Fallon nodded cheerfully at him, then looked away down the street. He raised his arm and waved at an imaginary figure. The man automatically turned his head to look, and Fallon took a quick step into the foyer, the CZ appearing in his hand and pressing hard against the man's ribs. The man stiffened.

"Now then, God bless all here," Fallon murmured. "Are you alone?" The man nodded. "Sure now? I wouldn't like any surprises."

"I'm sure," the man said.

"Good." Fallon said. "Now who's upstairs?"

"Nobody," the man said quickly.

Fallon grinned at him. "I don't believe you. Let's go up, shall we?"

"There ain't nobody there," the man complained.

"Then why are you here?" Fallon asked. "Move."

He pushed the man in through the foyer to the tiny lobby inside the converted warehouse. He glanced around: they were alone. Across from them was an elevator with a wooden grate. He pushed the man to it. "In the lift," he said. The man took a step inside, and Fallon followed.

"What now?" the man asked sullenly. Fallon nudged him with the pistol.

"Now we go up," he said.

"I'm telling you: there's nobody there," he said.

"Let's be checking," Fallon answered. "Maybe they came in through the back door." He jabbed the pistol hard in the man's back against his spine. The man gasped from the sudden pain and closed the grate, throwing the lever to UP. The elevator began to rise.

"You won't get out of here, Fallon," the man warned.

"So you know me, then. Good," Fallon said. "But how did you know I'd be coming?"

The man suddenly started to turn, his hand darting inside his coat. Fallon took a quick step to the left and brought the pistol around hard against the man's head. His hat flew off and he fell, his head bouncing off the floor of the elevator. Fallon bent and quickly searched the man's pockets, finding the pistol under the man's arm. He removed it and tucked it into the left-hand pocket of his own coat as the elevator ground to a stop.

"You should be more careful," Fallon said to the unconscious figure. He stepped over him and slid the door open and stepped out into the top floor of the warehouse.

A lot of money had been spent to convert the floor into a spacious apartment. One wall was glass, looking out over Boston and the harbor. Thick rugs covered the highly polished parquet floor. Comfortable chairs were scattered islands throughout the spacious rooms with small tables between them. At one end, a bar stood, heavy with suspended glassware above it, the back a gold-flecked mirror. Three short flights of stairs climbed to the kitchen on his left, complete with stainless cookware hanging from a black-iron grate, a butcher's block in the center, then continued upward to a large sleeping loft.

Fallon took a quick glance around then moved soundlessly up the stairs to the sleeping loft. He smiled to himself: Anne Ryan lay curled around a pillow in the middle of the king-sized bed. He walked carefully to the left of the bed and looked quickly into the bathroom: a large, black sunken tub, mirrored walls and ceiling, but they were alone. He walked over to the railing and looked out over the rest of the apartment: it was empty. He returned to the bed and pulled the covers down. She lay naked beneath them. She muttered crossly in her sleep and groped for the covers, but Fallon threw them off the end of the bed and stepped back, waiting.

She sat up, rubbing the sleep from her eyes. "Damn you, Tommy! Why'd you—" She stopped suddenly as she saw Fallon standing away from the bed, his hands crossed in front of him, the pistol dangling from his right.

"God bless all here," he said. He smiled at her. "And where is this Tommy you are needing?"

"Fallon," she said. She shook her head, the blond hair flying behind her in a tousled mane. "He's out."

"I can see that," Fallon said. "But where? Out is a big place."

She shrugged, her breasts rising with the gesture. "How'd I know? I was sleepin' before he left. And you seem to have taken care of that." She yawned and stretched, then leaned back to show her nakedness to full advantage. She gave him a sleepy smile, her hands casually slipping under the pillows.

"Let's try again, shall we?" Fallon said. He unclasped his hands, the pistol dangling negligently at his side. "Now let us imagine that you suddenly needed to get in touch with him. How would you go about it?"

"Well." She slowly licked her lips, moistening them. "I would try his father, I guess. Or his uncle."

"His uncle? And who might that be?"

"Donovan O'Brien," she said. "Have you heard of him?"

Her hand suddenly moved, then froze as he lifted his pistol. The bore seemed to center between her eyes.

"No. You tried that in Dublin, remember?" he said softly. She stared into his eyes. Her flesh pebbled against a sudden chill. Her eyes wavered. "It's no good," he said. "You'll never make it."

Her shoulders convulsed and her hands streaked from beneath the pillows. The right one clutched a tiny automatic. A bright flower seemed to grow from the end of Fallon's pistol, and she watched in fascination as it expanded and slapped her in the middle of her forehead. The back of her head blew apart, driving her back onto the bed. The automatic fell from nerveless fingers. Fallon stepped forward and leaned over the bed, collecting it.

"And Michael John is all right," he said to her corpse. Then he turned and walked from the apartment. He stepped outside and paused, leaning back against the doorway to let his eyes adjust to the light from the dark of the hallway. Something slammed into his shoulder, staggering him. He fell to one knee as a bullet ricocheted off the wall above him. He rolled to his right as another bounced off the pavement where he had been kneeling. Then he reversed his direction and rolled back, spinning on his good shoulder and leaping to his feet. He staggered again as he fell through the doorway back into the building and huddled against the wall. A shot whizzed by and smacked into the stairwell. He hobbled around the stairs and down the corridor. He came up against a fire door, opened it, glanced outside, then stepped out, shutting the door behind him. He made his way down the alley, fighting off a wave of dizziness. He reached under his coat and pressed against his shoulder. No pain. But that, he knew, was shock only. The pain would come and soon. He glanced at the blood on his fingers then took a handkerchief from his pocket, wadded it up, and pressed it against the wound. He pulled the strap of his shoulder holster over the handkerchief, anchoring it to the wound. Then he took several deep breaths and walked quickly down the alley.

SIMON KENTON SLIPPED THE TELESCOPE FROM ITS TIP-OFF MOUNTS and unscrewed the silencer from the end of the carbine's barrel. He folded the carbine stock back against its barrel. He slipped the telescope and silencer and carbine into the backpack on the floor beside him and left the empty office. He closed the door firmly behind him and walked down the stairs and outside. He paused on the stoop then turned left and walked away. He felt angry at missing Fallon again, but content that he had hit him and the hollowpoint .222 bullet would have done a fair amount of damage that would need a doctor's attention. And there weren't that many doctors one could use who would not report a bullet wound to the authorities.

A tiny smile played along his lips. Now the stalking began.

A familiar excitement ran through him as he walked jauntily down the street.

46

TOMMY COUGHLAN FROWNED AS HE HALTED HIS APPROACH TO THE apartment on Milk Street. *Where is that bastard Dick O'Farrell?* He frowned, shuffling from foot to foot, thinking. Then he slid his hand inside his coat, touching the comfort of the pistol.

He walked into the building and took a quick glance around the tiny lobby. It was deserted. He crossed to the elevator and threw the wooden grate back. He paused as he spied the senseless figure on the floor. His stomach lurched, and he pulled the pistol from under his coat and stepped into the elevator, putting his back against it. He panted, feeling the shortness of his breath. He quickly pulled the grate shut and threw the lever forward. The elevator lurched upward. He knelt and checked the man on the floor. The man was alive, but wouldn't come around for all of his shaking. He stepped away from him, cursing, as the elevator jerked to a stop.

He threw open the doors and waited. Cautiously he moved out into the apartment, sliding his way along the wall.

"Anne?" he called. "Where the fuck are you?"

He listened to the beating of his heart in the silence. His mouth grew dry, and he licked his lips, trying to make spit. Slowly he mounted the stairs, feeling the quiet press in on him. The pistol felt slick in his grasp, but he was afraid to change hands with the pistol and dry them on his coat. He stepped up into the bedroom and immediately found the body on the bed, her blood a fine spray on the wall above. He gagged, then suddenly fell to his knees, sour coffee and doughnuts spewing from his mouth.

And then he ran for the bathroom as he felt his bladder begin to weaken.

FALLON FELT FAINT AS HE MADE HIS WAY INTO THE BUILDING AND took a deep breath, forcing his eyes to focus on the steps leading up to Pegeen's apartment. He bit his lip to divert the pain beginning to throb in his shoulder and forced himself to take one step after another. He counted each step softly under his breath. Still, he thought he would never make it and then suddenly the door appeared in front of him. He knocked gently against it until it opened.

Pegeen's eyes widened as he staggered inside and pushed the door shut behind him. He leaned against it and tried to smile at her.

"Sorry—" he began, but then his concentration failed him and he slid down to the floor. She stepped forward and tried to catch him.

"Goddamn you, Fallon," he heard, and then a great blackness swept over him.

FALLON BLINKED AND FOUND HIMSELF STARING AT A LARGE CRACK zigzagging through the plaster of the ceiling above him. He felt the softness of a bed beneath him and a thick pad covering his shoulder. Beneath the pad, his shoulder throbbed, but there was no pain and he rolled his head to stare into the intent black eyes above him.

"Well, you're back. That's good," a voice said.

Fallon blinked as the face pulled back. A few wisps of iron-gray hair had been combed over a gleaming bald pate. The black eyes were deep inside heavy cheeks above a large red nose as round as a snooker ball and dotted with blackheads. A white shirt was buttoned tight against a collar and a green tie, the knot disappearing beneath the flesh of his jowls and chin.

"Who are you?" Fallon croaked. He raised his hand, slipping it beneath his pillow. The man frowned and shook his head.

"Don't worry," he said. His voice was soft but there was strength beneath it. "You have a very wise girl here." He nodded at Pegeen standing and looking worried off to his right. "She knew the right people to ask down at the Black Rose to get me. I'm John Riordan. Retired doctor. You've lost a lot of blood, but the bullet did no permanent damage. Surprising. Usually when a hollow-point hits it shatters when it strikes a bone and then bounces around inside you, tearing you up. But you would know that, wouldn't you?" He reached onto the table next to the bed and picked up Fallon's pistol. He looked at it for a moment, then shook his head and handed it to him. "I think you might be needing this. Whoever did this"—he pressed the bandage on Fallon's shoulder—"will still be looking for you, I'm thinking. And for all that you are, you shouldn't be without a chance. Otherwise I'd throw that thing in the bay. I have a hunch it's put quite a few people in the ground over the years, hasn't it?"

Fallon took the pistol from him, recognizing the weight of it in his hand and knowing that it was loaded. He pulled the slide back fractionally to see the bullet seated in the chamber, then set the safety and laid it beside him on the bed. He tried to glance at his shoulder, but lifting his head made tiny black dots swim in his vision and he laid his head back down on the pillow.

"So why didn't the bullet bounce around inside me?"

Riordan shook his head. "It glanced off your shoulderblade and exited. I took a small sliver of bone out—nothing much to speak of—and sewed the hole shut around a small tube. You have to let it drain for a few days and heal inside out. I'll check back daily on you to change the bandage. Meanwhile, you need to eat and rest." He rose and picked up a small bag that had been lying on the floor next to his feet. He placed the bag on the bed and picked up his coat from where it lay over the footboard. He shrugged into it with difficulty, his beefy shoulders settling the coat around his shoulders. He stared thoughtfully at Fallon. "You must have been turning when the bullet struck you. It came out below the shoulderblade, just missing the muscle mass. That's a one-in-a-million shot. You were very lucky. If you had to be shot, that was the place. The bullet traveled right through you, missing everything except a few minor blood vessels. Whoever shot you must have been up very high. Any idea who?" Fallon gave him a small smile. "No, you wouldn't say even if you did, would you?" He sighed and rubbed his eyes tiredly. "I don't know who you are, but I know what you are and I don't like it. There're enough people killing in this town without bringing others in. I suppose you're with the O'Briens or O'Farrells. Doesn't matter really. One group's just as bad as the other. I hope they're not starting up again. We had a bloodbath in the city ten, fifteen years ago. A lot of innocent people got hurt in that one before Blackie Cassidy put a stop to it."

"And Coughlan?" Fallon asked.

Riordan paused and peered closely at him. "You know about him. Well. That explains a bit, I suppose, though I don't know what."

"Enough that a man like you should be able to figure it out, I'm thinking," Fallon said dryly. "But I'm not with any of them. And I would appreciate you keeping this to yourself."

"The rules of the game," Riordan said absently. He picked up his bag and studied Fallon again. "You are alone in this, aren't you?" He glanced at Pegeen. "And you stumbled onto her. Good luck for you, but bad luck for her." He shook his head. "I'd advise you to heal quickly, my friend, then get out of here as fast as you can. And take her with you. The best thing would be for both of you to disappear. I won't say anything, but she had to ask enough people to find me that someone will drop a hint here and there and whoever is looking for you will pick it up and follow it back here."

He crossed to the door and opened it and left. Pegeen followed him, shutting the door behind him, then leaned against the door and stared across the room at Fallon. Tired rings made her eyes look bruised and her hair was rumpled and the ends hung limply, half-curling against her cheek. She wore a thick sweater in a fisherman's weave and faded blue jeans. She was barefoot.

"Hungry?" she asked. He shook his head. "A glass of water would be nice," he said.

She nodded and went to the tap, filled a glass. She opened a drawer, found a straw, and put it in the glass and brought it to him. She held his head while he sipped thirstily, then sank back gratefully against the pillow.

"Better?" she asked. He nodded. "Wouldn't be taking much to heat up some soup. Chicken noodle or rice? I've got both."

"How did you find him?" Fallon asked.

"The doctor?" He nodded. "From Billy at the Black Rose. He'll keep it to himself, if that's what you're thinking."

"Doesn't matter. Riordan's right, you know," Fallon said, nodding toward the door. "You need to get away from all of this."

She sighed and sat in the chair Riordan had vacated. She leaned forward, clasping her hands between her thighs. She rocked slowly back and forth. "And what about you?" she asked. "Should I just be leaving you here for whoever comes through that door?"

"If they come through that door, they come through that door. Won't be making a bit of difference Sunday or Monday if they do and you're here or not. And there isn't a thing you could do to stop them. Pegeen," he said softly, "it's something you ran away from. You don't want to be taking it back upon your shoulders. Leave."

She shook her head. "I don't think it is something that one can leave behind. It is something that will follow anyone who leaves Ireland. You can't get away from that once you're born into it. I thought I could, but you see—" She gestured around her and smiled brokenly. "It's fate. We can't escape it. Like Deirdre of the Sorrows. Remember?"

He nodded. It was an old story from the time of the Irish kings. One of the "Three Sorrows of Storytelling." Deirdre had tried to escape her marriage to Conchobor, the Ulster king, and fled with Naisi to Alba where she lived happily until Conchobor pretended to forgive them and sent Fergus mac Roich to bring them back. He killed Naise and tried to force Deirdre to marry him, but Deirdre killed herself rather than submit to Conchobor's demands. The story was often identified with the story of Ireland herself.

"Yes," he said. "I know it well. And Ulster, once cursed, has never been without bloodletting all these years."

"There is something to the old stories," she said, trying to smile.

"But they are only stories," Fallon said pointedly. "Just stories. People are what they make of themselves. And if they bring the stories into their lives, that gives the stories their lives."

"But the stories," she said softly, "are all that we are. We are the stories, the stories are us. It makes no difference, Tomas: you are here in my home and with you came the Troubles."

He said nothing but held out his arm. She glanced down at the pistol lying on the bed beside him. He picked it up and placed it on the table then held out his good arm again. She slid from the chair and lay gently down next to him, curling herself into him, resting her head on his good shoulder. He held her tightly as tears slid down her face and fell warmly onto his chest.

A great sadness filled him along with a great weariness.

47

FALLON RESTED FOR THREE DAYS BEFORE THEY LEFT. DURING THAT time, Riordan returned twice a day to change Fallon's bandage. On the third day, he removed the drain, gave Fallon another shot of penicillin against the possibility of infection, then showed Pegeen how to clean the wound with a cotton swab dipped in witch hazel, and left. He cautioned them again not to remain long and the next day, moving carefully, Fallon dressed in a pair of washed jeans and a black turtleneck sweatshirt Pegeen had found for him in an army surplus store. His shoulder was too sore for the shoulder harness, but he placed the pistol at the small of his back and slipped into a lined canvas barn coat with a corduroy collar two sizes too large that fell roomily around his hips. He pulled a scully cap low over his eyes and together they left, moving cautiously along the streets away from Pegeen's apartment.

They took a bus out of Boston north to Salem and found a bed-and-breakfast there overlooking the harbor where the hosts were all too happy to take them in out of season. For three weeks they played at being happy but everywhere they went, Fallon's pistol went with them, riding first tucked into the small of his back beneath his belt, then in the holster snugged beneath his arm. When he held her, he hugged her with his right arm, and when she wrapped her arms around him, she carefully made certain that she did not touch the pistol. But it was still there, between them, a constant reminder of the past.

They visited the Custom House and the famous seven-gabled house and Fallon bought copies of Nathaniel Hawthorne's *The Scarlet Letter* and *The House of the Seven Gables* and they read them together in the warmth of their bedroom, snuggled in the bed with a thick comforter over them and an electric heater warming the room. They talked about the books when both finished, then traded and each read the other's. During the day, they walked the narrow streets, visiting the museums and tiny tourist shops. Fallon bought her a small crystal on a chain from a self-described witch's store. She hung it around her neck, dropping it inside her blouse where it dangled snugly between her breasts. The next day, he bought her a moonstone in a simple silver setting and she wore it on her little finger and pretended that they were engaged to be engaged to be engaged. And they laughed at that and walked again along the harbor and he pretended to be placed in a set of stocks and she giggled at his mugging, covering her mouth with her hands.

And so they pretended that they were normal.

Until one day Fallon glimpsed a man dressed in a pea coat and watch cap who looked familiar lounging against a street lamp outside the restaurant where they were eating. When they left, ambling slowly down the walk, he glanced into the store windows they passed, pretending an interest, but watching as the man moved away from the street lamp and casually followed them. Pegeen felt the muscles tighten in Fallon's arm and looked up at him questioningly. He smiled down at her, but she saw his eyes flicker back to a window and dropped her arm, shoving her hands inside the pockets of her jacket.

"It's starting again," she said softly.

Fallon shrugged. "I don't know, Pegeen."

"And?"

"You knew that it was only a matter of time," he said quietly. He glanced again into a store window, stopping to look at the display. The man stopped behind them and pretended to look at his watch, then moved into a doorway, but he didn't enter the store and Fallon sighed.

"We're being followed," she said dully.

"Yes," he answered.

"What now?"

"I think you know," he said. "There's no sense in pretending that you don't. That *we* don't," he amended.

"So it's been grand and all of that but it's back to the war? Is that it? We could go away, Tomas. Elsewhere. It's a big country. Maybe Chicago. Or San Francisco."

Fallon smiled down at her and placed his left arm around her shoulder. She felt the pistol nudge her and pushed slightly away as he casually unbuttoned his coat.

"The entire ocean wasn't big enough before," he said. "You said it yourself, remember, Deirdre?"

She sighed. "I was hoping to be wrong."

"So was I," Fallon said.

She twisted her head to look up at him. "You're not just saying that, now, are you, Tomas? I really wouldn't want that. A lie, I mean."

"No," Fallon said. He squeezed her tightly, then gently moved a little away from her. His hand slipped beneath his coat and she felt his fingers as he loosened the pistol in its holster. "I mean it. The past weeks have been—the best in years."

Tears glistened in her eyes. She turned her face away from him. "Goddamn them," she said fiercely. "Goddamn them all."

"He has, I'm thinking," Fallon said softly. "But there you have it."

"And now what?" she asked again.

"Back to Boston. And get you away from it all," he said quietly.

"I'll—"

"Leave," he interrupted. She looked up at him. He shook his head and smiled. For a moment she saw what he could have been and then a hardness fell over his features. "I don't want to be watching you and your back along with mine. It's better that way."

"Alone, you mean." She tried to laugh. "Sinn Fein—ourselves alone." He remained silent and an awkward silence grew between them. "I could be useful, Tomas."

He paused and turned, taking her face in his hands. He kissed her gently and then draped his arm around her shoulder and walked her slowly down the street.

"There's a pub in New York City called Brennan's. A good man owns it. I want you to go there and tell him that Father Fallon sent you." He smiled faintly at her raised eyebrows. "My brother's a priest back home. 'Tis on his passport I'm here and Brennan knows me as a priest. Tell him that I sent you and then tell him why. He'll take care of you."

"How do you know this?"

Fallon laughed. "Because he wishes he was one of us and this is as close as he'll be getting to all of that, and in the years to come he'll be able to tell his grandchildren how he took a hand in Ireland's fight for freedom like his grandfather did before him in the Easter Rising."

"But he won't really know what it's all about, will he, Tomas?"

"No, God help him. And I hope he never does," Fallon said. "Now, you go to New York City and when I've finished with all of this, I'll be coming there for you."

"And?" she asked. "Then what?"

"Then, maybe we'll see if we can lose ourselves truly in this great country. At least, we can give it a try."

"Is that what you're thinking?"

"That's what I'm thinking. It's worth a try. Anything is worth a try."

"But you don't hope."

"No. I tried for four years and here I am once again."

They walked in silence for half a block before she stretched her arm around his waist, hugging him to her as they walked.

"Four years, now. Well. That can be a lifetime too, you know. It's all in the way of your thinking."

"Then you'll go to New York?"

"Aye," she said. "But first I have a few things to pick up back at my apartment. And to close it, you know."

"No," he said. "Don't do that. Leave it for the landlord to come around and do the closing. That will give us a bit more time."

"All right," she said. "But I do want a few things from there."

"Better not," he said.

"It's not negotiable," she said lightly. She stood on tiptoes to kiss his cheek. "I'll be careful. And," she added, giving a slight nod to their rear, "if that is the only one who has found us, we can befuddle them by splitting up a bit. They'll be looking for the two of us, but when we leave here, it's you he'll be following. I'll go back and get my things and go on to New York."

Fallon shook his head. "We'll go back separately, but you wait at the apartment for me. I'll take you to the train myself and put you on it."

"Tomas—"

"Enough, woman," he said gently. "There you have it."

"And then?"

"What is San Francisco like?"

"Ah," she said brightly. "It's a grand place. Or so I'm told."

48

FALLON STOPPED IN THE HALLWAY TO PEGEEN'S APARTMENT, FLATTEN-ing himself against the wall. His hand slipped inside his coat and emerged with the pistol. He thumbed the safety off and stood waiting, listening hard to the silence. You're getting old. You should have heard the silence before this. Too quiet. He glanced at his watch: only 2:00 P.M. Maybe Pegeen was out shopping. Maybe she wasn't.

Carefully, he checked both ends of the hallway. Then he reached out, grasped the doorknob, gave a sudden twist and threw it open, flattening himself against the wall, waiting for the blast or shot. But nothing came, and he moved carefully into the studio apartment, spotting her at once, naked and tied to the kitchen table. A piece of duct tape was across her mouth, shutting out her screams. Only she wouldn't scream, now, he saw: she was dead. A hard death, he noticed from the burns and cuts across her body. Her wrists and ankles were bloody from struggling against the wire holding them tightly to the legs of the table.

"Ah, Pegeen," he said softly. "You were right; you couldn't get away from it, could you?"

He slid the pistol back under his arm, freed her arms and legs, and gently carried her to the bed, placing her in it, and pulled the covers over her.

"Thank you, colleen," he whispered.

Then he left, securely locking the door behind him. He stopped in the next block and used the telephone. He dialed the overseas operator and waited. A mechanical voice answered. He started to speak, then caught himself. An answering machine could be heard by a lot of people. "Uncle Dan, I'm moving from the last number I left to another place. You remember your song? Well, there's a pub here by that name. Try to find MacCauley and tell him I need help. You can find me there. I'll wait for your call."

He hung up, hesitated, then called the police, reported Pegeen's death, and left, walking rapidly south toward the Black Rose. He didn't notice the two men slip in behind, following him.

WRIGHT LOOKED UP, IRRITATED, AS LOUDON ENTERED HIS OFFICE. He would have to speak with him about that, he decided. "Yes, what is it?"

"We have found Fallon," Loudon said, coming to a halt in front of the director's desk. "He's in Boston at a bar called the Black Rose down near Quincy Market."

"Excellent," Wright said, leaning back and smiling. "How did you manage that?"

"We placed another watch on Edwards's apartment. He and the woman left this morning for Boston. We followed them. This time, I made sure there was more than one agent on them. They went to the Black Rose immediately. Fallon wasn't there, and so they waited. He just walked in a couple of minutes ago. I've kept the line open. What do you want done?"

"Let me have it," Wright ordered. Loudon leaned across the desk and pressed the director's intercom.

"Gladys, please transfer the call on my line in here."

Moments later, the telephone rang. Wright answered it. "This is Richard Wright," he said. His eyes rolled. "Yes, that Richard Wright. Is Fallon there now?—With whom?—Yes, very well. Please dispose of them. All. Discreetly.—Yes, all of them. It can't be helped." He replaced the telephone and leaned back in his chair, rubbing his temples.

"Is there anything I can do for you, Richard?" Loudon asked.

"Yes, there is. Please leave," Wright said curtly. Loudon looked in amazement at him. "It's over now. You may go back to whatever it is you're doing in Operations."

Loudon turned and walked away from the desk, his ears burning from embarrassment.

"Oh, and by the way," Wright added. "Next time, knock before you enter. Junior officers owe that to their superiors."

Loudon hesitated at the door, then nodded and left.

THE BLACK ROSE WAS EMPTY EXCEPT FOR A HALF-DOZEN PATRONS who sat at the bar, nursing pints as they visited softly among themselves when Fallon walked through the door. He started as he saw Con and Maeve sitting at a table in the back. Maeve smiled and waved at him. He nodded back and crossed in front of the empty stage. The bartender nodded at Fallon as he passed.

"Tomas," Maeve began warmly, then stopped as she saw the expression on his face. "What's wrong?"

"Everything," Fallon said. "Someone I met a month ago is dead. A hard death it was, too."

"Jesus," Con exclaimed, leaning against the back of the booth.

"Oh, yes, I hope so," Fallon said, but there was no humor to his words. "What are you two doing here?"

"Con found out some information about the man in the apartment," Maeve said, leaning forward. "We thought you could use it, so we came up here. We've been coming here every day for three weeks, looking for you."

"That was a stupid thing to do," Fallon said coldly. He stared at Edwards. "You shouldn't have let her talk you into this."

Con flushed angrily. "We thought you could use the information," he snapped. "But if we're wrong, we can always go." He made to slide from the booth, but Fallon reached out his hand, staying him.

"Let it go," he said. "Sorry. But you may be complicating things. You could have been followed."

"By who?" Maeve said. "We had the man, remember?"

"Did you stop to think he might not have been working alone?" Fallon asked.

"Damn," she said, shaking her head and biting her lip. "Sorry, Tomas. I guess I've been out of it too long."

"We all have," Fallon said, relenting. He rubbed his shoulder and moved it slowly, working the stiffness from it. "And not long enough. How did you know where to find me?"

"We didn't," Con said. "I asked around for the most likely place to find an Irishman and a friend told me about this bar. He said all Irishmen usually wind up here. We started here every day and worked our way around to the others."

"Good thinking," Fallon said. "What did you find out?"

"The man worked for someone named Simon Kenton, who owned a bait shop down in Key West," Con said, pitching his voice low and hunkering over the table toward Fallon. "It seems like Kenton used to work for the Agency in Vietnam and was canned after the fall of Saigon. We don't know why, but I put in a call to a Colonel Black I knew in Vietnam who's now in Germany. Black told me that Kenton was one of the bad boys who used to work with Air America when they were doing their thing in the Golden Triangle. Running drugs," he said to the query in Fallon's eyes. "The CIA used to buy the opium crops of the war lords at top dollar in exchange for the war lords' waging a little guerrilla warfare on North Vietnam. It was an effort to keep some of the armies at home. It wasn't very successful. But, and this is important, the opium seemed to disappear and, Black says, nobody knows where it went."

"Kenton?" Fallon asked.

Edwards nodded. "Might be. MI—Military Intelligence—also suspects that he was part of a rogue operation being run out of the Agency by someone. Black didn't know who, but Kenton did put up a lot of money to resurrect an old arms factory in Egypt. It closed after fourteen months just as Black's people found out about it. When they went into the factory, they found the machinery and tools, but no weapons. The place was empty. From the look of things, however, they were making AK's."

Fallon nodded slowly. "And the guns that showed up with the drugs in Ireland were AK-47s. But with Russian markings."

Edwards smiled. "Anyone can stamp a weapon various ways."

"How did the Agency get the money for that? I don't know much about your government, but I know there have to be auditors."

"They ran it through a now-defunct bank called Nugan Hand in Australia."

"I see," Fallon said. The door opened and two men dressed in business suits and carrying briefcases entered. They crossed to the bar and sat, placing their briefcases on the bar. The bartender took their order and moved down the bar to fill it.

"It gets curiouser and curiouser. The *Times* bureau in Washington tells me that it appears a pretty important person in the Agency got canned lately."

"The one who put together the operation?"

Edwards shook his head. "No. At least they don't think so. They're picking up rumors that he was a Judas goat."

"Very strange," Fallon said. His eyes wandered back to the pair at the bar, then shifted quickly as the door opened and three other men wearing business suits entered. He glanced up at the clock over the bar: 3:00 P.M. He frowned.

"Fallon, what's wrong?" Maeve asked.

Fallon shook his head. "I'm not sure." He glanced over at Edwards. "What time do your businessmen break for lunch?"

"What?" Edwards's eyebrows came together in confusion. "What does that have to do with anything?"

"Nothing," Fallon said. He looked back as the three men took a table beside the door. "But isn't it strange now that so many businessmen would be stopping off at this time of the afternoon for the odd pint? And tell me: when you drink at the bar, do you put your bag on it? A bit awkward that, don't you think? Or is that usual?"

"Jesus Christ," Con muttered, glancing at the men at the table and bar. "No, it isn't. Do you think—what do you think?"

"I think it would be best if we all got out of here," Fallon said quietly. "You two first."

"Fallon," Maeve began.

"Now," Fallon ordered.

Con rose hurriedly and took her arm, pulling her to her feet. "Now, darling," he said loudly. "We have to be going. The kids are waiting, you know."

They took three steps away from the table, and the men from the bar suddenly slid away, their hands diving into the briefcases and appearing with pistols.

"Freeze!" the oldest one shouted. A woman screamed. The younger one stepped quickly in front of Maeve, spinning her around.

"Here, now! What do you think you're doing?" Con shouted indignantly. He reached to free Maeve and yelped in pain as the man chopped his pistol across his wrist.

"You're under arrest!" the man said. "Move back against the wall! Now!"

Con hesitated, and Fallon took the opportunity, dropping on one knee behind the table. The CZ slid smoothly into his hand. He raised it. A bullet slammed past his head. He turned slightly and shot the man at the bar. The man holding Maeve raised his pistol, but Maeve grabbed his arm, pulling it down. The bullet struck the concrete floor and ricocheted away. Fallon sighted quickly and shot him in the forehead. He flew back away from Maeve.

Fallon crouched and took three quick steps to his left away from Con and Maeve. The three men at the table were rising, pulling pistols from beneath their coats. Fallon fired twice, killing two. The third froze, his hand half out of his coat.

"You have a choice," Fallon said loudly, his ears ringing from the gunshots. "Chose wisely."

The man shrugged and dropped his pistol to the floor, raising his hands. Dimly, Fallon heard a woman keening, then a slap, and the keening stopped. He risked a quick glance at the bar: it was empty, all lying on the dirty concrete floor. A tight grin spread across his face. Yes, it's an Irish bar. They know what to do.

He glanced at Maeve and Con. They were white-faced, shaken. "Are you all right?" he asked. They both nodded. Con placed his arm around Maeve, holding her close, and she turned her face momentarily into his collar.

Fallon nodded and stepped by them to the man at the door. "Now," he said, softly. "Who are you?" He whipped the pistol across the man's face, dragging the sight harshly across his cheek, ripping it.

The man yelped and raised his hand to his cheek. Fallon raised the pistol and jammed it under his chin. The man gagged.

"Who are you?"

"O'Brien!" The man gasped.

"Who sent you?"

"Tommy Coughlan!" he said.

"And the others?"

"These are mine." He indicated the men by the table. "I don't know the others."

"Federal officers," the bartender said from the floor. Fallon glanced at him. He held their identification folders in his hands. "It's best you're away. And now, before others come."

"Where'll I find Coughlan? Quick!" Fallon said.

"Quincy!" the man gagged. "He's got a safe house there! Off Faxon Park on Hardwick!"

Fallon stepped back and shot the man in the knee. The man screamed and fell to the floor, clutching his leg, rolling back and forth, trying to get away from the pain.

"You best get away," Fallon said to Maeve and Con. Maeve pulled herself free. "No, stay with him," he said gently. "He's a good man, Maeve."

Maeve frowned and bit her lip. Con stepped forward and again placed his arm around her. "Thanks, Fallon," he said quietly. She stood rigid, trying to pull away from him, then suddenly a look of relief came over her face and she stepped close and hugged him around the waist.

"May you die in Ireland!" Fallon said. He stepped through the door and walked rapidly down the street. They watched him disappear around the corner.

"What now?" Maeve muttered.

"Now? Why now, we get away while we can," Con said, pulling her to the door. She looked at him.

"Sure, now, and you're going to leave this story behind?" she said.

"Yes," Con answered firmly, pulling the door open and pushing her outside. "I am." He grabbed her arm and together, they walked rapidly away, losing themselves in the crowd of curiosity seekers beginning to form down the road leading to Quincy Market.

TOMMY COUGHLAN ZIPPED THE LAST BAG SHUT AND GLANCED AT his watch: 4:30 P.M. It would be close, but he would be able to catch the boat. He glanced at the eight suitcases standing by the door and smiled. The hell with it. Why not just leave it all behind?

He had the pubs in Ireland to fall back on and there was a good amount of money in the bags that NORAID would miss but no fuss would be raised. And with the cease-fire on and, from the looks of it, the accord not far ahead, why it would be easy to get lost in the shuffle. And there was a man in Hanover he knew about that for the right price could give another any kind of papers he wanted.

"Take the bags down to the car," he ordered the two men waiting by the door with the luggage. "I'll be down in a minute."

They nodded and picked up the bags, leaving. Tommy heard the door to the garage open and shut, then crossed to the small bar and poured himself a large whiskey. He drank it quickly, then poured another. He lifted it, squinting at the rich gold color as the light spread through the whiskey, creating a warm glow.

It's all for the best, he thought, remembering Anne Ryan lying naked and dead on the bed. Now you're out of it and with a lot of money. Let dear old Daddy and Blackie fight it out among themselves with—

"Hello, Coughlan," the voice said quietly from behind him.

His throat closed. Slowly, he placed the glass on the bar and turned around. A slim man wearing a barn coat over a black turtleneck and jeans stood inside the door. He glanced over the man's shoulder.

"We're alone," the man said. "The others won't be bothering us, now."

"Fallon," he said past dry lips. The other nodded.

"The same. I've been awhile looking for you. You've got some answering to do."

Tommy looked wildly to his left, and Fallon shot him in the stomach. The bullet knocked him to the floor. For a brief second, he lay dazed, then the pain knifed through the shock and he screamed. Fallon stepped forward and looked impassively down at him.

"That's for Pegeen," he said quietly.

"Who—the fuck—is that?" Tommy panted through gritted teeth.

A strange look crossed Fallon's face, then cleared. "Of course," he said. "It wouldn't be you, now, would it?" He leaned close. "So. Who was it?"

"I . . . don't know," Tommy gasped. "Ah! God!"

"There's bravery, then there's foolishness," Fallon said. He rapped him gently on the forehead with the pistol's muzzle. "Who?"

"I don't know!" Tommy said.

Fallon stared hard at him for a moment, then said, "Of course, you wouldn't know, would you? Your father wouldn't be that stupid."

"Help me," Tommy pleaded.

Tiny muscles knotted around the corners of his jaws. Tommy moaned and Fallon looked down dispassionately at him.

"We kill traitors," he said. "Didn't you know that?"

Carefully, he shot him in both knees, then raised the pistol.

"No," Tommy said. "Ah, God! No!" His bladder emptied itself.

"Oh yes," Fallon said, and pulled the trigger once more, sending the bullet into his brain.

He looked without expression at the dead body on the floor, then turned and walked away, gently closing the door behind him.

JOE COUGHLAN LOOKED UP FROM HIS DESK AS FLYNN WALKED INTO the room. "Yes?" he said. "What is it?"

"Tommy's been killed," Flynn said softly.

Stunned, Joe fell back against his chair. His heart hammered in his chest as the blood drained from his florid face.

"What?"

"About three hours ago," Flynn said. He crossed to the hunt table and poured a large whiskey, carrying it back to the desk.

Coughlan took it and swallowed twice, convulsively. "Some of O'Brien's boys were with him. They'd taken some luggage down to the car."

"Luggage?"

Flynn nodded. "Yeah. And get this Joe: there was nearly two hundred grand in it."

Coughlan swore and drank another large draught. "Where'd he get that much money?"

"Probably from NORAID. Stands to reason. Tommy's been making the runs for us, you know. I think he's been skimming."

"How long you been thinking that?"

"Quite a while," Flynn said. "But it was just enough not to raise any questions."

"So," Joe said, shaking his head. "The kid wised up a bit, eh? Good thinking."

"Good thinking that got him killed," Flynn said, reminding.

"And what happened?"

"Fallon. I'm certain. Couldn't be anyone else. He killed them first. Then he went upstairs and killed Tommy. He died hard, Joe. Real hard."

Tears came to Coughlan's eyes. He pulled a handkerchief from the breast pocket of his jacket and blew his nose into it. "How'd we find out?"

"The guy called the cops after he left." Flynn hesitated. "We're gonna have a time of it, Joe."

"What about Tommy?"

"The cops have him for now. I've alerted Kelly's Funeral Parlor."

"Fallon," Joe said.

Flynn nodded. "Looks like it."

"Where is he?"

Flynn shrugged. "Who knows?"

"Find him," Joe said through tight lips.

Flynn shook his head. "Joe—"

"Goddamn it, he killed my boy!" Joe screamed, throwing the glass across the room. It struck the wall and shattered.

"Tommy was no good, Joe," Flynn said quietly. "He's gone now. Nothing's going to bring him back. It could have been anybody. Tommy didn't make many friends."

"It was Fallon!" Joe shouted:

"Probably, but you better know for sure. The dagos are going to be watching to see what you do. You run off like a wild man now, and they have the excuse they've been looking for to come down on us. You know that. You gotta be strong, Joe. That's all that's keeping them away."

"I don't give a fuck," Coughlan said. "Find him."

"Ah then, I'll be saving you that trouble," a voice said.

They froze and looked at the door. Fallon stood, a slight smile on his face, his hands empty. Coughlan glanced toward the French windows and Fallon shook his head. "There's nobody out there anymore."

Coughlan turned toward him, his face red. Flynn stood impassively, his drink held lightly between thumb and forefinger, his eyes watching Fallon carefully.

"Fallon," Coughlan said thickly. His neck swelled against his shirt collar. His face turned the color of old liver.

"Yes," Fallon said, but his eyes stayed on Flynn. "Well?" he asked.

Flynn let go of his glass, his hand darting inside his coat as he turned sideways, dropping to one knee. The bullet took him in the center of the forehead, snapping his head backward as the top of his head blew out, spattering his brains over the desk and floor behind him.

"Sonofabitch!" Coughlan said thickly. He leaped for his desk, then folded as the second bullet severed his spine. He fell, dazed, to the floor, willing his nerveless legs to carry him around the desk to where the gun waited in the drawer. Fallon's foot caught his shoulder and flipped him over on his back. He floundered, fluttering his arms like a turned turtle, wondering why his legs wouldn't move.

Fallon stepped over him, looking down, the pistol held negligently beside his leg. "Now," he said quietly, "we must have a little chat. You've sent someone after me.

"Who?"

"—fuck yourself," Coughlan said.

Fallon shrugged and stepped over Coughlan and walked to the drinks table. He placed the pistol on the table and poured a large whiskey then turned back to the room, leaning against the table, sipping.

"A good whiskey," he said. "Not Bushmill's or Jameson's, but good nevertheless. What do you call it? Bourbon?"

"Be done with it," Coughlan muttered.

Fallon shook his head. "No, not until you tell me where to find the one I want. And you will. I'm in no hurry. You're in shock now, Joe. But that shock will wear off in a little bit and then you'll feel the pain. And the pain will be bad, Joe. Very bad. And you'll ask me to kill you. But I won't. Not until you give me what I want. And then I'll kill you."

"Fuck you," Coughlan said thickly.

Fallon smiled. He picked up his pistol and crossed to sit in a chair near Coughlan. He sipped his whiskey and leaned back. He smiled down at Coughlan. "I've got the time for you," he said.

It took three drinks and a little over an hour for the pain to begin seeping through the numbness and Coughlan began swearing, tiny beads of perspiration appearing on his forehead. He began screaming an hour later.

And shortly after that, Fallon burned down the Coughlan house.

49

KENTON CHECKED THE STUB OF A TOOTHPICK STILL BENEATH THE top hinge where he had placed it after locking his door. If someone had opened his door, they wouldn't have seen it fall. Simple, but effective and much harder to detect unless one was lucky or knew enough to look for it. Much better than the hair around the lock or a piece of paper wedged in that would fall to the floor and possibly be seen by someone opening the door. No, the tiny toothpick stub was enough.

He unlocked the door and stepped inside, yawning and stretching. He carefully locked the door behind him and threw the deadbolt. Another day shot and no closer to finding Fallon. He had to give the Irishman credit: he had never had trouble running a person to earth before, but this Fallon was different. Much different. He would take great pleasure in killing him when he found him and he would find him, of that he was certain. He knew he was still in Boston. The Agency had the terminals covered and car rentals, but that didn't make any difference. He knew Fallon was still in Boston. He could feel him still in the city, like a predator feels his prey before he finds it. He just knew—

"And a good evening to you, Mr. Kenton," a quiet voice greeted him.

He froze, his coat in one hand, a hanger in the other. Slowly he turned to look into the darkened living room of the small apartment he had taken on Winter Hill Street. A light snapped on and he saw Fallon sitting on the couch, facing him, the pistol steady on his knee.

"Fallon," he said. He grinned. "Well now. Fancy meeting you here."

"The pleasure's all mine," Fallon said quietly.

"I've been looking for you," he said. He turned to hang up his coat.

"Uh-uh," Fallon said. He stopped and looked back over his shoulder. "Turn around now, like a good lad. Slowly. Let me see your hands first."

Slowly, Kenton turned, his hands still filled with coat and hanger. "You're a careful one, Fallon."

"I have my moments," Fallon answered.

"I know." He grinned. "I almost got you a month ago."

"Your second run at me," Fallon answered.

Kenton nodded. "Yep."

And at that moment, he threw the coat and hanger into the air and spun behind a wall. Dimly he heard a shot and something slammed into his back, driving him forward. What the hell? He couldn't shoot through walls. He rolled to his feet and lurched down the hall and into his bedroom, slamming the door behind him. A bullet plowed through the door and he fell to the floor reflexively. He put his hand behind him and felt his blood and swore. He reached up onto the bed and removed the pillows, pulling them from their cases. He knotted the cases and placed the knot over his wound and, taking a deep breath, tied it tightly around him. He coughed and spat in his hand and nodded satisfactorily. The bullet hadn't cut a lung. Good. Of course, there's no telling how much damage was done inside. But he might have time.

He reached under the bed and found the Colt .357 magnum in the clip holster attached to the bed frame. He slid it from the hol-

ster and opened the cylinder to check the loads, then closed it and
thumbed the hammer back, cocking it. He rose slowly to his feet
and took an experimental step. Gingerly he twisted and felt no
pain. But he knew the pain wasn't far behind and when it came he
would have a bad time of it.

You'd better make this quick, he thought. He slipped his shoes
off and crossed to the door and, taking a deep breath, threw it
open and leaned against the wall. He glanced quickly down the
hall. Empty. He frowned. The bathroom? Possible. It was the only
other door before the end of the hallway.

He crept down the hall, the pistol pointing ahead of him, his
finger already taking up the slack. He stopped by the bathroom,
took another breath, and carefully edged his head around the
doorway. Empty. He moved rapidly down the rest of the hallway
and stopped before the living room. He glanced into it. Empty.
He frowned. Surely not the kitchen. He took a deep breath and
started across the living room when he heard the door open
behind him and he knew that he should have checked the deadbolt instead of taking it for granted that it was still locked and Fallon had stayed in the apartment.

He spun on his heels, firing as he turned. The cap snapped on
the cartridge, but no recoil came and he felt the blood draining
from his face even before the shot took him in the stomach,
knocking him backward over the coffee table onto the couch. He
raised the Colt as Fallon walked across the room, but suddenly the
pistol was too heavy for his fingers and fell away from him. He
swore as Fallon bent and picked it up. He watched as Fallon
opened the cylinder and let the cartridges fall into his hand. He
showed them to Kenton. The bullets had been pried out of the
casing and the powder dumped.

"Blanks," he breathed. "Clever." He tried to smile. "An accident,
you know. You getting me. Nothing more."

"Oh," Fallon said, dropping the Colt back on the floor. "It was a bit more than that. Now the question is, how did you manage to find me all the time? Who is the gombeen man?"

Kenton grinned. "Why, look to your own, my friend. Surely you can figure that out."

"Yes," Fallon said softly. "It would be two or three. But which one?"

Kenton shook his head. "No."

"I didn't think so," Fallon said. He sighed. "I guess that's all to be said for it. You killed the girl, didn't you?"

"Oh yes," Kenton said. A wave of pain shook him. "Jesus." He took a deep breath and let it out slowly. "I thought she knew where you were. But she didn't."

"She wouldn't have told you anyway," Fallon said.

"Oh, I think she would have," Kenton said. "They always have. It just takes a bit of time."

Fallon shot him in the knee and he screamed from the pain. "Well, then," Fallon said mildly. "Maybe you are right."

"Ah, Jesus!" Kenton said.

"I don't suppose you'd like to tell me anything else?" Fallon asked conversationally. "How did you manage to always find me? Who's the one who turned?"

"Figure it out for yourself," Kenton gasped.

"Oh, I already have," Fallon said. "I just thought you'd like to confirm it."

"Go to hell," Kenton said.

"You first," Fallon said.

He raised his pistol. For a moment Kenton felt a surge of fear as he realized at last that Fallon was through talking. He opened his mouth and tried to speak, but the bullet smashed through his forehead.

50

HELEN, THE SENATOR'S WIFE, MOANED DEEP IN HER THROAT, HER LEGS
locked around Wright's waist as he moved slowly upon her. He
pushed up on his arms, looking down at her full breasts, the nipples
taut and rigid beneath him, the sweat glistening on their bodies.

"No," she moaned. "No, don't leave! Don't leave!"

Wright grinned and at that moment the flash went off, freezing
him. Eyes shut, she continued to move against him, grinding hard
as she grabbed his buttocks, pulling him tightly to her.

The flash went off again.

He swore and tried to push away. She gripped him tighter,
wrapping her legs around his waist and locking her heels together.
Her net stockings rubbed harshly against his flesh.

The flash went off again.

And then she came, keening high, her head thrown back, muscles rigid in her neck, breasts arching up toward him.

And again the flash.

"That's enough," someone said quietly.

And Helen fell away from him, gasping for breath. He rolled
away from her toward the nightstand on the far side of the bed.
She grunted in complaint and the flash went off again. She cried
out, opening her eyes in fear, throwing herself over on top of
Wright. They floundered together for a moment, then he pushed
her away and grabbed for the drawer.

"I don't think so, Mr. Wright."

He stopped and took a deep breath, then swung his legs over the side of the bed. He reached down and found his robe and stood, shrugging into it and tying the belt around his waist.

"No, no, no," Helen moaned. She pulled the covers up, tucking them under her chin, looking fearfully at the four men standing around the foot of the bed.

"I hope you know what you have done," Wright said coldly, facing them. "Do you know—"

"Who you are? Yes, I think so."

Wright turned to look at the fourth man in the room. "Kelly!"

"Oh yes," Dave Kelly said calmly. He held up his hand. A badge glinted in the pale light of the bedroom. "Federal Bureau of Investigation. You are under arrest, Richard Wright, on charges of conspiracy and treason. If—"

"Oh shit," Helen said. She pulled the covers up over her head.

BLACKIE CASSIDY LOUNGED ON HIS BED, IDILY SIPPING A GLASS OF Irish whiskey as he thumbed through a magazine. He glanced irritably at the bathroom. What the hell was keeping her so long? Jesus! A man could come twice while a woman primped and preened herself only to be mussed up while fucking.

The door opened and Mary Dunne walked out, her pear-shaped breasts bare, a red-and-black thong low above her pubic hair. She wore a black garter belt with black lace stockings held up at her creamy white thighs. His throat thickened. The wait had been worth it. Ah yes. Well worth it.

"Come here," he growled, setting his glass on the table beside the bed.

She held up her hand. "Wait a minute," she said. She walked to her purse on the bureau. "I forgot something."

"Ah, Christ!" he complained. "I thought we cleared that up. I'm not wearing a rubber! You know that's a sin."

She turned, smiling, and he stared at her breasts, then suddenly registered the pistol in her hand. She shot him in the forehead and he slapped back against the bed, his eyes staring in astonishment at the ceiling.

"So's this," she murmured. "But it's only one after many others."

She walked to a closet and pulled out a skirt and slipped into it. She pulled a sweater over her head and picked up her purse. She looked over the room, then crossed to the clothes tree and removed his wallet from his pants hanging there. Then she left, walking carefully over the stone path down to the road where a Ford Cortina waited. She opened the door and got in. A man leaned forward from the front seat.

"You got him?" MacCauley asked.

She nodded and passed the wallet back to him. "Yes. And I took his wallet to help it look like a robbery."

"That's a good lass," MacCauley said. He took the wallet and opened it, removing a thick sheaf of bills. He handed them over to her. "You might as well have the cash. We'll take care of the wallet."

"And my mother?" she asked quietly.

"Ah yes. Don't be worrying about that. You'll find her in her own home in Sligo and a goodly sum to carry her over to her grave. And there's ten thousand punts waiting for you in Geneva with an apartment at the lake for all of that to help you in your time of mourning."

"Good," she said and leaned back against the seat, closing her eyes as the driver put the Cortina in gear and pulled away. He glanced down at her thighs where the skirt had risen above her stockings, showing a garter black against the creamy smoothness. He shook his head and turned his attention to the road, remembering the story of black widows.

WHEN THE TELEPHONE RANG, WILLIAM CASSIDY LEAPED IN HIS CHAIR and leaned back, staring at the instrument on his desk. He leaned forward and took it on the third ring.

"Hello?" he said.

"Mr. Cassidy, is it?" a voice said over international ether. His heart began to hammer in his chest.

"Yes?"

"It's over, now. And we'll be giving you our heartfelt thanks. We know that it was a terrible thing you had to do, but it was for the good of the people, you understand."

"Yes," he said dully, and again, "Yes?" Then, he realized he was listening to the hollow ether sound of emptiness on the other end of the telephone. He replaced the receiver gently in his cradle. He stood and walked to the small hunt table and filled a glass with Scotch whiskey. He drained it and filled it again, choking back the gag instinct at the harsh afterbite in the back of his throat. He raised his glass and looked into nothingness.

"Here's to you, Blackie," he whispered. "I'm sorry. I know you don't understand, but it had to be. I have my own life, you know."

And he drank again and this time it wasn't the whiskey that brought the tears to his eyes.

Epilogue: Ireland

THE SUN HAD SET OVER DAGDASKILLEN AND A LOW GLOAMING stretched over the hills as Father Brian Fallon left his Romanesque church with the stained glass windows and slowly made his way down the hill toward his cottage. A great weariness slumped his shoulders and his head and knees ached from the long vigil he had kept at the altar rail. He had been praying for over three hours straight—ever since a Protestant firebomb had killed the three children in Ballymoney. In a land that had seen countless acts of violence over the past thirty years, the firebombing of the Quinn home had drawn instant reaction from across the nation as all, Protestant and Catholic leaders alike, had denounced the killing, marking it as worse than terrorism in its senselessness.

The firebombing came on the heels of a Catholic protest at a planned Orange Parade in Drumcree near Portadown. Protestant hardheads had held that they had a right to parade on July 13 in recognition of William of Orange's victory over the bloody Catholics and James II at the Battle of the Boyne in 1690. But the parade was really only to rankle the Catholics and heap fuel on a smoldering fire, and cooler heads refused to allow the Protestants to march from Drumcree Church where hundreds of Protestants had gathered in protest. Some of the Protestants had decided to retaliate and firebombed what they thought to be a Catholic house, but only the mother, Chrissy Quinn, was Catholic. Her boyfriend, Raymond Craig, was a Protestant. The three children, Jason, seven, Mark, nine, and Richard, ten, burned to death in their beds in Ballymoney.

He shook his head in sorrow as he opened the door to his cottage and entered. There had been too much killing, he reflected. Far too much. Was freedom worth the price of so much innocent blood? The children. That was enough. But it had always been enough. First the nine-year-old Kevin Rooney who was shot dead when he sat up in bed, disturbed by the Falls Road riots in the small hours of August 15, 1969. A machine gun bullet had struck him in the head. And that was the first of more than a hundred children who would become innocent victims.

But we are all innocent victims, he thought, lifting anguished eyes to the crucifix hanging on a nail beside the door. He kissed his fingers and touched it gently. Why do you allow it to continue? he asked.

"Hello, Brian."

He froze for a moment as he recognized his brother's voice, then turned and looked at the figure sitting quietly at the table, a cup of tea in front of him. Another cup had been poured and sat on the table opposite him. Tomas gestured at it.

"I'm sorry," he said apologetically. "I'm afraid it's gone cold. I saw you at prayer and didn't think you'd be this long. The Ballymoney children?"

Brian nodded and pulled the chair out, sitting. He lifted the tea and sipped: lukewarm.

"It's all right," he said quietly. "We can make more later. So. I take it you were successful? Otherwise, you wouldn't be here."

Tomas nodded and sipped from his tea. "Yes, that I was. It's over. For now."

"Will it stay over?" Brian asked. He started to rise, pointing at a tin of Walker's shortbread biscuits on the counter beside the kettle behind Tomas. "There're some biscuits—"

"I'll get them," Tomas said. He rose and brought the plaid tin to the table, opening it. Brian took one and gestured.

"Help yourself," he said.

"No, thanks," Tomas said. He sat, watching as his brother dunked the biscuit in his tea and bit, washing it down with a swallow.

"Whatever happened, Tomas, I don't want to know," Brian said.

"It's too late for that, isn't it, Brian?" Tomas said gently.

Brian stared at him for a long moment. He sighed and placed the cookie on his saucer and sat back away from the table. He folded his hands in his lap. Deep lines suddenly appeared in his face and a gray pallor appeared on his cheeks.

"So, you've figured it out, have you?" he said.

Tomas nodded. "Pretty much. You gave up the woman in Belfast after your time in Crumlin Jail and Castlereagh. But that really wasn't it, was it,? Brian? The question was why she was so important that the Brits and the Prods were willing to let you go after you gave them her. And why she was killed."

Brian stared with anguished eyes at his twin across the table. His lips were a thin compressed line.

"We all thought it was an accident that MacCauley's wife got caught up in the net, but it really wasn't, was it, Brian? We didn't blame you as you had taken a beating—or had you?" Brian covered his face with his hands. Sobs began to wrack his body. "I don't think so. What really happened in Castlereagh, Brian?"

He waited until his brother sighed and wiped his eyes with the sleeve of his cassock. He lifted his cup and took a long drink, then replaced it in the saucer. He looked away from his brother, staring at the crucifix on the wall.

"They raped me," he said softly.

Tomas remained silent.

"Again. And again. Five, six, I no longer remember. Sometimes I remember, though. In the night. I remember. And I awake and forget." He looked at his brother. He shook his head. "You have no idea."

"I think I do, Brian," Tomas said softly. "It wasn't even that, though, was it? How did they know about the woman? You had no way of knowing about her except—"

"Her confession," Brian said. He looked again at the crucifix. "I knew from her confession."

"And you violated the confessional," Tomas said.

Tears broke again from Brian's eyes and fell on the front of his cassock. "Yes," he sobbed. "I broke the seal of the confessional. God forgive me!"

He dropped his head onto his arms on the table and again the sobs wracked his body. Tomas leaned over and placed his hand on his brother's head.

"He has," he said softly. "But you can't forgive yourself."

"No," Brian said through his sobs. "That's not it: I can't forgive Him."

Tomas waited for a moment, then removed his hand and rose and left the cottage, leaving his brother crying bitter tears over his loss.

A THICK MIST CLIMBED OUT OF THE SEA AND SCUDDED ACROSS THE strand. The sun turned bloodred behind it. He paused, watching the curraghs struggle against the lead gray sea in the Bay of Tralee, the men carefully keeping a distance between the sides of the curraghs and the schooner rolling with the wave action as hands unloaded crates from the deck of the schooner to the waiting men in the curraghs. The schooner was sixty feet, gaff-headed, the top of the Herreshoff schooner design. But her owners had been careless with her: her brightwork had weathered gray; the sails had been patched, and the rust-flecked winches had been oiled, but not cleaned; the varnish on the low cabin was white-flecked like leprosy.

Fallon turned his head and looked at the old man standing, watching the unloading of the schooner. The thick, crescent-shaped thatch of white hair blew back off his forehead. He held the stump of a briar tightly in his teeth, his hands thrust deeply into the pockets of his oilskin. As if he sensed Fallon's stare, the old man turned and watched as Fallon approached. He stopped in front of the old man, his eyes locking with the bright blue eyes watering from the cold.

"Hello, Uncle Dan," Fallon said. The old man nodded.

"Tomas," he said around the pipe.

They stood for a moment, watching the schooner being unloaded, then the old man sighed and removed his pipe.

"Brian?"

"Killed himself," Tomas said quietly.

"Dear God," the old man said, crossing himself. "Took his own life, he did?"

"Yes."

The old man nodded. "This bloody war," he sighed. He took a large, soiled handkerchief from his pocket and blew his nose noisily and wiped his eyes.

"Brian wasn't at war, Uncle Dan," Fallon said. "Except with himself. At the end he couldn't forgive his God and so he kept his soul from Him."

"How did you figure it out?"

"At first I thought it was you. But then I knew it wasn't. Couldn't have been."

"Why's that?"

"For the same reason it had to be Brian. He wasn't in it long enough to grow the scars."

The old man thought a minute, then nodded. He brought out a packet of matches and turned his back to the wind, relighting his pipe. "It's so," he said.

"Yes. Your scars were too thick for you to become a supergrass.

We've lost too much to give up anything more. Brian came too late into the horror of it all and hadn't time to grow the scars to cover his soul. He hadn't learned to live on the hatred. Or maybe he couldn't. It doesn't matter, does it?"

"No," the old man said. They turned to watch the unloading. The old man sighed. "But now, at least, we have the hope that others won't grow those scars."

"Perhaps," Tomas said.

The old man turned his head to look at him. The cold wind made his eyes water. "But we have the accord, now, Tomas. That's a start."

"Yes," Tomas said. He pointed. "As long as we can keep that from happening."

"Ah that," the old man said with sudden relish. He pointed at the bay. A gunboat was sailing around the point, making its way toward the schooner. From the shore, four lorries suddenly appeared, blocking the trucks from the road. Gardai swarmed down from the lorries toward the beach. The old man looked at Tomas. "We have to try, Tomas. We have to try."

"Yes," Tomas said gently. He turned and walked away, leaving the old man alone upon the strand. He turned his face into the wind, letting the cold scrub his face, cleansing him with its bite, baptizing him anew with its salt spray from his journey through the region where the hosts of the dead lived and waited. He felt his own identity fading, slipping on the tide into the universe, joining those whose names had become air, their bones dust, their souls lost, the land they walked slowly being eaten by the sea, gray and heavy, rolling into the land and out again.

He watched the whitecaps dancing on its turgid swell, infinite, rolling out into the bay and from the bay to the sea, and he heard its song in the heavy roll, the song of eternity, singing down through the ages from the Shannon and the tiny country streams, the same song, endless and mournful. The land was temporal and the people who walked it more so, but the sea was there, forever, singing its song throughout the universe, pure and clean, washing itself constantly from man's abuses, the endless sea, singing a mournful song.